STARLING

GRYPHON INSURRECTION BOOK 3

K. VALE NAGLE

STET PUBLISHING

Cover art by Jeff Brown.

Interior art by Brenda Lyons.

Interior graphics by Crystal Gafford of Crafty as a Coyote.

Author portrait by Murphy Winter.

Published by STET Publishing, Denver

WWW.STETPUBLISHING.COM

WWW.KVALENAGLE.COM

Trade Paperback Edition
ISBN: 1-64392-021-9
ISBN-13: 978-1-64392-021-4

BELAMURIA
ALABASTER EYRIE
REEVESPORT
WHITEBEAK
CRESTFALL PALACE
DUCKBILL
ABYSSAL NAZE
ARGENT HEIGHTS
CRAC S
NIGHTSKY
NEW EYRIE
ALWREN
CL RA
JADEBEAK MOUNTAINS
EMERALD JUNGLE
FLOWER OUTPOST
SUNKEN EYRIE
STORMTAIL
KING'S REACH
RAFTWORK
SUBMERGED FOREST

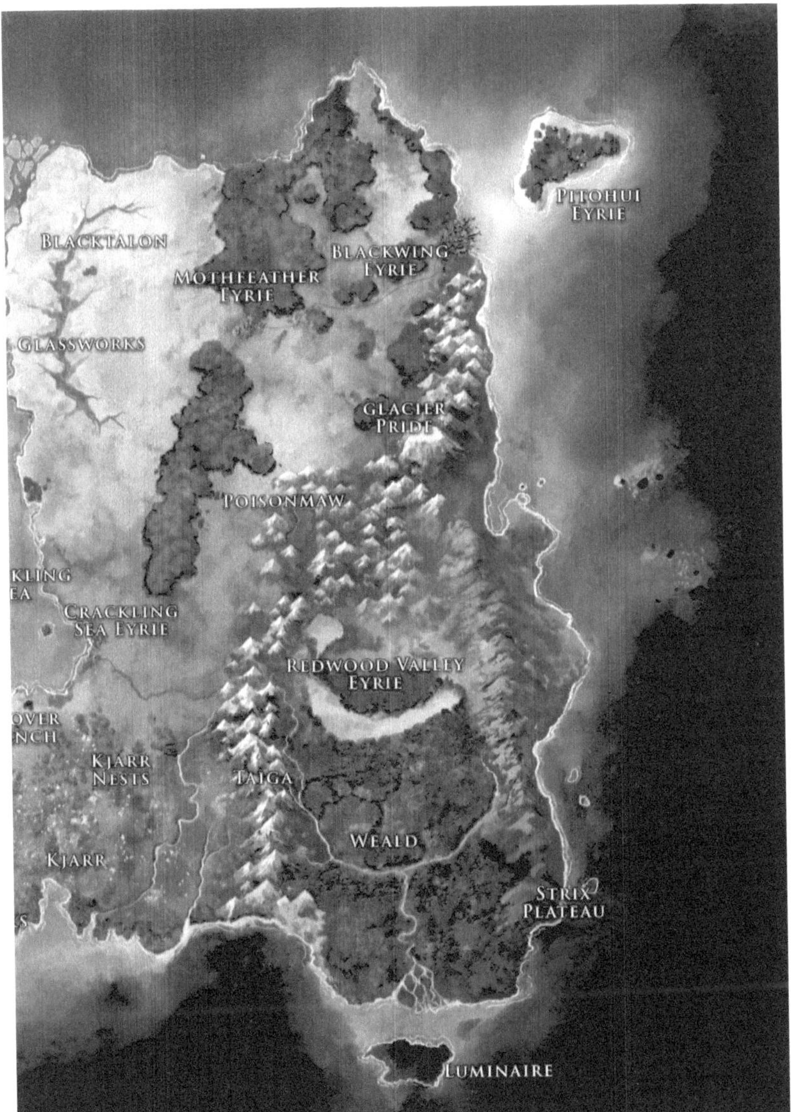

BLACKTALON
MOTHFEATHER EYRIE
BLACKWING EYRIE
PITOHUI EYRIE
GLASSWORKS
GLACIER PRIDE
POISONMAW
KLING EA
CRACKLING SEA EYRIE
REDWOOD VALLEY EYRIE
OVER NCH
KJARR NESTS
TAIGA
WEALD
STRIX PLATEAU
KJARR
S
LUMINAIRE

*For Griffen O'Brien. He made everyone he met a little happier.
In his absence, I've attempted to do the same.*

RANGER LORD ELLORE
CRACKLING SEA OPINICUS

THE FLOWER

Ranger Lord Ellore stuffed an old Crackling Sea badge into a pocket of her harness. The paint on it had split, revealing a different design hidden underneath. If New Eyrie fell, that badge was her passport to the lands north of the sea.

The gryphon armies of the Ashen Weald would be upon New Eyrie any day now. If the refugees of the Crackling Sea and Redwood Valley were going to survive, they needed food and lumber. Unfortunately, two months ago, the last opinicus outpost in the bog went silent. It was up to her to find out why, preferably before New Eyrie found itself under siege.

The ranger lord—a temporary promotion that only became permanent if she saved New Eyrie—ordered her troops to land at a lumber mill north of the bog. Her ragtag group of rangers, their front halves resembling blue herons, descended to look around. All showed hints that their ancestors had bred with gryphons. Her second-in-command had the long legs of a kjarr gryphon. Several others had tufted tails like the weald inhabitants. Ellore herself resembled the snowy taiga pride. She'd considered living there once, long ago, before Satra, the head of the Ashen Weald, had drowned Ellore's daughter. Before the weald and taiga gryphons found out about Vosk's betrayal.

She shook her head. She hoped he was okay, but if not, revenge would come later. For now, there were a thousand refugees who needed to be fed and an escort of twenty rangers who had all suffered wounds from the taiga pride and needed her guidance.

They split up to search the lumber mill. From the air, it had appeared empty.

She found the whole situation with the missing rangers disconcerting. At the waystation on the goliath bird pass, she'd understood what had happened—an army of wingtorn. Blood, bodies, and pawprints testified to the battle that had gone on.

Here at the lumber mill, there was no sign of conflict. There should be twenty or more opinici working this mill. There were none. Her rangers found no blood stains among the processed wood and laborer nests.

They did find signs that someone had left in a hurry. Nests overturned, a few sentimental things taken. No weapons remained, so they must have felt threatened. But if they had, why hadn't they flown to the safety of New Eyrie or the Crackling Sea Eyrie?

"The attackers must have come from the north. I can't think of anything else that would make me flee into the bog," her second-in-command said. His name was Bruen, and he looked like hell. A blood-soaked taiga gryphon had charged him through two tents and a wall. Only his reassurances that he looked worse than he felt had convinced Ellore to bring him along. That, and his trust lay with her before the eyrie. He had kjarr blood in him and was tired of having his loyalties questioned.

"Was it sailfins?" another ranger asked. Ferrick was nursing a nasty bite that had come at the beak of a blood-red taiga gryphon. While most rangers assigned to the kjarr had been half-breeds or Jonas loyalists, Ferrick had just been too incompetent to trust with anything important. He'd once knocked himself out with crackling jelly toxin and had never lived down the tale.

Bruen scoffed. "I don't know about you, but I'd just fly over sailfins. How many miles of monitors would there have to be to stop you from flying to N'Eyrie?" Swelling around his beak truncated New Eyrie in a way the other rangers would be imitating for the rest of the trip.

"Oooh, good point," Ferrick said. "Say, if Ellore is ranger lord now, does that make you our leader?"

The other rangers looked up. Many were interested in her old job, but if it went to anyone except Bruen, it'd just lead to fighting. He was the right combination of likable and competent.

"Bruen is in charge of you," she said. "Consider me...a valuable asset that you still have to listen to."

"Right, so as I was saying," Bruen continued, "something that can fly came from the north."

While he continued his brainstorming session, Ellore walked around the mill. It was fairly open except for a wooden shed where the chemicals were kept. The shed's door was shut tight, so she headed north instead and inspected the ground as she went. She didn't know of anything that could stay in the air forever. If there'd been a gryphon ambush, she might find feathers or paw prints.

Or an opinicus ambush. Her blackwing allies camped nearby, watching and waiting. Before she'd left New Eyrie, the mad peafowl Impir had met her in a supply tent. He hadn't entrusted her with his plans, but he'd given her the Blackwing Eyrie badge and told her to meet him in Crestfall when all hell broke loose. She resisted the urge to reach into her pocket and make sure the badge was still there. She'd already started wearing down its Crackling Sea veneer.

She wandered through the grasslands north of the lumber mill when another thought occurred to her. What if the missing lumberjacks weren't killed by gryphons or opinici? What if it'd been a sea monster?

She took to the air. The old reeve had kept a massive serpentine whale as a pet, which had gone feral after his death at the talons of blackwing assassins. It had been known to leave the safety of the water for short bursts if it thought there was a meal nearby.

The grasslands between the lumber mill and the shore far to the north were undisturbed. *Not a sea monster, at least.* Something green sparkled below her. She landed and wandered through the scrub brush until she found a starling feather. A gryphon-sized starling feather.

She flew back to the mill in time to see her rangers splitting up. She passed Bruen the feather. "It was gryphons."

"A wingfeather," he grunted. He twisted it so it caught the light from several different directions. "Couldn't be the wingtorn then. You think it's the kjarr survivors who fled into the bog when Jun surrendered? I don't remember any of them being this color."

She'd heard reports of hit and run attacks across the bog, though her position on the far eastern edge of the kjarr had left them free of such worries. The most her rangers had to deal with were rumors of bog wisps and strange noises, gryphonic skeletons that haunted flowering bushes, ghosts of wingtorn with glowing blue wings —superstition, nothing more. Not that she could blame them. There was something unsettling about occupying the kjarr nesting grounds, a feeling of being watched by the dead.

"No," she said, "not the wingtorn. There's a pride of starling gryphons who live in the rainforest. I think they've become emboldened since the kjarr pride disappeared. I was given orders to capture one and bring it back so they can interrogate it. I found the feather north of the mill."

Bruen didn't question her. He'd served under her for so long, it didn't even occur to him that she might be lying.

The only order New Eyrie had given her was to find the missing rangers in the bog. The mad peafowl Impir, however, would need to know if another gryphon pride was in play. It was the sort of information their blackwing masters liked to be kept apprised of.

Bruen scratched at the patch of feathers under his chin. "If these starlings are all over the bog, it would've been mighty nice of the previous ranger lord to keep us informed."

Ellore wasn't so sure that Grenkin had any idea about the starlings. She'd only recognized the feather because the Blackwing Eyrie had a special interest in the gryphons of the southern continent.

Ferrick poked his head around a wooden building nearby. "Hey, Captain, hey, Ellore. Maybe they're just playing a joke? I think the shed is full of squirrels."

She and Bruen looked at each other. She decided she

needed to have Ferrick's wounds checked to make sure they weren't infected.

"That opinicus is *nuttier* than a shed full of squirrels," Bruen grumbled, but there was a sound coming from the shed.

"No, I hear it, too," Ellore said.

Ferrick knocked on the door and was greeted with a loud chittering. It didn't sound like a shed full of squirrels, though. It was more like one large squirrel. There was an automatic latch on the door that kept it closed to animals. Without taloned claws, could a gryphon work it from the inside?

"Don't open it!" she ordered.

She was too late. Ferrick opened the door.

The starling tumbled out, knocking him down. Its eyes had a silver sheen over them. She wished she'd asked more questions about the starlings. She didn't know if that was normal.

Its feathers weren't just green, they glistened in the light. Their iridescence was marred only by white speckles. It didn't talk, but its beak kept chittering.

Bruen stepped forward. "If you surrender yourself peacefully, you won't be harmed. We'll give you food and medical care."

Whether it didn't understand or didn't care was unclear. Ferrick untied his metal talons from their leather bracers, slipped them over his foreleg, and dipped the prongs into the paralyzing jelly toxin. He was starting to stand up when the starling charged him.

"Help!" Ferrick yelled as the starling bit his foreleg. It clamped down over his talons, but the thick brace kept the starling from closing its beak all the way. That was the only thing that let him keep his limb. The starling shook Ferrick's metal talons back and forth until one of the prongs caught on its cheek. The toxin took ten seconds, but the starling lost consciousness.

"You're lucky to still have your foretalons," Ellore told him. "But good work. We can drop him off at New Eyrie and be on our way."

Ferrick was too shaken to speak. Another ranger had to come over and start treating his wound. She was tempted to leave him behind to recover, but New Eyrie was so short-staffed, she was sure someone would put him on the front lines when the Ashen Weald began their assault.

"I thought you were gonna end up like Grenkin for a moment!" Bruen knocked Ferrick on the head. Ranger Lord Grenkin, the opinicus who had surrendered the Crackling Sea days ago, had famously had most of the digits on his left claw bitten off by a wingtorn. "But you put the pointy end in someone else for a change `n it paid off."

Ellore muzzled the starling and relinquished it to four of her rangers to fly to Impir's carrot garden outside of town.

"There should be something to secure it with there," she told them. "Make sure the muzzle stays on tight."

They nodded. "I don't think this muzzle is going to last, Captain. Ranger Lord. Ellore."

She didn't correct him. They'd figure out her new title in due time. "It'll last long enough. I'm not wasting the good one. Hurry along. We'll wait for you at the first outpost in the bog. Don't dawdle."

They nodded and set off. The starling was small by

gryphon standards and emaciated. Four opinici would likely be enough to fly with it. It must have been stuck in that shed for a while to have lost so much weight. She went to take a look inside, but small red-and-black bugs were crawling on the door handle now. Probably just some kind of bog termite, but she felt itchy just looking at them.

She hated bugs.

On Impir's orders, she and Rakesh had used parasite eggs to infect the game around Sandpiper's Dune. They'd have infected the whole weald had they not been stopped. She'd never gotten a good look at what the eggs hatched into.

Probably a bug similar to the ones she was seeing now. It looked like *N'Eyrie* wouldn't be getting its lumber from here.

She turned back to her remaining rangers. "Alright, let's get to the bog. I've had enough of this dry ground."

IT TOOK Ellore and her rangers a few days to work their way south. The first few outposts they found were the same as the lumber mill—empty, but with starling feathers nearby. There was a little blood at one of them, but it wasn't yet clear to her whether the opinici stationed there had been killed or simply continued to flee deeper into the bog.

Early into their occupation of the peat bog, small bands of escaped kjarr gryphons had used guerrilla tactics to make life hard for the rangers. While the opinici had the numbers, they didn't know the bog the way the kjarr pride did.

When the rangers attempted to open up fishing villages on the ocean coast, the gryphons would sneak in at night and steal away all the food. The raftworks, built in the hope that offshore fishing would be harder to disrupt, was under constant guard. Caravans of goliath birds had followed a new boardwalk path through the bog with supplies up until everything went silent.

It was a cool, clear day, and visibility was high. She could make out the Crackling Sea to the north, the taiga to the east, and the ocean to the south. Somewhere west was the starling's jungle. If the Ashen Weald took New Eyrie, she'd be boxed in. She could feel the noose tightening. She needed to get north while the skies were still friendly.

She was surprised to see they were nearly to the center of the bog. A large outpost had been built here to stockpile food in one place that could be easily defended. It gave the rangers a central, fortified location to send flights of backup to all corners of the bog. If the missing rangers had been in trouble and couldn't get to the eyrie, this was where they'd have gone. It was her next stop.

The location hadn't just been chosen because it was in the middle of the map. On the contrary, for reasons she didn't understand, this was one of the few stretches of dry land in the bog. Dry was a relative term, but it was sturdy enough to build on.

Beyond the main compound, a circular boardwalk had been built around the edges. It was constantly sinking into the water and being rebuilt, but its height above the muck added another layer of protection against sailfins wandering into the camp—they were terrible climbers. A small fence along the main path served a similar purpose, with the goliath bird trail passing straight through the attached stables before snaking south to terminate at the raftworks.

The building at the center of the boardwalks was a wooden great hall like Reeve's Nest with four connected towers that had sprung up on each corner. The rangers affectionately referred to it as *the Flower* because of how it looked from above.

She hadn't seen any opinici flying in the air around the Flower, so she assumed she'd find it abandoned like the other outposts. Now that they were above it, however, she could see that the wooden planks of the boardwalk were stained with blood.

She trilled a command, and the rangers landed on the path just north. Half slipped on their metal talons while the others untangled nets. Her reports from Rakesh hinted that their fisherfolk cousins had made fishing spears. She'd be happy to find a method of combat that kept the beak and claws of gryphons far from her face.

She was afraid to approach the Flower on foot. Gryphons had the advantage on the ground; opinici did better in the air. She flew a circle around the boardwalk, but there were no signs of starlings or rogue bog gryphons. The moss-laden trees made it difficult to be certain, but at the least there wasn't a horde of starlings in the brush.

Her rangers split into teams. She took the front door while Bruen checked the tower entrances.

Ferrick went with Bruen. He'd been shaken up by his encounter with the starling and didn't look like he'd been eating. He was starting to appear as thin as the green, speckled gryphon had been. Ellore was polite but firm when she saw his talons shaking. She wouldn't let him use the toxin, just in case. He'd nodded, but there was an anger in his eyes she hadn't seen before. It must have come from the events surrounding his demotion to the kjarr nesting grounds. She hadn't meant to insult him, but she also couldn't risk a mishap when ranger lives were on the line.

Bruen's head looked over the edge of the roof. "The towers are all boarded up."

Ellore stared at the massive door in front of her. During hurricane season, the goliath birds could be housed inside. The chimes she'd normally use to announce her presence were missing, probably broken in one of the starling attacks.

Were the starlings just filling the gap left by the kjarr pride or were the two allies? Why had they left one of their sick behind? It was possible the primitive gryphons didn't have doctors as opinici thought of them. She'd heard of the weald's medicine gryphons. There hadn't been any among the captured kjarr and bog pride.

She pounded on the door and hoped she wouldn't be greeted with the angry sound of squirrels like back at the shed.

Nothing.

She knocked again and adopted an official tone. "Is anyone inside? This is Ranger Lord Ellore from the Crackling Sea Eyrie. I've come with reinforcements. Are there any survivors?"

This time she heard sounds from the other side. They sounded soft, like murmurs, through the thick wooden door. Bruen, Ferrick, and most of the other rangers watched from above in case there was trouble. Four others patrolled the sky in case the starlings showed up.

The door opened a crack.

"Ranger Lord Ellore? Not Grenkin?" the voice said. It

had a strong Redwood Valley accent, more musical than a Crackling Sea opinicus would consider appropriate.

"Grenkin perished when Satra the Kjarr took the Crackling Sea Eyrie." Wishful thinking, she supposed, but possibly true. "I've come to see why New Eyrie is starving and why the outposts have been abandoned."

The door opened wider.

"Hurry inside!" the voice said.

A SINGLE BRAZIER LIT THE common room of the Flower. It had been designed in the manner of most ranger outposts, with a large open area that allowed flight. The tall walls were lined with nests all the way up to the tower access points on each corner. Ellore walked in and assumed command of the band of twenty-some survivors.

The ranger who let her in, Mia she said her name was, sported colors only seen at the Redwood Valley—bright red with hints of green and blue. Ellore expected Mia to be relieved to have support, but instead Ellore smelled shame, embarrassment, fear. It put her on edge.

"You're the ranger lord now? I recognize you. Rakesh used to report to you." These words, full of the Redwood flourish, came from an opinicus with a circlet marking his rank as a captain in the Reeve's Guard.

"Used to, Captain?" she asked. There were a good number of Redwood Valley opinici who'd joined the ranks of the rangers, but none of them wore tiaras. The opinici silly enough to put on headgear for battle were all Reeve's Guard through and through. This songbird was out of his element. Bruen came inside and sighed when he saw the two reds.

"Ah, you wouldn't know up north," the Reeve's Guard captain said. "The fisherfolk retook Sandpiper's Dune. Rakesh died failing to hold it."

Mia rolled her eyes, and Ellore made a mental note to find out her version of events.

Rakesh had been strange but loyal. Ellore remembered a time before the war with the kjarr when he'd first signed up to be a ranger. He'd been one of their best and brightest then. Something he'd seen in the bog had warped him. A lot of things happened before the rangers took the kjarr nesting grounds and put an end to the conflict. The Crackling Sea had been starving then and more than willing to follow Jonas's machinations if it meant their children would get to eat.

It would be impossible to pinpoint the moment where Rakesh had changed, but it hadn't been gradual. He'd been assigned to something deep in the bog, and he'd come back different, strange. Off. It was important for the rangers to take care of their wounded—whether the wounds were physical or psychological. She'd hoped peace would rekindle some of his former self, but peace had become a precursor to future conflict.

"I recognize you now," Ellore said. "Rakesh held Sandpiper's Dune, and you were the one in charge of the rafts. How is our floating fortress?"

The captain frowned. "It was lost in the battle."

This time it was Bruen who spoke up. "You lost...there must have been sixteen rafts! How could you lose them? They took the floating fortress from you?"

The captain shifted. "No, it was destroyed."

Ellore shook her head and looked to Mia, hoping she had something to say that would make sense.

"They have a way of controlling the large sea

serpents," Mia said. "Rafts are only wood and stormcloth. This thing was as long as the entire fortress. We retreated to the raftworks, but it was empty, so we came north."

Ellore looked around the room. Controlling the larger sea serpents, the serpentine whales, was a neat trick. If the rangers could acquire that power, it would open up the eastern half of the Crackling Sea to fishing again. Maybe if she interrogated everyone here from the raftworks, she could figure out the fisherfolk's method.

Now that she'd found the missing rangers, however, her first order of business was to restock and get north. If the raftworks were gone and these were the last of the survivors, there was no reason for her to stay. She'd rejoin the forces at New Eyrie. Their chance of success was slim enough as it was. If the starlings were allies of the Ashen Weald, she'd be needed to help with the defenses. *Or I may be needed further north.* She reached into her harness and placed a talon on the disguised Blackwing Eyrie badge.

"How many of you were stationed in the bog?" she asked. No one raised talon or wing. "How many of you were assigned to Sandpiper's Dune or the rafts?" Everyone raised an appendage.

She took another look around. Excluding the rangers she'd brought with her, there were another twenty opinici here. The captain and Mia were the only Redwood Valley survivors. The others were blue herons—Rakesh's troops.

While her own mission was to bring home as many rangers as she could, she knew Ivess's concerns lay in supplies. "I assume there are still crates upon crates of fish in dry storage, and I saw a few wagons outside, but no goliath birds. We'll need to recapture them before we can leave."

"They were eaten," the Reeve's Guard captain said, "down to the bone. Then the bones disappeared."

Ellore frowned. "What about the ones at the raftworks?"

"Also eaten," Mia said. "We found their bodies on our flight north."

Ellore went through her mental calculations. She had enough food here to feed the Crackling Sea and New Eyrie for a month but no way to get it north. The Ashen Weald would take the goliath bird ranch before they came south, if their starling allies hadn't already killed everyone there and eaten the birds.

She put a foretalon into her pocket. There was no saving New Eyrie without food, but she could save these rangers. She could find them sanctuary in the north with the blackwings. It may not be a good life, not all of them would be willing to join the eyrie that had murdered their reeve, but it was better than starving or licking mud off Satra's paws.

"Is this everyone?" she asked. She'd seen the abandoned outposts on her way south but wanted confirmation. Rangers didn't leave anyone behind.

"Yes," the captain said.

"No," Mia countered. The captain frowned at her, but she continued. "We have three prisoners. Two are fisherfolk—a gryphon and an opinicus. The third was here when we arrived. He, uh... Maybe you should hear it in his own words."

The captain nodded.

"Alright," Ellore said. "Lead the way." She gestured to Bruen, and he stepped outside to check on the patrols. Something was wrong here. There was something she wasn't seeing, and she wouldn't be caught off guard a second time, not after the taiga pride's ambush.

ELLORE MADE her way down the stairs. To call where she was going a basement was misleading. It was an under-level, buried slightly into the soil to keep food and supplies cool. It was lower than the level of the boardwalk, which made it a sublevel of sorts.

With the ranger lord here, the captain had lost some of his prestige among the rangers from the raftworks. None of the other Reeve's Guard seemed to have survived. If Ellore had to guess, the rangers seemed to want to follow Mia, who should have been promoted when Rakesh died. Instead, the Reeve's Guard had held the power for himself. Ellore made a note to make it clear that Bruen was in charge if something happened to her.

"When we got here, we were attacked," the captain said. He preempted Mia, making sure his version of events came first.

"The starlings?" Ellore asked. "We saw one trapped in a shed, but otherwise there've just been reports."

The captain shook his head. "No. Well, later, yes. But when we arrived, it was dark. We were pounding on the doors to be let in, but no word came. We'd seen the starling feathers at the raftworks but didn't know what they meant yet. Our pounding attracted attention from the bog. Not gryphons, though. Opinici."

He stopped at the bottom of the stairs, waiting to open the door to the sublevel until he finished his tale.

Opinici? Ellore wondered. "Blackwings from the north? Escaped criminals from Crestfall, maybe?"

"No, they were blues, like you," he said.

She raised an eyecrest. While the slang was common on both sides, she didn't think she'd be brave enough to stand in a group of forty Crackling Sea rangers and call them blues.

"*Not* like you," Mia said to Ellore, shooting the captain a look. Mia, at least, had enough understanding of politics to try to avoid calling her allies *blues*. "He means they were colored blue. Um, like Crackling Sea Eyrie opinici normally are. The blue ones."

"Ah," Ellore said. "Continue, Captain?"

"Yes, sorry. Their eyes had glazed over, and they tried to kill us. One was tangled up in its own net. They weren't...they weren't right. We had to put them down." He looked helplessly to Mia, who nodded her agreement of his assessment.

He preened a bit to calm himself before continuing. "When we finally got the door open—we had to dismantle it using tools from the raftworks—we found more dead bodies inside with a single opinicus standing over them holding a butcher knife. We locked him up."

The captain opened the door. One side of the spacious room had crates of supplies. This had been a major hub along the trade route, after all. The other side had five cells, three of which were full. An empty cell stood between each occupied one.

"I am Ranger Lord Ellore. Identify yourself," she said to the first prisoner. He was a white crane opinicus with a red head. Fisherfolk came in all shapes and sizes, but this shape and size didn't come in a non-fisherfolk version.

"The dead of Crane's Nest will be avenged!" he proffered in lieu of a name.

"I call him Beaky," Mia said. Giving descriptive nicknames was more of a gryphon thing, but the red stains at the end of his long beak affirmed the epithet. "Don't get too close to the cage. You should have better luck with the other one."

"And who are you, little gryphlet?" Ellore asked, but she saw at once she was wrong. What she had taken for forepaws were actually some sort of device covering opinicus talons. Based on the webbing, they looked designed to help with swimming. She couldn't think of another purpose for them. If they had some combat value, they'd have been confiscated before the fisherfolk was put in the cell.

"My name is Quess. You should know it so you can tell the dead of Crane's Nest who sent you to the star ocean to keep them company."

"If nothing else, the fisherfolk have a flair for the dramatic." Ellore smiled. "I like your flippers. And no ears, too bad. I'd have liked confirmation, but I suppose I don't need it. I've seen those flank patterns often enough. You come from the kjarr."

Quess bristled. "I come from Crane's Nest. I don't have any ears to show you, but if you open the cell door, I'd be happy to acquaint you with my beak and claws."

Ellore was surprised to see that Quess's crane companion was unfazed by the comment on her kjarr heritage. Ellore had heard that the fisherfolk were accepting, but after the wingtorn destroyed their towns, she would have expected a suspicious eye would be turned to the fisherfolk with blue heron front halves, kjarr-patterned flanks, or black-backed ears.

Ellore and Bruen had faced enough discrimination from the Crackling Sea Eyrie opinici, and they were much more sophisticated than fisherfolk. Maybe simplicity was necessary for this level of acceptance.

The opinici with foreign blood had all disappeared from the Crackling Sea Eyrie after the blackwing invasion. Most had left on their own, but she'd found several dark-winged opinici left for dead along the waystation route, still wearing their Crackling Sea harnesses.

"Yes, yes," Ellore told the petrel fisherfolk and turned to the last cage. The ranger in there still had his pink fish harness on and was standing at attention. While Quess's avian half was petrel, she and the ranger shared the same kjarr fur. It was likely why he'd been assigned to the bog.

"Ranger, I would hear your report now," Ellore said.

"Grenkin is dead?" the prisoner asked.

She nodded.

His demeanor relaxed. "Ranger Darion, reporting in. The starlings killed all the opinici stationed here except me."

"The truth, Ranger!" the captain commanded.

"It is the truth. We'd heard some chittering in the bog, concentrated around a university dig site west of here." Darion paused when he saw their skepticism at anyone digging in the bog. "It's just an expression. Every now and then the bog spits something back up, old but looking like it just died yesterday. A scholar was here from the Redwood Valley, name of Neider. He said something about acidity preserving things. They set up a camp to study the bog bodies in the dry patch near the group of lakes in the west. That's where we first saw the starlings."

He stopped to catch his breath and drink. He'd been given a bowl and meager rations like the two fisherfolk despite the crates of food in the other room.

"So yeah," he continued, "soon after that, there were hundreds of them all around the Flower. We don't normally keep the towers boarded up—sailfins aren't much for climbing, thankfully—and so they swarmed in and killed everyone except me. Then your captain and crew showed up."

The captain rolled his eyes. "You left out the part where we had to dismantle the doors to get inside and we found you cutting up your comrades."

"That's because they were full of bugs," Darion said.

The captain scoffed. "As you can see, he's as crazy as the mad opinici who ambushed us outside. Deranged. It's likely caused by a chemical imbalance. Our scholars at the Redwood Eyrie, led by the same Neider who established the dig sites out here, discovered that time at sea or away from civilized cuisine can lead to all sorts of diseases. I've made sure all of the opinici under me consume a proper amount of lichen for the vitamin and minerals the bog lacks."

Mia's face showed what she thought of the required lichen rations. Ellore had brought dried fruit. It had a brackish taste to it from the salted fields but got the job done. The Crackling Sea scholars had found a way to counteract the same nutritional imbalances without licking scuzzy trees. It did explain why everyone's breath smelled the way it did.

The captain looked ready to go on, but Darion spoke first. "Little black-and-red bugs. They lay their eggs in wounds, and it drives an opinicus crazy."

"More madness—" the captain stopped when Ellore held up her foreclaw.

She was thinking—of Rakesh's reports, of Impir's clay jars, of the lumber mill's 'termite' infestation. The red-and-black bugs could be the adult form of the infecting agent she and Rakesh had used on the taiga. Her orders had been to infect chickens and send them to the weald. She'd been promised it would end the conflict without the blackwings having to invade again. Rakesh's orders had been to infect the gryphons of Sandpiper's Dune. He'd died before reporting back to her.

She'd thought the parasite just made gryphons sick and hungry. What if there was more to it than that? What if the starling in the shed had been infected?

There was only one way to find out.

She turned to the captain. "The bodies of the opinici, what did you do with them?"

"The ones he chopped apart we burned," the Reeve's Guard said. "Then we sanitized the area, just in time for the gryphon invasion. We're lucky we didn't get stuck inside with the bodies."

"The others we buried outside," Mia said. "Shallow graves because of the bog, but the sailfins haven't dug them up yet."

Ellore took a look at the prisoners again. A white crane with white fur. A petrel with kjarr fur. A blue heron with kjarr fur. If Impir was right about the beasts of the kjarr fighting off all infections, it would be good to know now, before the pumpkin vials ran low.

"Bring the prisoners. Release the ranger, but shackle the fisherfolk and grab some shovels," she said. It was time to confirm her suspicions.

ELLORE WATCHED the skies while several of the rangers dug up the bodies. Quess and Beaky were secured to posts, and the strange ranger prisoner, Darion, stood next to Ellore.

"They don't come from the sky," Darion said.

"Hmm?" Ellore replied.

"The strange green gryphons," he said. "They *can* fly, but they mostly walked. It's sort of like how you see insects buzzing, but you don't see them buzzing up high, right?"

"We call them starlings," she said. "They resemble a bird from the north."

"Huh, always a bird for every gryphon," he mused. "I wonder if they evolved from birds?"

She didn't point out the irony that he resembled the blue herons that caught fish along the Crackling Sea coast. There were things one could say about gryphons that couldn't be said about opinici, at least not in polite company.

It was why she'd been forced to take her gryphon daughter Mignet to the taiga after she'd hatched. Ellore knew how cruel opinici could be about breeding and wouldn't see her daughter subjected to it. If only Ellore had known she was sending her daughter to her death.

She wondered if Mignet's father, Vosk, was still alive. By the way the taiga pride had destroyed her camp a week ago, there was a good chance he was dead.

She pulled herself back to the present and Darion. "So everyone was exposed to the bugs, but you were the only one who didn't get sick?"

"Eh, a few of us didn't get sick." He frowned. "The starlings just ate the other ones. They thought that just 'cause the starlings like to walk it meant they couldn't fly and made a break for the north. Didn't get very far."

She took that in. "I guess you were just the healthiest. It must've hit the sickly first."

Mia interposed herself between the prisoner-ranger and Ellore as a safety measure. Ellore imagined she had a permanent bodyguard until she assigned the rangers here to Bruen or promoted Mia.

"Ha! No, I was always sick as a chick," Darion said. "I swear every storm blowing off the Crackling Sea would make me sick as a clam."

Ellore wasn't sure how sick clams got, but let him continue.

"No, it's just that once I got away from the salty sea air, I stopped getting sick. Getting assigned to the bog is the best thing that happened to me, up until everyone got murdered."

"I can see how that would put a damper on things," Mia said. "Tending to the pumpkin patch was fun, too, until the fisherfolk attacked and called upon their beasts to destroy the raftworks. Once Rakesh died, the patrol schedule got messed up. If we'd known where the fisherfolk were hiding, we could've gotten them first."

Ellore looked up at the sky. It was still afternoon, but the light was starting to turn. How long ago had Bruen gone to patrol with Ferrick? The bodies had nearly been dug up.

"Has anyone seen Bruen?" she asked. "Or Ferrick?"

The rangers here were all from the raftworks and didn't know the names.

"Bruen has kjarr blood," she explained. She hated to use those terms, but expediency won out. Bruen was just as likely to refer to Ellore as taiga-backed. "Ferrick is the only one of my rangers to look like the rest of you but wounded."

"Oh, I saw them," one of the raft-assigned rangers said. "Well, I saw a wounded opinicus who was having trouble flying over the bog. The kjarr-blood flew down to help him. It was just a few minutes ago."

"Stop digging," Ellore commanded. "We need to make sure they're okay. Anyone acting strangely should be considered suspect after the story I just heard, and he should've reported in by now. Show me where you saw them," she said to the ranger. Then she turned to Darion. "How long did it take the infection to take hold?"

"A couple of days," he said. "The raftworks rangers have been here long enough that if any of them were infected, we'd know."

"It's not them I'm worried about," she said.

FERRICK WASN'T FEELING WELL. He hadn't been right for days. Either the starling or the scary taiga gryphon must have passed something along to him when they bit him.

He hated to ask for time off to rest after he'd earned back some respect by subduing the starling all by himself, but he was afraid his foreleg was infected. When they were just checking out waystations, it didn't feel like the right time to speak up. But now that they were at a real outpost with supplies, maybe it was time to see what kind of medicine they stocked.

His feet grazed the top of a tree and he realized he'd been getting closer to the ground with each circuit. He was out on patrol, all on his own, but he just felt so dizzy when he flew higher.

He began to fly lower, and then, when he felt like he was going to throw up, he landed. He'd probably eaten too much. His body was fighting off something, and so he ate and ate but didn't get any fuller. On the landing, his foreleg lit up with pain. He stumbled onto his stomach and then settled onto his back legs.

There was a little blood on the bandage, but he couldn't tell if it was new. It wasn't dark like dried blood, but it wasn't bright like new blood, either. He was afraid to remove it and look, but he had to know how serious it was. He'd seen a few infected limbs in his time. If he were going to throw up, he'd rather do it here, away from the others.

He closed his eyes and unwrapped the bandage.

To his surprise, when he opened them, his foreleg looked fine. Sure, there were marks where the starling had bitten down, but there was no sign of infection. It must all be in his head.

"Ferrick?" a voice called from above.

Bruen.

Whenever Bruen or Ellore told him something, Ferrick had started feeling so angry. It began with Ellore—*Ranger Lord* Ellore, as if she deserved that title—taking away his toxins like he was a fledgling. She hadn't just ordered him not to use them, she'd had Bruen take away the vials like he was a chick. Well, he'd shown her. He'd stolen back the vials while Bruen had slept and put them in the bottom of a harness pocket. He wished she'd fall into a swarm of crackling jellies and drown.

And Bruen was made captain. Bruen! Ferrick could think of a dozen rangers more qualified. By the crackling depths, he was more qualified! He should run this troop.

No, that wasn't right. Ellore had done a lot for him. And Bruen: oh, Bruen was standing before him now.

Ferrick blinked. He'd had trouble seeing his friend

because his eyes weren't focusing right. His salt ducts were producing some strange, silvery substance. He wiped at his face but couldn't get it all.

Bruen was talking at him. "I'm here, Ferrick. You're okay. Let's get you back to the Flower, alright? Can you fly? We can walk if you need to. We're not that far from the boardwalk. I'll lift you up and we'll be good."

"I, um. I, then. I, okay. Captain." There was an emptiness between the words now. The anger fell into the emptiness, then rose again as hunger. He needed to eat something right now or he'd die.

Ferrick got down on all fours. He wasn't thinking about his wounded foreleg anymore. His muscles tightened and his talons dug into the ground. The strain opened the wound, and a trickle of blood wove its way down his leg and into the soil.

Bruen was still trying to talk to him, but Ferrick couldn't understand the words anymore. He was so hungry.

ELLORE DIDN'T HAVE time to put on her metal talons, let alone apply the paralyzing toxin. Ferrick was on top of Bruen biting at him. Bruen was trying to keep Ferrick's beak away from the important bits, but he'd already been bitten several times. Rather than let Mia or the other rangers handle it, Ellore dove, catching Ferrick in the ribs.

He was knocked back several feet but landed on his paws. He let out a sound that wasn't the chittering of the starlings but wasn't proper opinicus speech, either. Ellore kept her focus locked on him.

There was a little clarity in his eyes, and he was panting. Whatever had come over him had passed. He was trying to say something to her.

She slipped her foretalons down to Bruen, who gave her his net.

Ferrick began to cough. Then he began to knead the ground. Several of the other rangers were watching from the skies. He was under the cover of trees now, but where Ellore and Bruen stood, the cypresses had lost their leaves in preparation for the fall.

Ellore called out to Ferrick.

Clarity left his eyes. He charged.

She threw the net at him and pushed off, flying straight up. The net caught him in the face, slowing him down but not catching his wings. He snapped at her, just missing the soft blue feathers of her tail. The other rangers' nets caught him midair and he dropped, hitting the ground with a *thud*. He writhed in the net, despite a wing that must have broken on impact.

Mia, metal talons fastened, approached Ferrick. She looked ready to put him out of his misery.

"Stop," Ellore ordered.

Mia complied, confused. Ellore reached into her harness and pulled out some wrapped leather she used to repair harnesses. The rangers pulled the net taught, but Ferrick still writhed around, biting wildly.

She approached him and slipped the leather into his mouth to keep his beak from closing. Then she pulled out a vial of pumpkin extract and poured it down his throat. He was still trying to talk, but most of it went down.

She checked herself for bite or claw marks. None. Then she looked down at Bruen.

"Got any of that for me, Captain?" he asked.

"Lord. It's ranger lord. You're the captain now." She

hesitated. It was common practice to grow pumpkins for food in most ranger outposts in the bog and kjarr, but she didn't know if there was a pumpkin patch here. They might have a limited supply. It was also as good a chance as any to test out her theory.

"Do you trust me, Bruen?"

He nodded.

"Then I'm going to wait. I have the vial right here if we need it. But it took Ferrick a few days. Let's see how you are, okay?"

He shivered, but it was a testament to his character that he obeyed.

By the time Ferrick had been knocked out with crackling jelly toxin—from the same vials that Ellore had confiscated from him—and Bruen's wounds had been treated, albeit without pumpkin extract, Ellore arrived back at the makeshift grave to find both prisoners gone. Their cut ropes lay in a pile, and Ellore could make out two shapes flying southeast.

Both Darion and the Reeve's Guard captain had remained to watch the prisoners. Their bodies lay next to the graves. Darion's wounds had come from a crane-like beak, but the Reeve's Guard captain had several deep, clean cuts on him. The sort of cuts that didn't come from claws or beaks.

Since their harnesses had been confiscated, the petrel-opinicus must have hidden a primitive dagger in her flipper. It was a pity. Ellore had a lot of questions for that opinicus—questions about flippers for swimming, questions about how to control the giant sea serpents. Now she wouldn't have that opportunity.

"Should we go after them, Ranger Lord?" Mia asked.

"No," Ellore said. "I think it's more important that we figure out our situation here and return north. I don't want to risk any more lives. You've all been through a lot. Let's bring you home once we see if the pumpkin worked on Ferrick."

The raftworks rangers around her visibly relaxed. They moved the bodies to the graves.

"We should leave now, before the starlings return," Mia said. "They flew east, towards that bluish-brown mountain in the distance, but could return at any time."

"Hoarfrost." Ellore's great grandfather said the nests there were carved deep into the mountain. He said if you called loud enough from inside the caverns, your words would echo into every nest. Hoarfrost had been alive with gryphons once. He'd promised to take her up there and show her where all of her gryphon relatives had once lived.

He'd died before he got the chance. She hadn't bothered to ask Vosk if she could go to Hoarfrost. Despite her great grandfather's view on the matter, it wasn't a home. It was a necropolis.

"Stupid prisoners," Mia said. "They should've gone towards the ocean. If the starlings didn't make it across the taiga, they're flying—"

Her words proved prophetic. A mass of green mangrove and bog detached itself and swarmed straight up. Beaky was a hundred yards ahead of Quess. The starlings clamped onto him, and he plummeted with their additional weight.

Quess slashed out with her long knife at one of the starlings who came near and caught it across a wing.

It fell.

She started to fly south, but the ocean was a long way away. She turned and flew back towards the Flower. The starlings followed.

Bruen and Mia swore in unison.

"Everyone inside!" Bruen ordered. "Secure the gates. The starlings are coming back!"

Ellore hesitated before going in.

"Ranger Lord, we need you to be safe," Mia said. "You'll have plenty of time to observe the starlings."

But Ellore wasn't staring at the starlings; she was watching the fisherfolk. Bruen followed her gaze.

"You can't be serious," he said, forgetting her rank. "She's one more mouth to feed even if she doesn't try to murder us before we can capture her. If a single starling gets inside, there's both fisherfolk and infection to worry about."

Ellore still waited. Quess was halfway back. "The greater risk is if her kin come to rescue her and only find us. The fisherfolk wouldn't hesitate to raze this place to the ground. It's wood. It burns quite well, and we've put the idea of burning things into the heads of every gryphon south of Crestfall. If we have Quess, they can't burn it, and we may be able to strike a deal. The only backup coming to this forsaken place may be fisherfolk."

Bruen nudged Mia. He was still bleeding from Ferrick's bites.

"Ranger lord," Mia said, "you're too important to risk outside. I'll wait for the fisherfolk. You go in. If I cry out, close the gates."

Ellore let Bruen lead her back, but after a short trip to

the sublevel, she stayed near the door to make sure they didn't close it early. She waited for another two minutes before they heard the sound of a hard landing. Quess and Mia pushed inside. Ellore looked through the open gate to see if there were any starlings, but all she caught sight of was a large bog blossom bush.

She frowned. Bog blossoms only bloomed in the spring. Before she had time to take a better look, her rangers pushed the gate closed and barricaded it.

Quess reared back and held the long knife in front of her. Ellore recognized the design from the relics Rakesh had sent back. It was used for cutting through beaked whales and other thick-skinned ocean life. He'd been quite taken with it. She could see why. It had made quick work of the Reeve's Guard captain.

Quess was panting.

Ellore walked straight up to Quess and gave her back her harness and metal talons. Ellore recognized the engraved moth on the claws, but decided she'd wait to ask how Rakesh's weapon had come into Quess's possession.

"I'm sorry for your friend," Ellore said.

Quess, still panting, pulled the harness on and slipped the knife into a long sheath. Then she walked past the rangers to where the water was stored and began to gulp down as much as she could, thirst overcoming suspicions for the moment.

"What happens next?" Bruen asked. He'd been confined to a nest on the far side of the room until they were sure he wasn't going to turn like Ferrick had.

The sound of the starlings outside was like being in the center of a swarm of locusts. The buzz of their chittering filled the air, making it hard for the opinici to hear each other.

"Now we wait," Mia said.

Bruen shook his head. "For how long?"

"Until something new comes along and draws them away." Mia shrugged. "Darion said he was stuck here for at least a month before they left last time. I hope you know some good stories."

Everyone looked grim except the fisherfolk, who was still panting, and Ferrick, who was unconscious.

1

———

THREE MONTHS PASS

The early winter winds picked up the snow covering the taiga, swirled it around Younce, and dropped it on the next mountain. One gust at a time, snowflakes were making their way across the mountains. When the next icy migration lifted off from Snowfall, several gryphons went with it, gliding off the ledge with ropes and supplies.

Younce's eyes had turned blue with the season, and his winter coat made him look twice as large. He wiped snow out of his eyes, a habit he'd picked up while recovering from the parasite.

Nearby, Snowfall's nesting grounds were full of traders from different prides. As medicine gryphons certified the wildlife in different parts of the taiga free of infection, Younce would send his hunters in to find prey to trade. In return, he received promises of parrots, red fern, and honey come spring.

It wasn't just weald gryphons, either. From the kjarr nesting grounds, Satra the Kjarr's wingtorn worked tirelessly to build a path across the taiga. Here at the halfway point, Younce's pridemates worked to construct a path up Snowfall Mountain. The design had come from Askel and Triddle, who were on loan from the Ashen Weald, but was overseen by the wingtorn Thenca, who'd gone stir crazy being stuck on top of a mountain for the past few months.

Rather than have the kjarr fledglings, still inexperienced at flying through calm weald skies, attempt to cross the winds of the taiga, Satra had decided they would remain at the Strix plateau until a path could be built, and then the wingtorn would escort their children to their ancestral home. While there was a goliath bird pass up near the ruins of the Redwood Valley Eyrie, strange things had been sighted in the north, and no one was willing to take children there.

With the arrival of Askel and Triddle at Snowfall, Hatzel had returned to the weald to lead her ever-growing pride. Younce missed her guidance even now but understood why she'd been reluctant to develop a friendship with another taiga pride leader. He'd reaffirmed the promise of Vosk, his predecessor, to let her pride hunt in the aneda forests until the weald wildlife recovered. From here on out, Younce hoped to keep up relations with all of the prides, old and new—a thought which brought him out of his mental snow-gathering and back to his present visitor.

"I would like your permission to take over the abandoned Snowfeather nests in the north," Ninox of the Strix Pride said.

"I just don't know," he told her. "It's always been a part of our heritage."

She tilted her head. Her feathers and fur were thick from living in the northern mountains, but he could see her shift to try to stay warm. "You hope to resettle Snowfeather?"

It had been an unspoken hope among the taiga gryphons that, with their days of neutrality behind them, the pride would grow large enough to fill all of the old nesting grounds.

In the wake of the victories in the kjarr and the Crackling Sea—and the intermingling that happened afterward—all of the taiga gryphons who wished to lay eggs had found opportunities. The spring would bring many new gryphlets into the fold. And when the eggs hatched in other prides, he hoped to have a few taiga gryphlets brought back here once they'd fledged. There were many old nesting grounds lost in the Connixation he hoped to open again, but Hoarfrost and Snowfeather had been top of the list.

"I'd like to see them all resettled, in time. There are still some descendants of Snowfeather"—he motioned to Biski's assistant who lacked the black rosettes and long fluffy tail of most taiga gryphons—"who may wish to reclaim them. With the starling swarm in the southern kjarr, we've had to hold Hoarfrost jointly with the fisher-folk. Now you're asking us to give up our northern-most outpost. Some of our elders used to tell stories of how the taiga prides once owned the entire mountain range, from coast to coast."

She watched him speak without moving. He was used to Deracho's snowy owl mannerisms but still found it hard to read the lack of ear movement in the weald's owl gryphons.

"You seem more practical than that," she said. "Would you rather have a long expanse of open mountain range lie empty for years until invaders cross it or see

Snowfeather stand as a first line against those who will soon come? If there are any who believe Snowfeather is their heritage, I will allow them to stay there." She looked down the cliffs at Askel, Triddle, and several of the fantail gryphons who'd come with them. "If you wish to remain independent of the Ashen Weald, you would benefit from having other pride leaders as your allies."

Younce found Askel and Triddle, despite their ties to Merin's Pride and the Ashen Weald, to be harmless enough. He'd met them briefly back when Reeve Brevin still ruled the Redwood Valley.

When Thenca had suggested the duo could help build a path through the mountains and up to Snowfall, he'd indulged her out of a sense of guilt—he'd sent her lover, Deracho, south to help the fisherfolk reopen Hoarfrost and knew she couldn't follow him. The mountains were too treacherous, and two of the fisherfolk clans had forbidden the wingtorn from crossing south of Glacial Run. The third fisherfolk clan, Crane's Nest, wouldn't let a river keep them from their revenge but had yet to act on their threats.

Hence the need to build the path north of Glacial Run for the kjarr fledglings. Askel and Triddle had earned their keep quickly and seemed grateful for the opportunity to get away from the weald and kjarr for a little. Askel had been held captive in New Eyrie, and now Triddle wouldn't let Askel out of his sight.

"And what would Orlea think if I gave you permission?" Younce asked. Orlea had turned a collection of opinicus refugees into a gryphon-like pride. They controlled the eyrie ruins and associated hunting grounds, grasslands, and dam. These were strange times when opinici formed prides.

"She is my next stop. I need not tell her that you have already said yes." Ninox licked her paw and cleaned some of the errant snowflakes from her face.

He looked south, where several gryphons were taking shape in the sky. He recognized their black-and-white patterns. Petrel gryphons from Crane's Nest, the one village that hadn't reached a peace agreement with the Ashen Weald. The wingtorn had nearly wiped it off the map. Most of its survivors now lived in camps on Luminaire, an island off the coast.

Younce knew he should take the time to talk with the other taiga gryphons about Ninox's proposal, but after Vosk's death, they seemed to enjoy having a leader who made decisions and didn't mind if they questioned him later. His decisions had given them medicine gryphons, soap, potential mates, and new friends.

"I'll give you the Snowfeather Highlands for fifty years," he said. "After ten years, we'll talk about whether you want to continue or not. That's with the understanding that taiga gryphons will always be welcome there."

Ninox bowed slightly and her stomach scraped the snow. He saw for the first time that she'd flown up here pregnant to make sure she had a nest for her gryphlets in the spring. He'd seen her talking with Triddle like they were old friends and glanced over at the gryphon scholar.

"Not Triddle." She shook her head. "My brothers will have stupid children who are good hunters. They cannot help themselves. My pride, the Strix pride, will have smart gryphons who are good hunters. Triddle is not a bad choice. Maybe he will catch the eye of one of my pridemates, if they can get him away from Askel. But not for me. Not this season."

Younce saw her shiver a little in the wind. "You should consider adding taiga stock to your gryphlets if you want to survive the winters."

"I do not think you are quite smart enough to meet my standards," she said.

He blushed, but then saw her twitching tail and blinked eyes and laughed. "You're probably right. If I find any smart gryphons, I'll send them your way. I think the best of us is already spoken for, however."

Thenca, managing the Ashen Weald workers far below them, had heard the laughter and was staring up at them with a look of curiosity.

"I also understand you are more of an opinicus in these matters," Ninox said. "I hear they mate for life."

He turned to ask her what she meant, but she was already gliding east down the mountains and towards the weald. He turned back south and saw that the contingent from Crane's Nest was nearly upon him. He used the time to groom.

YOUNCE WAS polite enough to fly down to Thenca to wait for the fisherfolk to land. Together, they were both extremely well-preened. Unfortunately for Thenca, Deracho wasn't with the new arrivals.

Younce felt bad for her. Despite her wingtorn status, she'd climbed a mountain and leapt across a chasm to reach Deracho. She'd remained here ever since, serving as the Ashen Weald's ambassador to the taiga.

They'd chosen their representative well. Most of the taiga gryphons remembered the death of Mignet and blamed Satra. Had the Kjarr herself come, she would have found a cool reception. Both Deracho and Thenca were popular, and her daring heroics had earned her fans among the gryphlets and fledglings. They'd be sad to see her go when the path was done.

If Younce had anyone he trusted half as much as Deracho, he'd have sent them to manage Hoarfrost and Williwaw instead and saved Thenca this heartache. Deracho was reliable and competent. Hopefully he'd forgive Younce for assigning him to the southernmost outpost because Younce was starting to suspect that Thenca might not.

He chirped a greeting to catch the attention of the procession. The fisherfolk changed direction and landed down by them. They weren't all petrels. He saw Naya's sandy fur next to Tresh.

"Two fisherfolk leaders?" He licked his paw, groomed down his already-impeccable ears, and stood straight. "To what do I owe the honor?"

Tresh rolled her eyes, but she was just as well-preened as Thenca or Younce. She must have insisted they stop nearby before she saw him.

"Do people normally come this high up to honor you?" Naya asked. Of the three fisherfolk leaders, Naya of Sandpiper's Dune was the only one to make regular trips up north to trade with the opinicus refugees and weald prides. Unlike its sister cities of Crane's Nest and Swan's Rest, both the city and its people had survived the Crackling Sea's assault—first by virtue of having surrendered, then later because the battle to liberate the city had taken place at sea. There were still rumors that the dune opinici had willingly joined the rangers, but Naya had chosen to forgive everyone rather than root out individual loyalties.

It didn't hurt that the other fisherfolk factions had set

up camps outside the city, ostensibly to help with the salvage operations. Using the rafts they'd stolen from the rangers, the fisherfolk had started fishing deeper waters and trading their extra catches for goods and information.

Thenca looked past Naya to see if there were any others coming.

"Sorry, Thenca," Naya apologized. "Deracho wanted us to make this run north before the winter storms start in earnest. It'll be him and his thick taiga fur making the rest of the supply runs until spring, for what it's worth. You should see his eyes. They're bluer than the ocean."

Like all of the taiga pride, Deracho's eyes had begun the shift to blue when the weather changed, around the same time winter coats seemed to double everyone's size. Younce had already begun to plan this year's Blue-eyed Winter Festival.

While the taiga pride's change was most drastic, all gryphons were feeling the cold. Naya's colors had darkened with her winter coat. In the summer, her feathers and fur were a similar, sandy color. Here at the start of winter, her feathers had turned whiter and her fur darker.

Younce and Naya talked trade and logistics for a few moments. Sandpiper's Dune controlled the bamboo forest and mill, which provided the lumber for reinforcing Hoarfrost. Hoarfrost's old nests had been opened up and were housing some of the overflow from Luminaire while Swan's Rest and Crane's Nest were rebuilt. The small island had once been a popular place to visit, but now makeshift nests and refugees covered it from shore to shore. Rebuilding Swan's Rest was a priority as it had more survivors, which meant that Hoarfrost was a mix of Crane's Nest refugees, Sandpiper's Dune builders, and a pawful of taiga gryphons.

Without the threat of the wingtorn, fishing had opened up again, leaving the fisherfolk in a better position than many of the weald prides—or the opinicus refugees. Naya had set up trade with Orlea, using an old goliath bird trail from the shore to the Redwood Valley Eyrie ruins.

"How're your people settling in?" Younce asked Tresh. She was looking at the construction, so he added, "They're adding a bridge further east, so the path will empty out north of Glacial Run. They remember their promise to Rorin."

Younce and Tresh had spoken at length of Rorin, the leader of Swan's Rest, and his promise to remain neutral as long as the wingtorn stayed north of Glacial Run. Tresh had snuck up here alone a couple of times under one pretense or another to be with Younce. For a gryphon who'd been born and lived her life among the fisherfolk, this was the furthest from shore she'd been. She'd admitted a desire to see the Crackling Sea and compare the water, but relations were still tense between the fisherfolk and wingtorn. She'd only just gotten used to Thenca's presence.

Tresh shook her head. "It is a different matter that brings me north. You remember Quess?"

"Yes, of course." He remembered saving the petrel opinicus from a net when they destroyed the Crackling Sea's floating fortress. She was less muscular than the petrel gryphons, but being able to use knives and tools had made her an invaluable part of Tresh's team. More than that, Quess had been mated to Tresh's brother until the wingtorn's raid killed him and their children. Only the fact that Quess was out diving with Tresh had spared her.

Tresh shivered. He resisted the urge to put a wing

around her. They'd decided it was better if they waited to tell others about their relationship, though by Ninox's teasing, it was an open secret.

"Quess and her pair were tracking the rangers as they fled Sandpiper's Dune," Tresh said. She spoke slower than most gryphons, the result of having nearly shattered her beak as a gryphlet. The triangular scars had come from a rock crab's carapace but resembled the toothy grin of a shark. "They followed the rangers north into the kjarr but did not report back. The starling prides are holding the mangrove swamp, and we have not been able to come in from the south to search for her. We have been trying for months, but there is a concern about leading the starling prides around the mountains. I would like to come in from the north and look for her."

"You?" Thenca's voice raised an octave. "As in you *personally* would like to come in from the north? Or you would like to send fisherfolk? Satra's not going to allow you or anyone from Crane's Nest through after you promised to kill her."

"I would like to go. Quess was close to my brother." When no one spoke up, Tresh offered, "I will not kill Satra until I find Quess, if it will make her feel better."

Younce shrugged. "It can't hurt to ask, I suppose."

Thenca seemed to be considering her words carefully but finally spoke. "Satra is at the kjarr nesting grounds for the next few days." She looked to the other petrel gryphons who had come with the procession, then turned back to Tresh. "You should go alone and be mindful that many of the wingtorn were killed by fisherfolk, too."

Tresh bowed her head a notch. "I will go first thing tomorrow. My kin will help provide food for the Ashen

Weald workers in the name of cooperation. We have an idea about how to get fish out of the frozen lakes."

Younce was glad that the new road hadn't yet brought more wingtorn here. Housing the wingtorn and the refugees of Crane's Nest would be a nasty proposition.

"Was that one of the Strix Pride flying away as we approached?" Naya asked.

"The great Ninox herself," he said. "She wants the old Snowfeather nesting grounds."

"Is she still refusing to turn over the invaders she caught?" Naya asked.

His eyes grew wide and his ears both went straight forward. "How did she capture them? How do you know about it and I don't?"

"I still correspond with Orlea when we send fish north," Naya said. "She says the Ashen Weald is demanding Ninox turn over both prisoners, but Ninox is holding off."

"I'm not sure why she'd do that, but it explains why she wanted allies," Younce said. The news left him troubled. For all the talk of invasion, he'd never seen any of these supposed invaders. Ninox had warned that she was a vanguard, the first line of defense against the next attack. If she was already taking prisoners, the threat was more immediate than he'd given credence.

One of the petrel gryphons was stepping back and forth impatiently, and Tresh gave Younce a nudge.

"Oh, welcome to Snowfall," he said. "Fly on up and we'll get you situated with food and nests."

Tresh led the fisherfolk up into the nesting grounds, leaving him alone with Thenca.

"We need to talk about your fisherfolk amour," Thenca said.

Younce nodded. "Later. Let me take care of them, and I'll come back just before night. Do you have everything you want here? Need anything sent down?"

Thenca looked at her small, makeshift nest set back from the construction. They'd had to lower her down with ropes to get her back to ground level from Snowfall.

"No, not unless you have a spare Deracho flying around," she said.

Younce laughed. "Not even you seem to have a spare Deracho. If you want, we can see about getting you to Hoarfrost. I don't know how long it'll take on foot."

She looked wistfully to the south. "No. I'm wingtorn, remember? It would break our agreement if I crossed south of Glacial Run. I'll stay here and wait for the road to complete. Snowfall has been pleasant, but I want to see the kjarr again. It's been too long."

He nodded. For all their talk of borders and factions, he still often forgot his friends held their own ideologies and allegiances. He put a paw on her shoulder, mindful of her scars, then set off after the fisherfolk.

2

THE BLACKWING PRISONER

Cherine tapped against the metal tip of his beak with an errant talon while he read through the confiscated papers and maps. He'd moved several small braziers into the secret workshop to provide light and had taken over the table and bookshelf for his own use. In cleaning it out, one of the owl gryphons had found a sealed ventilation passage behind the bookcase, and with a little ingenuity, they'd opened it up. They'd also discovered the mechanism for unlocking the door from the inside.

Between the clean air and way out, he felt much better about setting up inside the workshop. In addition, several owl gryphons stood guard, inside and out. The workshop had one large open space with several stalls, two of which currently contained the Blackwing Eyrie prisoners. There were only two side rooms, a small library and a slightly larger room full of chemical stains and bones. He'd insisted they bury the bones in one of the strange graves that dotted the mountains this far north, near where they'd buried the body of the third Blackwing Eyrie prisoner, a long-eared gryphon.

Cherine paused over a glyph that looked like two birds fighting midair, reached for his quill pen, and then stopped and put it back. He tapped his beak again.

"Will you stop that?!" the black cockatiel opinicus shouted from his cell. The horror on his face at being locked into the stalls had told Cherine he knew exactly what had taken place here. Based on the graves and egg shells Cherine and Ninox had found in the surrounding foothills, he suspected experiments on opinicus mothers, their eggs, and their children had been conducted here by the infamous exile Mally the Nighthaunt.

Several of Mally's assistants and close scholar friends had fled during the events at New Eyrie. Bario the Phoenix, inventor of saltpeter, had left gryphon and opinicus bodies in his wake. Impir the Mad's part wasn't public knowledge, except that he'd been seen fleeing north. Because of the Strix Pride's shaky relationship with the Ashen Weald, Cherine hadn't been able to find out more. Impir had been locked up before Cherine became a scholar, but he knew Bario from having spent a semester at the flameworks. There had definitely been something off about him.

The black cockatiel's "Will you stop that?!" echoed through the small cave. Several of the owl gryphons hissed.

"Stop what?" Cherine asked. He picked up his favorite quill pen, rescued for him by Kia.

"The tap-tap, tap-tap, tapping. I thought the quiet was bad, but your tapping is worse. Can't you do that outside?" The cockatiel's eyes were bloodshot. He'd over-preened most of his feathers and undergroomed his fur. He looked patchy, like he'd caught mange. As a precaution, Ninox had trimmed his feathers to prevent flight, but he'd done such a number on himself, it hardly seemed necessary. In his zeal, he'd broken a blood feather.

Cherine had insisted the prisoners be treated with civility. He didn't know that Ninox would be cruel, but he knew she had a different view of right and wrong as an owl gryphon—even compared to the other weald gryphons.

Next to the cockatiel, the blackwing opinicus said nothing and had said nothing since being caught. Cherine took the prisoner's calm to mean he felt he would soon be rescued. It was too much to hope that no more invaders would show up.

In the meantime, Cherine had devoted himself to trying to crack the code the maps and papers were written in. So far, his research hadn't been interrupted by any further incursions. Ninox's owl gryphons kept watch on the northern mountain range up to Poisonmaw Valley, the abandoned saberbeak hunting grounds where Hatzel's relatives had once lived. Since the creation of the Strix Pride was still a point of contention with the Ashen Weald, they gathered information circuitously.

Ninox's brothers had been understandably upset when she staged her coup and half the pride came with her. It weakened their standing in the Ashen Weald. Where their unhappiness had turned to anger was when they found out she'd named her pride after their father, Strix. At that point, they'd sent word through Orlea that none of Ninox's pride were welcome in the old owl hunting grounds and plateau.

Cherine started to move a talon towards his beak then stopped. "Sorry, I didn't realize I was doing it. I must have picked up some bad habits away from the university."

The cockatiel *tsked*. "No, you did it back then, too. You

always used to tap your beak while thinking. In lectures, you'd do it whenever something started to make sense. You just didn't make that feather-rotting clinking sound back then."

The brazier light flickered against Cherine's metal-tipped beak. He cocked his head to the side. He'd seen the cockatiel with Neider many times but didn't remember him in any of the lectures. Had he been a student, or had he just attended classes to take notes for the headmaster?

Cherine stood up and walked over to the prisoners. The blackwing opinicus looked healthy enough. The cockatiel was doing much better than he had been, considering they hadn't given him any red fern. The first month he'd begged, screamed, shouted, and tried to kill himself. If he ever got free, he'd probably go back to the drug, but for the moment, he was clean. Cherine wondered how many years it'd been since the cockatiel had last been drug-free.

"I can't seem to recall," Cherine said. "What was your name again?"

"How rude," the cockatiel replied. "You should've paid better attention."

Cherine motioned to the blackwing opinicus. "Does your friend have a name?"

The cockatiel rolled his eyes. "I didn't catch it."

"Can you read this language?" Cherine asked.

The cockatiel chewed at a feather. "I must have skipped that class."

Cherine tried another question. "Where is the headmaster?"

"Goodness, he should be around here. I guess we just misplaced him. Did you check the university?" The cockatiel laughed, but the laughter had an edge to it.

Cherine changed tack. "Who did you come here to meet?"

"What?" The cockatiel hadn't been given this question before. He looked to the blackwing opinicus, whose posture had stiffened. They'd had the same questions every day for the last month. This was the first new one.

"I've been looking over your map of the eyrie. The scrawled notes on top of it are different from the other papers; I think they're yours." Cherine stared at the cockatiel, who looked away. "Some of the important locations are labeled with different sets of characters that I think represent names: Reeve's Nest, the university, the Reeve's Guard station, Snowfeather Dam. But there are other locations marked with glyphs that repeat. I think they're meeting points or drop offs."

"Oh, that." The cockatiel spoke with a practiced boredom, but his posture was stiff. "When we got back, I was going to go check on the fern growers, but my buddy here, he wanted to know where to get a good bite to eat, so I marked them on the map for him. They all serve underbough squirrel."

It was Cherine's turn to roll his eyes. The disadvantage of weaning the cockatiel off his drugs was now that he was lucid, he let less slip. There was no point in asking more questions, but it had broken up the tedium. Cherine went back to his desk and settled down by the inkwell and began to copy over the new characters.

There was one interesting aspect about the map he hadn't figured out yet, the fact it was necessary at all. Kia had said the headmaster had fled the night of the fire, but bringing a detailed map for a city that was now rubble suggested they hadn't known the extent of the damage. The Redwood Valley Eyrie hadn't just burned, it had burned down. It was ruins and ash. There wouldn't be anyone to meet because no one lived there anymore.

But that didn't mean that it wasn't a good place to leave a message. Who would notice parchment among the destruction? Even the scavengers had started ignoring the eyrie. It'd actually be much easier for a spy to leave coded messages now that it was abandoned.

He looked down at his quill and wondered how Kia was doing. He'd sent a letter asking for her help on this but didn't get a reply. They hadn't parted on the best of terms, but he still worried about her. More than anyone else, she'd been affected by the violence around her—the ranger she'd killed to protect the gryphlets; Xavi's son, who'd lost his sight escorting her from the explosion; and the hundreds, maybe thousands, of opinici who died the night of the Redwood Eyrie fire.

He'd visited Hatzel's nesting grounds only to find out that Kia had never returned. He hoped she'd found some sort of solace with the fisherfolk. He was starting to get comfortable among the owls, though he wasn't under the impression that he was one of them.

He tapped the metal tip of his beak with a *clink*.

THE WARM COALS of cooking fires smoldered along the western beach of Luminaire Island. The sun was going down, and the two rocky points resembling an open beak were only just visible against the dark water.

Having done his part to help prepare the fish, Zeph sought out Rorin near the shore while Kia helped pack the fish into crates. She had a good head for figures and was helping keep track of how much food was stored for winter and how much the fisherfolk could afford to trade with the weald.

Not that Zeph was bad with numbers—he'd made a living trading parrots to opinici, after all—but he preferred the hunt to the after-hunt. There was no thrill in plucking the feathers off a ground parrot. It was just a necessary step before he ate it. Still, he had to admit that Kia's attention to detail had helped improve catch sizes.

The fisherfolk populations may have been at an all-time low, but their ability to trade food to the starving gryphons and opinici of the north had helped them rebuild Swan's Rest and secure Hoarfrost against the starlings across the taiga.

Kia had made herself a local hero by getting a crop of winter squash grown, picked, and stored at Sandpiper's Dune before the first major frost hit. Even Zeph had started to tire of fish, and the prospect of vegetables all winter long was a happy one. If Kia could find a way to eat the salamanders that had taken over the river delta, the fisherfolk might start naming islands after her.

Zeph found Rorin up on the rocks looking down at the water. Carru stood nearby, next to a folded net. The gryphlets and chicks called him 'The Goliath Bird' because of how strong he was. He'd kicked through several fortified doors during the battle to free Sandpiper's Dune.

"What's going on?" Zeph asked.

"We're hunting." Carru pointed to the water. "Several tasty schools of fish are off the coast."

If they hunted fish this late, they'd have to take care of them after, and the prospect of cleaning a school of fish was less enticing than going to bed. Still, Zeph had questions. "Why aren't you out there over the water, then?"

This time it was Rorin who spoke up. The large crane opinicus had led the defense against the wingtorn, killing Jun the Kjarr, and organized the liberation of Sandpiper's Dune from the rangers. In spite of these great deeds, he never seemed to lose interest in talking about fishing. "We're hoping the fish guts will lure them into the bay. The water here is shallow enough that we should be able to catch more with our net."

Zeph took a look at the net. Debris from the city of rafts had drifted to shore for a week after its destruction. Many of the fleeing rangers had left their nets behind, and the fisherfolk were becoming adept with them.

They hadn't managed to create their own yet, but Piprik, the old medicine opinicus from far away, had come up with some ideas involving bamboo fiber before he'd been sent north to the Crackling Sea Eyrie on a mission of diplomacy. The Ashen Weald had fifteen starling prisoners and no idea what to do with them. Since Piprik had worked with starlings before, Rorin had convinced him to go investigate. Piprik had left with a promise to return quickly, mumbling about how the war was too close already.

Zeph thought he was seeing a reflection of the moonlight until he heard a squeal from the beach, likely from a happy gryphlet or chick. It was later than the young would normally be allowed from the nest, but since so few children had survived, it was hard for the fisherfolk not to spoil them. The chicks and gryphlets rushed to the shore to watch as the bay began to glow a bright blue.

"We lured the shrimp in instead." Carru drooped. The slate color of his fur was intensified by the glow coming from the water. Between his distinctive beak and size, it was hard not to see Merin when Zeph looked at Carru.

Only Carru's kindness and color differentiated him from his father.

Rorin put a talon on Carru's shoulder. "It was a good idea. If it'd worked, everyone would be well fed and sing your songs tonight."

"Maybe the shrimp will sing your songs. They look well fed," Zeph said. "It's too bad they're too small to eat."

Rorin laughed, a deep sound that echoed across the bay. "I feel like we should consult Kia before we say anything is too small to eat. She carries around her journals and tells everyone what is or isn't edible."

"Don't worry, I don't think you're on the menu," Zeph replied.

While Rorin continued his laughter, Zeph looked to the beach. In the light of the shrimp, he saw a family of peafowl fisherfolk.

There had been rumors that their daughter had died in the attack on Crane's Nest, only for her to wash ashore weeks later. Her strange mannerisms were forgiven in the excitement of finding her alive. If she looked a little different, spoke in a strange manner, none of her friends had survived to call her out on it, and her family was quick to explain away the differences.

Their real daughter's body had already been given a deep-sea burial.

Zeph caught the 'daughter's' eye and nodded. Levin, youngest child of the deceased reeve of the Redwood Valley Eyrie, nodded back.

While it had meant keeping their grief private, the peafowl fisherfolk family had agreed to shelter the last of Reeve Brevin's children. Zeph wanted to check on her, but it was better if no one associated them together. While he didn't think anyone had spotted him taking Brevin's youngest away from the fighting, there was still a lot of speculation as to why the Reeve's Bane had disappeared in the middle of the Battle of New Eyrie.

Instead, he flew down to help Kia. Some of the bamboo crates were marked for Hoarfrost, and he would be going with them to check on Deracho. They needed to stock the outpost as securely as they could now, before midwinter set in and travel became even more difficult.

3

NINOX OF THE STRIX

Ninox caught the winds coming off the mountain and glided all the way down to the weald. She resisted the urge to dive at the birds flying out of the canopy. She didn't want to strain herself. Soon enough, she'd lay her egg and go back to hunting. Until then, she would keep it safe.

She didn't have much in the way of motherly instincts, but she'd seen too many prides drop to a dozen members and either die out or get absorbed by a larger pride. Her pride, the Strix Pride, was going to be strong, and that required diversity. The taiga pride leader had made a good point. The Strix Pride would benefit from taiga weather adaptations. She would have one of her pridemates make up a list of the smartest and fluffiest taiga gryphons.

Thinking back, she remembered that Zeph had been born in the taiga. His interesting hunting temperament and upside-down ambush style would be useful for hunting prey—or opinici. She'd have to ask after his family, see if any were still around. While she firmly believed that Strix owl gryphons were the best gryphons, she was willing to admit there was room for improvement.

Coming out of the taiga and over the weald, she was alarmed to see smoke rising from Hatzel's nesting grounds. She slipped under the canopy and settled down atop a redwood branch to investigate. There were the sounds of flight, the shuffling of feathers, the crackling of fire, and the trill of an opinicus talking. She flexed her claws.

At her father's insistence, she'd learned to remain undetected by leading incursions into other gryphon territories. It was one of the so-called hunting exercises he'd insisted his children participate in. She knew the Parrotface and Fantail territories as well as her own, but had never explored Hatzel's corner of the weald. It was too small and too far away to be of much consequence, an amalgamation of the remains of three failed prides. Who could have guessed Hatzel and Zeph would be held in such esteem now?

Ninox glided closer to the source of the fire, resisting the urge to bite at a chubby squirrel. She found a perch overlooking the nesting grounds and caught sight of Hatzel, calm and unfazed.

At the shoulder, Hatzel was nearly twice as tall as smaller gryphons like Zeph or Tresh. Her home pride—called saberbeaks after the long, fang-like features of her beak—had been hit hard by the monitor plague and had fled south looking for help, abandoning their home of Poisonmaw hidden somewhere to the north.

By the time the worst of the plague was over and the monitor population was back down to size, three prides had nearly been wiped out. Hatzel brought them together and turned them into a thriving community. While none of her home pride except for herself had survived, the magpie and copper hawk gryphons represented the others who'd come together under her leadership.

The last saberbeak was watching as several opinici ran wooden spears through monitor carcasses and held them over the fire. Ninox recognized the need to cook food from her time with Cherine. She slipped to the edge of the clearing and walked the rest of the way to Hatzel.

"Hello, Ninox," Hatzel said. "You're usually lighter of paw."

"I did not want to startle you so close to the flames." Ninox bristled. Closer inspection revealed that there were dozens of dead monitors prepared for the spit. "It is hard to believe gryphons are eating monitors again."

Hatzel shook her head. "We're not. At least, not yet. When winter goes into full swing, gryphons and opinici will both be hungry. Ideally, Orlea's pride will eat the preserved monitor meat, and we'll eat something else. If that's not the case, hunger should overcome squeamishness. I've been assured that cooking and salting the lizards kills the sickness." A magpie gryphon a few feet away shot Hatzel an alarmed look and she added, "Not that there's been any sign of the plague in years."

Ninox looked closely at Hatzel. The scars on the saberbeak's stomach weren't visible from this angle. The ones on her chest had healed but were still prominent. It made her look older, more dignified. There was some sadness in her, but whether that was related to the death of Vosk or the thought of eating monitor meat, Ninox couldn't intuit.

"Everything okay?" Hatzel asked.

"You look more ferocious," Ninox said. "The other pride leaders will be hesitant to challenge you now that you have killed Vosk."

"Envious?" Hatzel gave a sad half-smile with her jagged beak. "Maybe a few scars would help the Ashen Weald respect you more."

Ninox thought before she answered. "No. I am better without scars. They will understand that if I come to kill one of them, they will not get an opportunity to fight back."

When Hatzel seemed unsure how to respond, Ninox gave her a slow blink.

"So what brings you to our section of the weald?" Hatzel asked.

Ninox groomed her feathers. The warmth of the fire was nice. "You are on my way to see Orlea. Younce is allowing me use of the Snowfeather nesting site, but there are opinicus ruins nearby. The eyrie must have tried to build up there after the Connixation. I hope to get her support. There is increased pressure from the Ashen Weald to join them. My brothers hope I will reconsider."

"You have our support, at least as far as being independent goes," Hatzel said. "I don't mind what prides do as long as they don't interfere with anyone else. If you want to be independent, you should have that right."

One of the opinici offered Hatzel a piece of the salted meat, and she shook her head.

"I will stay here tonight if you will allow it," Ninox said. "It has been a long flight."

"Sure, of course," Hatzel replied.

Ninox looked around. "Is Zeph here? I have a question about his back paws."

"No, he's been with the fisherfolk, checking on Kia, I think," Hatzel said. "She's there cataloging animals and providing an *eyrie perspective* on fishing."

"Oh." Ninox was a little disappointed. She couldn't

risk flying that far south until her egg was laid. "I will ask later, then. If he is gone, I will sleep in his nest."

"He's been nesting with me in the main cave," Hatzel began.

"That is acceptable," Ninox interrupted. When Hatzel seemed unsure, Ninox added, "I do not bite in my sleep."

"That's not really what I was worried about, but sure, come on in." Hatzel led the way to the nests.

NINOX AWOKE EARLIER than was decent. She'd adapted to a daytime schedule when searching the mountains with Cherine, whose night vision left something to be desired. She'd maintained the schedule because she wanted to meet with Younce, Hatzel, and Orlea during the hours when they would be awake. The pressure on her bladder from the egg, maybe eggs, inside of her made sleeping through the night difficult.

She slipped out of Hatzel's nest and into the predawn morning to relieve herself. She didn't like the way the squirrels made noise all the time and went silent when she approached, nor the smell of the fire that made it hard to distinguish what was living in this section of the woods. This wasn't the way a gryphon's home should smell.

Still, preserving food kept everyone from starving. Her hunters were learning to take down the massive goliath birds in the northern mountains to make sure food was plentiful. They might benefit from learning to cook and salt it. They'd just have to keep the fire far from Snowfeather.

She'd just reached the edge of Hatzel's nesting grounds when she saw several large gryphons fly down from the clearing in the canopy. She backed into the forest and climbed to a branch with a good view. They formed a half-circle around the entrance to Hatzel's cave nest. Had they come for the pride leader or for her?

I am a pride leader now, she reminded herself. She only recognized one of the intruders, but their hooked beaks and large size marked them as Merin's offspring. One was blue, while the other two shared Merin's dark brown plumage. One of the brown ones' mother must have been a fantail by the look of his feathered rear end. They seemed to be waiting. *Blue, Boring, and Fantail. I will kill Boring first. Blue cannot hide under the canopy, and Fantail will have trouble flying here.*

Hatzel must have heard them milling about outside because she came out a moment later.

"How may we help the Ashen Weald?" Her voice was even, almost bored. She licked her paw and groomed the sleep from her eyes. Merin's sons must have been used to intimidating those they paid a visit to because they seemed unnerved by how casual she acted towards them.

"We wish to have a word with Ninox alone," Fantail said.

"On Ashen Weald business?" Hatzel asked. She was grooming her wings now and not bothering to keep an eye on Merin's thugs. Ninox half-expected Hatzel to swat them like gryphlets and tell them to be on their way.

After a long pause, Blue spoke up. "Yes. Ashen Weald business."

"Well, that's too bad." Hatzel stretched a wing and paw together.

"Too bad?" Fantail asked.

"Yep." Hatzel shook out her feathers. "You're not important enough to request an audience with a pride leader. What kind of deal are you going to strike? What authority do you have for your pride, let alone the entire Ashen Weald? Ninox is a very busy gryphon. Maybe you could send your daddy along, and he could set up an appointment to meet with her."

"You're quite rude for having such a small pride," Fantail retorted.

"You're quite stupid to come into my nesting grounds and say such things." Hatzel, now groomed, put her weight on her back paws and stretched high, a trick Ninox had seen Cherine do to look taller. This had the benefit of showing Hatzel's chest and stomach, laced with scar tissue.

Blue's fur rose up and back, looking like the feathered half of his body had been stuck on the back half of a much larger gryphon. He lowered himself to a crouch when Boring put a paw on him to calm him down. Unlike his siblings, Boring had taken a moment to look away from Hatzel.

The lightening of the sky peeled back the night enough to reveal forty gryphons along the edges of the clearing. Several hung upside-down from trees or watched from branches while others were on the ground, already crouching as though preparing to pounce on a ground parrot. Not all had the brown or magpie coloring typical of Hatzel's pride, nor were they all gryphons. Underbough opinici had flocked to the pride of the Reeve's Bane, as had gryphons who'd refused to join the Ashen Weald with the rest of their prides.

Hatzel was now stepping towards the unwanted envoys. "I hear your siblings who went to the Crackling Sea accomplished great things. I even hear that your fisherfolk brother is well-regarded. It's a pity the three Merin left behind turned out so useless."

She spread her wings, letting her primaries touch the trees on either side. "Would Merin notice your absence? His tenth, eleventh, and twelfth favorite offspring? The sun is out now. Perhaps you have some hunting you should be doing far, far east of here?"

Fantail lifted off first, his two brothers following. Only once they were far out of sight did the pride relax and Ninox glide down and land near Hatzel.

"I underestimated how much you annoy the Ashen Weald," Hatzel said. She settled back on all four paws and finished her morning grooming without the posturing.

"Yes. I have something of value to them now." Ninox looked at the upside-down gryphons. "The ones with the backward claws like Zeph, are any interested in breeding?"

Hatzel looked at Ninox's stomach. "I feel like you already found someone for that."

"Not for me. Not this year," Ninox amended. "The trait is rare. It may not exist outside the weald. I do not know. The invasion may come this year, but if it comes in three, having more gryphons like that could help us."

"It's late in the season, but I'll ask if anyone is interested and send them north to you," Hatzel said. "In the meantime, there's probably someone from the Ashen Weald watching the skies around our pocket of the weald. You may want to take advantage of an alternative route. One of our new opinicus pride members, after recovering from getting caught in a tangle of vines and bitten by a snake, started clearing out sections of the upper canopy."

Ninox didn't understand what Hatzel was getting at, not until Hatzel led Ninox up to a branch a hundred feet into the redwood canopy. Along the edges of the clearing, there were small glyphs carved into the trees, the same way hunting territory used to be marked. Past them, a hole through the vegetation had been cleared to allow someone to fly under the canopy quickly without getting tangled.

"It feels like an indulgence, I'll admit, after all the years of flying through the dense growth or having to rise above the treetops." Hatzel motioned to a magpie gryphon, who brought over some food for Ninox. "But it's been nice to allow pridemates to get through our hunting territory without hassle or prying eyes. I can send Xavi with you if you're worried about getting lost."

Ninox looked at the magpie gryphon. "Thank you, no. I can find my own way from here." And with that, she grabbed the food from Xavi in her beak and set off into the flyway.

4

THE ASHEN WEALD

Tresh awoke to the sound of shifting goliath bird pelts and the soft padded echoes of Younce slipping out of the nest. Her first thought was that it was morning, but based on how tired she still felt, she was certain she hadn't slept more than a pawful of hours.

She was tempted to stay curled up in the den. It was nice and warm under the goliath bird pelts, a good place to drift off to sleep, but Younce had seemed bothered, and she worried that something was on his mind. She'd spent enough nights flying out to Crane's Nest, digging through the wreckage, hoping to find something from her nieces or nephews, that she could understand the restless compulsion that came when the stars were overhead.

It had been Rorin who'd started staying up late with her until she felt well enough to sleep. She wouldn't have thought to ask someone for that kindness, and she didn't know if Younce would ask if he needed the same, so she pulled herself out of the den and into the brisk night air.

Younce's white shape didn't grace the skies, but she caught sight of his pale, fluffy tail as he dove off the cliff towards the construction. Intrigued, she crept to the edge and looked down. The bitter cold played havoc with her senses, and the wind stung her eyes. She thought she saw another gryphon down there, but not a taiga-white one. She was about to crawl back when the echoes of their conversation reached her.

"I don't understand why you're concerned," Younce was saying.

"You're not just sending her to Satra," Thenca said. "You're sending her to my brother."

"Urious?" Younce asked. His confusion mimicked Tresh's own. "Why does that matter?"

Tresh's hackles rose, but she preened them back down. Thenca was a wingtorn, yes, but she was also here as Younce's guest. Tresh's time with the survivors of Crane's Nest had made her suspicious of anyone who wasn't a fisherfolk.

She didn't know how Rorin had managed to forgive the wingtorn and rangers, let alone how he'd convinced Swan's Rest to go along with it. It would be nice to think the Ashen Weald wasn't their enemy, that the remaining Crackling Sea opinici were no longer a threat.

Perhaps it was Tresh's own guilt that kept her from letting go. When she was honest with herself, she knew that her own paws weren't clean of blood. She'd gone to Swan's Rest first. There was no way to know what would have happened if she'd taken the petrel gryphons to help Crane's Nest instead. Could she have saved her brother, her nieces and nephews?

The night sky shone, the ocean of stars full of her ancestors. She shivered. The world seemed cold.

Tresh shook off some of the snow. She should go back to sleep. Younce's business was his own. He was a good gryphon. He'd helped free the fisherfolk of Sandpiper's Dune. He and Biski had fought beak-and-claw against the Crackling Sea rangers. He'd nearly been killed. He'd earned her trust.

"When we reached the river delta, my brother and I split up," Thenca said. "I went to Swan's Rest. Urious led the attack on Crane's Nest."

Thenca's voice trailed off, and Younce offered no immediate response. Tresh was paralyzed, unable to return to the warmth of the den, unsure what to do with that information. The nameless, faceless gryphons who'd killed her nieces and nephews now had one name, one face. She knew enough about Thenca to know that her brother looked just like her.

"Who else knows it was your brother?" Younce asked.

"Just the wingtorn who were there," Thenca said. "Satra never asked. It's customary for the current Kjarr to disregard the actions of her predecessor. Jun was the same way. He never reversed his father's decisions when he took control of the pride, never condemned his father taking over the bog pride. It's why so many of my kin resented Jun. He could have released us from our pact, but he didn't." Thenca's voice was strained.

Tresh's eyes adjusted enough to see Younce take a breath in, but Thenca spoke first. "Hatzel. She hid me when the fisherfolk came to Snowfall. Hatzel knows. There may have been survivors at Crane's Nest who recognized Urious. I don't know. My brother doesn't talk about it. He was thinking of Ari's gryphlets."

Tresh was thinking of her brother's gryphlets.

"I don't know what to do with this information," Younce said. "What are you asking me to do? Why are you telling me this?"

"Convince Tresh to stay back, to send Naya to talk to Satra," Thenca said. "Think about it. What happens if one of Tresh's fisherfolk recognizes Urious? What happens if they kill him? Just because purging the weald didn't work for Reeve Brevin, it doesn't mean it wouldn't work for the Ashen Weald. If they felt threatened by the fisherfolk villages, they could wipe them all out."

Younce said nothing.

"I love Satra like she was my own gryphlet," Thenca said, "but she's responsible for thousands of gryphons and opinici now. The only way this heals is with time."

Younce shook his head. "No, I won't lie to Tresh or use our relationship to manipulate her. I believe she'll do the right thing. I believe it's her right to make that decision." He held up a paw to keep Thenca from talking. "But I won't tell her what you told me. You need to trust her. Get word to your brother if you have to."

I believe she'll do the right thing sounded to Tresh like Younce believed forgiveness was the right decision. He hadn't seen the small bodies of the dead children, wasn't in charge of their parents now. Whatever Younce—and Rorin, she reminded herself—believed was right, she couldn't agree. She'd do anything to find Quess, but she wouldn't absolve Satra. Only the dead had that right.

The stars shone in the sky.

Tresh's anger at Younce's promise to withhold this information from her gave her enough warmth to move. She crawled away from the edge until she felt sure she could fly without drawing attention to where she'd been. Maybe Younce would find her outline in the snow, maybe he wouldn't. She was too angry to care. She kept thinking about how much time they'd spent talking together.

Would he tell her anyways, despite his promise to

Thenca? If so, that made him a liar. Tresh re-entered the den and curled back up in the pile of goliath bird hides and waited.

Relationships were frustrating. She was glad she wasn't an opinicus.

She wanted to say something when he came in, see if he trusted her with the information. Instead, she kept her eyes closed and pretended to be asleep. She couldn't stay with someone she didn't trust. Either he'd tell her and she'd know he'd lied to Thenca or, worse, he wouldn't tell her and would keep the identity of her brother's murderer a secret. Either way, she'd lose all respect for the gryphon she'd spent the autumn thinking about.

There was only one solution. She slipped out before he awoke, denying him the opportunity to do either.

ONCE TRESH CAUGHT up to the path's construction on the other side of the mountains, it was easy for her to follow it to the kjarr. The wingtorn's ancestral home was nestled along a river that fed into the peat bog, though the grounds were solidly in the aneda forest. There were enough trees to provide shade and cover to the massive, lone kjarr nesting grounds, but farther out, the foliage had been recently cleared to keep starlings from sneaking up.

She knew from her own experience that any section of trees could house starlings. Despite their reflective green wings, they had an uncanny ability to blend in with the vegetation. Because they stayed close to the ground, there was no way to be sure where they were hiding.

The cold and the heights of the taiga had given them pause, but she worried they would follow the mountains south to the dunes and cross there. The cliffs and sharp winds by Williwaw might kill half the gryphons who attempted to fly around it, but that still left half of a starling horde arriving at Sandpiper's Dune.

Satra faced her own starling problem here, Tresh imagined. The Ashen Weald leader had reclaimed her home and nests but hadn't been able to retake the hunting grounds.

Before leaving the taiga, Tresh had awoken one of opinici in her escort to fill her pack with salted fish bars and other luxury gifts, then ordered them to stay and help the taiga gryphons. The gifts were a simple gesture, but she hoped to leverage any goodwill to help her get Quess back.

Months ago, one of Deracho's scouts had claimed he saw two fisherfolk trying to fly straight over the aneda forests. Tresh held onto hope that this meant Quess still lived. The eyesight of the snowy owl-gryphons of the taiga was unmatched by any of the fisherfolk.

She landed on the boardwalk outside the kjarr's nesting grounds and walked the rest of the way for the sake of the wingtorn. Being around Thenca, at least before last night, hadn't made Tresh nervous. A single wingtorn in a group of winged gryphons was one thing. Here, she would be one winged gryphon among hundreds of wingtorn.

She took a few steps before the gryphons milling about took notice of her. Several wingtorn looked up from what they were doing. Most resembled Jun the Kjarr, but she caught sight of pockets of masked wingtorn like Thenca. One of them gave a strange call, and more gathered.

A wingtorn with black ears and long legs pointed at

her dark plumage and petrel-like shape. Another pointed at her beak. All stared as she went by.

The illogical urge to spread her wings wide warred with an impulse to pull them tight against her body for safety. She resisted both and kept walking.

A crowd of grey, yellow, and brown wingtorn parted to allow her into the main nesting grounds. Some resembled the kjarr gryphons who had made up the bulk of the army that'd razed the fisherfolk villages. From these, she sensed outright hostility.

Others, the bog gryphons, just held curiosity. Except for Thenca and Urious, none of them had been part of the wingtorn raids. Naya said they'd been held in the depths of the Crackling Sea Eyrie.

More wingtorn noticed the scar pattern on Tresh's beak. A low hiss followed her on her march. She did her best to ignore them and looked around, taking in the scenery. She'd heard that the kjarr pride maintained one large home instead of several smaller ones despite their size, but the scale here was epic. The idea of *nesting grounds*, as compared to a fisherfolk city or an opinicus eyrie, suggested something small. What she saw here was larger than all three fisherfolk villages combined.

It also looked off, at least to her eyes. There'd been no markers on the tree tops, no splashes of color to help guide winged gryphons and show them where to find things. Before she'd landed, all she'd seen was a mix of browns and greens. Whatever the nesting grounds had looked like four years ago, now it was a city for those without flight.

Huts similar, yet alien, to the ones the fisherfolk used had sprung up all around the river. Each aneda tree had several domiciles at its base. There were no sounds of gryphlets or chicks. It made sense as they were all trapped in the weald, hence the need for a path. The fisherfolk had lost most of their gryphlets and chicks, but the ones who survived were all loud.

This was a nesting ground without any gryphlets.

It felt wrong to her.

It is a wrong they are trying to set right, she reminded herself. The new path that went by Snowfall would be finished soon, and the gryphlets would return to their families. These were all parents.

These are all monsters. Her hackles rose. They felt justified doing terrible things to protect their children. The refugees of Crane's Nest felt justified seeking revenge for their dead. Was it the same? Rorin and Younce would say no.

The boardwalk led to a large building that spanned the river. She couldn't imagine gryphons building that on their own. It must be a gift from their new opinicus allies.

Several weald gryphons perched atop the building, keeping watch. She recognized the fantails and feathermanes from their shared border with the fisherfolk. Several hooked beaks, similar to Carru's, hinted at Merin's pride. The feathermanes seemed close to the Merin pride gryphons, leaving Tresh to wonder if they'd always been that way or if it was a new change since Zrim Feathermane's death.

A small pack of parrotfaces waddled across the bridge on foot, oblivious to both Tresh and the crowd of wingtorn around her.

There were a few clicking beaks, but the mass of wingtorn parted to allow her into the building. She went inside expecting it to be dark, but stormcloth-covered holes in the ceiling let the light filter down. She couldn't see past a crowd of Redwood Valley opinici—or would that be New Eyrie opinici?—in front of her. While Orlea controlled the Redwood Valley ruins, Tresh hadn't heard what had happened to the refugees who had fled across the Crackling Sea to found New Eyrie. She caught snippets of conversation.

"But, Foultner, surely..."

"You're welcome to find work at the goliath bird ranch or with the trappers, but until you have a leader and some organization, there's no one to make agreements with. You're welcome to join as part of the Crackling Sea, if you'd like."

There was some grumbling about reds and blues not mixing, the once-mighty heritage of the Redwood Valley opinici, but then it settled down. It seemed that while the underbough had opted to form their own independent pride, the upper class who'd fled to New Eyrie hadn't been allowed into the Ashen Weald yet.

The discussion continued for a few minutes, with a few reds renouncing their old reeves and swearing to help the Ashen Weald, before they dispersed and Tresh could get a look around.

Spread out on cushions was a council of sorts, including one wingtorn—Urious, unless Thenca had somehow crossed the mountains on foot ahead of Tresh— and several winged gryphons of all shapes and sizes. The fisherfolk, while mostly cranes and petrels, contained defectors from all the weald prides. She saw their reflections here. She didn't see any of Carru's kin, discounting the guards outside, but there was a fantail of near-starling coloring with its tail mostly burnt off, some parrotfaces, a strix owl with nasty facial scars, and two opinici who were now staring at her.

The blue heron opinicus had seen better days. He was missing an eye and had long silver talons on one foreleg to replace missing digits. The refugees of Crane's Nest didn't have the sorts of scars that the Crackling Sea opinici had. The attack on the fisherfolk villages had come so suddenly that most had been killed outright. There were few mutilations or disfigurements. This opinicus must have seen a different kind of combat.

The opinicus next to him was more subdued but wore a black armor unlike anything Tresh had ever seen. She wore bracers with metal talons, a swirled grey, that she fastened over her claws when she caught sight of Tresh.

Satra sat in the center of the half-circle. An unremarkable, brown songbird leading the most powerful gryphons and opinici in this corner of the world.

"I am not here to kill you," Tresh said to Satra. "I have a favor to ask."

"Tresh of Crane's Nest?" Satra asked. She wore no harness nor any other sign of her importance, but the way her chest feathers were crushed in a cross shape told Tresh that Satra had been wearing one regularly in the past and had yet to molt since then.

When Tresh nodded, the Ashen Weald's leader examined the scars on Tresh's beak. "Ask away."

"Two of our scouts were following the rangers fleeing to the raftworks. One is probably dead, but I believe the other still lives. She has been cut off. The southern kjarr and mangrove swamp are full of starlings. We cannot get across to find her. I would like to come in from the north and bring her home. I have twenty more fisherfolk waiting at Snowfall who could aid me with this." Tresh unhooked her harness and laid it down. "I have brought gifts."

"Thank you," Satra said.

The smell of the fish perked up some of the weald gryphons who knew the taste. The owl gryphon came forward before any of them could stop her and grabbed the fish bars.

"Blinky, don't just eat that," the black-armored opinicus was saying, but Blinky ignored her friend, and soon, her eyes were watering with the salt.

Tresh looked to the strange council, who seemed unsure what to say or do. There was a weird energy, which Satra also seemed to notice.

"I can't allow twenty fisherfolk from Crane's Nest to enter the kjarr lands, but I may have an alternative. We can talk about this in private. If the rest of the Ashen Weald wouldn't mind?" Satra asked. Most of them took the hint, Blinky took the hint and the fish bars, but Urious and the black-armored opinicus remained.

"Foultner, Urious, you two can wait outside," Satra reiterated, but neither moved.

"It is okay," Tresh told them. Her eyes were on Urious. "They can wait here if they prefer. If I wished to kill Satra, I would not use this...deception, but I am not offended by their presence. You have no reason to trust me."

"Why do you want to go in person?" Foultner asked. "Who is this opinicus that you're rescuing? And why do you think we'll allow you, let alone twenty of you, into our lands?"

"Her name is Quess. Quess of Crane's Nest." Tresh watched Urious while she spoke. "She was close to my brother, the mother of his chicks. There are so few of us left alive, I cannot leave her to die so far from the ocean. As a leader who must take care of her own people, you may understand. If you understand, you may allow us to get her. It is, as Rorin says, the bamboo upon which peace is built."

"It sounds to me like you'd just be wasting twenty more lives," Foultner said. With her short neck and coloring, she resembled an underbough opinicus. Tresh wondered how she had come to be part of this council.

Foultner looked to Urious, but he remained silent. His tail had twitched when Crane's Nest was mentioned.

"They are all worried for Quess and know the risk. Most have tried to cross from the south, between Williwaw and Hoarfrost." Tresh saw the opinicus's eyecrest rise. Had Younce not told the Ashen Weald that there were fisherfolk in the southern taiga? Despite her current trust issues, she hated to think she may have just betrayed him. In truth, she'd started to regret leaving without talking with him first. "This is less dangerous than flying directly over the starlings. You said you had another option for me?"

"It's not just one scout lost in there. There are rangers unaccounted for and some other...precious goods." With this, Satra shared a look with Urious. "And not just the rangers from Sandpiper's Dune. Entire outposts have gone silent, going back before the Ashen Weald arrived. I'm not saying yes, but before we go further, I would need your assurance that you wouldn't harm any of the Ashen Weald in the bog."

"So long as they do not harm us, I will help them. But not at the cost of saving Quess," Tresh added. It wasn't quite the promise Satra was looking for, but Tresh wondered how rangers would react to seeing fisherfolk in the kjarr. If the missing rangers had been gone for months, they may not be aware of the current conflict. They wouldn't even be aware the Crackling Sea had surrendered to Satra. Was Satra doing this as a sign of good faith to her new allies?

The rangers who had fled Sandpiper's Dune, however, would feel differently. It would be enough to get Quess out, but Tresh worried about what they would do to Quess if they'd captured her.

Urious broke his silence. "I'll take her. If it was Thenca trapped on an island, I would be down there begging for help and access to the shoreline to get my sister back."

Tresh's eyes widened. She wasn't sure if this was the help she wanted or not. She wondered how much slower it would be to have to walk across the bog, but neither Foultner nor Satra acknowledged his disability.

Foultner did, however, roll her eyes. "Don't be stupid. You've waited this long to see your sister again. They'll get the path done soon enough. Then comes Ari and the gryphlets. I'll take the fisherfolk in. I've been setting traps and learning the kjarr."

"It's different in the deep bog," Urious said. "The sailfin monitors grow larger, the knife fish have enough charge to kill an adult gryphon, and it's hard to find clean water. Not to mention the turtles. Before Jun's father subjugated us, Thenca and I lived in the deep bog with our mother's pride. We know it like none of the kjarr wingtorn do."

Satra nodded. "You're right, but you shouldn't feel obligated to go. The wingtorn here need your leadership."

Tresh thought of the wingtorn outside with bog markings mixed in with the kjarr wingtorn.

"Grenkin said the rangers set up outposts in the bog while we were gone," Satra continued. "Surely some of them know the way."

"The same rangers who set up the outposts are the

ones who disappeared," Foultner quipped. "Either they're too scared of gryphons to show themselves, or they think they can wait out whatever happens next. I'd love the opportunity to give them a piece of my mind."

"No, I need you to go to Orlea. Urious will be enough of a guide," Satra turned to Tresh, "and I will provide the extra troops. I can either send them on their own, and we'll return Quess to you if we find her, or if you want to go along, I need your word that you won't be a problem."

Tresh looked at Urious. "As acting leader of Crane's Nest, I promise we will not harm Satra the Kjarr nor any of the rangers who do not fight until Quess has been reunited with her surviving kin."

Satra nodded but wasn't done. "Before you go into the bog, there's something you should see north of here. I'll have Erlock take you; they're already expecting her up there. Foultner can drop off a message to your kin at Snowfall for you."

"There's a goliath bird ranch shaped like a four-leaf clover just north of the bog," Urious said. "I'll wait there with the supplies and the rest of our group. We'll leave as soon as you and Erlock return."

5

ERLOCK CHARTAIL

Tresh followed Erlock Chartail, the strange fantail pride leader she'd seen at Satra's table, from the kjarr to an island on the Crackling Sea.

The water stretched far to the north. She couldn't see where it ended. Despite the stories of monsters and lightning-loving jellies, the surface was calm. It felt like a wasted opportunity to see the Crackling Sea when no storm filled it with light. She was unlikely to return.

Naya and Piprik had insisted upon infusing Tresh with information on all the weald politics when she'd taken over as the leader of Crane's Nest. Since then, she'd learned that Strix had passed away, leaving his pride without a clear leader in the Ashen Weald. No one had been able to give her a name for the leader of the Parrot-face Pride, but that had more to do with proximity. They were a northern weald pride who never ventured to the southern coast.

The fantails and feathermanes, on the other paw, had more dealings with the fisherfolk, though Tresh had never personally interacted with one before. When Erlock said she'd be coming along with the expedition, Tresh took advantage of the opportunity and plied the weald gryphon with questions Naya and Piprik hadn't been able to answer.

Erlock answered the barrage of questions as best she could while flying. "Well, no, the Chartail bit is new. I was Erlock Fantail before the explosion. The feathers may still grow back; we fantails molt slower than most gryphons. I can't speak for my pridemates, but I had exactly forty tail feathers. Yes, Satra was the one who doused me, Thenca right there with her, probably on the run from you fisher-folk lot."

Tresh took a moment to soak the information in. Rorin would use this as an example of how Satra wasn't all bad. Tresh, however, had not been impressed by the new Kjarr. She seemed just like every other gryphon, though maybe Tresh was underestimating her. Hearing Thenca's name so soon after Tresh's departure from Snowfall made it hard to be objective about anything she'd seen today.

Tresh realized that in her haste to ask about fantails and the Ashen Weald, she'd missed the most obvious question.

"Are you a starling?" she asked Erlock. While the fantail leader was a mix of brown and green, her stomach and wings had white speckles on them, and the green lit up in the light.

"Well, look at you, all thinking," Erlock mused. "I'd thought fisherfolk were more of the relaxed types. Swim, eat fish, be happy, don't think too hard about much of anything."

"You should try to live off fish, sometime," Tresh responded. "They can be craftier than you think."

Erlock threw back her head to laugh. "Ha, you're probably right. What isn't? Yeah, I'm half-starling. Well, some part starling, not nearly half. I wouldn't have thought it mattered, but you'll see here in a few when we get to the tower. I can't be too closely related. When was the last time anyone saw a starling in the weald?"

Tresh had no idea. None of the starlings had ever come to join the fisherfolk, which was unusual. Most of the nearby gryphon and opinicus communities were reflected in the makeup of the fisherfolk. While there wasn't any taiga stock on the mainland settlements, there were a few among the islanders who only came to Swan's Rest and Sandpiper's Dune to trade a few times a year. Younce had invited them back, but they'd declined.

Tresh and Erlock were drawing near to a large opinicus structure made of stone. Where the Crackling Sea Eyrie, barely visible off to the east, appeared to be carved into the cliffs, this structure had been built from the ground up. Many different rocks of varying shades of grey had been stuck together to make the tower. It stood at the center of the island, appearing taller because only diminutive trees and shrubs grew in the rocky soil. It was smaller than the redwoods on Luminaire but still dwarfed anything the fisherfolk had made.

"Welcome to the tower," Erlock said.

Atop its ramparts, Tresh saw a familiar face. An old opinicus, white feathers with dashes of grey and big circles of black around his eyes, stared up at her. His brow creased, but he waved hello as they landed.

"You look well, Piprik," Tresh said. Having the composition of the fisherfolk settlements on her mind, it occurred to her that Piprik had come from the furthest away, somewhere north of the Crackling Sea. He was lucky he wasn't a blackwing opinicus—assuming black-wing opinici had black wings. It was always possible they didn't match their name.

"Yes, yes. The assassins haven't caught up to me yet. You look well, yourself. Did Rorin send you to fetch me? I didn't think I was due back for another week." He turned to Erlock. "You, however, were supposed to come right back. Where've you been?"

"I have a pride to attend to. I'm a pride leader. It's what I do," Erlock Chartail said. "I'm not your lab pigeon. I only came back because Satra wants Tresh here to see what she's up against before she goes into the deep bog."

Understanding lit in Piprik's eyes. "Ah! You're going to rescue…"

"Quess," Tresh said.

"Yes! The petrel opinicus. Quite fascinating. One of a kind," he added. "It's important that you rescue her so there can be more petrel opinici. It could be very important."

"There are several at Sandpiper's Dune," Tresh said. "They just don't swim."

Piprik had lived in Swan's Rest since arriving at the fisherfolk villages. He'd always seemed concerned with laying low. She'd never seen him visit the other two settle-ments until the wingtorn arrived.

"Oh, well, you should still rescue her. But here, let me show you why they called me in." He led them into the tower.

TRESH WAS the first to enter the bottom level of the tower and was greeted by the smell of alcohol and pumpkins. A familiar voice was talking at them without looking up.

"We need to get some of the golden pumpkins and see—oh! Tresh!" Biski, a bundle of blues and oranges, bounded over and softly headbutted Tresh to say hello. From what Younce said, this was a Biski thing and not a traditional feathermane greeting. "How are you? How's Rorin? Is anyone making sure Younce stays groomed?"

Tresh returned the headbutt tentatively and noticed Biski had a lot more feathers. Tresh had known Biski was a feathermane but hadn't realized how young she must've been to only now be getting her characteristic mane of plumage. Younce had said she was only an apprentice, but it hadn't registered at the time.

"Rorin is well," Tresh replied. "Kia tells him where and what to hunt, and he flies out to sea and returns with his catch, happy as a salamander. Without your soap, Younce is impossible to keep clean. Every day he says thanks in your direction for turning him back to white, but I miss the pink Younce. I am well but worried for a friend. I was told there was something I should see here before going into the bog?"

Piprik was complaining of the effect the Crackling Sea air had on his joints when he caught up to them. He seemed to understand the concept of stairs better than Tresh had but was still much slower at them. "We need to get some of the golden pumpkins, Biski. Don't let me forget."

Biski rolled her eyes. "Yes, Greyfeather Pip. Why don't you use the ointment I made? You'll feel like a new opinicus. Then I can call you Newfeather Pip."

Piprik scoffed. "If I put that greasy stuff on my fur, I'll

be cleaning it out all night. Maybe if you assign one of your kin to help me?"

The feathermanes milling about the laboratory gave him a dirty look and then went back to their work. The medicine gryphons had jurisdiction here, despite their plea to send Piprik in to help. They were boiling, concentrating, mixing, and changing pumpkins of all shapes and colors into tinctures. One feathermane was saving the mixtures into small glass vials.

Tresh's first thought was that Piprik had allowed them to repurpose his own vials, but then she saw that the glass was a different color, the same color as Kia's glass baubles and trinkets. Had the Crackling Sea Eyrie traded for these, or could they make them here?

"Fine, fine. Be that way," Piprik said. "Come along, Tresh. They're in the cages in the back, around the corner. No, don't look at me like that. The cages were already here. I think this used to be the Crackling Sea Eyrie's version of a prison. They love their feather clipping, and no one wants to try to swim through jelly-infested waters."

"It's not the jellies so much as the sea monster," Erlock grumbled.

Tresh followed Biski and Piprik past the curtains to the back. Four starlings were in cages; three still had muzzles on. Erlock slipped in behind Tresh.

"Feels wrong to have gryphons locked up, doesn't it?" Erlock said.

"Yes," Tresh replied. "Are they still infected? Why the muzzles?"

"To stop the chittering," Piprik said. "No worry of the parasites. I cured the infection."

"*We* cured the infection," Biski corrected. "That's the good news. Tell them the bad news."

"They started with fifteen, and that's just the star-lings," Erlock said. "That's the bad news."

"Started with?" Tresh shook her head. "Just the star-lings? What does that mean?"

"Some of the cured refused to eat," Piprik said. "They were too far gone. Then we caught some infected rangers in the bog."

Tresh's face couldn't hide her skepticism at what had happened to the rangers.

"Don't look at me like that, it's not like they came to us pristine," he scoffed. "The starlings were pulled off the battlefield in nets. We had to force feed them. Before the muzzles, when one started chittering, they'd go crazy. They'd harm themselves trying to push through the bars. It was absurd."

"The infected rangers, too?" Tresh was looking at a massive cage, now empty, wondering how many prisoners it had held.

"No, that was my fault." Biski looked more uncomfortable than Tresh had ever seen her. "The infected all seemed to get along so well that I put the rangers in with the starlings. The starlings tore them apart."

Piprik mumbled something that sounded like "green wing altruism."

Tresh's mind was swimming. She hadn't given any thought to what Piprik was doing up here, but she hadn't expected this. She wasn't sure why she was being told now. It made her feel complicit, like when Thenca told Younce about Urious. Instead of wanting to leave, she wanted all the answers. She pointed at the one without the muzzle. "What about that one?"

"That's our best and brightest," Piprik said. He pushed Tresh close to the cage, and she tried to dig her claws into the stone. He was much stronger for his age than she would have guessed.

"Stop!" she said. Her beak was against the bars, and she didn't know if she trusted that the parasites were gone.

The unmuzzled starling ignored her.

It seemed to be scratching something into a sheet of bark. Along the back of the cage were sketches. They seemed to be of many small gryphons around a large... gryphon? Opinicus? There was evidence of him trying to give it wings several times. It had been drawn in such a way that it looked like both while having the definitive traits of neither. Were those talons or dewclaws? They were on both the front and back feet, too high for talons and too low for dewclaws. The front feet weren't quite gryphonic but weren't clearly avian, either. The front and back claws were identical but looked more like opinicus foretalons. It was poorly drawn, and if not for the level of detail on the starlings, she would've thought the prisoner was a bad artist.

"Go on, talk to it." Piprik released her. "Wave at it. Do anything. It'll just ignore you."

Biski frowned at Piprik's use of *it*. "*He* took to the pumpkin better than the others, but he's not entirely there. That's why we needed Erlock. Up until she left to take care of her pride again."

On cue, Erlock walked up to the cage. "Hello, how are you doing today, darling?" she asked the starling.

Despite having a good idea of what was going to happen, Tresh still jumped when the starling came to life.

"Oh, hello, Er-lock Char-tail," he said. His voice was high-pitched, nasal-sounding, and the syllables came out choppy. He looked directly at Erlock, ignoring Piprik, who was waving his talons.

"It is like we are camouflaged," Tresh said. "This is brain damage from the parasite?"

"Yes," Biski said to Tresh. She turned to Piprik. "Well, sort of. This is all so theatrical. She has a friend to save, Pip."

"Some of this might be wrong, but if you're going in there, you need to be careful," Piprik said. "I think, normally, this parasite isn't so bad. It's not exactly the worst one I've seen, but I haven't encountered it before. Most of what lives in the kjarr, the gryphons who grew up there included, is extremely resistant to kjarr-born illness and parasites. You might say they've evolved to fight off the nastiness of their homeland. When they were pushed out by the Crackling Sea opinici, however, the starlings moved in. These new inhabitants had no resistance, so they became infected."

Erlock was speaking calm, soothing words to the starling. Even with the charred tail, now that they were beak-to-bars-to-beak, Tresh could see Erlock's starling ancestry more prominently.

Piprik continued, "So usually, when the infection hits the host, they become aggressive and thoughtless, attacking others to spread the parasite, then die. But with the starlings, I think their green wing altruism keeps them from hurting each other."

Tresh thought back to when she'd first heard the term, back on the beach when she'd originally brought word of the starlings. "Their total disregard for other gryphons, yes? They save their own at any cost but leave a different gryphon to die without a thought?"

This time, it was Biski who spoke up. "I don't think it's about hating other gryphons. I think it's more that their bond to other starlings is so intense, so pack-minded, they can't think anyone except other starlings matter."

Tresh's views on the term were less kind, but she kept her beak shut on that for now. All this *altruism* really explained was why the starlings didn't hurt each other even after the infection took hold. "How does this help me?"

"What?" Piprik said. "Oh, yes, help you. It's no use to try to cure a few starlings. They won't interact with you because you're not a starling. Subject Four here is slowly getting better, but if you're not spending months in the bog, save the pumpkin extract for yourselves. It's possible none of them will recover enough to be functioning gryphons ever again. They've just been infected for too long."

Biski's beak was pressed shut as though to keep her own words inside, but she didn't contradict him. Instead, she weighed in with her own advice. "From what we can tell, there are a few infected rangers still in the woods. They should be alone. But if a starling starts chittering, it's going to bring a whole lot more, and they don't tend to stop chasing, like, ever. Just ask any of the Ashen Weald about the battle for New Eyrie. You have to find a way to lose them, otherwise they'll follow you back here. We don't have a good way to deal with another mass of starlings. We might fight them off, but we don't have enough extract to save an army after using it on everyone who fought at New Eyrie, and it's not like we can really grow more pumpkins in the winter."

Tresh mulled this over. "So I need to rescue Quess, but I cannot come back with starlings chasing me?"

"See why Satra said yes?" Erlock asked. "You're probably going to get stuck in there. Now, we'd best get going.

One of the assistants will give us a few vials of pumpkin extract and go over the symptoms of infection."

Tresh started to leave but then turned back with one more question. "Are all kjarr gryphons immune, even the bog ones? I am bringing a wingtorn. The infection will not reach him?"

Biski and Piprik looked at each other. Piprik spoke up. "Who can know? I'd like to find out."

"But I won't let him infect new gryphons," Biski said. "It's unethical, even for an opinicus, and we're already working with a limited amount of the antidote."

This seemed to be an old argument, and as it flared up again, Tresh followed Erlock out of the lab. This was going to be more difficult than she'd thought.

They waited as a harness pouch was stuffed by one of the medicine gryphons and were about to head out when Piprik stopped them.

"You can let the Ashen Weald do this on their own, little shark," he said.

Tresh shook her head. "Quess and her children meant the world to my brother. I cannot save my brother or his children. It is too late for that. But I will not let Quess be forgotten."

Piprik turned to Erlock. She was also packed to go. "And you? Don't you have a pride to lead, like you always remind me?"

Erlock hesitated. "I do, but I worry for the starlings. Maybe it's a mistake. I just think someone needs to observe them and see if they can be helped."

This time it was Piprik who paused. "You should not go west past the bog."

Erlock ruffled a little.

"But if you do, there's a river that feeds into the bog

from the jungle, the Jadebeak River. Look for a cave next to the waterfall and show them this." He reached into his medicine bag and pushed aside several golden vials marked as saltpeter before pulling out an eyrie badge. On one side it had an opinicus wearing a spiked crown. On the other side, it read *Piprik*.

Erlock put the badge into her harness. Before she could thank him, Piprik turned and made his way back to the laboratory.

"Strange opinicus," Tresh said.

Erlock shrugged. "Aren't they all?"

Not like that, Tresh thought, and not for the first time.

TRESH TRIED to secure the satchel of pumpkin vials to her harness so they wouldn't get damaged during the flight. Considering how many starlings were in the bog, she couldn't help but feel that she had too few to be effective. While the feathermanes were hesitant to get rid of any of the antidote, the number of rangers lost in the bog was staggering. The raftworks, two lumber mills, something called the Flower, and the smaller outposts hadn't reported in. A team had been sent from New Eyrie before the battle but hadn't returned.

It was optimistic thinking, according to Erlock, but they could find a lot of sick rangers hiding out in the deep bog. Tresh was more concerned about a single fisherfolk.

"Should we be going?" Tresh asked. It was irresponsible to fly over strange water once the sun set. She wasn't sure what they were waiting for.

"Just a little longer," Erlock said. "A sense of adventure can be an overwhelming thing."

"Adventure?" Tresh looked back up at the tower. A blue face peeked down. The same blue face that had come along in the battle against the city of rafts to help the wounded. "I see."

Biski glided down. The pockets of her harness seemed to be stuffed full for a gryphon of her stature. Tresh noticed that Biski had several clear golden vials the same shape and color as the ones Piprik used, but these had their labels scratched off. Inside was a black powder, too dry to be pumpkin.

"I told you," Erlock said. "They've been hearing from the wingtorn about a golden pumpkin that's much more potent than the kind we eat for food, but only grows deep in the bog. It could make a big difference. Or it could be nothing. They've already tested six other types that were less effective than the ones we're using now."

"Hello!" Biski chirped, landing next to Tresh. "I liked Quess. She was plucky. Do you have a medicine gryphon already? Let's go!"

"I do not know," Tresh began, but without waiting for a response, Biski hopped back into the air and headed south. Erlock and Tresh caught up to her.

"Is that more pumpkin extract you have on you?" Tresh asked.

"Oh, no. We gave you what we could," Biski said. "These are ointments and things to rub in your fur and feathers. Just normal weald medicines."

Tresh gave her the side-eye, but Biski adjusted her harness pouch so the golden vials were no longer visible.

"She's very big on ointments," Erlock sighed. "They do tend to work, if you can get past the smell."

"Who cares about the smell? Have you seen the size of the flies in the aneda forest?" Biski shivered. "Can you imagine how big they must grow in the peat bog? Oh, I itch just thinking about it. Piprik also asked me to scrape some of the slime off a knife fish. I'm not sure how to do that without getting shocked, but maybe one of the kjarr pride will know."

Tresh looked to Erlock, who managed a shrug mid-flight.

6

THE OPINICUS PRIDE

Orlea was having a rough day. Before the sun had come up, she'd awoken to the sound of something scavenging outside her home. Cherine's description of the capybaras had been of tame, awkward critters a hundred times bigger than a squirrel. None of what he'd said had suggested they'd be capable of waging guerrilla warfare on Orlea's food stores, yet every night something new had been broken into.

The problem was their teeth. If they were determined to get into something, they'd gnaw their way through.

The merchants wanted metal locks made, a suggestion so laughable, she had, in fact, laughed. Despite its proximity to the flameworks, the metalworks had survived unscathed. Orlea had even tracked down two metalworkers who had returned from New Eyrie. What she didn't have was metal to work with.

She had a long list of problems to figure out, and opening a new mine wasn't on the list. Instead, she had her two metalworkers melting down scavenged scrap and turning it into something useful, like harness buckles. Her best opinici were attempting to locate the old Reeve's Nest building in the ruins, which should provide enough scrap metal for their current needs.

Orlea yawned. After scaring off the capybaras last night, she'd crawled back into her empty nest and reached a talon to where her mate no longer slept. Having a nest big enough to sleep two had earned her a few dirty looks while nesting material was so scarce. Some of those dirty looks had come from her mate's family, but the truth was far less scurrilous. She couldn't sleep in a small nest because she needed the illusion that he was there next to her to fall asleep.

She just had time to stretch before her first appointment of the day arrived. Later, she'd get to interview one of the prison guards who had worked the northern quarter. Now, however, she had merchant drama to deal with.

She opened the door to the abandoned ranger outpost that served as her nest and welcomed in several opinici who had been waiting patiently outside.

Didi, a blue opinicus merchant who seemed enamored with Zeph, had taken to leading the other tradesfolk when something happened that affected all of them. She acted respectable now, but Orlea had sold her an illegal turkey or two back in the day.

"There are thieves in our midst!" Didi began. The other merchants nodded affirmation. "We need guards stationed over the fields. Ten ferns are gone!"

Orlea yawned. Ten ferns weren't a whole field. It could've been hungry capybaras. "You already have guards. Where were they when this happened?"

"We have *daytime* guards," Didi said. "We need night guards."

As much as Orlea wanted to ignore the problem,

having enough red fern contraceptive would keep down the number of eggs they had to deal with in the spring.

The merchants were awaiting her reply. She wanted to ask the guards why they couldn't work at night. She wanted to suggest that, with so many merchants, they could each take one evening a week for night time guard duty themselves, though she knew none of them would want to risk their own necks.

"Can we hire an owl gryphon?" one of the merchants in the back asked.

Orlea and Didi looked at him.

"Well, they don't sleep at night, right? And they can see things," he added. "Like, in the dark."

A chorus of "spooky" came from the other merchants.

"Can you get us an owl gryphon?" Didi asked. "Ninox is your friend, right?"

Orlea tapped the tip of a talon on her beak, a bad habit she'd picked up from her time in the medicine gryphon cave with Cherine. "I don't know. I can reach out. What would you pay this owl gryphon night guard of yours?"

More discussion amongst themselves, then from their spokes-opinicus, "What would it want?"

The obvious answer was food. Ninox herself might want books. It got colder in the mountains than in the valley, so blankets or bedding might make sense.

Orlea decided to delegate thought responsibilities. "Take some time to think and talk among yourselves. Maybe find a gryphon to chat with. Then come back tonight with your best offers."

THE UPPER CANOPY flyway dropped Ninox at the edge of the grasslands. She made note of the marker on the tree in case she ever needed to get back to Hatzel's nesting grounds and flew low across the grass to the forest around the remains of the Redwood Valley Eyrie.

An opinicus chirped a greeting as she flew by. They were used to her kin stopping in to provide information and restock.

Ninox said her hellos—she took every opportunity to practice conversing with gryphons and opinici in common—but kept them brief and headed to Orlea's den.

The opinicus pride leader slept in a large storage shed that had once housed extra supplies for the Reeve's Hunting Grounds. It was one of the few buildings far enough from the eyrie to still be standing.

There had been a few rickety buildings constructed later, but most of the opinici were sleeping in makeshift nests in what had been nicknamed 'turkey territory.' The blue ocellated turkeys had all fled, prompting talk that they were hiding in the northern mountains.

Ninox often heard rumors of escaped domesticated goliath birds, capybaras, and turkeys living in her mountains, but she'd never seen any evidence of such a food paradise. Her pride were learning to hunt the shaggy feral goliath birds to get enough to eat. They'd been living off the fish in the Snowfeather River, but she wanted them to be prepared when it froze over.

Ninox remembered Orlea as a late sleeper, but the door to her makeshift nest was already open a crack. She often stayed up late at night interviewing everyone about what happened to the Redwood Valley Eyrie.

It was common wisdom among the refugees that the reeve had set the fire as part of some plan to purge the lower class opinici with the gryphons, but the flames had gotten out of control. Rather than assume anything, Orlea had been compiling everyone's accounts and trying to fill in the gaps. Ninox herself had used Orlea's notes to find information about her father.

Orlea snored loudly in her nest.

Ninox clicked her beak once.

Orlea's breathing and heartbeat changed. She rubbed her eyes. "Oh, hello, Ninox."

"Why open your door if you still need sleep?" Ninox asked.

"Because I have to steal sleep wherever I can find it. If I left the door shut while I slept, I'd never talk to anyone. What news from the north?" Orlea went through her morning grooming routine. It involved less spit than the gryphon grooming routine. No wonder she was so loud when she flew. Improper feather grooming led to poor hunting performance.

Ninox did not comment on the poor grooming. She had learned politeness from Cherine. "The reeve built and then abandoned several structures by the Snowfeather nesting grounds. I would like to make use of them and the nesting grounds, so I am speaking to both Younce and you for permission."

"I'm not the reeve," Orlea protested. "I don't own any of that."

"You are not the reeve, yes. But you have taken responsibility for all of this when no one else has. Now I wish to take responsibility for the northern mountains. The invaders will return." Ninox stretched her ankles. They had started swelling when she flew for too long. This was her first time being pregnant. It was less than enjoyable.

"Did you ask Younce yet? I imagine he'd be the harder sell," Orlea said.

"He asked me not to tell you what he said," Ninox replied.

Orlea laughed. "The fact that you're here means he said yes. I suspected he had a fluffy heart the first time I saw him and Biski together. Sure, you have my permission. Crater Lake might be a stickier point, but we can talk about that later. There's not much of a lake there after Kia blew up the dam. Before you go, I have a few questions for you, if you don't mind."

Orlea got out her quill and ink and opened a page. How she'd saved so much paper from the fire, Ninox couldn't guess.

"I do not mind," the owl gryphon replied, "but I need to get back. The Ashen Weald is not happy with my choices. They sent Merin's brats to find me at Hatzel's pride. Ask your questions quickly."

Ninox settled down, trying to take the weight off her paws while keeping her stomach safe. She ended up sideways, leaning against a stack of goliath bird pelts.

"Is it true you've been holding a Blackwing Eyrie scouting party hostage?" Orlea asked. "Is that why the Ashen Weald is upset with you?"

"Blackwing Eyrie? I have not heard this term." Ninox kneaded the air to keep circulation flowing. She'd left Cherine in charge of figuring out the prisoners. She had a pride to run.

"Some of the refugees spent time talking to the Crackling Sea inhabitants. That's what they call them," Orlea said. Ninox didn't respond at first. "Oh, come now. I gave you the north. You may have access to information no other gryphon or opinicus does. Is it true? Is that why the Ashen Weald is so angry?"

"Yes," Ninox said. "Though I think my problems with the Ashen Weald have more to do with me leaving and taking half my kin with me. They were not happy to get word that so many of their owl gryphons had left."

Orlea chewed on the feather of the quill. "I don't get it. Why not just turn over the invaders? What value do they hold for you?"

Ninox looked at the compiled tomes. Whatever she spoke would be added to them. "Wait to write this down, please, until later." She didn't know how much later, but Orlea put the quill down, and Ninox continued. "There were only three. One died before I arrived. They were not invading and already had maps. I think they have an ally or a hideout somewhere south. Cherine is working on their strange words. I have not told him what I think, but I hope he will confirm it on his own."

Orlea picked up her quill out of habit, then put it down again. "You think someone from the eyrie is working for them. You think we have a spy among the opinici."

Ninox nodded. "While one prisoner is from a foreign eyrie, the other is the cockatiel forger from your interview with Kia, Headmaster Neider's assistant. Their ally here could be someone he knew from the university."

Orlea's eyes widened at the mention of the cockatiel forger who'd disappeared the night of the eyrie fire.

"Or it could be a gryphon," Ninox admitted. "They had a gryphon I have not seen before with them. Owlish, fuzzy, no tail, with long ears. He died fighting. It may be that they have many spies. I trust my pride. I do not trust any other prides. Once the prisoners leave my care, I believe they will be killed or freed."

Orlea seemed to be thinking. "What can I do to help? Do you need more guards?"

This was what Ninox had been waiting around for. "We have them in a hidden location. I do not believe the Ashen Weald will take them by force. I do not think they can find the hiding spot."

The owl gryphon paused, searching for one of Cherine's longer words. "What I need is the solidarity of a large pride while remaining small. If the Ashen Weald attacks the taiga, it would take years to root out all of the Snowfall Pride, if they could do it at all. If they attack Hatzel's pride, they lose the large number of gryphons who see Zeph as the hero who killed the reeve. If they attack you, they risk their own opinici rebelling. I need a little of the protection all of you provide. Your support allows me to look north for threats instead of south."

Orlea nodded. "I never noticed, but you've become much better at talking. I've never met a more loquacious owl gryphon."

Ninox tilted her head to the side.

"Sorry, that's not what you asked," Orlea said. "I don't speak for all opinici, not even all of the refugees. I believe my hold here is more tenuous than you give me credit for. We're already seeing conflicts rise up between the old underbough and the northern quarter, as though either exist now, and between us and the blues. Still, I can't fix things between my people if I'm looking north. I'll do my best to give you support."

"Thank you," Ninox said. "That will let me no longer have to worry about the Ashen Weald, at least for now."

She turned to leave, but Orlea spoke up. "One more

thing, I almost forgot. If you could have anything from the opinici here, what would you want?"

Ninox turned her head to the other side. "That is an odd question. Why ask it?"

Orlea seemed unsurprised by her answer. "The merchants have a problem with someone stealing ferns from their fields. It might be capybaras, but it might be an opinicus or gryphon. They want someone to guard the fields at night when our own guards doze off or can't see."

"How much value does this red fern have?" Ninox asked.

Orlea started to answer, stopped, then began again. "It's very valuable to the merchants and most opinici here."

"You have teachers from the university who teach the opinicus chicks when they are young and as they get older. For one guard at your fields, I want one teacher at our nesting grounds to teach the young. When they fledge, we will send them here to learn more. And adult gryphons must have access to the university when it is up again." Ninox was surprised at how many words had come out at once, but she didn't know if she'd have another opportunity like this.

Orlea smiled. "I'll give your demands to the merchants when they come by later."

"And I would like to read your books now," Ninox added.

"Go ahead," Orlea said, "but I'm going to take a nap. Let yourself out when you're done."

KNIFE FISH BREAKFAST

Tresh, Biski, and Erlock arrived at the goliath bird ranch as the day was ending. Tresh missed being over the water. Once landed, the Crackling Sea was no longer visible to the north.

While the weald gryphons settled in, Tresh took the opportunity to explore. From the sky, the ranch was designed like a clover. The road heading south into the bog formed the stem, while three fenced areas formed circles like leaves coming out from a building at the center. Each 'leaf' was subdivided into different pens, but those fences were only visible once she was close. Several large rodents she recognized as capybaras roamed the western pasture. Goliath birds filled the east. The northern fences were still being repaired.

The large building at the center was a mixture of residence and common area. The bottom story had no walls, only supports, and the roof was open. The ground level offered places to congregate and eat. Above, the building rose several stories with nests on the top levels. Makeshift ramps, at odds with the original design, had been added to allow wingtorn access to the nests on the second story.

While there were a few Crackling Sea opinici, most of the workers were of the more colorful Redwood Valley variety. It seemed the old wounds between the sea opinici and kjarr gryphons hadn't healed entirely. She'd have to tell Naya when she got back with Quess.

Since becoming leader of Sandpiper's Dune, Naya had been on a quest to uncover the causes behind the deaths and fires of the summer. She had questions about Rakesh and the strange jars she'd found in his camp after Carru had killed him. It had led her into the weald and taiga, then eventually to the charred remains of the Redwood Valley Eyrie.

There, she'd found a kindred spirit in Orlea. Their shared crusade led to shared knowledge, which then led to the opening of a trade route between the fisherfolk and the strange opinicus pride. Most of the knowledge Tresh had about the Crackling Sea Eyrie came from Orlea by way of Naya. Neither of them had expected Tresh to be allowed in the kjarr, but Naya had stressed that Tresh should keep her eyes open if she were given safe passage.

Tresh had promised nothing. She didn't think of herself as a spy. Still, there were things about gryphons and opinici she wished to understand. So when a Crackling Sea ranch, full of birds once raised by Crackling Sea opinici, was now staffed almost entirely by wingtorn and Redwood Valley refugees, it stuck in her memory. She was so busy watching a wingtorn and blue heron opinicus argue that she almost walked into a stray goliath bird.

"*Mrooonk!*" the bird said.

She stared at it. It was twelve feet tall, four times her height. She'd seen a few of the taiga breed over the past months, greyish-blue monstrosities that could reach nearly twenty feet. This one was brown and seemed much less shaggy. It reminded her of Carru. Like him, it seemed friendly.

It stretched its neck towards her. "*Mronk?*"

"I do not talk to food," she told it.

"A good policy for a hunter." Urious's voice came from behind her. He wore leather bracers on each foreleg the way an opinicus might. Several wing feathers were tied to each bracer. While the feathers looked similar, somewhere between a mockingbird and a shrike, the set on his left smelled like Thenca.

Tresh didn't want to speculate on if he'd retrieved the feathers himself. Instead, she motioned to the other goliath birds in their pen. "This one is on the wrong side of the fence."

Urious laughed. "Tilly is a special case. She's more of a pet than a ranch animal. I think the blues used her to keep the others in line. In exchange, she was given free range. It also doesn't hurt that Tilly's figured out how to open the gates with her beak. There's really no way of keeping her in check."

Tresh watched the way he moved. Her first impression of him at the kjarr nesting grounds had been of a small gryphon, like her, but that'd been incorrect. He'd looked smaller without his wings, but he was an average size, a head taller than her.

The resemblance to his sister was striking, but Thenca had her thick winter coat in, adding to the illusion that Urious had been smaller. Tresh noted that he had scars on his tail that Thenca lacked in case she ever had to tell them apart.

Something struck Tresh as off about him. It didn't

come from his wingless stature, not directly, at least. His musculature was wrong. After the wingtorn's initial attack, she hadn't been given an opportunity to see a live one up close. Rorin's sentries had rained javelins down upon them until they retreated to the safety of the forest. Tresh herself had only killed their opinicus allies.

Now, seeing a wingtorn next to her, she could understand how their old leader had jumped as high as he did. Their leg muscles were well-developed. It must have come from having to run instead of fly everywhere. She was sympathetic. Since learning to dive and swim, soon after her run-in with the rock crab, her own shape had diverged from those of her nestmates.

Next to the petrel gryphons from Sandpiper's Dune, she looked strange. Her shoulders were broader. Her back legs were stronger. Her wings had more muscle, but her forelegs had less. Not that she minded. She didn't care how she looked, as long as she could swim, dive, and hunt better.

Urious was staring at the triangular scars on her beak. She tilted her head.

"Sorry," he said. "I know I shouldn't stare, but I never expected to see you up close. I remember when you killed one of our jailors. We'd never seen a gryphon like you before. We'd never seen a gryphon swim before. Not like you swam. We called you The Shark."

"No one expects to see their enemies up close unless they are trying to kill them," she responded.

His ears went back. "We weren't your enemies by choice. I don't think of you as an enemy even now."

She searched his face. A black band of feathers surrounded his eyes, giving her the impression of a mask, yet he sounded genuine. Thenca could sound like any gryphon she met, so it reasoned that Urious could do the same. This sincerity could be a trick of his voice.

Naya sought answers. Rorin sought peace, or perhaps safety by way of peace. What did Urious seek?

Tilly offered one final *mronk?* before wandering off towards the ranch building where gryphons and opinici were eating and getting ready to sleep.

"And Rorin? He killed Jun..." she searched for Naya's phrase, "Jun the Kjarr. He is not your enemy? My family meant everything to me. Did Jun mean nothing to you?"

Keep your head down, and don't say anything to get you in trouble, Rorin had told her. If Quess weren't so important to her, Tresh would have let one of the fisherfolk less impacted by the wingtorn go on this mission. If Rorin hadn't killed Jun in front of half the wingtorn, he'd have been better-suited by far.

"Jun was like family," Urious said. "His father was a tyrant. Demanded the deep bog tribes bring tribute to him. When Jun took over, he offered us our dignity."— *Though not your freedom, if Thenca's story was to be believed*, Tresh thought—"He figured out what offerings we'd brought over the years and returned the same amount back to us. He said we were an equal part of his pride and worked hard to win over most of us. Thenca and I were the first to become full members of the kjarr pride. I mourn him every day."

"And Rorin is not your enemy?" she prompted again.

Urious shook his head. "How could he be? We fought hardest for our gryphlets. We surrendered to the Crackling Sea to save them. I was in Crane's Nest when Jun died, but we all know what happened. Jun would rather have died to Rorin the Hunter than to a blue or a puffed-up red. Reeve Brevin and Jonas killed Jun. No one blames Rorin."

She looked at the line of wingtorn climbing up to their nests for the night. "No one?"

Urious raised an eye crest. "Are you worried? Your nest is on top, between Biski and Chartail. I'll keep you safe until we save your friend."

She didn't know what to say to that, so she just said, "Goodnight," and flew up to meet Biski and Erlock.

Urious was a strange sort of child murderer. He made her uncomfortable.

THE MIST COMING off the bog pulled, softened, and warped the morning light. With daybreak came breakfast and final preparations. As much as she wanted to get a good look at the strange capybaras, Tresh decided to forgo her investigation of the ranch in favor of making sure she had enough to eat. She wanted to save her salted fish bars for emergencies.

If fish were all she wanted, she needn't be worried because that was what they had for breakfast that morning. Long, cooked fish.

"Is this from the Crackling Sea?" she asked a blue heron who was seated next to her. She'd heard his friend call him Xalt. There was a slight pink hue to his feathers that suggested a Crestfall parent. It made her miss Younce.

Xalt gave her a horrified look.

"It's knife fish," Biski said.

"From the *kjarr*," Xalt added. Several of his feathers were frayed as though they'd been burned away and he hadn't molted yet, leaving Tresh to wonder if the damage had been done at New Eyrie or if he'd been among the rangers placing explosives in the weald.

"The fish in the sea have figured out they just have to stay east where the reeve's pet patrols and the blues can't get at them," a wingtorn chimed in. Tresh still wasn't sure what the reeve's pet referred to, or which reeve it had been a pet of, but didn't ask. "Until then, we're teaching them bog fishing. If it's not to your liking, the stew is sailfin meat with the last of the rimu olives from the parrotfaces."

While the opinici turned their beaks up at the cooked knife fish, she thought it tasted pretty good. Even as a gryphlet, she'd never been a picky eater—the scars on her beak proved that much.

"How do you catch it?" she asked. "The knife fish."

"Very carefully," the wingtorn said.

"Not carefully enough," Biski said. "The medicine gryphons have been complaining about all of the electrocuted hunters."

The other ranger, Jer, spoke up. Unlike Xalt, he'd mentioned several times that he'd been stationed at the Crackling Sea and had aided the Ashen Weald in the battle for New Eyrie. "We use nets, then a pointed stick to kill it. The moment you go for them, they jump at you. If they touch you, it's *zap!*"

He mimicked falling unconscious. While knife fish were specific to fresh water, Tresh's underwater exploration off the coast of Luminaire had led to the discovery of a type of ray that hunted with electricity. Every few years, a fisherfolk drowned when they startled a buried ray.

"Besides," Jer continued, "this is only temporary. We're setting up a fishing outpost on the island, and we're going to try fishing north."

Erlock looked up from her sailfin stew. Bowls had not been designed for use by gryphons. "Aren't you worried about the Blackwing Eyrie?"

"It's a big sea," Xalt replied. "We only stayed on the southern tip because we didn't need more. Crestfall is up farther north. They used to trade with us. They went silent after the Blackwing Eyrie's attack, but all the glass in the Redwood and Crackling Sea Eyries came from them. Either way, we haven't seen their rafts on the water. Winter brings squid to the surface. Enough squid and we might last until the crops are done growing."

Tresh finished eating and moved away from the food to finish her morning grooming. Her mouth felt oily from the knife fish. If she were swimming, she wouldn't mind the fish oil on her feathers. She wasn't sure she'd get to swim in the bog. The water seemed to be full of electric fish and monitors. Still, there was no way to know what the rest of the day held. She left Biski and Erlock and headed outside. Both seemed more intent on listening to the wingtorn and opinicus argue about whether they should eat all of the goliath birds.

AFTER GROOMING, Tresh went to where Urious was gathering their team just south of the ranch on a packed-dirt path. A glance north revealed a thunderstorm brewing over the sea. The warmth this close to the bog was oppressive, a stark contrast with the taiga in winter. Things still looked sunny to the south, so she didn't pay the rain much mind, instead putting her energy into speculating on what this Ashen Weald rescue team would look like.

She'd imagined they'd be made up of weald gryphons

and Crackling Sea opinici, but Urious was speaking with two wingtorn.

"Hello," she said to the three of them. "I am Tresh."

They didn't offer their names. Both had markings similar to Urious, but with their own twist. One had black mask markings that took up most of his face, and the other was different shades of brown, no black at all, and even his facial markings were white stripes.

Urious didn't apologize for their rudeness. "Don't mind Black Mask and White Stripe here, they're surly to everyone who isn't bog. They were searching for the rest of the capybara herds and found signs of opinici." He called out, and Jer, one of the opinici from breakfast, came over with a map. "They were searching here."

The map showed the bog with the kjarr nesting grounds on the northeast corner, the raftworks along the southern mangrove coast, and the Flower building in the center. At least, the words looked like they said Flower. The lettering was similar to how the fisherfolk opinici wrote, but they were drawn in ways she wasn't used to. Urious was pointing to a place away from the trail that went straight from their current location to the Flower, off the path.

"Satra seemed to think they were at the center. Is it better to check there first?" Tresh had no power to contradict him. She'd promised to follow his lead as a condition of joining the expedition.

"If the Flower was overrun, they may've come north," Black Mask said.

"If the Flower was overrun," White Stripe added, "you really don't want to go poke that bee's hive."

She looked from one to the other. "As you think is best."

Urious traced a paw over the center. "The opinicus maps don't show it, but the bog is drier there. It was once a nesting ground, and there are some old eyrie ruins nearby that provide some cover. It might have seemed a good place set up defenses if they were chased by starlings."

She nodded. With the trail, it seemed like it would be easier to go straight south first. She didn't know how the wingtorn would travel through the wetter parts of the bog. She decided against suggesting that the flyers check out the camp and report back to Urious. If it wasn't her place to call the shots, it definitely wasn't her place to say who had to stay behind.

"Oh, there's the rest of our team," Urious said. "Looks like they finally woke up."

Tresh turned around. Biski was lecturing Erlock on the proper way to handle a knife fish. Behind them, the ranger from breakfast, Xalt, spoke with a Reeve's Guard. She wondered what the opinici thought of old eyrie ruins. She'd never heard of a swamp eyrie before.

Gliding behind them was Urious's late sleeper, an owl gryphon. She landed next to Tresh, and Tresh could smell salt and ocean fish on her breath. This must be the gryphon who'd pounced on the fish bars back at the nesting ground. She tried to remember what the dark-armored opinicus had called her.

"Blinky?" Tresh guessed.

The gryphon blinked at Tresh. She sniffed at Tresh's harness for more fish.

Biski walked over. "Here, rub this in your fur, but don't get any of it in your beak."

Tresh wasn't sure how to do that and said so.

Biski was unfazed. "It's okay. I'll do it for you."

Urious climbed on top of an empty crate discarded

alongside the trail and spoke to the crowd. "Good morning! Thank you all for volunteering. We have several opinici and at least one fisherfolk trapped in the bog. You all remember the starlings that attacked New Eyrie. The largest swarm of them is stalled in the southeast, between the mangroves and the taiga. Now is the time to save our friends."

The two wingtorn capybara trackers were staring at Tresh. She did her best to ignore them.

Urious continued. "We've had reports of movement near an old set of ruins southwest of here. That means going off the trail. If they're ours, great! We're done early. We can come back here and have a party. If they're not, they could still use our help. They may have information on starling movements." He turned to look at the two trackers. "Or even information about our missing capybaras! I'm getting tired of sailfin meat, myself."

The trackers took their eyes off Tresh long enough to mumble their agreement.

"Okay, a few safety issues before we go in," Urious continued. "I'm in charge. The bog is dangerous, so if I give you an order, you follow it. If you disagree with the order, follow it now, then when you're safely back at camp in one piece because you listened to me, we can argue about it. I like to argue.

"Never go anywhere alone. Never go near the water. Sailfins and knife fish hide in the water. If you start to feel funny, talk to Biski. She's our medicine gryphon. You said the last medicine gryphon was hard to spot, so we color-coded this one for your convenience." Biski chirped something friendly and spread her wings to show off her blue plumage and spotted orange fur. "The rangers have extra water. Don't drink anything unless we tell you it's safe."

To their credit, the trackers didn't seem to like the rangers any more than they liked Tresh.

"Lastly, we cannot lead the starlings out of the bog. If we get detected, we need to either kill the starlings or lose them before returning home. The feathermanes have found a cure—with help from one of the fisherfolk, thank you for lending us Piprik—but we don't have enough to treat a large population. We used up all the stores after the Battle for New Eyrie, and it could be a year before we'll have that much, maybe two. Until then, we let the starlings have the bog. If you have a problem with that, take it up with Satra."

Tresh was surprised to see that one of the trackers scowled at Satra's name. Did they just hate everyone?

Urious hopped down from his crate. "Alright, one final supply check and it's time to go. There's an outpost with walls south of here. I'd like to make it there before dark. Opinici, check the harnesses of gryphons. Gryphons, if something is too tight, say so. Biski, you're making clinking sounds. If you don't want to be starling bait, give some of your vials to the rangers. I want you carrying essential medicines only: pumpkin, aneda resin, bandages. Let the others carry your ointments. Henders, do you have an extra water skin? No? Well, go grab one and fill it with clean water."

Tresh decided to seek the relative friendship of other gryphons and moved closer to Erlock and Biski with an uncomfortable pang of guilt. Down on the coast, she didn't tend to think of individuals as gryphons or opinici. Here, far from her friends and home, she realized she didn't feel comfortable around the Crackling Sea or Redwood Valley opinici. She associated both with the attacks on her village.

She tried to justify this by saying that the wingtorn made her uncomfortable, too, but she knew that wasn't quite it. There were cultural lines that existed here, and she felt forced into them. She resented it, but she was doing this for Quess.

"So, first time in a bog?" Erlock asked.

"No. I have been to the raftworks," Tresh replied.

"Oh. I've heard it's very impressive. What's it like?" Erlock asked.

"Abandoned," Tresh replied.

"Yes, I guess that makes sense." Erlock pawed the ground awkwardly. "Oh look, here comes our harness checker."

The Reeve's Guard was walking over. Tresh had been told that they'd disbanded, but his harness and medallion matched that of the Reeve's Guard captain who had led the attack on Sandpiper's Dune.

"Hey there, gryphies," the Reeve's Guard said. "I'm Captain Henders, but you can just call me Henders. No need to worry about formalities in a swamp, am I right?"

"Yes?" Tresh ventured.

Erlock rolled her eyes. "Especially as there's no reeve for you to guard and no guards for you to captain."

"Hey now," he scolded Erlock before turning to Tresh. "That's right. I heard someone say your name was Shark?"

"Tresh."

"Yes, pretty close. I can see the mistake. Foultner used to call me Sailfin because I bit the sailfin that bit me." He showed off scars on his foreleg.

"You should not have let it bite you back," Tresh said. "This is a lesson we teach gryphlets."

Henders gave Erlock a look that suggested that she'd poisoned Tresh against him. "I'm from the Redwood

Valley but currently serve the small population still at New Eyrie. Where might you be from?" His words came quickly and easily. He managed to check Erlock's harness without having to pause his conversation. He only stopped when Piprik's strange medallion fell out, and Erlock snatched it back with a paw.

"I came here from Snowfall," Tresh said. When he cocked his head, she added, "but I was born at Crane's Nest."

"A coastal bird. That explains the plumage. Erlock, you're ready to go. Biski, is it?" Henders asked. "I'm guessing a medicine gryphon knows how to work a harness. Looks like you've got our pumpkin vials. Don't lose `em, okay? Tresh, mind if I check yours?"

She shook her head.

He tightened the straps the smallest amount. "Huh, this is a pretty fancy harness you have here. And are those gryphon wooden claw things strapped to it? What're they for? What's the harness made of?"

"Serpentine whale," she responded. "The flippers are to help me swim."

"Wow, wow! A serpentine whale harness, huh? How does a gryphon or opinicus go about getting one of those?"

"You kill it and then skin it," she said.

"I guess you do, I guess you do. Say, if you have a moment later, I have a serpentine whale that needs killing northeast of here. But let's find our friends first, eh?"

He moved on to check Blinky's harness, but she wasn't wearing one. Urious seemed to be trying to convince her to put one on, talking about supplies and not being naked in the bog, but Blinky stood steadfast. At least, without words, Tresh guessed she was standing steadfast. She wasn't letting Henders put a harness on her, and she didn't blink. He seemed especially wary of her.

"Henders is a strange opinicus. I can never tell if he's joking or not," Erlock complained. "Foultner seems fond enough of him, though."

"Kidding or not, he should be careful," Biski said. "Tresh is likely to solve his whale problem for him. Wait until he hears about the city of rafts."

"Raft City?" Erlock asked. "That's a place?"

Biski looked over at the rangers. "Maybe it's better if we don't tell that one. Not the right crowd."

"I did not kill that whale on my own. I just led it closer to shore," Tresh said but let it stand. She trusted Biski's judgement in such matters.

"Alright, time to move out!" Urious called, and their expedition began.

8

LIGHTNING

Despite the well-trod nature of the path, Tresh grew tired of walking. She was hesitant to speculate what it would be like trying to cut through the bog itself. Despite her concerns about the wingtorn slowing them down, their journey began with stories of Ashen Weald gryphons and opinici flying too close to hidden starlings and being pulled out of the air. The moral was clear: they were *all* going to be walking in the bog.

The strange caravan continued through the morning before stopping at a glyph along the path that marked clean water. They followed a partially-constructed board-walk to a spring. The water looked a little funny to her, so she let the others drink first. The bog gryphon trackers went on ahead. Tresh felt more comfortable without Black Mask or White Stripe around.

Biski and Henders, the chattier members of their expedition, cooled their paws where the water spilled out into a small brook that moved to join the river.

"Watch your toes. The matamata might catch them," Urious joked. Once they were all fed and rested, he took over as lead. The winged gryphons followed along behind him with the opinici in the back. Where an hour ago there'd been no cloud cover to temper the sun's rays, now the sky was grey and an erratic yet strong breeze helped mitigate the heat. The storm they'd seen over the Crackling Sea would reach them soon.

"We found a few starlings who were too weak to keep up with the rest of the swarm." Urious was having no trouble with all of the walking. He was made for it. "They weren't too weak to try to take a bite out of our scouts, though. Every now and then we send a fast flyer over the bog closest to the ranch to see if we can lure any out."

Tresh didn't have anything to add, so she kept her beak shut and looked out at the bog. The slow-moving river, twenty feet across, inched south. Every so often a splash signaled a jumping fish. She'd started trying to spot the sailfins hiding their spines in the tall gryphtail reeds along the shore. Was there any way to spot a knife fish? The water didn't allow much visibility. It gave her the same ominous feeling as the dark water beyond Luminaire where the serpentine whales hunted.

"Piprik has been going over the maps night and day to try to find a pattern in the starling attacks," Biski said. "He wants to know if they were infected in the jungle and brought the parasites here, or if they moved in when the kjarr pride left and were infected in the bog."

"The starling you cured, did he say anything about where he was infected?" Tresh asked Erlock. Several conversations behind them stopped. Some of their traveling companions were unaware that a starling had been cured enough to talk, it seemed.

"No, he isn't entirely coherent," Erlock said. "It's a miracle he's able to form words and recognize me. We brought him some aneda trees and other plants from the east to see how far he'd ranged. He didn't recognize them. As best I could figure out from his rambling, his swarm stayed in the northwestern section of the bog. Mostly, he just draws his gryphon pictures and talks to himself."

Tresh didn't like the term swarm to describe a group of gryphons but couldn't argue that the starlings felt and acted like insects. "Oh, are they gryphon pictures? I was not able tell from the legs."

"He's not much of an artist." Erlock shrugged.

Urious laughed. "Do you know many gryphons who are?"

"My apprentice with the taiga pride does amazing things with snow," Biski said. "I always hoped they would construct a snow gryphon of me. I need to get back there to see it."

"I am sure if you asked the gryphons of Sandpiper's Dune, they would make a sand gryphon of you. You have many admirers there." Tresh was watching the path ahead as it went around a corner and turned away from the stream. The songbirds had gone silent.

Urious noticed the change and slowed his pace. Tresh lowered herself to the ground. Blinky moved in front of Biski. Henders strapped on metal talons while the two rangers took out their nets.

The sight of armed opinici raised Tresh's hackles. She tried to sooth herself—these were part of her expedition, after all—but she wasn't having much luck. Xalt noticed and scowled at her.

The wind picked up, waving the reeds and trees, and a flock of eight frost chickens flew around the corner with one of the bog gryphon trackers in pursuit. The chickens climbed two feet, four feet, six feet into the air before the wingtorn, White Stripe by his coloring, leapt after them. He managed to slash one of them with his claws and catch another in his beak.

The other six flew over the river and as far from the gryphons and opinici as they could get. Blinky hunched down. Her tail twitched in anticipation.

Urious made a quiet, hooting sound, and she relaxed. They watched as the birds flew above the reeds, climbing again to get above the gnarled bog trees.

The chickens had avoided the fate of their two kin but continued to put distance between themselves and the predators. They were in the clear, two hundred feet away, when an emaciated, iridescent shape fluttered above the tree line and attacked them. By the cry Tresh heard, at least one chicken hadn't made it.

"Starling!" Henders said.

"Shh!" Erlock hissed.

Everyone hurried around the curve in the trail and out of sight of the starling. Urious picked up the second, slashed chicken as he ran. Tresh listened to see if the starling would begin its strange chittering, but no sound came.

TRESH WATCHED the wingtorn eat the chickens while they debated. The moss in the cypress whipped about violently in the wind.

"We should move off the path," White Stripe said between bites. Black Mask had gone ahead to see if the nearest ranger outpost was starling-free. "We're too exposed on the trail."

"We make better time out of the muck," Urious said.

"With the storm brewing, we stand a better chance of reaching shelter before the rains if we follow the path, and part of what we want to know is if it's safe to send goliath birds down it again. If the swarm in the southeast is the only one left, we can mop up the other starlings and re-open the raftworks. That's another source of food. I'd rather not depend on squid and salty crops if I have other options."

His point was undermined by the fact that he and White Stripe were both consuming the frost chickens. If the kjarr pride could feed on the frost chickens, they had more options for food than the other gryphon prides, assuming they could keep a section of the bog starling-free.

"I wish they'd share," Henders said. The Crackling Sea rangers didn't seem to trust him, so he'd left their company and come to chat with winged gryphons while they watched the two wingtorn discuss their options.

"No chance there," Biski said. "The swamp grouses carry the parasite. You're stuck with monitors and fish. Only the kjarr gryphons get to eat the birds and any capybaras we find."

"Swamp grouse?" Tresh asked. "Not frost chicken?"

Erlock shrugged. "Kjarr bog, kjarr terms."

White Stripe twitched an ear. "There are no kjarr gryphons here. Only bog."

Biski was too busy inspecting a small lizard on a stump to notice his correction. "Piprik hasn't had a chance to get a good look at one to see if it's the same bird. They might just have the same general shape. The wingtorn eat them before we can catalogue them."

Henders's stomach growled.

Biski gave him a stern look. "The fact that the wingtorn *can* eat them means our other food stores last longer. Stop drooling."

His mouth was open so far that Tresh could see into his gape. His beak lacked the tomia—tooth-like serrations just inside the beak—of the fisherfolk. Had that come from their interbreeding with gryphons?

Rorin and Younce both had them. The few starling corpses pulled out of Hoarfrost had inward-facing, sharp tomia. Piprik often complained about food portion sizes, so he might not. He'd come to Swan's Rest as an adult, and the things he said suggested he hadn't grown up with gryphons as friends. She made a mental note to look into the mouths of everyone on her expedition and ask Piprik about it later.

Tresh looked up to see that Urious and White Stripe had stopped talking and were staring back at Henders.

"Did you want some?" White Stripe asked. He tossed a leg towards Henders, who was smart enough to jump back.

"Tsk!" Biski scolded. "We don't know how contagious the parasite is. There could be eggs in the blood."

Urious gave White Stripe a look but didn't reprimand him. "We're going to pick up the pace. If there's one starling, there could be others. As nice as the walls of the outpost will be, I don't want to get trapped in them. I want some time before sundown in case anything goes wrong. I know some of your paws are tired, but let's move out."

The two rangers in the back groaned, and for the first time, Tresh realized their bird-like forelegs might be even less suited for walking than her gryphon forepaws. She thought of offering one use of her flippers, but they were flat-footed and not designed for walking on land. They might make things worse.

Henders stretched out his talons.

"You okay?" Erlock asked him.

"Oh, yeah, I'm good. It's an old habit. I managed to break both wings when I fell off the market square and caught them on some vines on the way down. Back when I was a fledgling," he hastened to add. "My forelegs kept cramping up, so I fell in the habit of stretching them before I went out to play. Reeve's tail feathers, I miss the Redwood Valley markets. What I wouldn't give for some salty, smoked meat."

"You should show the rangers your talon stretch," Tresh suggested. "Make some friends."

He shook his head. "That's probably a lost cause. Without anyone advocating for us in the Ashen Weald, any of the Redwood Valley opinici who didn't join Orlea's pride are under suspicion. It isn't just the Jonas loyalists that Satra and Grenkin have been rooting out since the fall of New Eyrie. There's a lot of talk of Redwood Valley reeve loyalists hidden in our ranks."

Tresh would not have said that so close to the Crackling Sea opinici, but she was starting to realize that Henders was not the smartest opinicus in the flock. White Stripe ran on ahead, and they fell in line behind Urious.

"That's stupid," Erlock said. "Most of the Reeve's Guard at New Eyrie were poisoned. Not to mention Grand Reeve Ivess!"

"That's just it," Henders said. "Bario the Phoenix killed some of the rangers when he escaped the blues. And when they chased him to the island tower, they found a lot more dead blues than reds, pardon the language. There's still talk that some of Reeve Brevin's kids are alive. Things have gotten mighty uncomfortable for the peafowl-feathered opinici among us, or anyone who served in the Reeve's Guard. I don't think any are actually disloyal to the Ashen Weald, but if you start treating an opinicus like a traitor long enough, he's bound to start thinking things are better up north."

Tresh frowned at the mention of the former reeve's children. She was glad everyone's attention was on Henders's story. Her mind was in the past.

IT HAD HAPPENED MONTHS AGO. Tresh had been up late, lost in her thoughts again. She'd returned to Luminaire Island to be near the Crane's Nest refugees, but everyone had gone to sleep.

She flew around the island several times before settling atop the largest redwood. With the smell of burnt weald on the wind, she found it reassuring to be high in a healthy redwood.

Rorin, always clairvoyant when it came to Tresh, flew up to check on her. They were resting on the highest branches that would hold their weight when two small shapes crossed the water towards Luminaire.

She recognized one of the shapes. By the way he was moving, he was trying to get to the island without being seen. Rorin flew down and dismissed the sentries while Tresh flew out to a raft to signal their strange guests.

There wasn't any reason to think the rangers or wing-torn would attack again, but there hadn't been any reason to think it would happen the first time. Now, patrols were standard. With the sentries gone, Rorin caught up to Tresh and they met their night visitors just north of the island.

Zeph looked haggard. Tresh recalled he'd worn a

harness when he'd come with her to investigate the raft-works, but it was gone. Though he'd apparently waited until nightfall to cross the water, he was panting from overexertion. As she soon found out, Zeph and his ward had flown from New Eyrie all the way to Luminaire over the course of several days.

His traveling companion was small. Tresh mistook her for a chick at first, but her plumage was too well-developed even for a new fledgling. The moon's light was absent, covered by some late-night cloud cover, but Tresh was certain the peafowl opinicus before her was green and not blue.

"Why is the Reeve's Bane sneaking into a fisherfolk village in the middle of the night?" Rorin asked.

"To meet you two," Zeph managed.

Tresh kept her eyes on the peafowl. When Rorin called Zeph the Reeve's Bane, the peafowl's eyes grew wide and she shivered. Zeph coughed, then nudged her. She seemed to debate what to do next but finally spoke up.

"I wish to abandon my former life and join the fisher-folk," she said.

Tresh and Rorin shared a look with each other. Gryphons and opinici could be turned away. It'd happened in the past, but it was rare and for just cause. What cause could they have against one so young?

"I do not know what you are running from, but a green peafowl will have a hard time hiding anywhere," Tresh said. "What is your name?"

The peafowl hesitated, but Zeph nudged her again.

"My name is Levin. I was called Lei by those closest to me," she said.

"With all due respect, you're wrong, Tresh," Zeph said.

"One of the islander families are peafowl. I saw some of them restocking at Sandpiper's Dune. One is albino. His children could be green and no one would question it."

Rorin looked at Tresh. "Is that true? I never noticed before."

Tresh nodded. "They live on some of the smaller islands but had family in Crane's Nest. They were ashore when the attack came."

The name Levin meant nothing to Tresh when she first heard it. She thought of the peafowl family on the islands. They'd been searching for meaning in their despair. Losing a child was difficult. It was hard to know if asking them to help with this might make things worse.

Rorin reached into his harness and pulled out a flagon of fresh water and some fish bars. He tied them together with a loop so Zeph could hold them in his paws. "We'll take care of her, Zeph. You go back to the bamboo forest and return in the morning when the sentries are on duty. Tell them you've come to check on Kia. Don't seek either of us out until the end of the day."

"Thank you," Zeph said. "I have some news on the Ashen Weald and Crackling Sea, but Levin and I didn't stick around to see the end of it. I'll tell you tomorrow." He half-heartedly groomed one of Levin's feathers, then took the package and flew back towards shore.

"Can you fly?" Tresh asked Levin.

"Yes." Levin seemed a little calmer now. For someone who'd traveled such a long distance with Zeph, she'd become terrified when she heard his epithet.

Tresh looked out at the dark water to the west. The mountain range became guyots under the water, but several pushed above the surface and formed a string of islands going out into the ocean. On one of those islands was the peafowl family. "Can you fly for another hour tonight?"

Levin paused. "No, I don't think so. I'm not a good flyer. Zeph had to help keep me up over the mountains."

Rorin leaned onto his back paws and lifted her up. "She weighs nothing. I've flown with fish bigger than her."

"Tie her to your harness," Tresh said. When Rorin furrowed his brow and turned his beak to the side in protest, she added, "You drop fish into the ocean sometimes. Do not deny it."

"They're small," he protested. "I'm throwing them back."

Levin looked horrified.

Tresh realized the peafowl's request to join the fisherfolk had been left unanswered. "You are welcome with Crane's Nest, but there is only one family who can hide you. We will go to them now. Once they teach you to be fisherfolk, you will return with a new name. When you meet us again, any of us, it will be like the first time. Yes?"

"Yes," Levin said. "Thank you."

"Rorin may yet drop you in the water like a fish. Wait to thank us." Tresh did her best to keep Levin calm. She was afraid to ask what the peafowl had been through.

"Thanks for that," Rorin said to Tresh. He secured Levin to his harness and tried to reassure her. "You're flying with Rorin the Hunter. It'll be a smooth flight."

"Rorin the Fish-Dropper," Tresh corrected. She could hear the worry through Rorin's banter, but they played their part well. Levin relaxed.

It took an hour to arrive at the small island and locate the peafowl family. The conversation was not easy, but in the end, they agreed to take Levin in. Since everyone who'd known their lost chick had died in the wingtorn assault, they decided to call her Mi-Lei, so if they messed up and called her Lei, no one would question it.

Now, walking through the swamp and hearing that others were seeking the reeve's offspring, Tresh wondered if that had been wise. What were the repercussions if Satra found out they were safeguarding Reeve Brevin's child—possibly her last child?

Tresh had come to the kjarr for Quess, but she realized now that it was important for her to get this information back to Rorin. He would know what would need to be done.

9

THE FLOOD

Tresh and the rest of the party descended into the muddiest section of the marsh and were halfway to the outpost when the thunderstorm from the Crackling Sea reached them. The path ahead disappeared behind sheets of grey rain and rising mist. The gryphons and opinici closed ranks.

Erlock pulled a paw out of the muck and scraped it on a fern. "I can't believe I was sweating when this day started. I can't even see the path anymore. We're going to freeze if we stay out here. Can you get us there, Urious?"

Urious squinted at the mist. "They call this section the lowlands for a reason. The path ahead could fill with water in a moment's notice."

"That's not so bad," Henders said. He was covered in mud and needed a good bath. He was looking right, to the north, but the higher elevation was lost in the rain.

"It's worse than you think," Urious said. "When this area floods, the knife fish leave their ponds for new hunting grounds." He let out the call of an animal Tresh had never heard before. In the distance, it came back to him.

Tresh put a wing over Biski, whose mane was soaking up the water. Petrel feathers were better suited for this sort of weather. Out in the mist, Tresh heard a splash and caught sight of a dark shape moving in the distance. "Do you see that?"

Biski squinted. "Is that one of Urious's friends? Maybe they got turned around and ended up behind us."

Tresh hadn't seen any wings, but with the mist, she hadn't seen much. She'd gotten the impression of a light blue face. She'd heard rumors of bog wisps, tricks of the light that only happened in the bog and kjarr. Maybe that's what she'd seen. *Not a starling, at least. Probably our tracker friends.* She turned back to ask Urious but was surprised when White Stripe and Black Mask emerged from the path ahead, a different direction than the shape she'd seen.

"The opinicus outpost's gate is locked," Black Mask growled. "We'll need one of the *winged* to open it for us."

"Is the path flooded ahead?" Urious asked.

"Not any more than here," White Stripe replied. "It's faster to plunge ahead than try to turn back. You'll drown before you get out of the lowlands."

Tresh looked behind her, but the shape in the mist was gone. Blinky was staring intently at where it had been. The water was now over their paws.

The blue on the face hadn't been Crackling Sea blue, and she was sure she'd have been able to tell if the bog wisp had a long heron-like neck. She thought of Satra's comment to Urious about other 'precious cargo' lost in the bog. "Is it just rangers that were lost out here, or were there some wingtorn, too?"

"There might've been a few," Erlock replied. "It's hard to tell."

Tresh thought of Kia's obsessive note taking. "There are no records?"

Erlock opened her beak but didn't say more. One of the rangers spoke for her.

"A lot of kjarr gryphons surrendered," Xalt said.

Tresh nodded. She'd seen the size of the kjarr nesting grounds.

"But probably one in five died from the surgery." He paused. "Because of the surgery."

The other ranger, Jer, gave him a look of disgust. "What my companion fails to say is that infection was rampant. Some threw themselves off the cliffs into the Crackling Sea. Others were sick or 'troublesome' and assigned to the bog outposts and then abandoned. The thinking at the time was that we didn't have enough food and medicine, so why waste it on a gryphon? Without the outpost records, it's hard to know if any wingtorn escaped...or even just survived."

Xalt bristled. "Don't use that tone with me. I was only coy because I didn't want to scare Henders there. I'm all for our current Kjarr and the new, reformed Ranger Lord Grenkin; I'm no Jonas loyalist. You know what the Ashen Weald does to them."

While the rangers argued, Tresh stared out at the rising water. Perhaps she had just witnessed her first bog wisp. *Do bog wisps splash, though?*

"We're pushing on." Urious shouted over the opinici. "At any moment, this whole area could be full of knife fish. We need to be safe but fast. Keep track of who's in front and behind you. Don't lose anyone. It's not far now."

The parade of gryphons and opinici pushed through

the lowlands. Tresh's naturally oily wings and bristly fur protected her from the water better than the others—enhanced by whatever Biski had rubbed into her fur earlier. It would take some grooming and drying before the medicine gryphon or Erlock would be able to fly. If starlings attacked now, they'd be in trouble.

The water was almost to Tresh's shoulders. Along the edge of the lowlands, a section gave way, sending mud, rocks, and branches their way.

"Hang tight!" Urious shouted.

Henders lost his grip on Biski's tail when she splashed forward to dodge a fallen branch. Tresh stepped into a hole, plunging her head under the water for a second. When she looked back up, the water flowing down from the highlands was black.

No, dark red?

"What am I seeing, Biski?" Tresh asked. The mass of red was coming towards them. It squirmed.

Biski squinted, then let out a string of feathermane-specific profanity followed by, "Ants!"

She pushed off Tresh to flee back towards the opinici while Erlock flailed forwards, inadvertently kicking Tresh in the chest. Tresh coughed, then tried to leap into the air. The mud held her paws fast, not giving her the purchase she needed to get out of the water.

The mass of ants clung to each other. They were a good fifteen feet across, too wide for her to paddle out of the way in time. She couldn't see how far back they went. She spared a thought for how much they resembled the rafts from the battle for Sandpiper's Dune, then took a deep breath and pulled herself completely under the water, digging her claws into planks of the path.

The sounds of her companions disappeared. She

pulled her ears flat to keep any ants from grabbing them. As the squirming mass passed overhead, the little light that had pierced the storm was lost.

She waited in the darkness. Being eaten alive by ants wasn't how she wanted to go. She resisted the feeling of panic. She resisted the urge to count and waited for the light to return.

In the darkness, breaks of light appeared. A frost chicken—*swamp grouse?*—had fallen into the ants and was struggling to break free. It dislodged several insects that relodged their mandibles into Tresh's back.

She winced but kept her beak shut.

More chickens went by, but the water level had now risen to Rorin height. The lowlands were filling up.

Four minutes underwater felt like an eternity. There were moments back when she was teaching herself to hunt where she'd dove too deep and thought she'd drown before she reached the surface again.

A similar feeling crept into her now, until she heard something, a sound that was squeal, grunt, and neigh all in one. She could see some light breaking into the water ahead and just past it a herd of capybaras were being swept away.

If she could hold her breath for another twenty seconds the ants would pass her.

She relaxed her grip on the wooden walkway to push herself to the surface and was nearly swept away by the current. She let out a cry and watched bubbles of precious air escape. She latched back onto the plank. Her lungs burned. *Just a few more seconds.* If she were taken by the current, would she be able to find her way back, or would she be lost in the bog?

The wave of ants passed. She begged her body to hold on for a few moments longer.

The capybaras floated overhead.

Tresh pushed off and swam upwards.

She burst above the waterline in the middle of the herd. They squealed at her but were helpless to flee. She swam over to the largest, careful to stay away from its teeth, and climbed onto its back. It squirmed as its head went under, but that gave her just enough time to push off and get airborne.

Tresh made the saddest, wettest flight of her life north-west towards where she'd last seen the outpost. She looked back, but there was no sign of her expedition, only a thick mist.

As suddenly as the rains had started, they stopped. The clouds hadn't parted, and the mist remained, but the downpour dissipated.

Tresh took advantage of the lull to land on a rocky outcropping on the western edge of the lowlands. She'd been willing to stop at a tree branch, but the ones she'd seen were covered in ants. The entire lowlands had become a lake, and it was only here that she'd found a landing spot that, if not dry, was at least above water.

She got to work preening her feathers. She also secured the flippers to her feet. She didn't want to go back into the ant soup, but if it came to that, she'd be ready.

In the mist she heard the hollow cries of sailfin mothers searching for their young and the squeal-grunts of capybaras trying to locate their herds. To the north, a diving petrel cried out, its *ooo-awk* sound piercing the damp.

Tresh furrowed her brow. She hadn't noticed any diving petrels on her flight over the Crackling Sea to see Piprik. Perhaps they'd been blown off course by the storm.

The same *ooo-awk* sound echoed back. Not a similar *ooo-awk*, the pitch and timbre were identical. Her hackles raised. It was uncanny.

She moved under cover of several thick branches and continued preening. The distressed calls of animals continued, but the two petrels must have found each other because their birdsong didn't sound again.

Now as dry as the dark mist permitted, Tresh began to head north to look for the trail. Visibility was low. Memories of the starling earlier in the day kept her mostly on the ground, except for a quick flutter over another caravan of ants.

Her stomach growled. It hadn't forgotten the expenditure of energy it took to swim against the current and launch herself into the air from the back of a large rodent while soaking wet. There were some animal carcasses, victims of the flood, that the ants hadn't found yet. Her mouth salivated at the sight of the capybaras, but she knew they'd likely carry the parasites since they were fuzzy like a gryphon. Biski had cautioned them against eating anything with feathers or fur.

Biski! She'd been holding all of their antidote. Tresh looked back east to the lowlands, now a lake. There was no sign of the medicine gryphon or of anything else except thick fog.

The sun overhead was still fighting to find purchase against the mist. Once things cleared up, Tresh would be easy for the starlings to spot. If she flew before that happened, she stood a good chance of making it to the other side undetected, and if she did attract their attention, she still might be able to dive into the water or lose them in the fog.

She got a running start and flew low over the surface. Judging by the debris floating by, the initial surge had been the worst of it. The current was still moving at a fast pace, but she felt certain with her flippers on she could swim against it if she needed to,

"Biski?" Tresh shouted. The mist warped the word, made it sound like someone else had called out. The lowlands had been muddy and treacherous on foot, but in the air, Tresh crossed them in a matter of minutes. She recognized the gnarled tree that marked the start of the path and landed on the far shore to investigate.

A gold vial, some blood, and paw prints pointed towards her companions escaping the water. Having spent a lot of time staring at tracks in the mud during this expedition, she made her best guess at what she was seeing now. Judging by the lack of wingtorn tracks, she assumed Urious and the wingtorn had made it across while Biski, Erlock, Henders, and the rangers had been forced back.

She grabbed the vial and put it in her harness. She'd return it to Biski when she found the medicine gryphon. Their tracks disappeared into the water heading north. It looked like they'd followed the shore, and the shore had disappeared, but Tresh suspected if she followed the northern rim of the lowlands, she'd catch up to them.

She took a few steps into the mud, then checked the sun again. *The sooner I find them the safer we'll all be*, she decided and took flight.

She quickly realized why Urious had led them through the lowlands. The high ground to the north was a wall of vegetation. She landed a few times to stop and search for any indications of gryphons or opinici. Enough of the foliage had washed into the lowlands that it was hard to find any signs. She was nearly around the northern shore of the lowlands flood when she heard a splash and Erlock's cursing.

Tresh was about to call out to them when another sound interrupted her. The *ooo-awk* of the lost petrel had returned, and its mimic came from fifty yards away. Her ears went straight back. She landed and crawled through the tangle of vines and hanging moss to the sound, grateful she wasn't Rorin-sized.

Another *ooo-awk* called from ten feet ahead of her, and she stopped and hid under a large fern. Through the mist she could make out White Stripe. He was pacing.

There was a rustling of branches from behind Tresh. She resisted the urge to run and stayed put. Another wingtorn walked past her. She caught a sour, floral scent.

"You called?" the wingtorn asked. Tresh couldn't get a good look at her through the moss. Only her face was visible. Her mask was both white and black with flecks of bog-blossom blue. *Too little to have been the bog wisp earlier.* Her long, black ears were slicked straight back.

"Vitra? Is that you?" White Stripe asked. "We need to change the code."

The new gryphon, Vitra presumably, took a few steps to the side, giving Tresh a glimpse of a nasty set of scars. She'd seen Urious and Thenca's scarring, but those looked surgical compared to this. The tissue was thick and hadn't been stitched together well.

"Why's that?" Vitra paced around White Stripe. "Is there a bird enthusiast among the opinici?"

His feathers stood up. He kept his head lowered when

he spoke. "No, but they sent a fisherfolk with them. She'll know the call."

Vitra stopped. "You said Satra's Ashen Weald were at war with the fisherfolk."

"They are!" He frowned. "They were. It's just the one."

Vitra walked around him, pecking once or twice. Tresh thought it might be grooming, but there was a little blood on Vitra's beak. Punishment? Was this a wingtorn thing?

"Fine," Vitra said at last. "We'll switch to goliath birds."

"What do we do about the fisherfolk?" he asked.

Vitra's pacing now put her in front of Tresh's hiding place, her feathers blocking the view. "We'll kill her with the others. The rains kept them safe tonight, but the deeper into the bog they get, the easier it'll be. If we're lucky, the starlings will take care of them for us. Just keep them away from the nests and stop calling me out here or we'll feed you to the turtles."

Tresh felt something crawling on her tail but kept her beak shut. Hopefully it wasn't venomous. She parsed through what she'd overheard. The wingtorn were leading the rest of them into a trap, but why? What was the point?

She shifted a little to try to get a better look at Vitra, but the feathers were still blocking her view.

Not just feathers, primaries and secondaries. Wing feathers.

Vitra turned to leave, and Tresh finally got a good look at her: the terrible scars on one side, a full wing on the other. This was not one of Satra's wingtorn who'd been in captivity the past two years. This was a gryphon who had escaped mid-surgery. *How many more like her are waiting in the bog?*

Tresh waited until both Vitra and White Stripe had left, then flicked the bog crawler off her tail and slipped back to the lowlands.

An owl hooted after her.

DESPITE BEING DETERMINED to tell her compatriots about the impending betrayal as soon as she caught up with them, Tresh arrived to find a new problem. Biski and Erlock had made it around the flooding and found the path again. Henders and the rangers were nearby, just within earshot. The wingtorn and Blinky were nowhere to be seen.

Tresh chirped a greeting as she caught up to them.

"Tresh!" Erlock shouted, loud enough to attract any nearby starlings. "I was sure you'd drowned."

Tresh pulled the gold vial out of her harness and returned it to Biski.

"I thought I'd lost it!" Biski chirped.

"Where are the others?" Tresh asked. The rangers were giving her a dirty look. If this was an Ashen Weald trap, they'd be in on it, too. It'd be better to find a way to separate from the main group and slip away.

But everyone here is Ashen Weald, and the trap was set before Vitra knew I was coming. Perhaps it is for the opinici? Then Erlock and Biski would be in on it. I do not understand.

There was also the matter of Quess and the missing rangers. Tresh might not find her at all if she left now. She was unsure what to do, whom she could talk to.

Biski wrung out her mane. "Blinky flew off after something in the mist, and we haven't seen her since."

"She'll be fine." Henders said. He was helping preen Biski dry.

Xalt gave him a weird look. "You seem pretty enamored with the owl gryphon. Thinking of going fisherfolk?"

"It's not that," Henders protested. "My heart only flutters for Foultner. I just saw Blinky up close when the starlings attacked New Eyrie. You should be thanking her. She sent some of the blackwings to the depths during the battle. Saved Foultner and Askel. That's how she got the scars across her face."

"I didn't realize that was the same gryphon," the ranger apologized. "They're hard to tell apart."

"There were blackwings at New Eyrie?" Tresh asked. Neither Zeph nor any of the later information to reach the fisherfolk had mentioned blackwing opinici, just the starlings.

The rangers froze. They must have forgotten they had a fisherfolk among them.

Erlock rolled her eyes. "Oh, for all the parrots in the weald. What's the point in watching what we say?"

"The wingtorn would not like us giving information to the fisherfolk," Jer said.

"If you want to make allies of enemies, you do it by sharing knowledge," Erlock scolded. She turned to Tresh. "Not that you're an enemy, little shark, but I hope my point is taken."

Henders spoke up. "There were rumors that Impir murdered Grand Reeve Ivess. That he'd been working with the Blackwing Eyrie all along."

"They weren't just rumors," Jer said. "I was in the air

during the battle. I saw him flee north and a bunch of blackwings come to his aid."

"I have heard of the Blackwing Eyrie, though only recently," Tresh said. "I have not heard the name Impir."

"He was one of the reds," Xalt explained. "Some sort of scholar they kept locked up. Second coming of Mally the Nighthaunt or some scat like that. You know how red scholars are."

Henders raised his hackles. "It wasn't our fault someone let him out of his cage. Besides, you know how scholars get. They're all a little touched. Even the blues have their fair share of the crazy learn-èd."

It was Erlock's turn to bristle. "Not all scholars are bad. Biski and the medicine gryphons are scholars of a sort."

"Yeah, well, you try telling that to inquisitors," Jer said. "The scholars who don't disappear up north end up locked in the old wingtorn pens at the Crackling Sea as Jonas loyalists."

"It's not a good time to be a scholar," Henders confirmed.

A whistle sounded up ahead. The mist was starting to disappear, but so was the remaining light.

Urious padded through the mud and greeted them. "Enough grooming and chatting. The outpost is up ahead. We need a flyer to get inside before night. Let's get to it."

Tresh gave Urious a sidelong glance. White Stripe and Black Mask weren't with him.

10

THE LOST RANGER

The outpost shared the same architectural style as New Eyrie. Its walls were wooden posts with sharpened tops. Downward-facing spikes had been attached along its length to deter climbers. A single gate served as the only way in or out for the land-bound. Inside was a small courtyard with a single tower roost that looked like it would fit nests for ten opinici at most.

The branches of nearby trees had been cleared, allowing the sun's illumination into the courtyard and preventing anyone of a paws-on-the-ground persuasion from using them to leap over the fence. Whether this was a deterrent for wildlife or wingtorn was unclear. The lone gate's size suggested that at least goliath birds had been allowed in. There was a covered section in the back where they could rest away from the bog rains.

"What do I do?" Tresh sat atop a branch that gave her a view over the walls. She couldn't quite see the courtyard, but could make out the tower and the roof of the stables.

Despite a thorough preening, Biski was still carrying half her weight again in water, and the opinici all needed more room than the forest allowed to get into the air. Tresh would be the best option for getting over the fence and opening the goliath bird gate.

Urious seemed to be examining her size. "Try not to fly above the tree line. We don't want any starlings watching the skies to get a glimpse of you."

"All of the outposts share the same key," Xalt continued, "but most of them were stolen and melted down so the metal could be sold on the black market. We weren't able to get one before we left."

"But there should still be one up in the roost," Jer added. Like Biski, he didn't seem to be able to get dry. "The entry to the roost isn't locked, but it's designed to deter gryphons. Can you twist your paw into this shape?"

Tresh did her best, but the shape was like trying to wrap her claws around a perfectly spherical stone. She'd held spears for Rorin a few times, and while her paws didn't allow her to throw them, she'd become good at gripping things.

The rangers pushed her pads a bit to get the correct shape.

"That'll work," Xalt said. Unlike Jer, who was soaked through, Xalt's Crestfall heritage seemed to have made him particularly resistant to the humidity. "Once you're in, grab the keys. The main gate only unlocks from the inside."

"I will do my best." Tresh did a few practice jumps, but the clinking in her harness alarmed Biski, who came over to relieve her of her vials.

"Erlock's pouch fell open in the water and most of my ointments floated away," the medicine gryphon said.

"What a shame that is." Erlock snorted.

Biski bristled. "I notice Tresh isn't complaining about the oils. They kept her nice and dry!"

"Enough chatter, you two," Urious commanded. "Time for you to go up and over, Tresh. We need time to look around before the light's gone."

She backed up, and her entourage cleared the path. The final stretch to the outpost used wooden planks, sparing them the mud of earlier.

She got a running start and leapt into the air, flying just high enough to get over the wall. One of the spikes on top caught her back leg, leaving a little blood on the pillar, but she made it over and backbeat her wings to try to stop her momentum. She hit the roost harder than she intended but managed to hold onto a ledge and wait for the world to stop spinning.

Down below, the small courtyard was partially flooded. Whoever had designed the outpost had intended for the main gate to be opened to let the water out, it seemed. By the damp lines on the inner walls, the water was draining, just not in a timely fashion.

The flooded courtyard was too muddy for her to tell if any snakes had taken up residence. She missed the clean waters off the coast of Crane's Nest.

She climbed onto the platform that gave access to the roost. The strange door loomed before her with its circular locking mechanism. She twisted her paw into the shape the rangers had suggested, using her beak and other front paw to get it right, then gripped the device and turned.

There was a *click*.

The door slid open a crack.

The smell inside was terrible. For the first time since the expedition began, Tresh was prompted to wonder what'd happened to the rangers in the bog. Had they been caught unawares and eaten by starlings? By the smell of it, someone had become trapped inside and died.

She braced herself. The key should be just inside to the right. She pushed the door, but something was caught on the other side. She pushed harder. The door flew open with a *thud*. She reached up to the right to feel for the key as her eyes struggled to see in the darkened roost.

Her paw caught the key.

The shadows stirred.

She moved the keys to her beak and took a step back.

Something arose. Its shadow looked like an immense snake.

Following instinct, she dove off the roost and into the standing water as the shadow struck out where she'd been located a second ago. As the shadow's long neck hit the light, she saw an orange beak and blue feathers.

Tresh landed with a splash, but the water was only chest height and all four of her legs hurt. She struggled to get the key in the gate.

Above her, the infected ranger stepped into the sunlight and stretched its long neck. It was still wearing its Crackling Sea harness and medallion. It sniffed the air. The silver sheen over its eyes glinted. It spread its wings, but one refused to open fully.

Tresh fought to get the gate unlocked. She had two ways out: up towards the infected opinicus or out through the gate to her friends. She didn't want to spook it into flying above the tree line lest it attract the starlings. Even without green wing altruism, its noise and movement would draw them to the outpost.

She tried to push, but the gate was stuck in the mud.

The *click* of the metal key in the lock was met with a growling sound from the flooded goliath bird stable.

Goliath birds do not growl. What in the—?

The water by the stable churned and two sails poked above the surface and snaked their way towards her.

There must be a hole in the wall by the stables, she thought, but even in the back of her mind she knew the standing water precluded such an option. This was a trap, plain and simple.

Tresh kept pushing on the gate, heard Urious and Erlock pulling on it from the other side, looked up to see the serpentine head of the infected ranger staring down at Tresh.

The sailfin monitors were almost upon her. She finally gave up and kicked off the gate to leap over them. On her kick, Erlock pulled, and with a plop the gate flung open, sending the water and the monitors onto the path. The infected opinicus dove down from its perch after Tresh.

"Sweet floofy gryphlets are those *monitor* lizards?!" Biski shouted. The sailfin monitors growled in response.

The infected ranger fell into the draining water next to Tresh. It tried to spear her with its beak, but a last-minute wing tuck sent its face straight into the muck.

Tresh pulled herself onto the tower, but her claws were caked with mud and couldn't find purchase on the smooth wood. There was no water left inside to wash them off. She leapt to the roof of the stables. The opinicus began to flap its wings, trying to dislodge itself.

Urious poked his head in and looked to Tresh. "Don't let it get away!"

"Use your claws!" Biski was shouting to Erlock. "Use your beak!"

"You're not helping!" Erlock shouted back.

Urious called out to Henders and the rangers. "There's an infected inside. You need to pull it out of the air before it alerts the others."

"Are the nets ready?" Tresh shouted over the gate.

"Just about," Henders said. The infected ranger dislodged its beak from whatever it had impaled under the muck. "Okay, we're ready!"

As the monstrous opinicus rose out of the mud, Tresh pushed off from the tower and spread her wings to glide overhead, losing a tail feather to the infected's impressive reach. The muddy heron rose up after her, just able to get enough clearance in the courtyard for flight.

Tresh came over the wall first. One of the rangers, whether from nerves or calculated malice, threw a net right at her. She was forced to pull her wings in to keep them from snaring on the net and breaking as it wrapped around her. She crashed into the ground hard and tumbled into the underbrush.

The second ranger's aim was true, and his weighted net caught the infected opinicus across its good wing. The effort was enough to ground the infected, but not enough to disable it.

Tresh struggled against her bindings while the rangers struggled against one of their own. Urious led one monitor on a merry chase around the outside of the outpost while Erlock tried pounce and feint tactics against the other sailfin.

The sound of something moving through the branches behind Tresh nearly caused her heart to explode. She struggled to roll on her side so she could see what was coming. She saw feathers and thought it was White Stripe coming to finish her off in the confusion, but then saw the eyes were too big and the beak too small.

Blinky skulked towards Tresh and began biting through the net.

"Blinky, I'm—"

Blinky hissed at her to be quiet. Once the owl had finished freeing Tresh, she moved her beak up against Tresh's ear. "I could hear you listening by the lake. I, too, heard. Something is wrong. I will find out. For now, tell no one what you saw. Find your friend. Be the first one to go relieve yourself each morning. I will be there if I have something to report. Understand, yes?"

Tresh nodded.

Blinky blinked, then backed into the bog and disappeared. *She could have stayed to help*, Tresh groused but understood the importance of having someone else looking out for her. Even if this were a trap of some sort—and what was happening felt like one—the owl gryphons held the weakest ties to Satra or the kjarr pride.

Tresh pulled herself free of the net, crawled out of the underbrush, beat her wings a few times, and joined the fray.

She started by climbing up a branch on a tree in Urious's running path. There were none directly overhead as she would have preferred, the branch clearing efforts had been too industrious for that, but she managed as best she could. When he came by again with the second sailfin, she leapt as high as she could manage without breaking the tree line, glided, then dove on its back. The spiked sail kept her from catching it from behind and holding it, but she hit one side hard and latched her serrated beak onto the back of its neck.

The sailfin hissed. Its neck skin was too thick for her to do any real damage, but it still reared up, attempting to dislodge her.

When it did so, its belly was exposed, and Urious pivoted back and went in for the kill. They managed to flip it over, breaking its sail, and Urious finished it off.

Erlock and the first monitor seemed to be at a standstill until Biski reached into her harness pouch and pulled out a small pitcher plant, the top bound with vines. She snipped the vines with a claw, then tilted her head back and flung the pouch at the monitor lizard, splashing it with yellow liquid.

The smell was acrid and terrible in ways Tresh had never experienced before. All of the gryphons leapt back and covered their beaks. The sailfin monitor must have shared their sentiments because it let out an indignant chuff, hissed at Biski and Erlock, then fled into the woods.

"What was in that?" Erlock asked.

"Lace monitor pee," Biski replied.

Erlock's response was open-mouthed horror.

The infected ranger let out a haunting cry, reminding them all of the real threat. There was no time to ask questions about Biski's bag of horrors. They rushed over to help their opinicus allies. The rangers had it cornered with its back against the fence but were afraid to get too close. One bite or scratch and they could end up infected.

"Can you get its attention upwards?" Urious asked Tresh.

She nodded. She got a running start again. This time, Urious began his own run just behind her. She flew at the opinicus, getting just enough height to get over the fence again.

The infected ranger lashed out, catching her back paw. Without tomia, it was unable to hold onto her, and Tresh slipped over the fence and back into the mud of the courtyard with a gross *splash*.

While its attention—and spear-like beak—were directed towards the sky, Urious pounced and hit it right in the chest, pushing it into the spikes. Two went through the opinicus and nearly impaled Urious, too. He beat a hasty retreat.

"What in the depths was that?" a ranger swore. "And wasn't the plan to try to *cure* any opinici we found?"

"Why do you have a flagon of monitor pee?" Erlock shouted.

"It has antiseptic properties!" Biski shouted back.

"Good job, team," Urious said.

"What did you do to my net?" Jer asked Tresh. "I only brought two of these!"

The bickering went on until Xalt put a talon on his ranger companion's shoulder and said, "It's Ferrick."

Everyone went silent. The rangers examined the infected opinicus's harness pockets, pulling out a pair of metal talons and a few knick-knacks.

"Ferrick," Jer repeated. "I did my training with him. Sweet bird. Clumsy but always quick with a kind word."

Tresh had a dozen questions for the rangers about their friend and how he came to be locked in a roost. She had enough sense of decency not to ask them while they mourned.

Urious did not. "Where was Ferrick assigned? Is he one of the rangers lost in the bog?"

"New Eyrie, I think?" Xalt guessed.

"No, remember the mishap with the jelly toxin?" Jer asked. "Ranger Lord Grenkin called him a menace to eyrie life. He was assigned to the kjarr nesting grounds with the rest of the 'opinici of questionable skill or intent.'"

The kjarr nesting grounds. Younce had freed those. They'd had pens of infected frost chickens that they'd been using to infect the taiga and weald wildlife. The same infection that had ultimately claimed the starlings.

She spared a thought for what Younce was up to without her. She regretted the way she'd left him there. If Urious was in on the ambush, and she ended up killing him, what would that mean for the relations between Crane's Nest and the taiga? *I should have given Younce a chance instead of leaving in the middle of the night.*

She looked over and saw the expression on Urious's face. He seemed just as surprised as she was, but that could be an act. Was he leading each of them into a trap, whittling down their numbers, until there were enough for Vitra and her allies to finish off?

Tresh didn't know, and White Stripe and Black Mask were nowhere to be seen.

MOUNTAIN LIFE

A scavenged brazier, courtesy of the last trade delegation from Orlea, illuminated a cavern deep within Snowfall, giving Younce the light he needed to sort through his predecessor's belongings.

Younce had traded for the braziers so they'd have another source of warmth in winter, but as the days shortened, he found the traders and merchants who traveled to Snowfall appreciated the extra light.

His own eyes had just a glint of green left. In another few weeks, they'd be all blue, and he wouldn't need any help seeing the interior of the cavern.

For now, though, he appreciated the aid. Vosk had been a bit of a magpie, figuratively speaking, hiding small stones in every nook and cranny of his living space. Some Younce recognized from the weald. Others looked like fossilized coral.

He started pulling out a pile of goliath bird pelts to distribute among the pride when he found a hidden stash of feathers. He pawed at a long black one. When the light hit it just right, there was a hint of blue. It smelled like Hatzel. He placed it next to the pile of weald stones he'd collected.

Several long blue feathers smelled salty, like a Crackling Sea opinicus. He didn't recognize the scent, but he could guess: Ellore. Unlike Hatzel's feathers, Younce couldn't think of anyone who might want Ellore's. He put them in a pile to be thrown away.

He cleared out a few more pelts before he found two primary feathers, white with black bars. He sniffed at one and his eyes widened. It'd been a long time since he'd smelled—

"Mignet's feathers?" Thenca asked.

Younce jumped straight up and hit his head on the top of the cave. He hadn't heard her come in.

"Sorry," she apologized. "You seemed caught up in your work, and I didn't want to disturb you. Does Mignet have any living family now that Vosk is dead?"

Younce rubbed the top of his head, grateful for the extra winter fluff. "No one she was close to. Ellore, if she survived New Eyrie."

He'd been one of Mignet's hatchmates. So had Zeph, for that matter. Deracho had been one of her friends, but he was a little older.

Thenca held one of the feathers in her paw. "You could give it to Satra."

Younce looked at the wingtorn. She was wearing a harness so the larger gryphons could fly her up to Snowfall. "It's been a long time since Mignet drowned. Isn't it time Satra moved on?"

"Not everyone does move on," Thenca said. "Even among gryphons. Remember Triddle when Askel disappeared? Or even you. You've sulked every day since Tresh left."

Younce scratched at the back of his ear with an errant paw. It was sore from hitting the ceiling. Thenca was right, giving Satra the feathers was what Mignet would have wanted.

He pulled out the last of the pelts but didn't find what he was looking for. Thenca's ear twitched mischievously. He looked at her harness pocket.

"You stole it back from Vosk, didn't you?" he asked.

"I didn't want it to get lost after Hatzel killed him." Thenca pulled Mignet's bracelet out of a harness pocket. "Satra managed to hold onto it for years. Jonas would have melted it down if it didn't make her look more Crackling Sea."

Thenca placed it at Younce's feet. He picked it up. It looked small in his taiga paws. Now that he had a chance to see it up close, he could tell it had been made at the Crackling Sea Eyrie. There was a small heron engraved upon it.

"You should return it to her," Thenca said. "Talk about your lost friend. Find out what happened to Tresh."

"I'm sure Tresh is fine," he said, but he wasn't sure she was okay. She'd left without waking him, and he'd noticed the line of paw prints leading from the nest to the edge of the cliff. He wasn't just worried about her, he was worried about Thenca's brother, too.

"Maybe you're right," he said. "Maybe it's time to talk. Any message you want me to bring to Urious?"

"I'd ask you to tell him not to do anything stupid, but there's little chance of him following *that* advice." Thenca grinned. "The path should be done soon enough. Once Grenkin's rangers finish the last bridge, it'll be possible for me to walk home and see him myself while everyone tries to make the path safe for fledglings."

"You've been here so long that I've started to think of you as one of us." Younce's tail swished back and forth. "Any chance of you coming back in the spring? I need someone who can keep Deracho out of trouble."

Thenca laughed but didn't reply. She closed her harness pocket and headed past the brazier and out of the cavern, leaving Younce alone with Mignet's bracelet and feathers.

Satra, Zeph, Deracho, and even Younce. They'd all grown up while Mignet remained young in their memories.

He rubbed at his eyes.

AFTER A SHORT STOP in Sandpiper's Dune, the fisherfolk caravan made its way up to the taiga to restock Hoarfrost.

The logistics of moving food and lumber up a mountain by gryphon or opinicus helped Zeph appreciate the goliath bird pass in the north. Letting the hulking birds do the heavy lifting on a well-trod path was much easier than carrying it himself. It was hard to bring anything of weight up a mountain, let alone the correct mountain.

It made sense, looking back, that the taiga pride had always traded small things of value that could be carried easily. They supplied aneda resin to the medicine gryphons and bright, shiny stones to the opinici. They had no way of getting larger things up or down.

Well, not easily. Just behind Zeph, two crane gryphons were carrying a bamboo door from the mill. Behind them, two more were carrying pelts from beaked whales to insulate the door. The original inhabitants of Hoarfrost had been killed off by the Connixation, a blizzard that wiped out all but one taiga pride. The next attempt to inhabit Hoarfrost by sick fisherfolk had ended when the mountain was invaded by starlings. When the decision came to re-open Hoarfrost on a permanent basis, everyone agreed they needed doors thick enough to keep both the starlings and the weather out.

After crossing their first mountain, Zeph and Carru split off from the others to check on Williwaw, the small outpost at the southern edge of the taiga. While the fortification efforts were in full swing at Hoarfrost, Williwaw remained more of an observation post to make sure the starlings didn't try to fly south around the mountains over the water to the dunes. Since the taiga gryphons had the best vision in the cold heights, two of them were always assigned to Williwaw, taking turns keeping watch. A third fisherfolk stayed with them so if the starlings arrived, messages could be sent to both Hoarfrost and Sandpiper's Dune. Today, it looked like Deracho was on scouting duty.

Zeph had last seen Deracho on the flight north to aid the Ashen Weald in the final days of summer. Now that autumn was over, the taiga gryphon had his winter coat. The difference in size between a taiga gryphon in the summer and a taiga gryphon in the winter was the difference between Zeph and Carru.

The snowy owl gryphon turned and greeted them with a soft hoot. "Welcome back, you two. You're spending so much time in the taiga, Zeph, you might want to apply for readmission to your birth pride. Hatzel will have forgotten about you by now."

Zeph shook his head. "I just wanted to give the ground parrots a fighting chance for the spring. Besides, I hear the new taiga pride leader is a real lace monitor. No personality at all."

"Oh, that's not true. He has a lot of lace monitor personality." Deracho laughed, subdued sounds, like several short hoots. "What about you, Carru? Does the taiga hold any appeal? Do you miss the weald?"

"And give up all that fish?" Carru used his hooked beak to scratch at his back. "The taiga is pretty, but I'm not a fan of the black flies. As for the weald, I have more than a dozen siblings, and they're all crazy."

"A dozen?" Deracho asked, looking to Zeph for confirmation.

"It's true," Zeph said. "In thirty years, all of Merin's pride will be Carru-sized. That's the direction they're headed, at least. Which is sad because the smaller ones are the most fun. Just look at Askel or Triddle."

"I can't imagine providing food for that many large gryphons," Deracho said. "But perhaps larger does not always mean hungrier. To hear Younce tell it, Zeph became the better hunter because he ate so much and no one else would hunt for him."

"All I heard was, 'to hear Younce tell it, Zeph is the better hunter,'" Zeph preened.

Another taiga gryphon and a crane opinicus fisherfolk appeared in the distance.

"Our patrol has returned. They'll unpack your harnesses, then you can head up to Hoarfrost," Deracho said. "Let 'em know things are still quiet down here. Nothing but harsh winds and cold water."

WHILE CARRU HELPED MOVE supplies deep into the caves, Zeph took a tour with Dusty. The sand-colored fisherfolk, hailing from the dunes, had been one of the infected gryphons taking refuge in Hoarfrost last time Zeph came through. They'd worked together to lead the refugees through the catacombs until a timely taiga rescue had saved them all.

Dusty had campaigned for Hoarfrost to become a joint taiga-fisherfolk holding to watch for starlings, and Naya had assigned him to oversee it. Whether he would stay here all winter depended on just how warm the new doors kept things.

"Why hasn't the infection killed off all the starlings?" he asked. "It's been months. It would've killed us by then."

Zeph was inspecting the new caves that'd been opened up. While weald gryphons weren't big on doors, the taiga pride used a system of barriers to close up the old nesting grounds and insulate any supplies left inside them. Combined with fisherfolk hut entrances, they hoped having several barriers would help keep starlings and bad weather out.

Most of the entrances had been sealed up after the Connixation and were now covered in debris and frozen shut. There was debate about whether they should replace all the old entrances with barriers, but practicality won out. They only had so much bamboo and time before the winter blizzards began.

"I'm not sure we can say that for certain," Zeph said. His time with Kia had made him more inquisitive and less likely to accept things at face value. "You never got to see what would have happened if Biski hadn't gotten to you in time. You may not have died. Maybe you would've become like them, like beasts."

Dusty nodded. "Yeah, I'm not ashamed to say there've been a dozen fights on who gets to name their upcoming gryphlets Biski."

Zeph's ears perked up. "I've never heard of gryphons fighting over names before. Especially not when Biski is still alive. Who gets to be New Biski?"

Dusty grinned. "Actually, that's how Naya solved it. She said while Biski is still among the living, no new gryphlets or chicks can be Biski. So we have a Bisk, a Biskette, a Biskle, and the list goes on." His grin faded. "Do you think the starlings can be saved? Like, if we get some pumpkin in them? I know we don't have enough grown yet, but maybe we can catch a few of the infected. That coulda been me, y'know? I hate to think they're going to starve or get killed crossing the taiga."

"It's a good question," Zeph agreed. "I think Piprik is trying to figure that out. Word is, they captured a few at New Eyrie."

His estimation of Dusty went up a notch. Maybe it was a fisherfolk thing, but weald gryphons held their own prides in highest esteem, followed by the prides they interbred with. The starling prides hadn't been to the weald in his lifetime, so they weren't given the same consideration.

The current thinking, as word trickled down through Naya, was that the Ashen Weald planned to purge the kjarr and bog of starlings, then hold a bonfire of the infected bodies. All they were waiting on was the spring pumpkin crop.

Dusty opened up a barrier door, recently installed by the previous supply team. "Here, let me show you the inside. We took the old bolt hole we used to escape and made it a one-way door, so if we need to get out, it's still there. But we've been using fish oil to set up braziers in the center cave. I know it seemed tiny when we were running for our lives, but you're going to freak like a gryphlet with a crab on its tail when you get a look at it now." Dusty led Zeph into the darkness of Hoarfrost.

Zeph remembered the cave as being huge in the dark, just not in a vertical sense. They'd wandered through it for over an hour. Past the first two sets of barriers, the tunnel opened up, and light spilled down the corridor from the center. The breeze when they opened the doors suggested that there was some ventilation going on. In his memory, the ceiling should be scraping against the tops of his ears. Now that there were lights, he could see that the low ceiling opened up to a large cavern with enough room to fly around in. He was surprised there were no bats.

"This is pretty nice," he said. There were dozens of nests set up for the fisherfolk workers and taiga representatives. "Are you all going to stay here during the winter?"

"That depends on how warm we can keep it," Dusty said. "We got it hot enough in here to melt the icicles, but I haven't figured out how to keep it that temperature all winter without using a fish ton of firewood. It's kinda insulated, though you can't tell with fisherfolk like us opening the doors all the time, but I don't know if it'll be enough."

Zeph looked around. Maybe there was a warmer, longer burning fuel source. The braziers they were using for light used fish oil, but there might be other options. He didn't know if you could burn the already-burnt redwoods of the weald, but Luminaire could stand to lose a few trees, if someone could figure out how to cut one down.

He knew the taiga kept maps of mountain hot springs, but he didn't know if any were located this far south. Maybe they could redirect the water. Maybe a combination of both. He didn't know what was possible, but he knew who might have a few ideas.

"I hear Askel and Triddle are at Snowfall," he said. "You should send word. I'll bet they can warm this place up. Just, uh, clear the flammable nesting material out before you try any of their ideas. And make sure there's good drainage."

12

THE OUTPOST

The outpost was supposed to provide answers. Instead, it offered up new questions. As Tresh had suspected, there was no hole in the goliath bird stables. What's more, the bodies of two large capybaras were found inside, possibly the lure that drew the sailfins through the gate. The fact that the gate had been locked after them suggested opinicus or at least gryphon intervention.

Had Ferrick done this on his own as a deterrent to starlings? It seemed unlikely. As far as Tresh knew, the starlings were as likely to snack on sailfins as anything else in the bog.

By the accounts of his fellow rangers, Ferrick had not been particularly bright or adept. He wouldn't have thought of building a moat of sailfins. However, he wasn't idiot enough to have accidentally locked himself inside the roost, either.

While Urious and the rangers explored the outpost and debated the safety of staying there, Tresh used the last of the light to seek out a nearby stream to wash the mud off.

It gave her time to think.

And to report in to her owl scout.

Blinky materialized while Tresh had her head underwater. One moment, she was alone. The next, Blinky stood there. Instead of speaking, Blinky just tilted her head to the side. Tresh filled the owl gryphon in on what had happened.

Blinky looked at the blood in the water, then at Tresh's wounds. Blinky began to cough, and Tresh rushed over to help. Blinky held up a paw, and a moment later she coughed up a small vial of pumpkin extract. She batted it over to Tresh with her paw.

"Please do not tell me you want me to take that," Tresh said. She didn't know if it'd been stolen from Biski or recovered after the flooding, but either way, it was covered in owl drool.

Blinky pointed a paw at the claw and bite marks inflicted by the infected ranger.

Tresh grimaced and rinsed the vial off in the river before using a claw to pull out the stopper and down the slimy substance.

"You really need to start wearing a harness," she said. "Anything with pockets."

Blinky stared at her but did not blink.

"Fine, have it your way." Tresh's stomach rumbled from the pumpkin. She needed to get back and see what was for dinner. She rinsed out the vial—glass was too valuable to discard it—and slipped it into her own harness. Blinky lifted off without a sound and disappeared between the cypress trees while Tresh padded back to the outpost.

WHILE URIOUS HAD PROMISED secret knowledge of bog camps and hideaways at the start of their journey, he now claimed there was nowhere nearby safe enough to set up camp before dark. With the roost under quarantine by order of their only medicine gryphon, the bottom level of the tower was their only cover.

It was normally used for storage. They shifted around some boxes, opened some spare nesting material, and made do. The rangers set their nests up atop a pile of crates. Henders found a high point across the room after getting some glares from the Crackling Sea opinici. It seemed they still didn't trust anyone willing to wear a Reeve's Guard harness.

Tresh and Erlock huddled around Biski to keep her warm; her fur and mane were still damp to the touch. Urious slept alone on the hard floor. None of them talked about what it meant if this had been intended as a trap. They just blockaded the doors with crates and prayed they didn't end up trapped down here like Ferrick had been trapped upstairs.

Tresh couldn't sleep. Even here, as far from the fisher-folk village as she'd ever traveled, she continued to think of her nieces and nephews. The dead of Crane's Nest visited her at night, discontent to remain in the sky ocean above. They wanted vengeance. They wanted Urious and the wingtorn. They wanted to see their relatives taken care of. They wanted Crane's Nest rebuilt.

The celestial aspirations of the host of dead fisherfolk weighed upon the small petrel gryphon. When she closed her eyes, however, she saw no host, only her nieces and nephews. She knew what they wanted. They wanted their mother to be alive.

Tresh would find Quess. If the dead were still searching for her, if Tresh's nieces and nephews still haunted her dreams, it meant Quess had not yet joined them in the afterlife. That meant Quess was still out there somewhere in this kjarr, in this bog. Tresh could still save her.

Far in the distance, the sound of starlings chittering reached through the night. Their infected, mindless cries woke the gryphons and opinici hiding in the tower.

I will save you, Quess. The chittering grew louder and was joined by the squeal of a capybara herd caught unawares. The thought of Quess wandering the bog with silver eyes came unbidden to Tresh's dreams. *Or, if necessary, I will release you to be with your children among the stars.*

TRESH AWOKE with one side of her face still wet from being pressed against Biski's mane. Erlock had already gone outside and was talking to Urious and the rangers. Tresh stood up and began to shake off her wet side.

"Stop, stop!" Henders shouted from above her. "Do that outside!"

Tresh's nares turned red. "I did not know you were still in here. That is just what you get for sleeping in."

"I wasn't sleeping, though you're one to talk," he protested. Biski snored, oblivious to the two of them, and pawed the air. "I was going through these crates of supplies."

Tresh climbed up next to him. He'd opened a dozen of them. "Did you find anything useful? Pumpkin extract?"

He shook his head. "No, nothing like that. I found a lot of vellum and ink. Weird for a swamp outpost, right?"

"Yes." Tresh looked at the crates again. Painted on each was a green peafowl feather. "Those were Redwood Valley Eyrie crates?"

Henders looked at the same symbol. "Oh, hey, you're right. Oh wow, almost all of the crates in here are from the Redwood Valley. What gives?"

Xalt walked in as Henders asked his question and answered. "There was a dig site near here. They found it searching for swamp iron. The reds sent scholars to investigate. It was set up by Jonas, our reeve's consort, right after the wingtorn were subjugated. Your headmaster led the effort. I remember them coming through the Crackling Sea."

Henders frowned. "Jonas and Headmaster Neider set this up? That's not good."

"Does it matter?" Tresh hadn't heard the name Jonas outside of the strange term *Jonas loyalist*. It was a name she'd pass on to Naya. "It is just paper and quills."

"*Mostly* paper and quills, not *just* paper and quills. There were also a bunch of these." Henders lifted a clay jar out of a box, and Tresh let out a hiss louder than she would have thought herself capable of.

"Put it down! Do not drop it!" she shouted. She was too late. Her hissing had startled him, and the jar was already halfway to the ground. It hit the hard floor of the storage room and shattered.

"Out!" she commanded. Biski had been startled by the exploding jar but squawked awake when she saw what had broken. The four dashed out the door and stared back inside at the broken pottery.

"I left my harness inside," Henders said.

Xalt stared at him. "What?"

"I sleep naked," Henders replied. "I forgot to put it back on."

"What's going on?" Urious arrived with Erlock in tow.

Biski and Tresh pointed at the broken clay jar. They were both staring intently at the strange thick sand pooled on the floor.

"Those were the crates we found at Sandpiper's Dune, where Rakesh was infecting the wildlife," Tresh said.

The rangers hissed, "Jonas loyalist," at the name of the ranger who had led the fisherfolk subjugation efforts.

"The taiga pride found them at the kjarr nesting grounds, too," Biski said.

Urious looked in. "If Blinky were here she could confirm it, but I believe Impir was carrying something similar when he fled, if the reports to Satra were accurate."

Henders and the rangers stepped farther back from the jar.

"I do not see anything moving, do you?" Tresh asked. They watched. Nothing writhed in the sand. "It is...empty?"

Biski stepped forward. Henders gasped.

"The salt seemed to keep the ones we found in hibernation," she said. "I think it's a way to transport the parasite or its eggs. Piprik poked around a lot before the fisherfolk sent him north to help with the starlings. We talked a little about the jars at the kjarr nesting grounds, too."

"How would someone know how to do that?" Urious asked.

Henders pointed up at the Redwood Valley Eyrie crates and his harness. "Maybe this is where the parasite came from. Or maybe they released it here first."

Tresh turned to the ranger who had spoken earlier. "Do you know where the dig site is? Can you show us?"

The ranger nodded. "It's south, a little deeper in."

Urious laughed. "A dig site? In the deep bog?"

"You'll understand when you see it," the ranger said. "The bog does the digging for you."

Urious shook his head. "Okay. This is too important to ignore. The inquisitors will want to know what we found here, especially if it relates to Rakesh using the parasites as a weapon."

"Not just Rakesh," Tresh said. "Biski said the kjarr nesting grounds had jars. That is where Ferrick was assigned, yes?"

The rangers nodded but frowned. "Not just Ferrick. The last expedition sent from New Eyrie were all originally watching the kjarr nests."

Urious stared at the jar. "Our orders haven't changed. We rescue them either way. We need answers. We need to know who ordered the jars' use and what information those rangers were given about the parasites. Whether they're victims or have something to do with the infection, we need to locate them. Get your things. It's time to head out."

While Henders attempted to climb around the broken jar up to his harness, and Biski tried to preen more water out of her feathers, Tresh sidled up next to Urious. He was on a dry patch of the path away from the courtyard, next to a fallen tree that smelled bitter and floral despite not being a flowering tree.

"Have you heard from your wingtorn friends?" she asked.

"Hmm? Oh, yeah," he replied. "We spoke first thing this morning before everyone else woke up. With the lowlands flooded, I sent them to find a path to the Flower. There's a pack of starlings to the north that've cut us off from skirting around the lowlands back the way we came."

Tresh was skeptical but didn't say anything to draw attention to the question. Instead, she changed the subject. "And Blinky?"

Urious shook the courtyard mud off his paws. "Nothing yet, but she's a strange bird. My friends are looking for her. They're excellent at finding things in the bog. Don't worry, they'll catch up to her sooner or later."

13

THE DIG SITE

Hundreds of tiny streams flowed through the bog like cracks in a jar, emptying the flooded lowlands into a dozen ponds, creeks, and wetlands beyond. What should have been a twenty-minute flight from the outpost had turned into a four-hour hike by paw. There was a chill in the morning air dusting the plants with frost.

While the rangers had flown over the dig site years ago, the landmarks below the tree line were different now.

Urious commented that the land shifted with every flood, making it difficult for anyone except experienced bog trackers to find their way around.

"Too bad our bog trackers are conspicuously absent," Erlock groused.

Urious gave her a look. "They're surveying the flooding to find us a path southeast to the Flower once we're done with the dig site."

The expedition walked until Jer and Xalt would normally have complained, but since they'd been put in charge of navigating, the rangers remained silent. Tresh began to sweat through her paws when the sun came out and melted off the frost.

She was starting to understand the danger of the bog. She never finished drying, and the temperature could swing wildly based on access to the sun. She was also getting tired of seeing blue flowers and hanging moss everywhere she went.

Biski kept shaking her mane, to the chagrin of anyone in her splash zone. "It's going to be ruined. And I spent so much time grooming it just right."

The tenth time she complained about her mane, Urious spoke up.

"Hey Biski, see those roots?" He pointed a paw towards a hill that'd been eaten away by the flooding, leaving the roots of a gnarled tree visible. They were sweating a white sap.

"Oooooh. What's it called?" She bounded over and wrestled through her pack for an empty vial.

"Kashow sap," Urious replied. "When I was a gryphlet, the medicine gryphons would use it to numb an area. I had to soak my tail in the stuff after a particularly nasty bite."

"Why's it called—" Biski began but then went into a sneezing fit. "Oh, I guess that's why you call it that."

Urious was trying to explain to her that the tree was named before they found out its smell made gryphons sneeze, but Tresh's attention was drawn to a mark high up on the tree. It was a light blue streak. Combined with the fact that the roots had been cut to allow the sap to bleed out before they arrived, it left her wondering if someone had been out here harvesting the trees recently.

Biski finished gathering a few vials of the sap to bring back to the medicine gryphons, and they went on their way. The roots had distracted her from her complaining, but Urious now found himself pelted with questions about the bog's medicine gryphons. He remained tight-beaked about them. He only offered that none of the medicine gryphons from his pride had become wingtorn, a statement which raised more questions than it answered.

Other than a nagging feeling they'd never find the dig site, things continued without incident, excluding a mishap where Henders attempted to clean off his talons in a creek and was shocked by a baby knife fish. He seemed fine, albeit a little dazed. Biski and Erlock did their best to keep him from wandering off while he recovered.

When Tresh asked how to spot knife fish, Xalt said the key was to make sure someone else touched the water first. Considering Urious's comment back at the kjarr nesting grounds that the knife fish out here grew large enough to kill an adult opinicus, that seemed irresponsible. She resolved to find a better way than sending Henders in first and hoping the shock didn't kill him.

The rangers perked up as they passed by some rock formations and began to whisper amongst themselves, then pointed due south. Urious nodded but commanded everyone to stay silent from here on in and divided them into pairs with orders to move ahead only as he gave the birdsong to indicate it was safe. Tresh was up front with Urious, Biski and Erlock were in the middle, and the opinici moved to bring up the rear.

Urious told Tresh to stay close but kept twitching his tail and hitting her in the face with it. Her patience was gone, and she was one tail swipe away from biting it when they crested a rock formation and looked down upon the dig site.

While the strange stone formations were fascinating, and the dilapidated scholar buildings were of a construction type she'd never seen before, it was hard to concentrate on either with the sea of dead bodies that lay before them. The ground was littered with unmoving starlings. They radiated out from the edges of a lily pad-covered pond; its verdant green becoming their moribund emerald.

"Stay here," Urious commanded. Before she could protest, he added, "and keep watch. If you see any of the starlings so much as twitch, make the sound of a coastal bird."

She watched as he made his way down the rocks to the outpost and tried to think of a coastal bird she could imitate. None came to mind. She'd never played birdsong as a gryphlet. Her shattered beak had prevented it.

He checked each body in turn. Many of the starlings' eyes hadn't glazed over yet. Either they were in the early days of infection, or they'd been healthy when they died. The fact that their bodies were fresh enough to tell meant they had been alive a day or two ago.

Atop another stone formation, there were scorch marks and the burned bodies of several starlings. Urious, as the only one of their expedition immune to the parasite, dragged the new bodies to the unlit pyre. To the credit of her comrades, his efforts took hours and none of them complained. When he finished, he sounded the all clear, and the gryphons and opinici in the rear caught up and began their own exploration of the dig site.

"Is it safe to talk?" one of the rangers asked.

"Yes, word this morning was that the starlings are east

of the flooding and north of us," Urious said. His tone was hesitant. His scouts hadn't told him of the dead starlings here, if Tresh had to guess.

"The opinici have flint and tinder fungus," Biski said. "You should let them burn the bodies. Otherwise, scavengers will find them and spread the infection."

Urious nodded and began to move wood from a pile by the camp to the stone pyre. Biski inspected several of the bodies but seemed unwilling to risk infection by cutting into them with her claws. Henders got the fire going, and the camp warmed.

ONCE THE FIRE was in full swing, Jer took over managing it while Urious went in search of any remaining bodies. This left the other gryphons and opinici time to explore.

Tresh and Biski remained by the pyre until the ranger tending it suggested that it might be safer if they left, then they went to see what everyone else was doing. They found Henders first. He was clearing the moss and pungent vines from one of the stone structures.

"What're you up to?" Biski asked him.

He waved them over. "It's the rocks here. Someone's carved words into them."

Biski peered up at them. "Oh, it's a picture. An opinicus."

Or a gryphon, Tresh thought. It actually resembled the starling prisoner's poor drawing attempt, complete with three-part wings. Seeing it up close, the front legs weren't clearly meant to be talons or claws. They didn't match Henders's avian forelegs, nor did they really match Tresh's, either. The back feet looked the same as the front, and all four legs had long feathers coming off them. *This must be where Piprik's starling got the idea from.*

"Yeah, maybe," Henders said, "but under here is the word for *eyrie*. Most of the monuments we had to patrol in the Reeve's Guard used the old glyph-based alphabet, so you sort of get used to seeing it around."

"What does this say down here?" Tresh asked.

"I'm not sure," he admitted. "The glyphs are the same ones. It's the right alphabet, they're just not in any order I recognize."

Biski stood on her back legs and rested her forepaws above the drawing. "Want some help clearing off the rest of the moss?"

"Sure, that'd be great," he said. "With the two of you helping, maybe we can find more stone artist pictures."

Tresh stretched her forepaws out. They were still cramped from working the opinicus doors at the outpost and trying to twist the key. The thought of standing on her back legs after Ferrick had bitten one of them didn't seem like an enjoyable endeavor, either.

"You will have to proceed without me," she said. "I think I will find Erlock Chartail."

Tresh made her way to the pond, where the fantail pride leader was pacing. While Erlock's own tail feathers had been burnt down to the base, she'd had donor feathers imped onto hers to help her fly until her next molt. Judging by the bright red color and short length, they'd come from a cardinal opinicus and not another fantail.

The stony outcropping where Tresh had watched Urious move the corpses hung over half of the pond, but with all of the runoff flowing into it, it had become a small lake. There were still a few bodies in the water Urious hadn't moved yet.

She interrupted Erlock's pacing. "What agitates you? The dead starlings?"

"They look like gryphons," Erlock said.

Tresh had been facing off against the starling horde along the taiga border for months. She understood what Chartail was getting at. The infected were emaciated. They didn't speak in words. Their eyes were glazed, and they looked like animals.

No, not animals. Monsters. It was easy to forget they'd once been gryphons.

The bodies here were different. Clear-eyed. Meat on their bones. Panic etched on their faces. They hadn't been picked over by scavengers yet.

Tresh reached a paw towards the water, then thought better of it after Henders's knife fish mishap. "They were new starlings. The Emerald Jungle is still sending gryphons here, perhaps trying to find their missing kin."

"Emerald Jungle?" Erlock asked.

"It is what Piprik calls the starlings' home," Tresh said. "A jungle that lies past the bog."

Erlock looked west, but below the canopy, all anyone could see was hanging moss and the scholar's camp. It was in surprisingly good shape. While the pyre burned, the rangers were making their way to look around the buildings.

She looked back to the water. "My heart goes out to the starlings. They're searching for answers, too."

"Yes," Tresh agreed, "but if they continue to send expeditions, it explains why the infected have not died off yet. Their numbers are being replenished."

"How many more starlings can remain to be infected?

I saw the dead bodies at New Eyrie. We burned them, too. A bonfire with more gryphons in it than my entire pride has now." Erlock looked back reflexively to the east, the direction of the weald. She wore Piprik's badge on her harness. "Fire is reclaiming us all."

Tresh put a paw on the pride leader's shoulder. "We have a cure. We just do not have enough of it yet. Kia, Piprik, these are smart opinici. They will find a way to grow enough pumpkins. In the meantime, the starlings may be without end. Piprik said they tolerate no opinici, no other gryphons in their jungle. We would be wise not to stray too far west."

Erlock stared at her reflection in the pond. Enough light came through to show the white spots hidden in her plumage. "Someone needs to warn the starlings to stay away. Someone needs to tell them of the antidote."

"The infected will not hesitate to attack you," Tresh said.

"Not the infected." Erlock looked up at Tresh. "Someone needs to warn this Emerald Jungle."

Tresh stared back at Erlock's reflection. She no longer saw the dark plumage or starling spots. Instead, she saw—

She saw the imprisoned starling's drawing brought to life.

Beneath the water's surface, covered in some sort of scaffolding, was a mummified gryphon. *Opinicus*, she corrected herself. *No, not opinicus*. The back legs were wrong. They were too bird-like.

Tresh shoved her face under the surface to get a better look. Yes, this was the strange creature of the drawing.

Erlock pulled her back up. "What're you trying to do? You'll get infected in that water! It's full of dead starlings."

Tresh shook the water off her head. "Not just starlings. Look at the center. That is not a starling."

Erlock peered into the pond. The ripples from Tresh's dunk obscured it for a moment. Then it came into focus. "I see it!"

Tresh started to hop in, but Erlock grabbed her.

"No, you'll be infected!" Erlock scolded. "Stay on dry land."

"Why is it secured down there, beneath the surface? Do you see the restraints?" Tresh asked. She didn't know how to tell Erlock she'd taken a large dose of pumpkin the day before without bringing up Blinky.

Biski had decided not to dose Tresh since she wasn't showing any symptoms, saving Tresh from having to reveal her meeting with the missing owl gryphon. Erlock seemed trustworthy, and Tresh realized now might be a good time to bring it up, but the rangers were running over with their own news.

They must have caught Tresh's question because Jer had an explanation. "The water level isn't usually that high. Normally that section is no more than a few inches deep. The rains flooded it."

"You knew of the mummified opinithing?" Erlock asked.

"Opinithing?" He shook his head but looked into the water. It took a moment for him to see it. "Oh! That is gross. No, that wasn't here when I did my supply run. Or maybe it was covered up. Bog bodies often show up in this section of the kjarr lands. I'm not sure why, but every so often, things wash up here after a heavy storm."

"That's not why we came over, though," Xalt said. "We found something at the camps. Things aren't the same as when we were last here."

Erlock and Tresh followed the rangers. At first glance, this outpost resembled the last one they'd come from, except without a sailfin moat. There was the tower, complete with a storage room at the bottom and a roost up top. There were no walls this time, but there was a covered stable for goliath birds. Without a boardwalk trail leading here, Tresh didn't want to speculate at how you'd guide the giant birds through the muck. Inside were more crates and jars.

Scrawled on the outside of the tower, sometimes in a color suspiciously similar to dried blood, were sketches of the bog body. Surrounding it were brightly colored markings in blue and green.

"Looks like more gryphon magic," Xalt said. "So we thought you'd be able to translate."

"It seems like the starlings worshipped the thing in the water," Jer added.

"Gryphon...magic?" Tresh tilted her head to the side.

"Maybe fisherfolk don't have it," Xalt conceded. "Weald gryphons put mystical wards on trees to repel monitor attacks."

"Yeah, and if you get too close, you get cursed and red fern stops working for you," Jer added. "That's what happened with my first four kids."

Erlock laughed. "There's a lot to unpack there. Where are you getting all of this from?"

The rangers shared a look.

"We were, uh, passing through the weald a while back and saw the magical wards on the trees," Xalt said. Tresh was left wondering if their weald expedition included crates of saltpeter.

Jer nodded. "Yeah, and the effigies above the trees."

Now it was Biski's turn to laugh. "Those aren't mystical. They're territory markers."

"And the effigies aren't magical, either," Erlock said. "They're there to help fledglings find their way back to the nest when they're learning to fly. You two are dumber than parrot scat, you know that?"

Tresh examined the blue and green markings up close. "These are kjarr territory markings, then?"

"No, not kjarr," Urious said, joining the conversation. The smell of ash still clung to him. "The kjarr symbol is a black and goldenrod paw, symbolizing the long legs and golden feathers of past Kjarrs. The blue comes from the deep bog prides. It's the color of bog blossoms. You probably think of the kjarr as extending from the aneda forests to the jungle, but the deepest parts of the bog used to be independent. Anywhere the blossoms grew, that was bog pride territory, not kjarr. It was our symbol before Jun's father," here he paused, "brought us into the fold."

"The green doesn't match the weald prides," Erlock added. "It could be the starling marker."

"How old are these?" Tresh asked. "Are we in danger of getting in the middle of a territorial dispute?"

Urious shook his head. "There's no more bog pride. We're all kjarr now. Thenca and I were two of the last eggs to hatch before the prides combined."

Biski pushed Tresh out of the way to get a better look. "Sorry, sorry. See where the markings are next to each other? The blue is on top of the green. We know this wasn't here when our ranger friends were here a few years back. This mark is newer than that. Well, all of this would have to be newer, otherwise they'd have noticed, right?"

The rangers nodded. Urious frowned but said nothing. His tail twitched.

Caught in a lie? Tresh wondered. *Or surprised some of your kin survived?* She needed to bring Biski and Erlock in on her secret before it became too dangerous. She'd just needed another minute or two with Erlock.

"So what's the plan?" Xalt asked. "Are we staying here or heading to the Flower? We've wasted two days already."

"We don't know anything more than when we got here," Biski said. "We're not any closer to figuring out the parasite."

"We know what happened to one ranger, Ferrick," Tresh said. The rangers glared at her.

Urious turned from the stables and headed towards the tower. "We know there are more starlings coming into the kjarr and getting infected. This isn't a problem we can outlast."

"So let's rescue anyone left at the Flower and get out of here," Jer said. "If we leave now and camp on the way, we should get there tomorrow night, right?"

Urious hesitated. "No, our scouts haven't returned. They were supposed to meet us here. I've been calling for them, but I'm not hearing anything back. We'll wait here until they report in."

Tresh's hackles rose. The dead starlings here could just as easily have been killed by wingtorn as by infected. Someone could slip out of the tower, barricade the door, and light it on fire in the middle of the night.

"Do you want us to go through the crates for supplies?" Xalt asked. He was the bossier of the two rangers.

A clay jar like the one from the previous outpost stuck out of the top of the crate.

"No, better not." Urious looked at the sky. There was plenty of light left. "Let's set up traps and see if we can catch a capybara or two. It's a good opportunity to replenish some of our food. I'm sure the scouts will be hungry when they catch up to us."

While Urious and the rangers went to set up traps, Biski was using charcoal dust to trace the starling and bog pride symbols into a journal. While her attention was caught up in territory markers, Tresh's rested on the drawing of the bog body.

14

SHATTERED

Tresh and her compatriots passed the night without incident. This time she slept in front of the door to keep Urious from sneaking out and talking to White Stripe and Black Mask without her noticing. Urious seemed surprised that she'd taken over guard duties but didn't protest.

Outside, the wind howled. Whatever warm front had pushed the rain down into the bog continued its assault. The next day, the sun was shining, and there was no frost.

"What're we up to today?" Biski asked.

Tresh yawned and padded around the tower a few times. "We wait for Urious's friends."

Erlock stretched and scratched the side of the tower, leaving behind her fantail scent. "We'd best hope the starlings didn't get them, then."

"At least our friend seems to be doing better," Biski said.

"Henders? Is playing with rocks better for him? It just makes him weirder," Erlock complained. Off in the distance, Henders was scraping moss off a statue.

"No, our other friend." Biski pointed to the pond. The runoff from the north had dried up and most of the pond overfill had drained away. The *opinithing*'s ears and wing tops were above the water line now.

"How does that happen?" Tresh asked. "Why did nothing eat it? Why did it not decay?"

Biski shrugged. "You'll have to ask Piprik when we get back. I'll bet he learned all that as a chick."

"Where's he from?" Erlock asked Tresh. "Was he Crackling Sea? Redwood Valley?"

"He is from Swan's Rest," Tresh said.

"No, before that," Erlock pressed. "What type of opinicus is he?"

Tresh bristled. "He is not an opinicus. He is fisherfolk."

"You know what I mean." Erlock's hackles were raised now, too.

"We do not speak of where we came from. Once you are fisherfolk, who you were does not matter." Tresh internally admitted a curiosity to Piprik's origins. She'd never seen an opinicus like him. He was as white as Rorin, but with a raptor countenance and black circles around his eyes. She'd seen neither bird nor opinicus with similar markings.

Erlock sighed. "So you're not a gryphon, you're a fisherfolk, then? Despite the paws? Despite the ears?"

Tresh nodded. "Yes. I am fisherfolk."

"And you're going to tell me you feel comfortable around opinici?" Erlock pushed.

Tresh's ears went flat. "Yes. *You* would call Quess opinicus. *You* would call my brother opinicus, my mother and father opinicus. They are not. We are all family. We are all fisherfolk."

Erlock was at a loss for words. She must not have considered that Tresh might be the only gryphon in a family of opinici.

Biski let out an exasperated sigh and put both of her front paws on her cheeks and opened her beak slack-jawed. "This is you, Erlock. This is how you look right now."

Erlock started to say something, then laughed. "Okay, okay! I'm sorry. I was being a lace monitor. It was inappropriate."

"The rear end of a lace monitor," Biski said.

Tresh looked back and forth. She'd heard that fantails and feathermanes had a friendly rivalry, as the two prides controlled the southern weald. She'd never seen that rivalry up close before now.

Biski shook a damp, sweaty paw, nearly hitting Erlock with the spray. "I'm sweating and it's the start of winter. How is this possible? I'd have stayed in the taiga if I'd known it was going to be hot down here."

Tresh looked over at the pond. Their *opinithing* was halfway revealed now. She was about to suggest Biski get a drawing of it when Henders began shouting from the nearby woods.

HENDERS'S EXCITEMENT was not proportional to his findings. His excitement would have been more appropriate for finding a golden pumpkin or warning of incoming starlings. What he found were none of these things. Not even in the same general patch of forest as those things, if Tresh had been asked to weigh in.

He'd found more rocks.

"They have glyphs on them, too!"

Erlock, who had run over the fastest, was not impressed.

"But what's really exciting is the angle. Look!"

They were all staring at the rock. The corner of the rock.

"See here? Now look at the other pillars."

Pillars?

"Other rocks."

Everyone did so. They seemed pretty boring to Tresh, and she let him know that.

Henders enthusiasm wasn't dampened by his audience's lackluster reaction. "It's the same construction type as the Snowfeather Dam. See? I think these were meant to fit together."

In the distance, the rangers were rushing over much as Erlock had. Urious was standing on his back legs and stretching high to try to see what was going on. Tresh waved a paw to let him know it was just Henders being Henders. Urious shook his head.

"Ah, my opinicus brethren," Henders said. "I think I made a new discovery in the name of eyrie scholarship."

They stared blankly. One poked at the picture.

Henders pointed to the corners of the rocks again. "I think these all fit together. I think there was a stone building here. Maybe it was made by the same opinici who built the dam and carved the Crackling Sea Eyrie into the cliffs."

"Why'd they build it in a swamp?" Jer asked. "Didn't they know it'd sink?"

"You knew this was a swamp," Tresh said, "and you kept building outposts."

"Your people tried to build a city on sand," he countered.

Tresh was reminded of having to spend a night in a nest covered by sand with Rorin when hiding from the rangers. It did seem like Sandpiper's Dune was one heavy storm away from becoming a dune itself.

"Maybe they didn't *know* it was a swamp," Henders said. "Maybe it *wasn't* a swamp yet."

Xalt looked around. "Does that mean there might be stormcloth buried here?"

Urious, perhaps feeling left out, finally padded over. "Gryphs? Opies? Can we get back to hunting and trapping?"

"Hey Urious, are there more ruins like this?" Henders asked.

Urious twitched an ear. "Ruins? Oh, the carvings on the rock. Yeah, they go all the way into the heart of the bog."

"We built the Flower at the heart of the bog," Xalt said. "It's dead center. There are no ruins there."

Biski poked at the ranger's middle, then moved her paw up and to his left. "The heart isn't in the center. It's off to the side."

Urious gave Biski a curious look. "Yes, she's right. The medicine gryphons used to tell stories of a giant blue gryphon battling a monstrous lightning bird. The bird died north of here, and its blood became the Crackling Sea, its body the crackling jellies. The gryphon fell back and cracked the earth, allowing the water to flow through it. The wildlife of the kjarr and bog sprouted up from its corpse. Its head fell into the ocean, and the blue from its feathers stained the water that color. The bog blossoms sprouted from its heart, from which the bog pride was born. Our original nesting grounds were located there. It's sacred ground."

No one said anything. The rangers didn't believe in gryphon mysticism, as they'd said on several occasions. The weald gryphon beliefs were unknown to Tresh. Her own were different from Urious's, but the fisherfolk were such a mishmash of cultures that it was hard to scoff at anyone's beliefs.

"I'd like to see the stones at the heart of the bog," Henders said at last.

Urious smiled but shook his head. "No, I don't think so. Terrible things happened there. It's not safe anymore. Only the medicine gryphons travel there to collect bog blossoms in the summer. And they all abandoned us during the war."

"Why?" Tresh asked.

He hesitated.

Jer spoke up. "Because Jun salted the land. You said the land is sacred, right?"

Urious looked away for a moment but didn't deny it. "Yes. The spilled blood from the conflict feeds the gryphon spirit that still empowers the bog. To salt the lands, though, to make it so nothing grows—that was Jun's crime. That's why the medicine gryphons turned against him."

Another moment of silence, but this time Biski interrupted. "Don't we have hunting to do? Those scouts should be back any moment. We want to be ready when they return!"

Tresh nodded and left to join them, leaving Henders to continue scraping moss off rocks. She spared one glance back at the unfolding mural. Most of the words meant nothing to her, but the drawings told their own story. There were no recognizable gryphons or opinici on them.

By the third day at the dig site, everyone was getting nervous. Tresh wandered from gryphon to opinicus to gryphon again, leaving when she sensed she was annoying them. Everyone was on edge, and their ongoing disputes faded in favor of wanting to leave the abandoned dig site.

Biski was counting her supplies for the tenth time. With Urious's help, she'd even captured some ants for medicinal purposes. Having missed the signs with Younce, she insisted on giving Tresh checkups three times a day to make sure she wasn't showing any indication of infection.

Henders was using Biski's paper to trace the ruins. While not a scholar, and clearly unsure how to use the paper, he seemed to think what he was tracing would make him famous back home.

Whatever happened to 'it's a bad time to be a scholar?'

The rangers were searching for any signs of hidden caches of stormcloth when they weren't checking their traps. Urious imitated birdsong with increasing despair. And then there was Erlock.

The fantail pride leader stared at the shrinking pond. The remaining dead starlings rested in the mud. The bog body was entirely above the water now and drying out in the sun. Sometimes she'd wander off for a few minutes to eat or drink, but she always returned to stare at it.

"This is not healthy behavior," Tresh told the weald

gryphon. "You should go hunt or scrape moss. Do something normal."

Erlock shook her head. "I feel like I need to see this. We'll be gone soon and maybe next time it floods this'll wash away. The chains holding it in place have nearly rusted through. I'll probably never come back here. I don't want to forget."

Tresh looked at the bog body. Its back feet resembled the front, neither talon nor paw, but something in between. While most had been destroyed, there were still some feathers coming off the legs, something no gryphon nor opinicus had. "What is there to forget or remember?"

"I'm not sure," Erlock conceded. "It's just...what would you call that? The body is so long. If it was in your pride, what would you call it? Gryphon? Opinicus?"

"Fisherfolk," Tresh said.

Erlock returned her smile half-heartedly. "Maybe it was a lost fisherfolk. The product of gryphon and opinicus breeding."

Tresh's ears went back. The gryphons and opinici were overly concerned about breeding. "Not everything needs a label."

"I suppose."

Back at the camp, the rangers were arguing with Urious. Snippets reached the pond.

We can't stay here. The starlings could arrive at any moment.

We're staying here until the scouts return. Without the scouts, we don't know where the starlings are located.

The shouting continued. In three days, Tresh had become worried, but not for the wingtorn. She hadn't seen nor heard from Blinky in that time. She hoped the owl gryphon would let her know if there were more wingtorn being led to their location, but she couldn't be sure of it. *Actually, while Urious and the opinici are occupied is the perfect time to tell Erlock about—*

"Tresh, step back slowly." Erlock's voice was quiet but commanding.

Tresh obeyed the order. She looked up at the rocky outcropping over the pond. Iridescent green feathers were breaking through the thick vegetation.

They were halfway to the camp when the starling finally got through the tangle of moss and looked down at the dig site. Its glossy eyes didn't see them, but it was sniffing the air.

When the starling went back into the brush, the petrel and fantail gryphons dashed for cover. Urious and the opinici saw Tresh and Erlock coming their way and found hiding places around the camp.

"Where are Biski and Henders?" Tresh hissed to Urious.

"Biski is napping inside," Urious replied. "Henders is playing with rocks."

There was a gentle snoring coming from inside the tower. Tresh considered making a dash for the rocks where Henders was, but the starling arrived at the pond before she could try it.

The infected gryphon was covered in mud. Swamp grouse feathers stuck to its face. *Is this the same one we saw back at the trail? Did it track us this far?* If they could track prey through days of flooding, that held terrible implications for their escape plan.

It poked at the dead starling bodies. One it ignored. The other it began to feed on. Everyone stayed silent while the sounds of cannibalism echoed on the rocks. Tresh felt sick.

It took an hour to finish its meal. It was just starting to crawl away when Biski awoke from her nap. She pushed open the door of the tower and was in the middle of chirping a greeting when Tresh stuffed her paw in Biski's mouth and Urious pulled her behind a crate.

The starling's ears perked up. It began to walk slowly towards the camp.

"This is bog turtle luck," Urious whispered. Tresh had yet to see a bog turtle but understood the tone.

The sound of birds to the north drew the starling's attention. It began to crawl up the stone incline when the inevitable happened.

"Hey, I found more rocks!" Henders shouted.

The starling's chittering cry filled the camp.

Urious sprang into action. "Kill it before it attracts the others!"

Henders tried to reach into his harness for his metal talons and fell beak-first into the ground. Even from his face-down position, he wrestled the weapons into place. Biski rushed to his aid.

"Bloody Reeve's Guard," Xalt said. The rangers scrambled to get their nets from the tower.

That left Tresh, Urious, and Erlock to deal with the starling. Its head was in the air, and its whole body shook as it chittered.

Tresh tried to pounce it, but it slipped out of the way, nearly catching her with its claws.

Erlock feinted a few times without success. She tried talking to it, but unlike the starlings Piprik had cured, this one held no love for her. She was mid-sentence when she became distracted by something near the pond.

"Need your focus here, Chartail," Urious snapped.

"Urious, look. Do you see that?" Erlock asked.

Tresh spared a glance for the pond. Something was crawling out from the *opinithing*. It looked like sand moving on the dunes. They were the size of mites, red and black, and they were flowing towards the chittering starling.

"Bog turtle luck," Tresh said, echoing Urious's comment from earlier. "We have to shut it up."

The starling had gone back to its call, head in the air, body shaking.

Tresh got a running start and tried to dive bomb it but was slashed across her chest for her trouble. Her whale-leather harness took the brunt of the attack.

Urious tried to ram it, but it fell back and latched onto him. It clawed at his back and sides. The rangers arrived and managed to each snare a foreleg with their nets. When Henders reared up to slash at it with his metal talons, it kicked him in the stomach and sent him sprawling.

Urious tried to bite its throat, but it caught his shoulder in its beak, and he cried out.

"End it!" Biski shouted, but none of them had the courage to bite into an infected.

Tresh saw a chance to do nothing and let the starling finish off Urious.

It was a cowardly thing to do.

Cowardly like raiding the fisherfolk villages and slaughtering their children.

There was a part of her that would have allowed it to happen. She was not Rorin. She was not so quick to forgive the unforgivable.

But she was her parents' child. She was an aunt to her nieces and nephews. Quess was still out there, and Urious was the best opportunity to find her.

Tresh slipped past the thrashing wings and back legs and bit down as hard as she could on the starling's neck. It was tough, grizzled. Muddy. The bite should have sent a normal opinicus into shock. The starling did not stop moving, did not stop biting, did not stop chittering.

Tresh bit down harder. Pain lanced through her beak, racing through every bit of scar tissue like a lightning strike. The fulgurite of her past folly flared up. She could feel her beak starting to give along the cracks. Blood spilled out like magma, tracing the shark-tooth-shaped lines along her mouth.

The starling stopped its chittering.

The starling stopped breathing.

The starling went limp.

Erlock pulled Tresh off the corpse and looked at her beak in horror.

The rangers were pulling Urious back from the tide of mites moving towards the dead starling. Jer said, "By the depths, they're just like the ones from Impir's jar."

As Urious passed by Erlock and Tresh, he gasped through the pain, "Good shark."

"We can't stay here," Henders said. "We have to get out now."

"Henders, go grab the packs from the tower before the mites spread that far," Urious ordered between gasps of pain. Henders flew back quickly to get their supplies.

"Are those the same mites from the jars? Why else would those jars be here?" Xalt's voice cracked.

Erlock stared at Tresh's beak. The blood had flowed out from the cracks and changed her beak from black to dark red.

Biski was the only one unfazed. "Urious, can you walk?" A yelp of pain answered her question. "Erlock, you're going to carry him. Rangers, help lift Urious on top of Erlock."

"Don't get any funny ideas while you're up there," Erlock grumbled, but she lowered her stomach to the ground so the rangers could balance Urious on top without damaging her wings.

"Tresh, dear, when the adrenaline wears off, you're going to be in a pain I can't imagine," the medicine gryphon said. "Before that happens, I need you to choke down this vial of pumpkin."

Tresh didn't nod, but she managed to get her beak open and swallow. As much blood as pumpkin went down her throat. She was watching the mites. New ones flowed out of the dying starling and moved towards their kin from the bog body.

This was where the starlings were getting infected. They probably set up camp along the shore and the mites got them in the night. Only the flood waters had kept her expedition safe.

Henders arrived with their gear. At Biski's command, he grabbed Tresh's harness and pulled her in line with the rest. They headed southeast, towards the Flower.

Tresh did her best not to let her beak chatter, but she was shaking all over. Biski was still treating Urious's bite marks. He and Erlock looked strange in front of Tresh. Two tails, eight legs, two heads, but one set of wings. A *gryphonithing* to go with their *opinithing*.

Her mind began to shut down, but her body allowed Henders to continue to guide her deeper into the bog.

15

FEATHERMANE INGENUITY

Tresh wandered for two hours before Biski called for a halt.

"I need time to bandage everyone properly," she said.

Urious gave the rangers instructions to the nearest safe drinking water, and they went to fill up. Erlock followed behind them, happy to be rid of her passenger for a little.

Henders served as Biski's nurse. He was looking at the vials of pumpkin. "It's a good thing Urious took the worst of it. We might run out of pumpkin before we reach the rangers and fisherfolk." When Urious glared at him, he added, "Um, you know what I mean."

"You'd be lost in here without me," Urious said. "Don't forget that."

Tresh watched Biski with fascination. Weald medicine was different from fisherfolk medicine. While kjarr gryphons were resistant to most infections and diseases, they weren't invulnerable. Wounds still needed to be cleaned and kept dry, not an easy task in a bog. Their expedition hadn't even managed to keep their medicine gryphon clean and dry.

Biski grumbled about the weather and mused out loud whether her ants would be put to better use on Urious or Tresh while she sharpened her claws with a stone Piprik had given her, prompting Tresh to wonder if Piprik's mysterious golden vials were still in Biski's pack somewhere.

"I do not understand," Tresh said to Urious. "Do we eat the ants? Are they medicinal?"

Urious grimaced. "Definitely don't eat the ants. You'll see in a moment. I think she's decided."

Biski opted to use treated aneda resin held in place by Tresh's harness to bind her chest-wound closed, allowing Biski to use the ants on Urious.

"I wish I'd grabbed more," she said. "It wasn't easy to catch them with paws. Some days, I wish I were an opinicus. If only they weren't so ugly."

"I'm right here," Henders said. "That's no way to talk to your friends."

Biski made a *tsk* sound. "I'm sure you're very pretty to other opinici. Your gaudy feathers, which provide no camouflage benefits, are probably all the rage at New Eyrie."

"Erlock's butt looks like it's on fire with all those red feathers, and you're orange and blue," Henders countered. "Where do you expect to hide?"

"There's a pumpkin patch by the sea at Sandpiper's Dune," she said. The Reeve's Guard was at a loss for words, so she continued. "Now reach in and grab an ant."

Henders put his claws in and had his digit bitten. His profanity was real and akin to what Carru said when experiencing his first jelly sting.

"No, bad opinicus!" Biski scolded. "Don't waste them!"

"It won't let go!" the Reeve's Guard wailed.

Biski put down the sharpening stone and cut off the ant's body, then vivisected its head to remove it. Tresh made a mental note to ask Younce for one of those sharpening stones for the Blue-eyed Festival.

If I get back in time. If Younce and I are still together after this. If I can forgive him for hiding things from me. If he can forgive me for leaving.

"Carefully take the ant between two claws," Biski directed Henders. "Don't let it touch flesh. Leafcutters never let go. Be careful not to squish it. I imagine you have some strong feelings about ants right now."

"I have some strong feelings about gryphons with star-berry front halves and pumpkin back halves right now," Henders grumbled.

Biski had treated Urious's wounds with aneda and was now holding one of them closed. "You want a mandible on either side of the laceration."

Henders did as she said, and the ant's mouth clamped shut, holding the wound together. Biski cut off the ant's body.

"It's stitches for gryphons." The annoyance had left his voice. "How long does it stay like that? The jaws don't release when it dies?"

"Nope," Biski chirped. "It'll last for a few days at least. Okay, grab another ant. If we're careful and don't squish any more, we'll have just enough."

Tresh watched with morbid fascination as the medicine gryphon and Reeve's Guard fixed up Urious. He grimaced every time the ants bit down but seemed to be doing okay. She imagined he'd been through worse when he lost his wings.

She looked again at his scars. They were jagged but had clearly been stitched and treated, unlike Vitra's. Though, now that Tresh was looking at the puncture marks left by the ants, she thought she remembered similar markings along Vitra.

"Do the bog medicine gryphons use the leafcutters, too?" Tresh asked.

He nodded. "They're all over the bog but pretty rare in the weald. Kjarr gryphlets get into a lot of trouble."

"Ah, like your tail?" Tresh asked.

He laughed, annoying Biski and Henders, who were trying to keep him still. "Yeah, I'm lucky it was a baby sailfin and not an adult. I think Thenca was even madder than I was. She had this vision of us switching places during hunting lessons with no one the wiser. That wasn't an option until my tail healed up again."

"I can see how that would be an issue." Tresh held up her paws. "I did not have that problem with my brother."

"I can imagine. Not just the paws, but I imagine your brother didn't share your beak scars." Urious became pensive. "You said you came from Snowfall? Did you see Thenca? How's she doing?"

Biski and Henders finished with the ants and went to try to find any bog blossoms that had survived into the winter for Tresh's treatment.

Urious gave them instructions to pick a vine with thorns, too. "On the off chance the starling tracked us by smell, the vine has a bitter scent that hides the smell of gryphon."

"Honestly, if it'll hide the smell of opinicus, we should just use it all the time," Biski quipped as they left.

Tresh and Urious sat without speaking for several minutes. She started to say something a few times, then thought better of it. He was trying to preen the blood out of the wing feathers on his bracers.

"Sorry, I'm being rude," Urious said. "The starling we saw the first day and the one at the dig site have been on my mind a lot. Almost as much as my sister. You were saying?"

"Thenca seemed well," Tresh said. "She misses Deracho. He is in charge of Hoarfrost and watches for starlings trying to get around the mountains. It is too far and too high for her to follow him there. I think she waits for the path from Snowfall to the kjarr to finish so she can see you."

"Deracho," Urious said. "That was his name. It feels like a lifetime ago. Sounds like you know more about what my sister is up to than I do. Please, would you mind telling me everything you know?"

Tresh nodded. Erlock had said that sharing information was how you made friends of enemies. She'd just started when Biski returned.

"Charred manes, what're you doing?" Biski cried. She'd returned with Henders in tow.

Tresh looked cross eyed at her own beak. The bandages were soaked red again. She started to say she was sorry, but Biski hissed at her.

"No, don't say *more words*. We don't have a lot of painkillers, and we don't have time to wander the woods looking for more kashow trees. You want this to heal as much as it can today because you're going to have to try to do without all day tomorrow," Biski fussed. "Henders, help me unwrap this loquacious idiot's beak. We're going to re-soak the wraps in aneda and bind it again."

As Biski reached over, Tresh caught the same bitter, floral smell that kept cropping up around their camps coming from the thorned vines Biski had gathered for Urious.

Erlock and the rangers returned to camp. In addition to fresh water, they'd also caught some swamp grouses.

"That's more than I can eat right now," Urious said. He seemed to have given up hope of White Stripe and Black Mask catching up to them.

Biski looked up from the wraps. "We dosed Tresh pretty well. Cut them very thin and feed them to her before I re-wrap her beak. Just don't overfeed her. I don't want to redo these if she throws up."

Tresh enjoyed the flavor of swamp grouse but had to admit it was identical to frost chicken. They were probably two words for the same animal. Her beak was starting to ache again in spite of the painkillers.

Through the forest, birdsong repeated. Tresh saw Urious's ears perk up. She listened closer. It did feel like she was hearing some of the same birdsong repeat, but she couldn't be sure. She'd never given much thought to birds before this expedition. She made a note to listen for them more often.

Biski finished with Tresh's beak and checked Urious's ant stitches. "We should spend the night healing. We have fresh water. There's a good selection of herbs and edible mushrooms. It'll give me a chance to look for more of that sap. Is there a safe place to camp?"

Urious took a moment to think. "There used to be some hunting hideaways nearby, but I never used them personally. I can tell you what to look for, though."

WHETHER OR NOT IT was the shelter Urious remembered, the rangers did locate some form of cover near the water. It was a wide hole big enough to fit even Erlock. Urious had demanded they check it for turtles before piling inside.

The rangers had each brought a small portable brazier. With Urious incapacitated and unable to sneak out in the middle of the night to warn his conspirators, Tresh's biggest concern was that Vitra might see the fire or smell the smoke and come to investigate.

Thankfully, food stores were just low enough that they decided to save the braziers for cooking. It'd be hard work to cook anything larger than a fish over one, but Tresh didn't correct their assumption. Instead, she positioned herself between Urious and the way out.

It was hard to keep her beak shut. She'd spent the beginning of her life silent. She hadn't spoken a word during her fledging years on the advice of a medicine gryphon. He'd suggested that her beak wouldn't heal if she talked before she was fully grown.

It had taken a lot to get Tresh talking again after she'd fledged. It'd taken even more to weather the teasing and learn to form her words properly. Ultimately, what had drawn her out of her shell was an opinicus tinkerer. She'd had an idea that would help her dive and swim better, and she needed the tinkerer's help to make it a reality. Those early designs had become the paw-flippers that all petrel gryphons used now.

She made sure she was the first one out of camp the next morning and went to the watering hole. She couldn't really drink without Biski pouring the liquid into her throat, not without risking wet bandages, so she just stood around. Tresh didn't know what *beak rot* was, but she didn't want to find out. She was just about to head back to the turtle hole when Blinky poked her head out from behind a tree and beckoned Tresh over.

Blinky looked worse for wear. There weren't any clear bite marks, but she had scratches, and there was a little dried blood around her paws and beak.

She pointed at Tresh and waited for the update.

Tresh pointed at her wrapped beak.

Blinky frowned.

Tresh tapped one paw impatiently.

Finally, Blinky gave in. "My common is not good. Do you speak owl?"

Tresh shook her head. She'd never met anyone except an owl gryphon who could speak their language. Many of the words were at a frequency that normal gryphon ears couldn't detect, making it a fool's errand to try.

"Was this starlings? Vitra? Wingtorn?" the owl gryphon asked.

Tresh nodded, shook her head, then shook her head a final time.

Blinky thought. "I need you to steal some pumpkin."

Tresh pointed at Blinky's wounds.

"I am uninfected, I think. It is for—" Blinky suddenly flattened herself and slipped backwards into the brush.

Tresh turned around and exited out of the bushes to the watering hole. As a testament to Blinky's hearing, it was twenty seconds later before Biski appeared. Tresh couldn't think of anything to say to explain why she'd been out on her own. With her beak wrapped, she didn't have to.

"I heard talking. Tresh, was that you?" Biski asked.

Tresh shook her head.

Biski frowned. "I'm sure I heard voices."

Tresh shrugged.

"I need to talk to you." Biski pulled out an empty vial, the one Blinky had coughed up. Tresh had kept it because glass was so valuable. "This was in your harness pocket. I found it when I was fixing up your chest wound. You've been stealing medicine."

Tresh said nothing.

"It's been washed. That means you were hiding your tracks." Biski's voice held an anger Tresh had never heard before. Apparently, the bubbly feathermane had no patience for medicine thieves.

Tresh weighed her options. She'd never be able to steal the medicine now, but she may not need to. She beckoned for Biski to come closer. To her credit, Biski did so. Then Tresh whispered into her ear. "Blinky."

Biski's eyes got wide. "Blinky! We need to tell the others."

Tresh shook her head.

Biski frowned. "Why not? What's going on?"

The petrel fisherfolk traced the outline of a wingtorn in the dirt with one claw. She did her best to make it look angry.

"There are wingtorn out here? Other than our wingtorn? That's good. We could use the extra help."

Tresh shook her head, mindful of the bandages, then took a moment to think. She drew the bog pride territory marker next to the wingtorn.

Biski's eyes got wide. She watched as Tresh then drew a tower with walls around it and wrote *trap* next to it.

"Okay. I follow. You think those wingtorn were behind it? How would they have got over the walls after locking the door?"

The sound of branches moving out of the way heralded the arrival of a wingtorn. They both jumped.

Urious limped over. "Everything okay? I woke up and both of you were gone."

Tresh nodded. Biski chastised Urious for walking down here but swished her tail back and forth as she scolded, destroying Tresh's drawings.

"Yeah, yeah. Thanks, den mother," Urious said. "I'll be walking all day today. What's it matter if I come down here to drink first?"

"Ask that again after hour five of hiking through the woods." Biski took her medicine kit out of her harness to put more aneda on Urious's cuts.

While their backs were turned, Tresh slipped two of the pumpkin vials out of Biski's kit and placed them where she'd last seen Blinky. Tresh reached up and scratched the tree. Hopefully the scent of tree sap mixed with Tresh's own would bring Blinky back to find it if she weren't already keeping watch.

Tresh followed the wingtorn and feathermane back up to camp, where the three opinici argued over their map in the morning light.

WHAT THE JAILOR SAW

Ninox had gotten lost in the tomes of new information in Orlea's library and forgotten about the threat of Merin's kin. Once she saw a journal marked *Reeve's Guard: Founding to Disbanding,* curiosity got the better of her, and she looked inside. She skipped past the creation of the guard to the end, then worked her way backwards.

During the conflagration, most of the Reeve's Guard perished in the fire, attempting to save the lives of civilians.

She felt disheartened. Strix was mentioned as participating in the rescue effort and battling Commander Wolden, but his family weren't mentioned at all. On the one paw, this would make gryphon-opinicus relations much easier. On the other paw, did anyone think all of the Reeve's Guard had vanished in a fire?

Strix had put her in charge of holding the Reeve's Guard headquarters. Ninox herself had over twenty clean kills. Her siblings had spread out and covered the other stations. There were many good kills there that hunters were not getting credit for.

Orlea snored in the corner. Ninox looked at the sleeping opinicus. *Clean kills* might be the wrong words. An opinicus was not food. Nor was it a gryphon. She knew it was not right to hunt gryphons, but food was also not the right distinction. Sometimes, she'd hunted things that were not food with her father. Every few years, for reasons she didn't understand, the population of weald monitors would explode out of control in the spring, and they would need to be killed. They were not food, but they counted as hunting kills.

Orlea was not food, prey, or a gryphon. Orlea was a friend. Many of the opinici in this pride were interacting with gryphons. Eggs being laid in gryphon prides could hatch as opinici in the spring. Her own egg could hatch as an opinicus. It was a possibility she hadn't considered until now.

Her hunting instincts were the same for hunting opinici as monitors. If the invaders came, her pride would have to hunt opinici. Thinking of it as hunting made it easier, gave satisfaction to the kill, made it a game. When something was a game, owl gryphons learned faster and became better at what they were learning. She should think on this longer before she shared her thoughts.

What if the Ashen Weald were to attack? The thought came out of nowhere, but it presented a new problem. What if she needed to learn to hunt gryphons? If that were made into a game, what would the implications be? Implications was a word Cherine used a lot. It was not one Strix had ever used, not in front of his children.

She went back to her reading. After beaking through several other tomes, she found no explanation for how the eyrie fire started. Cherine's account was not in here, except in little hints. She'd hoped that once she and

Cherine were closer, he would tell her his story. So far, he had not, and they were very close now. Orlea had shared a recovery cave with him, but Ninox didn't feel comfortable asking Orlea for information on Cherine. Ninox would wait and ask him if he took too long to tell her.

Looking closer at the accounts, none of Merin's pride had given their stories. She'd wondered about Satra's rescue, but the only version of it came from Hatzel, who'd arrived after Satra had been freed.

The chimes outside Orlea's hut made their musical sound, waking the sleeping opinicus.

"Oh, Nox, you're still here," Orlea said. "Is everything okay? What's on your mind?"

"Just food," Ninox said.

"Oh, I don't have anything here," Orlea replied. "I'm sure one of the merchants will give you something to eat. I'm supposed to interview a prison guard about the night of the fire. He was working the northern quarter. You're welcome to stay, but would you mind coming back after the interview?"

"I should have left already. Cherine will be worried. He is a gryphon who worries a lot." Ninox realized she'd called Cherine a gryphon and suddenly felt her nares turn red in embarrassment. Orlea didn't seem to notice her discomfort. "Thank you for use of your books. I will be back when the Snowfeather nesting site is settled."

She slipped outside and past an opinicus in a guard harness, startling him. He went inside and closed the door behind him.

The opinicus camp was unusually quiet this time of day, and Ninox groomed her flight feathers while listening in on the conversation through the door. It was rude, but she couldn't help herself.

Most of it was pleasantries, background on how the opinicus became a Reeve's Guard, why he started to work at the prison. Just as she took flight back to her nesting grounds, however, she heard the guard say, "So we're always watching mad 'ole Impir, but then they come in with the gryphon who started the fire that burned down the whole place!" She was about to fly back down, but several merchants, led by a blue one, had shown up outside Orlea's door and were waiting for their turn to talk to her, so Ninox continued on. She'd have to come back later and find out about this gryphon who had been locked up in an opinicus jail.

W*ITH* N*INOX* on her way back north, Orlea could move on to the next order of business. Not that she minded the owl gryphon's visits. As much as Orlea taught Ninox about opinicus culture, Ninox also presented Orlea with an opportunity to learn about owl gryphon culture.

She'd quickly come to realize that each weald pride had its own peculiarities. A fantail didn't have the same concerns as a parrotface. Hatzel's pride was always willing to help but could be a little boastful when it came to their hunting prowess. The feathermanes were busy planning the recovery of the southern weald in the spring. The parrotfaces made good neighbors, as long as Orlea's hunters didn't go past the grasslands. And Ninox, well, Ninox wanted knowledge and training. She saw something in the future that none of the other prides saw yet, and Orlea appreciated that.

Since Ninox was essentially guarding their northern border for free, it made sense to give her the Snowfeather

Highlands. *Maybe we should start calling it the owlfeather highlands?* Orlea would just tell the other opinici that it was a permanent security outpost to guard against invasion.

Crater Lake might be a problem. Were it still in its original condition, it'd be a good place to fish. Several less-practical merchants had already come to her asking when the dam would be rebuilt. The massive, cobra-statue-adorned dam had been built before anyone could remember. She'd let them know food was the priority and rebuilding would come later, but she'd heard their concerns.

Thankfully, Ninox hadn't asked for the lake. The owl gryphons would probably still fish from the river, but Orlea didn't think anyone would complain about that just yet. For now, the opinicus refugees were staking out their own section of the old Reeve's Hunting Grounds, and turkey still held its novelty.

Orlea was groggy from her nap when the guard arrived. Foultner, her old poaching nemesis, had made friends with some of the Reeve's Guard by—and just thinking this made Orlea laugh—joining it.

Foultner had been a poacher for longer than Orlea. Orlea had been driven to the role by desperation, but Foultner seemed to enjoy making herself unpopular with authority. Most of her pre-conflagration life had been spent avoiding arrest. This new *if you can't beat them, join them* mentality was just her sort of solution. That kind of thinking, to Orlea's mind, was like getting in trouble for hunting the turkeys in the Reeve's Hunting Grounds, so deciding to become the reeve.

That thought gave Orlea pause. Some would say that's what she'd done. She didn't think of herself as a reeve.

She'd grown up hating the reeves. Not just Reeve Brevin, all of them. She'd never heard any of their names other than Brevin, but the fact that they lived out there, ruling cities while she starved in the underbough, made her angry. When one of the gryphons helping with the fire-fighting efforts slipped up and called the opinici *Orlea's pride*, she knew she should embrace that idea rather than shy from it. It had the added benefit of making the gryphons feel safer.

"How does the morning find you?" the guard asked.

"Well, though busy," Orlea said. "If you're looking for work, the merchants have need of a night guard. Now, if you don't mind, tell me about the night of the fire?"

The guard had a flair for the dramatic and began by laying his jailor's keyring on the floor between them. Orlea examined it and resisted the urge to have it rushed to the metalworks to be repurposed. They'd melted down the last set they'd found, only to discover several locked caches excavated from the ruins of the market square. She'd have to find a safe place to hide these. Chances were good that they were just jail cell keys, but one was ornamented and might go to something in Reeve's Nest.

He settled in and began his tale, beginning with how he'd come to join the Reeve's Guard and the minor offense that'd led to him being shipped off to prison duty —minor extortion, with his emphasis on the word minor.

His upbringing landed him in the northern quarter prison, where the rich opinici lived. Only important prisoners were kept there. Prisoners like Impir, the opinicus who reminded everyone that intelligence or scholarship didn't mean you couldn't be a monster. Why he hadn't been banished with his master, Mally the Nighthaunt, she didn't know. While she was sure there were stories to hear about Impir, her interest was on the other prisoner, the gryphon.

"This gryphon, what had he done?" she asked. "Why was he there?"

"They brought him in back when they thought the fires were just a merchant quarter thing. I didn't catch all of the details. Honestly, I don't believe any of it. It's a bunch of capybara dung."

His voice went up a little as he spoke. Orlea wasn't sure if that meant he was lying or just nervous to be talking to her. He'd expressed an interest in staying here instead of at the Crackling Sea Eyrie. Without a leader or organization, the reds at New Eyrie were having a bad time of things. Few were willing to remain in the tents outside the city walls with starlings to the south and invaders to the north, not if they had a choice.

She settled onto her cushion. "I'll be sure to note your skepticism, but I like a good story as much as the next opinicus. What did the arresting guard say the gryphon had done? What was his name again?"

"Askler, I think," the guard said. "Gryphon names are all sort of nonsense, aren't they?"

Orlea wrote down Askel. While she didn't necessarily agree with the guard's assessment, she had run into problems with their penchant for using nicknames more than hatch names. For all of her interviewing, she'd yet to meet a gryphon who could remember what Pink Paw's real name was.

Not that opinici didn't have their own quirks. None of Orlea's pride ever called Zeph by his name. When he was among the opinicus refugees, he was always Zeph Parrotbane or Reevesbane.

The guard continued. "They said he'd sabotaged the

aqueducts, flooded the butchery, and tried to light it all on fire. Also, there was a hole in the middle of the merchant quarter. Let them tell it, he was Jun the Kjarr, waging war on the world, doing great and terrible deeds."

"Yes," Orlea agreed. "There is a prestige to arresting the most exciting gryphon rather than just another onlooker."

The guard nodded. "Yeah, that's right. You shoulda seen him. He's not one of the big ones. Not like the one with the hooked beak looking into the scholars."

Orlea put a question mark in her journal. Several of the New Eyrie and Crackling Sea opinici had said it was a bad time to be a scholar, but she'd yet to get anyone to explain what they meant by that. She only knew of five scholars: Neider, Impir, Bario, Cherine, and Kia. Three of those had fled north to join the Blackwing Eyrie, Kia was down with the fisherfolk, and Cherine was on loan to the owls.

"How's a gryphon going to do any of that when he can't hold anything with his little paws?" the guard contin-ued. "Anyways, he was in shock. Just stood there, looking out the window while 'ole Impir talked his freaky ears off. So Bario, that's Felicio's brat, shows up with the new reeve and claims this Askler had saved him at the flameworks. Anyhow, they had us release the prisoners, then they left. Once they were gone, we didn't have any prisoners to guard, so we high-tailed it out of there."

He seemed parched, so she slid a bowl of water towards him. Water purification had become more exciting without the aqueduct and waterworks, but they were making do. Once he'd had something to drink, she asked a few followup questions. The arresting guard had died defending the Crackling Sea Eyrie. The description of the gryphon, reddish brown with a feathered tail, matched her recollection of Askel. She thanked the guard for his time and let him go.

Now Orlea had a problem. Askel and Triddle had come to the medicine gryphon caves the night of the rescue operation. Triddle had been sent to blow up the flameworks to make a diversion. The flameworks were commonly blamed for causing the fire, but they'd been chosen by the insurgents because they were far from the eyrie.

This wasn't the first time a flameworks had blown up. It wasn't even the first time that particular flameworks had exploded. It'd seemed a safe diversion. It was one reason she'd been happy to go along with the plan to save Satra: no one should have gotten hurt.

She remembered Askel being in her team when Triddle left for the flameworks. Askel was supposed to stay with the rescue effort, helping get the kjarr gryphlets out safely, but he and a few of his pridemates had disappeared once they were past the gates.

She'd given a lot of thought to where he'd gone, but she'd never considered that he'd gone to the oil canisters in the market district. Askel had a reputation around the inflammable. Would he have caused such a big fire? Unlike the opinicus guard, she had no doubt that a determined gryphon could work the saltpeter bombs. Her question was whether or not he would, and why.

The answer made sense when she looked back over what the guards had seen. The line for the aqueduct overhead had been redirected through the oil, then lit on fire. That was the waterfall of flames she'd seen down below. The one that had nearly killed her. The one that had killed hundreds of opinici as the eyrie ignited. The smoke had killed more than the fire.

This was her problem. Askel was a popular gryphon because he was smart. He'd saved gryphons with a makeshift dam that flooded a section of the weald that was burning out of control. His other half, Triddle, had done a lot for the weald. They were both building a road for the Ashen Weald now with the help of the taiga gryphons. Zeph and Hatzel both spoke highly of Askel. There were a lot of reasons to let it go.

But now that Orlea had heard the guard's story, she couldn't. She'd seen this behavior before. Some opinici couldn't help but set fires. They were arrested or locked away. Before Felicio and Bario had claimed *phoenix* as a title for someone who ran the flameworks, it was the term used to refer to such opinici. Gryphons didn't use fire the way opinici did, so they didn't know this was something that happened. The eyrie and weald were only just recovering. If Askel were a smart gryphon who could not help but start fires, hiding behind his reputation for stopping fires with Triddle, he needed to be locked up.

Askel being a compulsive firestarter might be the most likely scenario, considering the guards said he was just staring at the flaming oil when they caught him, but it wasn't the only possibility.

Each gryphon pride was like its own eyrie with its own reeve. All of the pride leaders had heard about the wing-torn and the explosives in the weald. What if one of them had ordered Askel to set the fires? What if they'd only agreed to the rescue operation in order to kill off as many opinici as they could? Orlea didn't believe that Hatzel would let that happen, but the other pride leaders could have made the decision without her.

Orlea put a question mark next to Strix and Merin's names. She needed answers. She needed Askel.

She placed the keys on a peg by the door and was just opening her journal to jot down a few more notes when the wind chimes outside sang their song. The second-best trapper in the eyrie walked in, her black armor and swirled metal claws glistening in the light.

Orlea smirked. "Welcome back, Foultner."

17

THE FLOWER REVISITED

If nothing went wrong, Tresh would get to see inside the Flower by mid-afternoon. This was not the sort of expedition where things failed to go wrong. It was, in her opinion, the opposite sort of expedition.

Despite Urious's protests, the rangers had climbed a tree and poked their long necks above the treetops to get a look at the Flower. It still stood, though at this distance, it was tough to tell if it was occupied. The flooding that had emptied from the northern bog was still draining this far south, the saturation of the mangroves holding it still.

The Flower rose above the tree tops, a great hall with four watch towers atop it. Its wooden walkway *petals* were lost beneath the floodwaters. The boardwalk dipped in and out of the water as it approached the Flower and then continued south towards the raftworks on the coast.

It was good to have confirmation that the Flower hadn't burned down or fallen into the swamp over the past few months, but that raised several more questions. Should they just go up and knock on the door and introduce themselves? Should they try to sneak in? The gryphons and opinici found a stretch of dry land within sight of the Flower and sat down to weigh their options.

Henders said yes, they should go in the front door. Opinici were civilized and would let them in. The Flower held stockpiles of food and medicine, not to mention doors and barricades. Had anyone made it there, they should still be safely inside.

Urious said no. If they knocked and it was full of starlings, the chittering would begin, and soon the starlings in the eastern bog would appear. The eastern swarm was the largest of the ones being tracked right now by far, and they were within its territory. Besides, as their discovery of Ferrick had revealed, there was also the possibility that the opinici had locked themselves inside and then succumbed to infection.

"We could have Urious peek in and see what's going on," Henders suggested. "He's the quietest of us and he doesn't have to worry about getting infected."

Erlock scoffed. "Just how is he supposed to escape if it is full of starlings? Stun them with harsh language and limp away in the confusion?"

"It is like reaching into a hole and not knowing if it is full of hornets. Or turtles," Tresh added for Urious's benefit. She winced at the pain of speaking but wasn't about to be left out of this conversation.

Urious wasn't looking great, either. His ant stitches had held up, but he didn't look ready to escape from a swamp grouse, let alone a starling.

"Ferrick couldn't open the door, right?" Biski asked. "So if there are infected inside, we could open a small door, then close it again, and they wouldn't get out."

"There's probably a way in through the towers, isn't

there?" Urious asked. "Those should be easy to close behind us."

Xalt shook his head, the light catching the pink among his blue plumage. "It's pretty cramped in there. It'd be easy for a starling to wedge itself in the access hatch and keep it from locking. And even if it's not already full of starlings, if we climb down one and open the door to the great hall and it's full of infected, it's pretty hard to squeeze back up and out of the tower in a timely fashion."

"Damn," Urious said. "I wish we knew what was in there."

The raised boardwalk was flooded around the front door to the Flower. The water covered the bottom level. Tresh thought back to the knife fish and sailfins of the past few days. She didn't want to go in the muddy water, but she couldn't think of another way to see what was going on inside.

"With the Flower partially submerged, I could swim underneath and listen for sounds," she said. "That would give us an idea if something is alive in there."

"And if they're sleeping?" Erlock asked.

"With your leg and beak?" Henders added. "Is that safe?"

Tresh shrugged. "It is worth a try."

Xalt squinted his eyes and scratched the back of his head. "How well do the starlings swim?"

"About as well as any gryphon, I imagine," Urious replied.

"No, that is not true." Tresh whispered. Her beak hurt like hell, so she tried to limit her words, but memories of Williwaw and her past attempts to get a glimpse at the kjarr came forward. "They have trouble with heights. They get disoriented, unbalanced. It is why they have not passed Hoarfrost. They cannot safely fly at that height. It is the same for the mangrove coast. They would not follow us out to sea. The few who fell into the water became unable to function and were eaten by sharks."

Biski's displeasure at Tresh's speaking formed itself into another *tsk*.

Erlock shook her head. "So lure them into water and hope they get eaten by sharks. Great plan. Too bad this is freshwater. We don't have any sharks."

"Actually," Urious began, "we do get sharks that swim up from the river by the raftworks."

"You mean to tell me you've been warning me about turtles when I could have been eaten by sharks in the lowlands?" For a weald gryphon, Erlock's fear of sharks was surprising. As far as Tresh knew, there were no sharks in the weald.

"Turtles, sharks, stop!" Jer protested. "You're going to scare the fisherfolk."

Tresh glared at him. She would not be coddled by a ranger. She had destroyed their city of rafts and reminded them of that fact, despite the pain it caused her beak.

He looked away. "What I mean to say is that there's an overhang where you can access the underside of the Flower from the bottom. The hatch is rarely locked because nobody wants to crawl around down there. Tresh might be able to swim up through it, look around, and if she's being chased by the infected, she'll do better under-water than they will."

Urious nodded. "I've seen her in the water. She's no turtle, but I'd rather deal with sharks than her beak."

"Nobody will be dealing with her beak as it is," Biski said. "As her medicine gryphon, I would have to advise against dipping her beak in this fetid water. But I don't have a better plan. Be careful, okay?"

Tresh nodded and got to work putting on her flippers. She pointed to Biski's sharpening stone. If Tresh didn't have her beak, she wanted to be able to rely on her claws. Biski hesitated but ultimately agreed, searching through her harness pouch for the stone. She sharpened Tresh's claws for her.

"If things get really bad, just head straight down the river towards the ocean and save yourself," the medicine gryphon said. "If we find Quess, I'll make sure she gets back to you okay. Here's some pumpkin in case you're bitten and can't get back to us." She pushed aside the two vials of the powder Piprik had given her before locating the stone and two pumpkin doses.

Tresh flexed her paws a few times. The flippers on her back paws held fast. She adjusted the ones on her forepaws so she would be able to use her claws if she came across any sailfins. *Or starlings. Or sharks. Or turtles, if Urious isn't just messing with us.*

After saving him from the starling, she'd felt herself soften a little, especially when he'd asked about Thenca. With the prospect of finding Quess—possibly dead at the talons of the raftworks rangers—Tresh steeled herself. White Stripe, Black Mask, and Vitra were still out there, waiting. They wouldn't let Tresh's expedition escape, and until they made their move, there was no way of knowing whose side Urious was on.

And that assumed the Ashen Weald really were on her side. She didn't expect them to betray her, not with Biski here, but there were a lot of ways to kill someone in a bog that might look like an accident.

Biski re-wrapped Tresh's beak with treated leather on

top of the bandages to try to keep the water out, then Xalt guided her up a tree to get a better look. "See the two towers furthest from us?"

Tresh nodded. One of the towers had a blue spot on it.

"It's along the edge of the great hall, about halfway between them," he said. "It's the same mechanism as the first outpost. Remember how to hold your paw?"

Tresh twisted her paw in the same shape. She'd been practicing every day before going to bed and every morning while waiting for Blinky, just in case she needed to get into another opinicus outpost.

The ranger looked impressed. "You're good at that. Okay, yeah. It's a pretty typical layout inside. Have you visited the eyrie?"

She nodded. She'd gone with the trade delegations a few times.

"Crackling Sea?"

She shook her head.

"Ah, Redwood Valley." He scratched at an errant feather under his chin. "Their architecture isn't really the same. I do remember something about fisherfolk selling fish. I guess that's where you got your name from, huh?"

She didn't respond.

"There's a basement level made of wood treated with waterproof resin." Here he paused. Erlock's advice on sharing information to make new friends from the start of their journey must have stuck with him because he offered more than was necessary. "If they took your kin prisoner, it's where she'd be. If they locked her up, she might be dead by now. I'm sorry."

Tresh nodded.

"Oh!" Xalt said. "You may end up needing this more than I do. I grabbed it from the gate. Don't lose it."

He handed her the key from the first outpost. She slipped it into a harness pouch. If what he'd said the first day was true about most opinicus cells using the same key, it might come in handy later.

"Other than the basement, the only side areas are dry storage and the four towers. The rest of the great hall is open. The hatch should surface in a space below the dry storage. There's an empty area for drainage, that's where you'll be. Look for another hatch above you. That goes into the dry storage. We'd better hope no one put crates over it. Once you're in, look around the corner into the great hall. That should give you an idea of what's happening. Take one look, if anything stirs, get out of there."

Tresh put a paw in front of her eyes.

"Blind? See? What're you getting at?" the ranger asked. "Oh, won't it be dark. No, there'll be some light. Before trade dried up, Crestfall tried to produce their own stormcloth. It was too thin, too heavy for how thin it was, and nowhere near as good as the real stuff. We ended up using it to make a hole in the roof. The fake stormcloth keeps the rain out and lets a little light in. Not a lot, but enough."

Tresh nodded and wondered if the stormcloth they'd scavenged from the raft sails after the battle of Sandpiper's Dune was real or fake. They'd hidden it on the island where Lei's new family lived until they could decide if they wanted to trade it or make their own sails. She also wondered if it'd be better to try to look down through the stormcloth on the roof.

It was probably too fuzzy to get a clear picture, but they might be able to detect movement. *At the cost of making ourselves visible for miles around to any starlings peeking out of the canopy.* Water it was.

"That's it. Look, I know after what Jonas and Rakesh

did, you probably don't care too much for us," Xalt said. "I get that. I don't care too much for the things I did in the weald, either, and when I first heard that there were rangers spreading the infection, I assumed it was just gossip. I would never have followed orders to spread a parasite like that, and I know Grenkin wouldn't have, either."

She noticed that he didn't apologize for the wingtorn or the raid on the fisherfolk, but she didn't need a reminder to keep her beak shut.

"If I hadn't seen the crates and bugs and jars, I don't know that I'd believe any of this. A lot of the rangers think the Crackling Sea lost its way when the Blackwing Eyrie invaded. We're trying to purge the remaining opinici who subscribe to Jonas's point of view. I'll do what I can to put in a good word for you and the fisherfolk." He seemed to want to say more, but the others were down below wondering what was taking so long. "Good luck in there, okay? I hope you find your friend, and I hope she's okay."

Tresh put a paw on the ranger's shoulder. She didn't blame all rangers or wingtorn for what had happened. Only those who had given the orders. She looked down at Urious. *And those who did the killing.*

She glided down from the tree and made her way to the edge of the floodwaters. With her luck, this would be where the knife fish had all washed away to. As she walked past some blue flowers and looked for a good place to hop in, she caught the sour, floral smell again. She'd have to ask Urious if anything else smelled like that vine. She hadn't seen any since the aneda trees had given way to mangroves.

Despite her resemblance to a diving petrel, Tresh erred on the side of a subtle approach. She took a deep breath and slipped beneath the water's surface. The bite on her leg ached in protest.

Several fish displaced by the flooding approached her curiously. Had her beak not been bound, she'd have made a snack of them. The advantage of slow-moving flood waters over the rush she'd experienced earlier was that it was clearer than what they'd passed on the way. She saw several eels but had spent enough time on the trail studying what knife fish looked like after Henders's encounter that she felt comfortable these were of the non-electric variety.

She didn't see any sailfins, sharks, or turtles. Well, she saw a few softshell turtles of the normal variety. She didn't see any that would have inspired Urious's scary stories. The current carried her towards the Flower. She caught the bottom of the building and listened against the wood.

Nothing.

The wood was thick and treated. Something would have to fall for her to hear it through the floor.

She made her way to the stretch between the farthest towers and located the hatch. She paused again to listen. Nothing from above, but she could hear splashing some distance off and the growling-chuff sound of a sailfin.

Great. Just what I want in the water if I need to make a quick getaway.

It took her a few tries, but she managed to get the hatch open and crawled into the empty area intended for drainage. One more door between her and the dry storage, then a hallway between her and the great hall.

She felt around in the darkness and found some opinicus tools she didn't recognize. She stuffed one in the latch. If she had to escape, she couldn't afford to take several tries to figure it out. She also didn't want to leave it completely open for a sailfin to come through while she was busy inside.

She caught her breath, preened her feathers dry, and shook out her fur, mindful not to shake her head too much. She took a few practice swipes at the darkness. Her beak would shatter before it'd let her bite down again like she had with the starling. She'd have to adapt her hunting style to compensate.

She sheathed her claws, bent her paw into the strange opinicus door shape, and tried to push open the door to the dry storage.

It didn't budge. She placed her paw pad on the metal and felt around until she found a place to put in a key. It took a little effort, but she managed to get it open and push further into the Flower.

The storage area smelled of salted fish. It was reassuring after the last week. Stacked supplies continued in the hallway, blocking her view of the great hall. There was a pile of empty crates in the corner. There'd been opinici eating here at some point. That was the only way she could explain why there were so many of them.

She considered climbing the ones blocking her view of the great hall but realized this might give her an opportunity to sneak into the basement and check the prison cells unseen.

She weighed the need for silence against the need to escape and kept her flippers on. She'd worn them enough that she felt confident she wouldn't *clomp* as she stalked.

She crawled around the corner and looked into the basement. There was a foot of water on the floor. It smelled of rotten food. She coughed and her beak exploded in pain. She went still and listened.

No starlings materialized.

Hanging from a peg, she saw a harness quiver with bamboo spears in it. Several charms hung from the quiver, mementos of children lost to the wingtorn. *If Quess was not here, the crane opinicus with her was.* There was no sign of Quess's harness or the gutting knife Tresh's brother had given her to commemorate the birth of their first child. Tresh wasn't sure if that was a good sign or a bad one.

She took out one of the spears. It took a few tries to get her paws around it, but she used it to probe the water. Nothing gryphon-sized lurked beneath the surface.

She considered bringing it with her but had no way to carry it and sneak. She put it back in the quiver and stalked up the stairs. There were just the towers and great hall left to check. She climbed up the crates to get a look.

The great hall was well-named. Nests had been built into the walls, enough to house fifty opinici in close quarters. Goliath bird pelts and cushions were arranged around small tables two feet high. Tresh had seen similar setups at the Redwood Valley Eyrie's market square.

Those, however, had not been darkened with blood.

The stains on the floor were deep. She could have attributed it to any number of red, purple, or brown substances were it not for the smell. An opinicus might not notice, but even with her beak wrapped, the whole place smelled like the end of a hunt to her.

Fifty nests, all empty. No bodies anywhere.

No. Forty-nine nests, all empty. There was a shape atop the fiftieth, nearest the tower access.

Tresh slipped back behind the crates. *One starling is not a lot. I could fight it or escape if I had to.*

Her leg ached in anticipation of more fighting. One starling wasn't a lot, but she hadn't looked inside the towers. If they were all full, that would be different.

If a starling were alive in here, that would mean the tower accesses are open. I could see the front door. It was definitely closed.

She considered her options, deciding that the best way to see if there were a wasp in the hole was to toss something at it. In this case, words.

"Hello?" she called. Her beak lit up with pain.

The shape didn't stir.

She gritted her beak and tried one last time. "Are you injured? Are you alone?"

She was about to start to climb up to check for a harness or badge when the shape stirred.

A blanket fell off the nest and drifted to the floor, revealing a kjarr flank pattern. Tresh suppressed a hiss. A wing unfolded, and she thought it might be Vitra, laying a trap for her. Then it turned around, and she saw its harness and opinicus foretalons.

No, not it. *His* harness and foretalons.

"Qu-quess?" His voice was raspy, rusted from lack of use. "Quess, why did you come back? You need to leave! It's only a matter of time before they return!"

"I am not Quess," Tresh managed though the bandages. "My name is Turresh of Crane's Nest. Who are you?"

He climbed down from nest to nest and inspected her, lingering over the beak bandages, then he cleared his throat. "Ranger Captain Bruen. I served under Ranger Lord Ellore."

Ranger Lord? Tresh was unaware of any such promotion. Xalt and Jer hadn't mentioned that. Tresh knew who

Ellore was. These were not the missing opinici the rangers were searching for. This was a Jonas loyalist from the kjarr nesting grounds.

Bruen laughed, sending Tresh back a foot, claws extended. "Sorry, sorry. Ha. It's just that Quess always said you'd come for her. I didn't believe it, not the first week, and certainly not after a month had passed. I thought the rangers would find us first. By the depths, Ellore was right about almost everything."

He laughed again, and Tresh stared at his eyes.

"Are you infected?" she asked. Madness could be an early sign.

"No, no, lower your claws." He did a twirl which did not inspire a vote of sanity. "Kjarr stock. I was bitten by an infected a month ago. Months ago? How long have I been here? I'm immune, is what I meant to say."

Along one of the walls was a set of scratch marks noting the passing of days. Tresh weighed her options. Her beak hurt too much for her to question him alone. There didn't seem to be anyone else here. It was time to open the front door and let the rest in. There was just one more thing.

"You served with Ellore? At the kjarr nesting grounds?" She waited for him to nod, then considered her words. "The wingtorn took the Crackling Sea."

A look of panic crossed his face.

"Grenkin reached a peace with Satra the Kjarr. There are rangers outside who came looking for survivors with us. They will kill you if they know you are a Jonas loyalist."

"Thank you for telling me. I don't hold any loyalty to Jonas, but I hold a hell of a lot for Ranger Lord Ellore." He caught his mistake. "Captain Ellore, I mean. Blood and feathers, I can't believe Grenkin is alive and still ranger lord, that bastard. Okay, so be it. How good are the records? How organized is everyone?"

"One eyrie is now ash." She remembered Erlock's talk of New Eyrie. "Two, though the walls of New Eyrie still stand. No one will know where you were assigned."

He nodded. "Alright, let's meet your friends."

Ranger Captain Bruen unlocked the gates of the Flower and opened them.

AT TRESH'S SIGNAL, Biski, Erlock, Henders, and the rangers had flown across the flood waters to the Flower and slipped inside. With the boardwalk underwater, Urious had stayed behind in the bog to keep watch on his own.

That turned out to be for the better, once they heard Bruen's tale.

Some of it, Tresh had guessed. *Beaky*, as Bruen called him, had been killed trying to escape with Quess. The starlings had pulled him out of the sky and eaten him. Quess had retreated back to the Flower and surrendered herself again.

The infection had hit Ferrick first. He'd been bitten by a starling at a lumber camp before they began their trek to the Flower. They never saw the western outpost, nor the dig site. They'd gone straight south.

Bruen claimed he'd been stationed at a station nearby and assigned to Ellore's group rather than admitting he was one of the kjarr nesting grounds guards. The rangers didn't show any sign of disbelief.

When his expedition had arrived at the Flower, all its original inhabitants except one were dead.

"Darion. Strange bird," Bruen said. "He was under arrest when we got there. We thought he was mad, but then, we didn't know about how the infection worked yet. The fisherfolk killed him while trying to escape."

He didn't specify which fisherfolk, but he went on to explain that the medicine never seemed to fully cure Ferrick's persistent infection.

Tresh was reminded of Sandpiper's Dune, where Rakesh had spread another version of the same parasite that seemed more resistant to pumpkins than the one in the north. Had Ferrick been bitten by Younce? She didn't give voice to her concerns.

Then Bruen talked about the starlings swarming outside and his team's decision to wait for reinforcements. They had enough food, they had the high ground, and the starlings had finally gotten bored and wandered back to try their luck at Hoarfrost and Williwaw.

"That sounds like a pretty cushy way to spend two months," Erlock said. "It doesn't explain where everyone else went."

"Oh, I'm getting there," Bruen said. They settled in to hear his story.

18

BRUEN'S TALE

*"*N*ow that we're settled," Erlock said, "tell us what happened next?"*

"Well, it started with birdsong," Bruen began.

"Why won't that petrel shut up?" Quess complained. Her tail swept back and forth in annoyance. She was sharpening her knife.

"It's not a petrel," Bruen said. "It's just a bird that sounds like one. We're miles from the ocean."

"I know what a damn petrel sounds like," she snapped. "That's why it bothers me. Fly away, little bird, dive into the ocean and escape!"

He laughed. For the first month, he'd been grumpy. After Ferrick's bite, his rangers were treating him like he was about to go full silver-eyed starling at any moment. It was the same skepticism they'd treated Quess with, which had given them a chance to bond with each other.

Once he made it through unscathed, they'd started treating him like their captain again. Ferrick, though still sick, had apologized, and everything was pretty good now, except that they couldn't escape.

They'd tried opening the door once or twice, but no one made it more than a few feet outside before a starling scout started chittering. It was like something kept bringing the starlings back to the Flower. It'd been a week since the last sighting, and he thought it was about time to give it another go.

Ellore and Redwood Valley Ranger Mia spent hours talking about family and the places they'd explored. Mia was smart in the analytical way that scholars usually were, and Ellore appreciated talking over problems with her.

Bruen would've felt a little jealous, except that Ellore had always awarded loyalty above all else. She'd made it clear that if anything happened to her, he was in charge.

In another situation, things would've been much different. Being secluded in the woods, surrounded on all sides, was a bad situation for any opinicus. The fact that the Flower was part of a major trade route and supplies were plentiful combined with the starlings' inability to open doors had allowed a kind of camaraderie to spring up. In fact, Bruen had considered seeing if Quess wanted to share nests.

"She was seeing someone. She has chicks," Tresh interjected.

"Looked single to me. Who was she seeing?" Bruen asked.

"My brother."

"Oh."

"Please stop speaking," Biski said. "My supply of bandages isn't unlimited. Do you just not want your beak to heal?"

"I am sorry," Tresh said.

Biski made a tsk *sound.*

"Anyways, as I was saying..." Bruen continued.

Quess was amazing, full of interesting fisherfolk facts, strange flipper technology, and a beak that could split a log. Bruen sensed she was taken and had chicks back home she was worried about. As an honorable ranger, he said nothing inappropriate towards her but took it as an opportunity to learn about another culture.

"Better."

"Stop. Speaking. Or I will tie your beak shut."

Ellore had one concern, which she reiterated every day. She was worried there were other rangers trapped in the bog. They tried making a banner to put over the gates to the Flower, but it'd been a stormy winter, and it wasn't long before the banner disappeared. The one thing no one had thought to bring with them from the raftworks were proper tools.

The petrel bird had been singing for a week now, the same song every day. As much as Quess hated it, it seemed to be keeping the starlings away. Their numbers lessened around the Flower until, one day, the opinici poked their heads outside and none appeared. It was a miracle.

They could already see storm clouds gathering in the north. They had a basic plan. South of the raftworks, Quess had seen an island. She thought that if they could get there, they could make a final stand, or perhaps the starlings would get confused by the water. Then they could regroup, rest, and make the flight to Sandpiper's Dune.

"The raftworks rangers wanted to go back to Sandpiper's Dune?" Biski asked. She gave Tresh a look that said she knew Tresh would have asked it if she hadn't, and she was just saving Tresh a scolding.

"Yeah, it wasn't a great plan," Bruen agreed, "but Quess promised to grant us safe passage. You know what's west? Depths-be-damned starlings."

"The Emerald Jungle," Erlock mumbled. Her paw was over

the badge on her harness. When everyone stared at her, she added, "Sorry, please go on."

They decided to wait out the storm. The island Quess had seen was small. It wasn't the place to winter a kjarr storm. Everyone had heard of the Connixation. No one wanted to weather that on a strip of land in the ocean.

Bruen thought they were pretty lucky the starlings had all disappeared right around when the winter storms started. Without proper tools, they weren't able to keep the prison cells water tight. The food they stored down there went rotten, and he wasn't looking forward to only living off dry rations. Despite their best cleaning efforts, the smell of mildew spread throughout the Flower. They got a few crates out and stacked them outside dry storage, then they packed up their things and got ready to go.

The day after the storm, they opened the door. No starlings. However, there was a note. Someone had left it under an ancient Crackling Sea badge and hung it outside the door to the Flower. It said there was a group of rangers to the west who had become trapped. They were hiding in some ruins, but the infection had spread. They wanted to know if the Flower rangers had a cure. Time was running out.

Rangers don't leave anyone behind. The ranger lord knew this more than anyone else.

"Ranger lord?" Jer asked. "Ellore started calling herself ranger lord?"

"We left as the Crackling Sea Eyrie was being invaded. Grand Reeve Ivess declared that Ellore was the new ranger lord if she could locate the missing rangers."

"I see."

Ellore took most of the antidote and most of the rangers with her. Bruen stayed behind with Ferrick,

Quess, and three others to hold down the fort. They were instructed to hang a new banner from the towers as a warning if starlings showed up.

"I'D LIKE to say I had a bad feeling about all of this," Bruen said as he handed out dried eel to everyone, "but honestly, I didn't question how they'd stayed safe all that time. I just thought Ellore would pick them up, bring them back, and we'd be on our way."

"As they're not here, I'm guessing things didn't go as planned?" Erlock asked.

Henders laughed. "When in the last four years has anything gone as planned for the Crackling Sea opinici?"

"The chick's got the right of it," Bruen said.

Ferrick was closest to the door when hell broke loose. The knock wasn't the one the rangers used. Rather, it was one the original opinici assigned to the Flower had used.

That was Bruen's first clue something was wrong. The second was a glimpse he got through the door. Ferrick had opened it a crack. Bruen could see a face that harkened back to Satra and Jun. It was the face of a Kjarr. Bruen could just make out part of a wing. At the stranger's feet, covering her paws, was the body of a wounded ranger. One of his rangers.

Ferrick opened the door to help the ranger, and the wingtorn flooded in. Bruen caught a full look at a one-winged gryphon, then grabbed Quess and shoved her into dry storage. He balanced an empty crate on the edge of the door so it would close over them when he shut the hatch, and they stayed hidden for hours.

"Wingtorn? What do you mean wingtorn?" Xalt asked. "Were these part of Satra's army?"

Tresh spared a look out to Urious, but he wasn't where they'd left him. It was possible he was looking for more vines.

"I don't know about that, but I'm almost done. Let me finish," Bruen said.

Once it became dark, Bruen and Quess made their way up through dry storage and looked around. Everyone was gone. They waited another day or two, hiding out in storage, but one of the starling scouts returned and they were forced to close the door and hope the wingtorn didn't return and find it suspicious.

Bruen looked at Quess. "You need to get word to your people. I'll stay here in case anyone makes it, but I think the wingtorn were killing the starling scouts. Now that they're gone, the starlings will be back. And once the wingtorn see the starlings are hanging out here, they'll just come back for the two of us."

Quess nodded, but they didn't have a way to sneak out. They ended up waiting around for weeks, waiting for a storm that would flood the lower levels and obscure her from the starlings' view. They finally got lucky.

"Was that the storm that hit us?" Erlock asked.

Bruen shook his head. "No, Quess left maybe two weeks ago. She's probably home by now."

"How often does it flood around here?" Henders asked.

"Well," Bruen said, "based on however long I've been here, fairly often. Just when you think it's going to be dry for a few days, the rains start again."

Tresh looked out to where Urious was missing. Was it true? Had Quess arrived home right after Tresh had flown north to search for her? It didn't seem possible, but how would Tresh know?

Quess accepted Bruen's help with her flippers. "With the flooding, I think I can escape south of here. If I can get to the river, I can swim the rest of the way to the ocean."

"Be careful," he said. "You'll hit rapids before then. You're going to have to stop swimming at some point. And watch for sharks."

"I'll come back for you," she said.

He laughed. "Get yourself to safety and don't ever come back here. Once I find out what happened to Ellore, I'll save myself. It's just that I'm going north instead of south."

"You didn't save yourself," Biski said.

"No, I wanted to go west and look for Ellore and Mia, but my courage failed me," Bruen said. He looked down at the stains on the floor. "The blood here was from the old Flower guards. I didn't see much fresh blood. They took Ferrick alive, but without regular doses of pumpkin, I don't know that he made it. With your help, though, we might be able to get them back. Who's in charge?"

Nobody told him about Ferrick's ultimate fate.

Jer looked out the open door across the flood waters to where Urious was supposed to be standing watch. "The wing-torn was in charge."

19

ESCAPE!

Tresh would have frowned if it didn't require moving her beak muscles. She'd come all this way, and Quess had already been saved. Was she safe? If she'd escaped successfully, why hadn't she arrived at Sandpiper's Dune?

With the mention of one wing and *a face that harkened back to Satra and Jun*, and who could that be except Vitra and her wingtorn, Tresh thought back on the things Urious had said. Half her mind believed he'd been leading them here as part of a trap the entire time. He knew the thorned vine could hide them from the starlings or hide other gryphons from the expedition. *That* was why Tresh hadn't smelled Black Mask or White Stripe. When they'd disappeared, they'd covered their scent. It was how the bog pride escapees had been living here without having to worry about the parasite. They had the kjarr resistance to infection and the deep bog hunting secrets.

Why had they taken the prisoners alive, though? *Ferrick they took to make a trap for us,* she thought. *What will they do with the others? Trade them for more wingtorn? Infect them and release them upon unsuspecting prides and eyries?*

Urious had been so candid about the bog pride, it made her question if he'd actually been in on it. If not for him, they'd have had no idea about the territorial marker at the dig site. She only knew about the bog's oppression under Jun the Kjarr's father because Urious had spoken of it first. And hadn't he served as Jun's right paw during the fisherfolk raid that had killed her family?

"Who is Vitra?" Tresh asked at last. "I saw her earlier. She is the one-winged gryphon."

Everyone went silent. The rangers looked at each other but didn't speak up.

"I heard Vitra speaking with White Stripe when we were separated," Tresh said. "It sounded like they were plotting against one of us. I did not know who I could trust, so I did not speak of it then."

Bruen looked skeptical. "Vitra was one Jun's offspring. The eldest, I think. She didn't surrender, but the rangers caught her in the bog later and killed her."

"That cannot be true," Tresh said. "I saw her."

Jer looked guilty but finally spoke. "She may not be dead. We assumed she was, but..."

Xalt continued, "She'd been plaguing us for a while after the rest surrendered. She'd try to free her kin, often without success, so she resorted to laying out ambushes for patrols. Eventually, we got the idea to use her mom as bait to draw her out."

Jer looked away. "Her mother had survived the procedure but lost her mind in the process. She kept chewing at the stitches and trying to fling herself off the Crackling Sea cliffs. It was only a matter of time before she found a way to kill herself or bled out in the night. Using her as bait was a cruel thing to do, but we thought we were saving ranger lives. We put her in a cage, lured Vitra in, and captured her and her raiding party. Her mom pulled out her stitches partway into the ambush and bled out before we could save her."

"We were both there for the trap," Xalt said, "but we left once Vitra was secure. We took the other bog gryphons to the Crackling Sea to have their wings clipped, but we left Vitra with the friends of the rangers she'd killed."

"We must have missed a few, though," Jer, the meeker of the two rangers, continued. "When we came back, we found a bloodied wing and ten dead rangers. We figured Vitra had bled out."

Biski looked pensive. Erlock said nothing. It was Henders who made the mistake of speaking up.

"That's...monstrous," he said. "You're monsters."

Erlock flipped the Reeve's Guard on his back and had claws at his throat before Tresh could blink. "The *reeve* you *guarded* dropped explosives on my nesting ground while we were still in it. You should think twice before you attempt to take the moral high ground."

To Bruen and the rangers' credit, they didn't try to defend their actions. There were some apologies, some more arguing, talks of an inquisition to root out the sort of opinici who had let the war crimes happen.

Tresh didn't have the emotional energy for that right now. She had other things to worry about, namely Quess and Mia. While her expedition splintered, Tresh looked out the front door again. Urious had not returned. They would need to decide soon what to do. She wandered back to see if she'd missed anything in dry storage. If

Quess and Bruen had been hiding there for days, maybe Quess had left a message. Tresh thought back to their wingtorn leader and his conspicuous absence. Either he was in trouble, or the rest of them were in deeper trouble.

Or it could be both.

Sudden paranoia gripped her, but she had no time to tell them to shut the door.

It was too late.

"How nice of you to open up the Flower again." Vitra said. There was blood on her beak. "If you'll put down your nets and metal talons, you'll all be coming with me."

The doorway filled with bog gryphons, winged and wingtorn alike.

Erlock's roar echoed in the great hall as she charged.

Tresh slipped into the hatch under dry storage and closed it behind her, taking the key out of the lock. She hadn't taken her back flippers off. She yanked the opinicus tool she'd jammed into the bottom hatch and pulled it open to the floodwaters. If she were lucky, even if the bog gryphons had heard her, they'd have trouble getting it open again without the key. She jumped into the water.

The current pushed against her. She had two options. She could go south, like Quess had. Quess, who had either been captured or was currently back at Swan's Rest recovering. Either that way was safe, or it wasn't.

While she hoped Quess was back among the fisherfolk, Tresh wasn't willing to flee the bog just yet. That left her with her second option: rescue. She wouldn't leave her companions behind. She just needed to find Blinky.

Tresh crawled along the bottom of the Flower upside-down with her claws gripping its underside and pushed off, using her wings to swim against the current. She caught the bottom of the flooded boardwalk path and followed it north.

Every so often the wooden walkway rose above the water line, giving her a chance to catch her breath. She planned her next move.

If she came up and the wingtorn were waiting for her, would she fight? No, she was outnumbered. She knew it was unlikely Vitra would let the rangers live, not after what they'd done to her and her mother, but she might not harm the fisherfolk and weald gryphons.

Tresh looked to the sky when she came up for breath. Should she fly? Maybe. She could reach the ocean on adrenaline and dive into it. If the wingtorn—no, bog gryphons, there'd been some with wings among them, probably the medicine gryphons who'd abandoned the kjarr pride—attempted to follow, the starlings would eat them.

If she were cut off from the ocean, could she make it to Williwaw? If she were being honest with herself, probably not. The starlings were so agitated, they might follow her up the mountain even if she made it. Williwaw's strange wind currents would work against her. It'd only take one gust to smash her against the rocks. The fisherfolk had been forbidden from flying there. Only the best taiga gryphons could handle it. By the time she reached Williwaw, she'd already be exhausted.

It was hard to estimate how far north she'd crawled following the boardwalk, but the water was shallow now. She'd need to leave it to continue. She pulled herself atop the planks and looked around.

She smelled the bitter, floral scent first. The wingtorn stepped out of the high grass and moss. There were ten of them, led by a winged gryphon.

The bog witch had the look of a medicine gryphon about her. A skull had been painted over her face in bog blossom blue. She spread her wings wide, revealing long bone patterns in thick paint. Her claws dripped the same color. She held herself with confidence.

The wingtorn around her had blue fire painted on their sides. *Bog wisps? These are the bog wisps?*

The medicine gryphon hissed.

The wingtorn crouched and skulked towards Tresh. She had an overwhelming desire to leap into the air, but she remembered Jun the Kjarr. The ones with black ears could pull her out of the sky before she could gain enough altitude to escape. She'd learn from Rorin's mistake.

"You should lie down and die," the medicine gryphon said. "It will all be over soon, little fish gryphon."

Well, there goes my hope that they'll let the fisherfolk and weald gryphons go free.

Behind the bog witch, a creature of moss slipped out of the tangle. Tresh's first thought was that the bog witch had summoned some sort of magical creature to aid her. Tresh's second thought gave her hope.

Tresh pounced the witch.

The witch let out a startled cry and did what any winged creature does when alarmed. She took to the air.

The moss creature had anticipated this. It had leapt a moment before, dislodging its disguise, then came down as an owl gryphon, catching the witch's head in its claws and shoving it into the boardwalk with a sickening *pop*.

The moss creature spared one blink for Tresh, then returned to the air and went after the wingtorn. Blinky's wings made no sound, and she remained low to the ground.

Tresh did her best to stay alive without making enough noise to attract the starlings, though she wasn't sure they would make this any worse. She led two of the wingtorn on a merry chase through the flooded board-walk. She'd seen the path from her upside-down expedition under the wooden planks, so she knew where the water was deep. She'd also caught a glimpse of something long and eel-like.

She crashed through each puddle, making sure to splash. The two wingtorn chased after, splashing through the same puddles.

She caught a rock in her beak as she ran, and on the seventh puddle, she dropped it in, using her wings to glide over the water.

The two wingtorn hit the puddle with a splash. They were halfway through when the writhing, agitated mass of knife fish sprang out at them.

One small knife fish had left Henders muddled for an hour. Tresh didn't want to speculate what four full-sized knife fish were doing in one small puddle together, but they hadn't appreciated having a rock dropped on their activity.

Both wingtorn fell unconscious. Tresh rushed back to check on her owl gryphon friend.

It was Blinky's turn to lead the bog gryphons on a chase. She'd feint a jump, and the wingtorn would leap into the air. Then she'd run off in a different direction, and they'd have to land and catch up.

One reared back to hiss at her, and she pounced, catching it off guard and its throat in her beak.

Tresh rushed the remaining wingtorn from behind,

surprising the closest. As she smashed it into the ground, its friend lashed out, one of its claws digging into her harness. Tresh slashed back with her sharpened claws, raking them across its face. It went limp, and Blinky came over and finished the other one off.

The bog wingtorn used tactics effective at bringing down rangers. Anti-opinicus tactics. They'd never seen an owl gryphon or fisherfolk before and were having trouble. *Well, mostly an owl gryphon. I wish my beak was in better shape.*

With their immediate pursuers dispatched, Blinky led Tresh deeper into the bog, arriving at a bog turtle hole that smelled of those acrid vines.

Tresh caught her breath. Inside, the light came through the vegetation and illuminated a face further back in the hole. There was a slight silver sheen in its eyes, but not the gooey, dripping level of infection the starlings shared.

Tresh recognized her at once. "Quess!" she cried out as quietly as she could. She reached out to embrace her lost kin, but Blinky put a paw on her chest to stop her.

"Still infected," Blinky said. When Tresh drooped, she added, "but she is getting better."

Tresh shook her head. "Blinky, where have you been? What have you been up to? How did you find Quess?"

Blinky blinked. Then she caught Tresh up on what had happened since the flood so many days ago.

SOFT PAWS

GRYPHON BOG WITCH

THE OWL GRYPHON WHO BLINKED

Back on the day of the flood, Blinky, as she referred to herself for Tresh's benefit, had followed Biski and Henders as they made their way across the lowlands. The others were still there, too, but Blinky was mostly concerned about the water. The rain wasn't letting up, and there was nothing Blinky hated more than drying off microfeathers. They were worse than fur when it came to absorbency.

She glared at the water running past her paws. She stayed angry for a full ten minutes, until fish began to wash by. She bit at them, managing to catch one or two. They tasted *not salty*, sort of wet and wriggly. They were fun to eat. She began to peck at the current, swallowing a beakful of water and a couple more fish.

"Blinky, don't eat that," Biski said. "Wait and catch a bigger one later. Those aren't going to do anything for your appetite."

As was the case most of the time when other gryphons or opinici spoke, Blinky heard the words, but decided they were not worth listening to. She could do nothing about the water. She could not stalk and bite it into submission. She could, however, catch these slippery snacks.

"Your stomach is going to be a pond full of minnows," Erlock scolded. "Do you want your tummy to wriggle?"

Blinky kind of did.

She struck again, but the water was deeper now, and she missed. She tried sticking her face under the surface, but the minnows avoided it, confirming her suspicion that she had a good, ferocious look about her.

She pulled her face out of the water and shook it dry, garnering cries of annoyance from Biski and Erlock again.

The minnows returned. Blinky tried to catch them with her paws, but where she saw them from above was not where they were actually at. Nor was her paw in the right place. She adjusted and grabbed again. Another fish slipped through the pads on her feet.

This time it was Henders who grumbled at her, but Blinky shoved her face in the water to scold the minnows with a squawk.

The minnows were smarter than they looked.

They had laid a trap for Blinky.

When she looked back up, a cascade of water was coming straight for her, bringing with it ants, trees, capybaras, and an upside-down sailfin.

Despite Urious's promise to get her a crate of salted fish bars if she didn't fly, she leapt into the air and took off. She did not want to be wet, covered in ants, and hit by a tree. Not even for a crate of fish bars.

Also, Urious had promised a separate crate of fish bars if she didn't bite any of her traveling companions, so she still had an opportunity to get snacks out of this.

She didn't head north. If the Crackling Sea overflowed, the water would flood the capybara ranch and spill into the lowlands. Instead, she headed west, towards the outpost. The opinicus buildings she'd seen had been built up, so if the entire bog flooded, it might provide her with a dry place to weather the storm.

Urious's friends were jumpy, so she stayed south as not to spook them, and so Urious wouldn't see her flying. Erlock might see her, but she was a fantail, and they never ratted out other gryphons. Biski, as a feathermane, might, but she could be bribed with help drying off. If things went Blinky's way, she'd still get both crates of fish. She'd sneak up on him and his wingtorn later and announce her presence.

Despite the heavy rains, she managed to glide across the water and settled in a broad-leafed tree. The flooding seemed isolated to the lowlands, at least for now. She got to work preening her wings and grooming her fur and microfeathers.

She'd adjusted to the sounds of the storm, but the rushing water and fearful animals threw her sense of smell off. That was the only reason she heard the wingtorn.

A gryphon's senses worked together to paint a picture. She'd smelled the strange, acrid scent throughout the forest but hadn't thought anything of it. She'd heard the sounds of animals moving through the scrub, but she hadn't realized they were gryphons because there was no gryphon smell.

Now, without her sense of smell to depend upon, she recognized the sounds of four gryphons running up the bank north of her to get away from the flood. She smelled wet gryphon mixed with acrid vine and understood what had happened.

She slipped behind the tree, taking a moment to catalogue each of the wingtorn who'd been following her and her traveling companions. Two had swirls on their sides in a blue paint that hadn't washed off in the rain like their vine scent had. The third, a young medicine gryphon, had a blue skull painted over her face but flowers painted on her wings. The fourth had blue feathers—their real color, not paint—on her face and a single wing. The single wing was notable, but the blue feathers on her face were what gave her identity away.

Vitra.

"You knew about Vitra?" Tresh interrupted.

Blinky nodded. Then she placed just the tip of a claw on Tresh's beak to keep it closed and continued her story.

There was a problem with Satra's claim to leadership of her pride. Neither her mother nor her sisters had surrendered with Jun the Kjarr at the nesting grounds. They'd waged their own war from the deep bog. Foultner, Blinky, Grenkin, and Merin had all been informed of potential threats to the Ashen Weald. Satra's family was one of them.

Blinky looked again, noting the nasty, jagged scars, likely healed with bog medicine. Vitra hadn't been on any of the paperwork Foultner had found at the Crackling Sea Eyrie. Vitra must've been captured by rangers in the bog who wanted to remove her wings themselves. Based on the reports of what she and her mom had done to the rangers they'd caught in the bog during the conflict, that was unsurprising, if alarming.

Satra had hoped to find her remaining family alive and wanted them brought to the Ashen Weald as allies. Merin and Foultner had other ideas. They saw these potential Kjarrs as rivals, as threats.

Blinky held little loyalty to Foultner, though she

considered the opinicus a friend after their New Eyrie experience, nor Merin, whom she considered full of himself, but she'd found a home in the Ashen Weald that she hadn't found in Strix's pride, even before the split. *Strix showed too much favor to his children. He was a good hunter and a bad pride leader. Satra is different.* Blinky had been happy to join the Ashen Weald when the split came. Still, she couldn't help but think that Satra had been hasty in asking Blinky to look for her family.

The owl gryphon remained unmoving on her perch as she thought this through. She decided she needed more information. She waited for the strange blue-painted wingtorn to disperse and then followed Vitra north.

BLINKY PURSUED Vitra through the bog. The kjarr gryphon—Blinky didn't feel comfortable using wingtorn for a one-winged gryphon—slipped through the brush and hanging moss with only the slightest of sounds.

Fortunately for Blinky, now that she knew what to listen for, she had no trouble tracking her quarry. Even when Vitra stopped at some thorny vines to re-mask her scent, Blinky was able to take the pungent smell into account.

Tresh opened her beak to say something, then thought better and closed it.

"For myself, I thought the acrid vines alone would not be enough," Blinky said. *"The wingtorn were using them to track each other. I needed something different to hide my own smell."*

Tresh nodded.

Despite Blinky's impeccable grooming habits, wet owl wasn't a smell she trusted to blend in with the bog. She'd mix some vines with hanging moss later and see if it hid her scent.

While the weald gryphon would have thought it a detriment, Vitra was adept at using one wing to balance as she ran along fallen tree branches. Blinky had seen the parrotface pride use their wings in a similar manner.

Chatter erupted ahead of them, and Vitra crouched low and covered her face with her wing. The specks of blue in her plumage resembled flowers, and her grey-brown feathers blended in with the forest detritus surprisingly well. She stayed hidden like that as Erlock, Biski, Henders, and the rangers walked right past her on their trek to the outpost.

Blinky committed the shape of a hiding kjarr gryphon to memory for later. Once the expedition had passed, Vitra's wing folded back, and she continued onwards. She seemed to be tracking a lost bird, returning its *ooo-awk* call now and then.

She almost got away when Blinky caught a glint of light shining off a glass vial filled with orange goo. Not having a harness, and having a sharp beak, she was forced to hold it inside her mouth. She might need it later.

When Vitra arrived at the bird, it turned out to be White Stripe, one of Urious's *deep bog* gryphon companions.

"You called?" Vitra asked.

Blinky stayed in the trees as they talked. Vitra had stopped along the way to note the paw and talon prints in the mud but had missed the flatter indentations left by Tresh's flippers, indentations that disappeared into the nearby vegetation. Blinky looked around. She didn't spot Tresh, but the flipper prints ended at a tangle of moss large enough to hide a petrel gryphon.

Blinky cooed once softly to let Tresh know she was there but didn't get a response.

If there is anyone unlikely to secretly be working with these rogue wingtorn, it is a fisherfolk. She'd swing back later and see what Tresh knew about White Stripe. With him here, Blinky had to consider that the whole mission might be trap. *Henders and the rangers are unimportant. Biski, too. No one knew Tresh was coming. Erlock? Is this an attempt to assassinate the fantail pride leader?*

Fantails only had one point of conflict that Blinky knew of and that was with the Crackling Sea opinici. Fantails thought of all blues as being like the ones who'd bombed their nesting grounds. The opinici at the Crackling Sea Eyrie, mostly unaware of what their rangers had been up to, had first been introduced to the Fantail Pride during the battle for the eyrie, where the fantails had been vicious in their retribution.

The only problem with that theory was that no wingtorn, even a deep bog wingtorn, would work with opinici willingly. Even within the Ashen Weald, tensions were fraught.

There was another possibility. Rumors had come that Ninox was searching for any allies she could find outside of the Ashen Weald. Her position would be strengthened the most by the wingtorn prides splintering, by the loss of one of the most outspoken proponents of the Ashen Weald.

The leader of the so-called Strix Pride was not like her brothers, nor was she like her father. Ninox was a smart gryphon, and Blinky thought it was dangerous to underestimate her.

Vitra slipped away and Blinky followed. She needed to

see where these new wingtorn were holed up before she returned to get information from Tresh.

BLINKY TRACKED the rogue Kjarr-aspirant as far as she was comfortable. She remained hidden and watched as bog wingtorn came and went from a small vine-laden den outpost. She wanted to get a closer look but needed to mask her scent first.

She found some dead thorn vine, removed the prickles with her claws, then combined it with newly-dead moss and kneaded the mixture before preening it into her feathers and fur. Once she was satisfied that she smelled like the bog, she slipped closer to the camp.

To her surprise, they weren't focused on the expedition to the north. They seemed relatively certain that things would go in their favor there. Instead, something to the west held their attention.

She counted fifteen gryphons in total. Vitra had slipped away to the south, talking about checking on the prisoners, leaving four medicine gryphons to guide the wingtorn here. What hadn't registered earlier but now caught Blinky off guard was that the medicine gryphons still had their wings intact. The sight of a fully-winged kjarr gryphon who wasn't Satra was shocking.

The young medicine gryphons ground up preserved bog blossoms and mixed them with a muddy paste to paint the wingtorn with flame patterns and send them out. Then the medicine gryphons painted each other, this time a skeletal design. One painted flower designs on the top side of her wings instead of bones. The wingtorn called her Soft Paws. She was called away to treat one of the prisoners Vitra had mentioned, leaving the others.

Blinky considered her options. She wanted to track the floral gryphon, Soft Paws, to Vitra deeper into the bog, but Blinky needed to know what was happening to her expedition and what held the wingtorn's attention to the west. The kjarr pride spoke common, but with a different accent than the weald gryphons and opinici used. It sounded like they were saying that starlings were fighting starlings, but that didn't make sense. She'd have to investigate later. First, she needed to catch Tresh alone and find out what was happening to the Ashen Weald troupe.

"Was Soft Paws the one we killed by the Flower?" Tresh asked.

Blinky shook her head. "She is still at their nesting grounds. Sit and listen. Stop asking questions. We will get there."

BLINKY SOON DISCOVERED she'd heard the bog witch's words correctly. After checking in with Tresh and giving her the vial of pumpkin, the owl gryphon followed the rogue wingtorn to the dig site, where she discovered a flock of newly-infected starlings starting to change.

The wingtorn hid in the swamp, but now that she knew what to look for, their bog blossom coloring gave them away. Having seen Vitra and the medicine gryphons, something about their paintings clung to the back of Blinky's mind.

At first, she thought it just might be how strange it was to see painted gryphons. In the weald, only the parrotface pride stained their feathers with starberry juice, though the opinicus refugees from the Redwood Valley were starting to change that. On her flight south from Tresh, however, her mind caught up to her senses, and she realized that bog blossoms weren't in bloom.

Tresh thought of every time she'd seen blossoms this week and felt a sense of vertigo.

Blinky blinked.

It became much easier to spot the hidden wingtorn after that. *What good is ceremonial camouflage that only works for half the year? Stupid gryphons.*

The rogue kjarrlings set up a vantage point to watch the dig site. What came next was something the Ashen Weald feared was happening but only now had confirmation of. New starlings were coming into the bog and catching the parasite, adding to the infected horde that already filled the kjarr.

More than half the starlings at the dig site had succumbed, leaving the remaining healthy ones to fight for their lives.

She couldn't remember having seen a normal starling before now. They were pretty gryphons in the sunlight. Under the moss-covered canopy, covered in blood, they lost most of their luster.

In the end, the uninfected starlings hadn't stood a chance. Just two healthy starlings and four infected remained. One of the healthy ones charged into the infected and chirped an order to its companion, who then fled back to the starling lands.

This was a cue for the rogue wingtorn, who rushed in to attack. The medicine gryphons, unconcerned about infection, flew overhead and caught the fleeing starling before it could escape, killing it. The wingtorn finished off the infected.

The last starling was wounded and probably infected

but looked healthy enough to attempt an escape. The wingtorn circled.

He looked at their blue flame markings. "Bog wisps. Are you here to lead me to my death?"

The medicine gryphons returned with the corpse of its friend and dropped it among the other dead bodies.

"Starlings made a pact," one medicine gryphon said.

"Starlings made a covenant," another confirmed.

"To stay in the jungle. To stay out of the bog," the third said.

To the starling's credit, it didn't seem afraid. Blinky hoped she could remain so calm when her death came. *Then again, with so many wounds, its mind may already be addled.*

The starling stood to face its captors. "We promised the Kjarr. You are not kjarr gryphons, bog witch."

The first *bog witch* laughed. "To be kjarr is to survive!"

The second nodded. "We have survived."

"We have our own Kjarr," the third said.

The starling looked at the dead body of the companion he'd told to flee. For the first time, Blinky could see the silver sheen covering his eyes. No wonder he'd told the other gryphon to make a break for it.

"Enough," he said. "Release my spirit."

The medicine gryphons had already seen his eyes, however. They whispered among themselves, too quiet even for an owl to hear, then one of them motioned to the wingtorn.

The wingtorn held the starling fast while one of the medicine gryphons stretched his wing as far as it would go. Another medicine gryphon used her wings to get airborne, then landed right on the wing joint.

The sound made Blinky shiver.

"A nice gift for our friend," they said, then ordered the wingtorn to retreat back into the woods.

Blinky watched as the starling began to crawl to safety. *No, not to safety.* It crawled north. *I would not carry the infection home to my pride, either.* She wanted to help him, but already she could hear a slight chitter coming from his beak. Without more pumpkin, there wasn't anything she could do. She frowned and tracked the wingtorn back to their hideaway.

Tresh and the rest would likely be okay. If the rogue kjarr gryphons thought one starling could finish off several weald gryphons and opinici, they must not have known about the antidote.

21

QUESS

I t took Blinky a while to relocate Vitra. Blinky had to fly at night, under the canopy to avoid detection. The farther south she went, the more she began to see markers on the trees. She located the Jadebeak River coming in from the starling jungle and followed it south until kjarr patrols made it too dangerous for her to continue.

Kjarr or deep bog? She'd begun to notice a pattern in the markings of the gryphons here, at least for the wing-torn who didn't cover their faces in skull paint the way the winged gryphons did. They all had variants of the white or black masks that Urious, Thenca, White Stripe, and Black Mask shared. While Satra had mentioned that Vitra's mother was a deep bog gryphon, Blinky hadn't understood what that meant at the time. She was starting to now.

From her scouting, it looked like the bog gryphons had taken control of a large section of the swamp, the southwest corner of the bog, though they shied away from the mangrove coast. Unlike at their hideaway in the north, down here they had guards, trackers, and hunters patrolling the area. Blinky couldn't get a good look at what they were protecting.

She wondered how good Tresh's night vision was. The starling-territory river flowed straight through the heart of the bog. Would they notice a petrel gryphon swimming through? Maybe, maybe not. Blinky could just make out the sound of a massive waterfall. She didn't know how good Tresh was with waterfalls. Blinky made a note to be more social in the future and ask anyone she traveled with how they felt about them.

She spent a few days watching the patrols, looking for an opportunity to slip past them. Every so often some starlings wandered through. When that happened, she took advantage of the commotion to pick off a few of the bog gryphons and leave starling feathers on their corpses.

It was brutal work, but they'd been brutal to the healthy starlings. Ever since that bog witch said, "We have our own Kjarr," Blinky knew her mission had changed. Merin and Foultner were right. It was better if Satra and her sister didn't reunite.

While Blinky pondered this, she tracked groups of medicine gryphons coming out looking for herbs, often led by the Soft Paws bog witch from the north. The flower pattern on her wingtops made it easy to distinguish her from the others. This gave Blinky her first look at bog pride fledglings. While she'd thought that the kjarr and bog gryphlets had all been taken prisoner, there seemed to be a lot of newly-fledged, flight-capable gryphons here. Some were bog witch apprentices, complete with skull and bone markings, but many others had been painted with blue spots and circles to distinguish them from the wingtorn.

The more Blinky observed, the stranger it all seemed.

Most of the patrols were new adults. She did see a pack of adult wingtorn she recognized as having gone missing during the battle for New Eyrie and some elderly medicine gryphons, but everyone else here was young. The elders looked too old to lay eggs. The wingtorn had been held in captivity until this summer, and their food had been dosed with red fern by the rangers to keep them from getting pregnant. The new adults she was seeing were only just fertile.

Where had all of these young gryphons come from? The only explanation she could think of was that the adult bog gryphons were all hiding downriver. That meant they were using their youngest to hunt and fight starlings. No pride would do that. It took several years of training after adulthood to make a productive member of the pride.

Blinky was just about ready to give up and go check in with Tresh when she heard several familiar voices echo across the bog.

Vitra's voice sounded similar to Satra's, but without Satra's slight rasp. "Take her out near the Flower and chain her up. Her chittering will lure the starlings in as a surprise for our Ashen Weald guests."

"Yes, of course," Black Mask said. He looked worse for wear. Whether his wounds had come at the paws of the bog gryphons, the weald gryphons, or the starlings, Blinky didn't know.

The last voice wasn't a voice at all. The sound she was making wasn't quite a chitter like the starlings made, but it wasn't a healthy sound, either. She sounded just enough like Tresh that Blinky felt certain she'd found the missing fisherfolk.

Soft Paws was taking care of the fisherfolk prisoner.

She seemed hesitant to release her charge into Black Mask's care. When Vitra and Black Mask weren't watching, Quess pulled a gutting knife out of her flipper and slipped it to Soft Paws.

Tresh looked at Quess, silver-eyed and sleeping in the corner. "Why did she do that?"

Blinky shook her head. "She is not able to say."

If Vitra had gone with Black Mask and Quess, Blinky would have taken the opportunity to kill Vitra. Blinky had seen enough in the bog now to be certain Satra's relatives were not allies of the Ashen Weald. Vitra didn't give her the opportunity. Instead, she headed back into the well-guarded nesting grounds with the young bog witch.

Blinky settled in and followed Black Mask and the four wingtorn guards who joined him. Unlike his escort, he lacked painted markings. Her first thought was that it was because he needed to be able to fit in with the expedition in the north, but it seemed to be more than that. The other wingtorn had an edge in their voices when they spoke to him. He was not one of them. *Because he fought for the Ashen Weald?*

She followed them for most of a day before they settled into a hunting hideaway for the night, giving her time to scout the area and prepare her ambushes.

She had a plan, but it required a lot of fish, copious amounts of mud, and a pitcher plant.

THE NEXT MORNING, Blinky was ready. She'd have preferred to fight them at night, but they were holed up in a literal hole in the ground. She needed them out in the open to be certain Quess wouldn't be hurt in the ensuing conflict.

Blinky would also prefer not to face them all at the same time, which was what would happen if one of them called for help. She wanted at least a few of them dead before they were alerted to her presence. Thankfully, spending the past few days observing their kin had given her a plan.

The bog pride respected their local wildlife the same way weald gryphons did. They knew how to deal with each plant and animal, knew the dangers each posed, and had begun to take them for granted.

In the weald, every year dozens of gryphons who became careless were killed by monitors. Respecting nature was something you had to do all the time if you didn't want to become a snack.

"This is especially true in the water," Tresh said.

Blinky turned her head to the side.

Tresh made it through sharks, jellies, and serpentine whales before her beak started to ache and she shut it.

Blinky hoped to take advantage of the carelessness that familiarity bred to hunt her quarry. To that end, she'd spent all night luring wildlife into places they wouldn't normally be.

The first bog wingtorn woke up and went to get something to drink from the nearby spring. The spring was small, so it was unlikely there would be any sailfins in it. Adding to her sense of safety was the clarity of the water. It was fed from an underground spring, and its transparency ought to make any sailfins easy to spot. To any reasonable observer, it should have been a safe place for a sleepy gryphon to get a drink.

Should being the important word. Blinky had dug up

gryphontail reeds from a nearby river and planted them all around the pond. She'd picked the tallest ones. The ones that could hide, say, the fin of a sailfin monitor.

Then she'd filled the pond with fish and left a trail of fish parts leading from the river to the pond.

When the bog wingtorn stumbled into the small pond to get a drink, she didn't notice the five sleeping sailfins concealed by reeds around the bank.

She did not get an opportunity to call for help. The sailfins followed up their fish dinner with gryphon breakfast.

Blinky waited in the canopy above for the next wingtorn to come looking. She didn't have to wait long. The next one cried out, but not an alarm that warned of hostile gryphons, which was unfortunate for him because just as he saw the sailfins' meal, Blinky dove down and ended him.

Rather than let the sailfins have this one right away, she dragged his body towards the river, careful to leave a feathered trail. The sleepy sailfins followed her and were surprised to see she'd left the body of the wingtorn in their nest. *They will think they are taiga gryphons, celebrating the Blue-eyed Festival.* She'd always wanted a monitor as a pet. She'd even picked out a name. *Sailacious.*

The third wingtorn who came out was smarter than the first two. He called for backup when he realized the previous gryphons had disappeared. The final escort came out, leaving Black Mask in the hole with the fisherfolk prisoner.

They found their half-eaten friend in the pond and followed the sailfin tracks to the river. They were too busy arguing about how to get their friend's body back from the sailfins to notice Blinky's trap.

The flood waters had created a lot of small ponds in the southern section of the bog that had yet to dry. The night prior, once the sailfins had been lured from the river bank, Blinky had gotten to work playing in the mud. Specifically, digging little holes and redirecting the river to fill them in. Then she'd stocked them with minnows, resisting the urge to eat more than a pawful on the way. It had taken most of the night, but eventually, knife fish had swum along the tiny canals to the little pools to eat the fish.

In the lowlands, the minnows had been a trap for Blinky. This time, they were part of Blinky's trap.

She then filled in the connections to the river, leaving her with a dozen puddles full of knife fish. They'd slither back through the mud to the river by midday, but she was counting on at least a few still being there now.

The wingtorn danced around the ominous puddles, trying to scare off the sailfins, hissing and rearing up on their back legs.

The sailfins were not impressed. They may not have been fast enough to catch a gryphon without luck or owlish interference, but they knew two gryphons weren't going to attack a nest of monitors.

One wingtorn jumped up and down, trying to intimidate them. His paw landed in the water, and Blinky tensed, but that puddle's knife fish had slipped back to the river.

The sailfins were too full and sleepy to care about a tiny splash.

The other wingtorn let out a high-pitched growl, startling everything on the river bank, including the knife fish in the puddle he was straddling. Its slimy, electrified tail-slap caught him across the face.

He dropped to the ground, unconscious, as Blinky dropped on top of the other wingtorn, killing her prey before the look of surprise left her face. Blinky pushed both bodies into the river and retraced her steps back to the hideaway where Black Mask and the fisherfolk awaited.

"Owl gryphons can be scary," Tresh said.

Blinky did not blink.

22

BLACK MASK

Blinky had one final trick to get Black Mask out of the hole. This one she'd picked up from watching the weald's medicine gryphons. They were careful to only harvest honey at night, when the bees wouldn't swarm. She'd emptied a pitcher plant of water, set it under a wasp nest, then clipped the branch holding the nest up with her beak, shut the top of the pitcher plant, and covered it with rocks.

Unlike the bees, bog wasps had been more than willing to swarm in the middle of the night. It was only thanks to shutting the lid fast enough that she'd avoided the worst of the stings. Since stealing their nest, their buzzing had died down. The pitcher plant was quiet for now.

Blinky placed it in front of the entrance to the hideaway, placing a single rock on top to keep the lid in place. She backed up to the wasp container. If things went poorly, she would have a lot of stings in unfortunate places. She'd practiced kicking pitcher plants in the early hours of the morning and thought she knew how hard she could kick it without making it explode.

She took a deep breath, hoped for the best, then kicked it with her back leg.

To the delight of her posterior, the pitcher plant went flying into the hideaway and didn't explode until it was inside.

Both Quess and Black Mask came flying out, pursued by wasps.

While the stings kept Black Mask occupied, they hadn't rendered him unaware of his surroundings. Urious had likely chosen him and White Stripe because they were good at deep bog hunting.

Blinky pounced, but Black Mask rolled and caught a pawful of her chest feathers in his claws. He'd managed to squish most of the wasps in the roll but hissed when one stung his ear. Quess had taken advantage of the confusion to dive into the pond to quench her stings. Blinky hoped none of the monitors had stayed behind.

She struck out at her wingtorn foe several times, but Black Mask returned bite for bite and scratch for scratch, trying to catch her wings. A broken wing had dire consequences without the ministrations of a medicine gryphon, and the only medicine gryphons out here were bog witches.

She protected her wings, backing up when he attacked, keeping them behind her. He pressed his advantage with a pounce and nearly caught her neck.

She feigned leaping straight in the air as though to fly back to the weald. He committed to a full leap before realizing she'd only jumped a small distance, then folded her wings again and fell back, landing in the spread-pawed technique of a downy fledgling.

The jumping capabilities of the bog gryphons were a sight to see. *He could nearly leap over the walls around the opinici outpost.* Unfortunately for Black Mask, his incredible leap bought seconds for Blinky to time her pounce to hit him just as he was landing.

Her momentum sent him back into the air, pinning him against a tree. Her claws went into his flesh and he dropped limp.

Prey going into shock.

Disappointing.

Ever since facing off against the blackwing opinici, a feeling had been growing inside of her, a need for new prey, stronger prey. She hadn't expected to get a chance to hunt wingtorn. Now that the opportunity had arisen and concluded, she was left wanting. She'd expected more.

She pulled her claws out, and he fell to the ground. Unlike his escorts, she left him alive. She confirmed the sailfin monitors had left the little pond and Quess was uneaten. Quess gave her a wary eye but remained in the water. *Maybe it is a fisherfolk thing.* Blinky would have to ask Tresh. Blinky hoped her expedition friends were doing well. It'd been several days since she'd last seen them.

She waited until Black Mask regained some of his senses. She patched him up as best she could, using supplies she'd found around the hideaway. She knew a little about patching up gryphons from her hunting days. Strix's pride hadn't had any medicine gryphons, so they all learned the basics.

An hour passed before he coughed and looked up. "What're you waiting for? Why did you bandage me up?"

"The expedition," she said. "Answer my questions. Who were you trying to ambush?"

He looked down at the puddle of blood, then at the bandages over his chest. "If I answer your questions, you have to promise not to kill me."

Blinky considered this. She'd never given any thought to lying before. There were few opportunities for it within the owl pride.

"Well?" he asked.

"I may have already killed you," she said, "but I will not kill you more."

"Fine," he said. "We were here to kill Urious."

"Kill Urious?" It made a sort of sense. He was loyal to Satra and the wingtorn. "Because he serves the Kjarr?"

"Because many of the deep bog wingtorn look up to him for saving them at New Eyrie and the Crackling Sea," Black Mask said. "As long as he's Satra's lap parrot, the bog gryphons in the Ashen Weald won't want to secede. They forget how we were treated under the old kjarrs. They forget how Jun's warmongering got our wings cut off. How he salted the lands, blasphemed against the sunken god. Urious blinds them to their subjugation. We need them to see."

Blinky took this in. She'd never considered Urious anyone important.

"Can I—" Black Mask fell into another coughing fit. "Can I ask you something?"

"Yes."

"Why did you come into the bog?"

"Because there were members of the Ashen Weald who needed my help." *And I was promised salted fish bars.* "And because there has never been an opportunity to help the fisherfolk before."

Black Mask tilted his head to the side. He was beginning to lose himself to the pain. "Isn't helping the fisher-folk working against the Ashen Weald?"

"No." She tossed over some roots she'd dug up by the river when creating the pools. If she'd observed Soft Paws correctly, they should help with his pain at the cost of clouding his mind. "The Blackwing Eyrie will come again. Only with the prides and eyries working together can we be safe. Satra believes we are better if we do not have to watch our tails for fisherfolk assassins."

"Satra believes or you believe?" He chewed the root. At this point, it might only ease his transition to the afterlife. "I'd rather live free than die Ashen Weald. Your owl pride leader had the right of it."

Blinky hissed under her breath. "Ninox is not my pride leader. She thinks forty gryphons can stand against an eyrie."

"How many weald gryphons went into the Redwood Valley Eyrie?" he asked. "About forty? Then it burned down."

"When the stories are passed down, her name will not be worth remembering," Blinky said. "Vanity and pride will erase her, as they erase all who are too proud. The blue opinici thought to control the kjarr and bog gryphons by cutting off their wings. Pride. The red opinici thought to cleanse the weald of gryphons because they were worth no effort to befriend. Pride. The bog gryphons paint themselves with skulls and flowers and think they can overthrow the Ashen Weald. Pride. It is our failure as gryphons. It is our failure as opinici."

His eyes glazed over as the medicine worked its way through his system. "When we die, we become the bog. Vitra has bog blood in her. When my kin in the Ashen Weald see that Satra is not the real Kjarr, that the real

Kjarr is half bog gryphon, they will flock to Vitra and return to us."

Blinky looked at his wounds. The bleeding had stopped. The fact that he had not yet died was a good sign. "Do you wish to return to the bog, then? I can end your pain."

He shook his head. "There is someone I wish to see before I die. Someone I need to apologize to."

Blinky looked him over. They were far enough from the patrols that it would take him a while to be found. She retrieved one of her kills from a nearby branch—protection against hungry sailfins—and left it by him.

"Thank you." He paused. "What is your name?"

"I did not take a name in common."

"What is your name in...owlish?"

She hooted the sounds that formed her name, though she did not think his primitive ears would allow him to hear all of it.

To her surprise, he repeated it back.

"It's a beautiful name. I will not forget it." He looked like he wanted to say more, but all he managed was, "Watch out for the flower traps," before he lost consciousness.

Treacherous flowers would have to wait, however. Blinky needed to take care of Quess first. If her eyes were anything to go by, Blinky didn't have much time.

23

MATAMATA

Tresh listened to Blinky's story, filling the owl gryphon in on what had happened to the expedition as they went along.

"So that's why you needed the pumpkin extract? For Quess?" Tresh asked.

"Yes," Blinky said. "She would not have lasted one more day."

"At Hoarfrost, some of the Sandpiper's Dune gryphons needed a higher dose to recover." Tresh pulled out both of the vials Biski had given her before she swam under the Flower. With some coaxing, they got more of the orange goo down Quess's throat.

"Tresh, you can't just bite rock crabs," Quess managed to say. She was staring at Tresh's bloody beak.

Tresh thought back to the rock crab on the beach and the first time she'd cracked her beak. Quess had been older, a friend of Tresh's brother. Tresh looked at the empty scabbard on Quess's bracer. The knife she'd given the flower witch had belonged to Tresh's brother. She wondered what had transpired that Quess had parted with it.

Quess began to speak again, but Tresh put a paw on Quess's chest and eased her down. "You do not need to speak."

Blinky looked at Tresh's beak. "Nor do you. We cannot re-wrap your beak."

Tresh started to speak up, but Blinky stopped her. "Tomorrow. After we sleep."

Tresh nodded. More than anything, she wanted to curl up next to Quess and comfort her brother's mate, but the chances of infection were too high, so she and Blinky slept across the tunnel from Quess.

Tresh was lost in thought. In her heart, she'd been certain she would arrive too late to save Quess. Tresh had come here because it was the right thing to do, not because she'd had any illusion of success. Rorin had tried to warn her against it, as had Zeph and Carru.

Kia had not. If not for her bright plumage and lack of field training, the opinicus scholar would've come along. She'd understood what Tresh was going through.

Tresh had promised to look for Mia. It was a promise she was tempted to break. With Blinky's help, the three of them could escape to the shore. That would mean leaving the Ashen Weald expedition behind. That would mean leaving Mia behind. Bruen's story had confirmed she'd at least made it to the Flower. That would risk making the Ashen Weald angry.

What Tresh wanted more than anything was to be curled up in front of a fire eating fish with Rorin and the fisherfolk. She never wanted to go back to a swamp again. She never wanted to swim through nasty, knife-fish-filled waters as long as she lived.

The Ashen Weald, comprised of the wingtorn who'd killed her nieces and nephews. Their opinicus masters. The weald gryphons who had sent word to warn the fisherfolk. *No, Xavi is in Hatzel's pride. It was not an Ashen Weald pride who warned us.*

Rorin's words came back to her, deep and resonate. "You cannot hate an entire group of gryphons and opinici, especially not one as diverse as the Ashen Weald." *I can. I do.* "To do that, you'd need to go meet every single member and hate each of them. That's a lot of energy." *I have a lot of hate in me now.* "Would you hate the Redwood Valley Eyrie, if it still stood?" *Yes, even burned to ash, I still hate it.* "Kia is from there. Do you hate her? What if Hatzel joined. Would you hate Xavi and Zeph?"

In the months since the wingtorn raid, Rorin and Tresh had debated for hours, most of her thoughts kept internal, but over time, he'd drained the bulk of the hatred from her, and she was able to sleep a little until morning. Then the survivors of Crane's Nest would come to her in the morning with their problems, with their vitriol, and fill her with hate yet again.

It was a cycle without end: days and nights, hate and exhaustion. She'd been living in that cycle for so long before she set out on this expedition, she had little left to give. Crane's Nest would not be satisfied until Satra lay dead. In Jun and Brevin's absence, the Ashen Weald's Kjarr represented everything the fisherfolk hated about the Crackling Sea and the wingtorn.

Tresh reached for her beak but stopped herself just short of causing more pain. She could not be the leader of Crane's Nest. She had no hate left to give. If she could just return Quess, maybe they would let Tresh resign. She could go back to fishing, to rebuilding. She was so tired.

I have saved Quess. She is here with me. That is my final act as leader. My first act as an individual is to go save my friends.

That would wait for tomorrow. With her hatred drained through memories of Rorin, exhaustion took over.

THE NEXT MORNING, Tresh's beak wasn't feeling any better. Without the painkilling root medicine, it felt worse. She could tell it was healing only because it now felt itchy.

This wasn't the first time she'd overextended her biting capabilities and been forced to recover. Having not learned her lesson with the rock crab, she'd attempted to bite the serpentine whale from the shallows. She hadn't been any better at resting her beak then, either. She missed Biski and her satchel of clean bandages and ointments. A surprising sentiment, considering her feelings about ointments on the first day of the expedition.

Tresh resisted the urge to yawn, though the fact that she could spoke to an increase in beak flexibility. Quess was at the back of the tunnel, still fast asleep. Silver tears stained the feathers below her eyes. Her breathing seemed better than it had the night before. Tresh held out hope that Quess would recover enough for their escape once they'd rescued the others.

Tresh emptied her pockets of the nonessentials, including the opinicus key, and left them by Quess's harness before joining Blinky outside.

The owl gryphon was kneading moss and vines. "I scouted the Flower while you slept. There is some blood but not enough for a killing. Most likely, they are being held in the heart of the bog."

"I was not sure, not with Erlock's roar. Any sign of Urious?" Now that Tresh knew he was the intended target, she worried for his safety. She sniffed. "What's that smell?"

"I saw no sign of Urious." Blinky was holding a mixture of vines and moss. "This will hide your scent until you get in the water. I believe the river that feeds into the bog pride's home goes all the way to the shore and safety."

Safety? Tresh wondered. She'd seen the shoreline when she'd led the expedition to inspect the raftworks. The coastal waters there had been full of sharks. It wasn't water she wanted to swim through in her current predicament. "That is a long way for the others to swim."

Blinky looked at her. "That is just in case. I have not seen the wingtorn to be good at swimming. While the air may be denied to us, I believe you could save yourself, should things go wrong."

"What if things go right?" Tresh asked. "Is there a plan for that?"

Blinky looked south. "Starlings are heading west. Whatever happened at the Flower after we left stirred them up. You can hide in the water while I distract the bog pride by leading the starlings into their nesting grounds. Then you all can escape over the sea."

Tresh mulled the details. If the starlings were moving west, it might give them some cover. *But if they continue west, they could infect the entire Emerald Jungle. Someone should find a way to warn the uninfected starlings.*

Blinky's description of the area from her scouting venture earlier had included a lot of opportunities for things to go wrong. Her scouting had not, however, given a description of the bog gryphons' home.

"If you did not see the nests, how do you know it is the right location?" Tresh asked.

"They all came from the same place," Blinky said. "There is a break in the trees like weald gryphons use. I saw a few rocks in the distance."

"Okay," Tresh said. "Show me this river of yours."

"First, you will need a disguise," Blinky began.

"First?" Tresh raised an eyecrest. "Why do I need a disguise for swimming? You are not going to put a shark fin on me, are you?"

Blinky blinked. "They are using a makeshift dam to keep the waters from flooding their home. We will need to sneak past it first. Now, spread your wings so I can rub this moss on you."

Tresh's eyes widened. This was going to be more difficult than she'd thought.

"This is your disguise," Tresh's owl mentor told her. "You just need to get past the dam and swim into the nesting grounds. When you need a distraction, make an *oo-awk* sound."

Blinky looked up for a moment as though trying to recall an important fact or piece of trivia. "The dam is diverting all of the runoff into a huge lake. That is not the river. The river is the one with the waterfall. Oh! Do not forget the waterfall. You are good with waterfalls? Yes?"

Tresh shook her head, dislodging a little of the moss. She looked like a pile of leaves and undergrowth woven together. Blinky had decided it would be best if she stayed up in the canopy while Tresh crawled her way past the dam.

Tresh was not entirely on board with Blinky's ideas—particularly the one about leaving Quess alone with food, water, and pumpkin while they rescued everyone else—but didn't have a better one. Had Tresh's beak felt better, she had more than a few words she'd have liked to say about Blinky's plan.

They waited for the scouts to go by, then it was showtime.

Tresh scuttled along the forest floor like a bug. Two of the fisherfolk who sometimes visited Crane's Nest, Levin's adopted parents, in fact, told stories of millipedes as wide as a gryphon and as long as two Rorins who would crawl the forest floor in the north and eat dead plants. Tresh felt like one of them now, creeping towards the sound of water. Twice her scuttling was interrupted by quiet warning hoots from Blinky. She was almost to the dam when she heard talking ahead.

"Ugh, I'm so tired of walking everywhere. We just made it to the dam. What is the point of having wings if I can't fly away from the nesting grounds?"

Adult, but with a bit of the trill of youth. Winged bog gryphon? Are their nesting grounds in a canyon if it lets them fly without being spotted by starlings? The only rocks we have seen are eyrie ruins.

"Don't let the wingtorn hear you talking like that. They're likely to gnaw your wings off."

Two voices. Two gryphons.

"Don't be gross," the first voice said. "And get away from the water. The flooding has made the turtles grumpy."

Tresh stood still. The bog gryphons were pulling up herbs and weeds and putting them in a pile. They passed by her hiding spot. She counted to ten before moving again.

One serpentine whale.

Two serpentine whales.

Three serpentine whales.

She'd made it to nine when one shouted.

"Hey, we missed some thorn vine back here!"

One of the young winged bog gryphons grabbed a pawful of the vines Blinky had woven into Tresh's feathers, then saw two eyes staring up at him and screamed.

"Bog monster!"

A nearby patrol of three wingtorn changed direction. Had his call been more descriptive, he may have received more help. Thankfully, *bog monster* was not a cry the wingtorn found credible.

Blinky dove down and intercepted one of the wingtorn in the middle of its back. "Go for the water!" she commanded Tresh.

Tresh tossed off the vine mesh and made a dash for the river.

"Don't let it get away!" the wingtorn commanded the herb-pickers. He circled Blinky.

Tresh was sure Blinky could handle the wingtorn. Gryphons and opinici who hadn't seen an owl gryphon in action tended to underestimate how they moved. That left Tresh with the two herbalists.

If the winged bog gryphons had been told about fisherfolk, they hadn't been told enough. Tresh made it past the dam, which was holding back a massive amount of floodwater, and leapt into the river rapids, her beak pulsing with pain as it hit the water. Her pursuers followed in after her.

Statues and chunks of carved stone pillars littered the river. Beneath the hanging moss and cypress trees, the river didn't follow a straight path towards the nesting grounds as she'd guessed. It wove back and forth. It was less a river and more a canal. Where the river curved, she could see it was eating away at carved stone, as though it had once been part of an irrigation system.

While another gryphon might have been worried, Tresh had trained in the currents around Glacial Run and was used to following their pull. She kept her wings folded halfway and flowed with the water.

Her two pursuers were not adept at swimming through rapids. One of them hit a half-buried statue and was tossed into the air. He spread his wings despite his friend's previous warnings against flight and dove back down at Tresh at the next curve in the river. His beak just missed her wing before the current pulled him under.

Tresh lashed out with her claws and managed to stain the water with his blood. Had she had use of her beak, she could have finished him a dozen times over. Fighting underwater was harder than she was used to when limited to just paws and flippers.

The second bog gryphon had just caught up to them. She opened her beak to bite and got a mouthful of water forced down her throat, buying Tresh time to swim underneath her.

After that maneuver, the herb-pickers' attention was firmly upstream. They surfaced to gasp for breath, came back down, and swam against the current to get at the wounded fisherfolk.

Behind them, erosion had worn through a section of the canal, collapsing it. Tresh could have warned them, but she needed to get into the nesting grounds undetected. Instead, they were just preparing a coordinated attack when they all went over the lip of the waterfall.

The whiny one caught Tresh's leg as they fell, sending them tumbling. She kicked him in the face, and he squawked in pain and spread his wings.

Tresh was weighing the virtues of trying to fly back up and catch him versus fixing her dive into the water. The water had soaked his feathers, and he was flying low, next to some pools formed by the waterfall runoff. The last thing she saw before she hit the water was a diamond-shaped head larger than the biggest gryphon she knew. It snapped out of the pool and crunched the bog gryphon in its reptilian beak.

Tresh's eyes were wide when she hit the bottom of the waterfall. Evidently, the other gryphon had seen the same things Tresh had. The surviving bog gryphon's eyes showed panic, but her fur and feathers were soaked through, and she couldn't get out of the current. It pulled them past immense, plant-covered pillars. Where the stone had been scraped clean, Tresh recognized some of the glyphs from the dig site.

She tried to catch up to the bog gryphon but kept getting snagged on lily pad stems. Tresh would need to get air soon but had no clue how deep into the nesting grounds they were, or if they were even in them at all. The strange river-canal had woven back and forth so often she wasn't sure where she was.

The bog gryphon caught hold of a pillar and started pulling herself above the water level, forcing Tresh to make a decision before her adversary called for help. She caught the next one down and climbed.

The tops of the pillars were free of aquatic plants, making Tresh wonder just how much of the floodwater had bypassed the dam. She pulled herself on top and looked across the water at the bog gryphon. Her adult plumage was in, but the look in her eyes was inexperienced.

Tresh found herself in Urious's position at Crane's Nest. She needed to keep the bog gryphon from sounding the alarm but didn't know how to do that without killing her. She'd just started her adult life and was coughing up water, oblivious to the danger.

"Slow down," Tresh's beak lit up with pain. "Slow your breathing. You will be okay."

The bog gryphon stepped back in surprise, one foot going over the edge of the pillar. "Who are you?"

"I am Turresh of Crane's Nest. I am here to get my friends." Certainly, that would be a relatable sentiment, she hoped. The beak pain she experienced from rolling the R in Turresh reminded her of why she'd chosen to just go by Tresh.

Upstream, near the waterfall, a section of the shore had given way and was floating in their direction.

"I do not need to hurt you," she continued, "but I do need you to stay away while I rescue them."

The bog gryphon didn't respond. She was hyperventilating. Tresh moved towards the edge of her pillar, but the bog gryphon stepped back and nearly fell into the water again. Tresh was worried the grassy chunk of floating rocks would startle her back into the water.

The chunk of rock larger than several gryphons

combined. With eyes. And four webbed legs. And a tail. And a diamond-shaped head.

Other sections of shore were pulling themselves into the water.

"Fly!" Tresh shouted but was too late.

The long neck and diamond head of the turtle snapped up the wet bog gryphon with a splash.

The turtle's neck and head were like the massive snakes that sometimes came through the northern weald. Its body was larger than a fisherfolk hut or Younce's den. Five gryphons could perch on top of it.

More turtles pulled their bulky bodies into the water, but she wasn't fooled by their sluggish pace: she'd seen how quickly their heads could move. For the first time, she realized how empty of gryphons or bog glyphs this section of the river was.

Tresh turned and dove back into the water, swimming down. Her claws cut through the algae and mud when she tried to hold onto the bottom, revealing cracked stone.

Is this section a bog on top of an eyrie outpost?

The shape of a turtle overhead blocked out her light, and she swam with the current. With any luck, the water resistance would slow down their strike until she could get some place safe, and the deep current would give her the speed she needed to escape.

Several changed course and began to swim down, their long necks nearly catching her tail as she darted past. The deep current was focused and easier to manage. Things were chaotic at the surface, where the large turtle that'd eaten the bog gryphon was shoving its way past the others to try to catch Tresh.

She was thankful she'd kept her flippers on. The current was growing stronger, and for the first time, it occurred to her that she was far past where Blinky had been able to scout. *I guess, despite my protests to Naya, I have become a spy of sorts.* Blinky had mentioned one waterfall, but if the turtles were concentrated along this strip, there had to be a barrier of some sort coming up.

The river snaked back and forth. Tresh could just make out the sound of falling water coming up. The large turtle was still chasing her, letting the current pull it around. Despite its webbed feet, it was spinning in its zeal to reach her.

Tresh swam to the surface and caught a branch that dipped into the water. She watched the largest turtle coming down river until she had a good idea of when it would be facing upstream or downstream, then dove to the bottom of the river, set her paws on the ground, and pushed straight up.

She didn't go flying into the air, but she managed to get just high enough to land on the back of its shell, right in the middle.

In her leap, she finally saw what lay past the waterfall. She'd been expecting a small river flowing past a clearing with a few nests, maybe a limestone cave. She'd swim by, spy on the bog gryphons, find her friends. That was the impression Blinky had given her.

Blinky had been wrong.

The break in the trees ahead of Tresh wasn't a clearing. It was a hole.

Along the outer edges, overgrown with trees, were circular walls, mostly collapsed. Now that she was this close, she could see that there were lined terraces with water pouring in from every direction.

Inside the hole, she could see tower ruins sticking up. On the far side, to the south, there was a gap where she could see the river continuing south towards the ocean. Across the gap was a bridge, or what was left of it. It didn't cross the span.

While the eastern edge of the collapsed eyrie was entirely overgrown, the western side had a clearing with several small huts on top and a path leading down the terrace and canals and into the depths.

It looked as though a sinkhole had opened up in the heart of the eyrie, swallowing it whole but leaving behind its walls and terraces for the bog to reclaim with cypress and moss and vines.

It was a lot to process, and the turtle wasn't giving her much time for thinking. To her surprise, the middle of its back wasn't far enough away from the mouth. Its serpentine neck swung around, and Tresh twisted away, nearly slipping off the shell as its beak came inches from catching her face.

She held onto the back of the turtle and beat her wings, helping steer it and build speed before it hit the end of the river.

The turtle's head thrashed back and forth, but Tresh was safe right above its tail.

They hit a submerged statue, and the turtle caught sight of the upcoming waterfall and began to try to backpedal with its stubby legs. It managed to catch hold of a pillar sticking out of the water, but Tresh extended her claws through the slits in her flippers and dug them into its tail.

It flailed around, and the stone slipped out of its claws, sending it spiraling again towards the waterfall.

Just when Tresh was certain the turtle was going to go over the edge, it managed to catch a cypress tree that had taken root on the river bank with its beak. The current was strong this close to the ledge, but the turtle began to pull itself towards land.

Tresh steeled herself, then ran up the turtle's back, onto its neck, and right before her claws could reach its eyes, it pulled its head into its shell, and they both went careening over the waterfall and into the eyrie depths.

24

PARROTFACE WAYLAY

Ninox flew from Orlea's camp through the ruins of the Redwood Valley Eyrie. Despite it having been months, flakes of ash still floated through the air, picked up by the winds coming off the mountains.

Pockets of opinici worked to try to excavate the old Reeve's Nest building so they could disassemble it and melt down the metal for more practical uses. Ninox cooed a greeting as she flew overhead, wishing them well.

Past the eyrie, burnt redwoods gave way to aneda trees and mountains. She was about to head back to her makeshift nesting grounds to give them the good news about opening up the old Snowfeather nests and check in on Cherine, but the sound of arguing came from the east, where an old trail led down into the parrotface territory.

Ninox landed some distance away and prowled towards the noise on foot. It was nice to get to stretch her paws one last time before the medicine gryphons would restrict her to a nest until it was time to lay her egg.

She was far enough south that she wasn't worried about this being blackwing opinici. Since capturing their scout and cockatiel forger, she'd been unable to find any more of the invaders.

Which wasn't to say they weren't out there. Every so often, her scouts would find evidence of newly-abandoned camps. It seemed that as Ninox's pride scouted farther north, their enemies pulled back and waited.

She stopped once she was in earshot. She recognized the voices from the incident at Hatzel's nesting grounds. It was Merin's three dumbest children, the ones she'd labeled Blue, Boring, and Fantail. They'd continued their search for her all the way into the northern mountains and were causing trouble.

"You should trade with the other Ashen Weald prides," Fantail said. His tail was spread to block the way forward. She remembered him as the first to flee from Hatzel. Ninox crawled through the aneda trees to get a look at whom he was blocking.

A trade delegation of parrotfaces was boxed in by several feathermanes on both sides. In the back, Blue and Boring kept them from returning the way they'd come. Parrotface gryphons, unlike their ground parrot counterparts, were capable of flight, but they preferred to walk. The trail was a good place to ambush them.

Ninox stayed low and downwind. While most of her scouts were in the north, she'd set a few to watch the border between her territory and the weald just in case. Likely, she had kin watching this same exchange if she needed them. Hopefully one had gone to fetch more of the pride.

"I'll trade with whomever I want," the head parrotface scolded. Her voice was deep, scratchy.

Ninox looked around the tree to get a better look. The

elder had small beaded jewelry and was decorated in blue circles made from the violet berry juice.

This wasn't just an elder, this was *the* parrotface elder who led their pride. While she wasn't as physically impressive as Hatzel or Merin, she controlled most of the unburnt weald. Merin's three dumbest children had chosen the wrong gryphon to pick on if they wanted to remain fed over the winter.

Ninox stepped out from her hiding spot and onto the path. She cooed once, too softly for other gryphon ears, and heard the sound come back to her twice. Two of her scouts were also watching the display.

She waited until she was right behind Fantail before whispering, "You are in my way."

The sound he let out was also half-scream. He dashed back to Boring and Blue, flying over the feathermanes and parrotfaces. "You said she hadn't left Hatzel's nesting grounds!"

"I hear she turns invisible at night," one of the feathermanes said.

"I hear she has a nest made from the beaks of all the opinici she's killed," another feathermane said.

Blue, perhaps emboldened after his hasty retreat from Hatzel, took charge. "Ninox."

She couldn't remember his name, so she just said *Merin's dumbest child* in owl as a response before addressing the parrotface pride leader. "It is a long walk for so late an hour. Would you like to stay at our nesting grounds? We would be happy to provide food. We have..." she searched for the word. "Starberries."

Before the parrotface elder could reply, her four pridemates waddled past them with a, "*Skraark!*"

They paused when their leader didn't follow them.

Ninox had never been able to tell the difference between a young parrotface and an old one, but by their haste and hunger, she'd guess they couldn't have been adults for too long.

"Yes, Ninox of the Strix," the elder said. "We would be happy to."

With everything formalized, the young parrotfaces waddled on, leaving the elder and Ninox to deal with the Ashen Weald cronies.

From what Ninox remembered, feathermanes had better hearing than Merin's kin. She made another quiet sound, and her two scouts began to circle around the feathermanes from the woods, making slightly louder cooing sounds.

At first, there was no reaction from the feathermanes. Then, Ninox saw an ear twitch. The feathermanes looked around, trying to figure out what they were hearing while Merin's kids remained oblivious.

The owl gryphons moved upwind, continuing sounds that the feathermanes could barely hear. The feathermanes shifted and whispered amongst themselves.

"Parrotface," Blue said in a formal tone, "do you really want me reporting to my father that you would rather trade with outcasts than with your allies?"

"Only if your father wants to eat," the elder said. "We've kept the Ashen Weald fed despite fire, flood, sea monsters, and other problems. I don't think we're in any danger of being kicked out, do you?"

Boring bristled and glared at Ninox, but he wasn't brave enough to speak. She licked a paw and washed an imaginary speck of dirt off her forehead.

"And you feathermanes!" the elder continued as though scolding gryphlets. "What would Zrim think of you hiding by paths, waylaying innocent merchants like common padfeet. What would your den mother think?"

The feathermanes were ready to spook at any moment. Boring, Blue, and Fantail's hearing wasn't good enough for them to pick up the sounds, but two more owl gryphons had joined in their quiet cooing. To Ninox's ears, it sounded like the forest was full of her pride.

In the stories passed around from pride to pride, the feathermanes were known for their bravery. Since Zrim's death at the claws of the starlings in the siege of New Eyrie, they'd been left leaderless. Normally, the leader of the medicine gryphons would take over the pride until a new leader stepped forward. Instead, the medicine gryphons had remained neutral, continuing to help rehabilitate the wounded. The lead medicine gryphon took it a step further, housing herself in Hatzel's nesting grounds to show what she thought of the Ashen Weald.

Blue, unaware that his feathermanes were about to leave him, crouched low. While he probably wouldn't hurt the parrotface elder, Ninox didn't want one of her pride to accidentally kill an Ashen Weald gryphon.

She lowed herself slightly so her pregnant stomach touched the sand on the path. While she would have liked to think she could take one of Merin's brats, a pregnant gryphon looked less threatening.

She walked slowly towards Blue. Her owls went silent, which seemed to unnerve the feathermanes even more. Their tufted tails twitched back and forth.

She reached up and put a paw on Blue's hooked beak.

"Thank you for escorting the parrotface pride leader here." She watched his eyes. They widened a little as he realized who the parrotface was and the trouble he could find himself in. "We will see to her care now. You may tell your father you kept the trade route safe."

She turned and walked away. The parrotface elder followed. Blue and Boring shared a look but didn't back down.

The feathermanes relaxed until owl gryphons began to materialize out of the forest and onto the path, at which point they decided they'd had enough and flew back to the weald. Blue, Fantail, and Boring followed their lead, though Ninox's ears picked up some rather unpleasant conversation about her as they left.

"You're less bloodthirsty than you were as a gryphlet," the parrotface elder observed.

"Until I lay my egg, I am attempting a new type of hunting," Ninox explained. "It is called diplomacy. I can always kill them later."

The parrotface elder laughed as though Ninox had made a joke.

Unlike normal traders, the parrotfaces hadn't brought goods with them. Instead, what they offered was knowledge. They knew how to hunt things that weren't meat: berries, fruit, bugs. They knew how to eat even in the winter. In exchange for two goliath birds, these five would show the Strix pride how to survive the winter up here.

It was a good trade.

As they walked back to the nesting grounds, Ninox felt a twinge. Her egg might not wait until the old Snowfeather nests had been cleared out.

25

THOSE LEFT BEHIND

Zeph and Carru landed back at Luminaire. There would be more driftwood to fly to Hoarfrost tomorrow, but tonight, Zeph's time was his own. While Carru went off to find something to eat, Zeph went in search of Kia. He didn't have to look far because she was also looking for him.

"Hey Zeph," she chirped. "Rorin wanted you to meet him. We were expecting you back before now."

"The winter winds are starting to pick up by Hoarfrost," Zeph said, "so it's slower going. I'm not sure it's going to be safe for fisherfolk to fly up there in another week. You'll have to see if the taiga gryphons can run supplies. Where did Rorin want to meet?"

Kia led Zeph towards the southern edge of Luminaire. It was nice to stretch his legs. The flight back from Hoarfrost was much easier than the one up the mountain, but flying in the cold always reminded him of why he'd moved to the weald.

"How've you been?" he asked.

"Food preparation is coming along nicely." She

slipped into her scholar voice. "I think Cherine would have gone into the burnt weald to try to find new sources of food, but with a few tweaks, the fisherfolk are catching a lot more fish than they need. Trading that north makes more sense to me, at least until things regrow.

Zeph thought it over. "Yeah, but how *are* you? You haven't been back north in two months."

"The same could be said of you," she countered. "Do you miss Hatzel and Xavi? Why do you stay?"

"I do miss them," Zeph admitted. "But I think having Williwaw and Hoarfrost ready for winter is more important. If one starling gets across the mountains to the weald, things could get bad fast here. I think about what happened at New Eyrie a lot. They say the grasslands sparkled from all the dead starlings."

"Well, that's your answer," Kia said. "I miss my family and friends—opinicus and gryphon—a lot, but what I'm doing here is too important to leave."

Zeph didn't respond. Just because something was important, didn't mean it wasn't worth talking about.

"And...I didn't feel useful at the university," she admitted. "I learned a lot, sure, but I was always someone's apprentice. I just did whatever Cherine or the other scholars asked me to do. Now that I'm on my own, I feel like I'm figuring out who I am."

They reached the southern edge of the island, where the tide was coming in. Waves crashed against the rocks and gnarled trees, wearing them down. There were no salamanders along the coast. They preferred the freshwater springs at the center of the island.

Kia and Zeph looked around.

"Rorin?" she called.

"Up here!" Rorin's voice boomed down at them from

halfway up a redwood. They flew up and settled in on the branches around him. The water glistened gold in the dying light.

Zeph looked south. "What's out there?"

The water past Luminaire was much darker than the water between the island and the shore. Several petrels— the birds, not the fisherfolk—dove into the waves and came out with fish.

"More islands," Rorin said. "According to Tresh, the mountains continue into the sea, and their peaks form a chain of islands. Has there been any word?"

Zeph shook his head. "No, I'm sorry. There was a patrol down from Snowfall. They said the fisherfolk who went with Tresh stayed to try ice fishing, but Tresh continued on alone to the kjarr."

Rorin stared at the diving birds. "The kjarr is a large place. It would take more than a few days to find Quess."

"And Mia," Kia added. "She's out there somewhere, too."

Zeph didn't say anything. Two months was a long time to be lost in the bog now that they knew it was full of star-lings. He worried that Kia staying here meant she'd given up hope.

He thought back to Xavi's disappearance. While Zeph had been worried, things were so chaotic, he'd believed Xavi had just decided to stay and help the fisherfolk.

With his mom, word of the avalanche and her death reached Zeph at the same time. There'd been no worry or waiting, just mourning.

He didn't know what to do to make either of them feel better. "I'm sure Tresh will find Quess and Mia and bring them home safely."

"Tresh is very resourceful," Rorin said. Another diving

petrel escaped the waves with a fish dinner. "Even on land. But what of you, Kia? What will you do when Mia gets back?"

"I hear she was good with the pumpkins," Zeph added. "Maybe Naya would allow her to stay."

"I don't think that's likely." Kia reached into her harness and pulled out a glass bauble she'd found with Mia's things at the ranger camp by the pumpkins. It caught the last of the light and splashed it into rainbows on the branches around them.

Zeph looked to Rorin, but he still stared out to sea.

"You're right, Zeph. I've been here too long." Kia put the glass away. "Cherine sent a letter with the last trade delegation asking me to help him with something. Said he had questions about what I saw in the headmaster's study, and he thought he'd found something that could help me make sense of it."

The air cooled. The waves hit their zenith.

"They're all out there," she continued. "Neider, Impir, Bario. Maybe even Mally the Nighthaunt. It feels like the rest of the world has forgotten about our little Redwood Valley, but that's not true. Most of our scholars are out there somewhere, telling them about us."

Before he'd met Kia, Zeph hadn't heard of Mally the Nighthaunt. When the opinicus refugees came to Hatzel's camp, their chicks began to tell tales to the pride gryphlets. In some versions, Mally was long and lithe, like a snake. In others, his eyes were all black. The only detail they shared in common was that his talons and beak were red like blood.

Thanks to the stories, now the gryphlets were just as likely as the chicks to have nightmares about the Nighthaunt. He'd been aptly named.

"Ninox is stealthy," Kia continued. "Hatzel is strong. The Ashen Weald is the largest army in living memory. But these are smart opinici they're chasing. It's going to take someone who knows how they think to find them. It's going to take me and Cherine."

Zeph's ears were forward. "When you're ready to go north, I'll go with you."

Rorin stood, nearly hitting his head on the branch above him. "I don't know about you two, but there's only one thing I'm ready for right now, and that's food. Swan's Rest is having a feast for the workers. If we hurry, we can get there before Carru eats it all."

Zeph and Kia laughed. Rorin launched himself into the sky, a white crane with a splash of red against the blue of the night. Kia followed behind, bringing most of the colors of Mia's prism with her.

Zeph looked out at the ocean. A diving petrel splashed into the waves.

He watched the water, but it didn't resurface.

YOUNCE FOLLOWED the river out of the taiga and into the kjarr, a frozen waterfall at his back, a bog to his front. This was his first trip to the kjarr nesting grounds since he'd taken them from Ellore's rangers months ago. A sense of unease grew as he remembered the anger and violence that had gripped him in the last stages of infection. He'd nearly lost himself. Only Hatzel and Biski's intervention had cured him in time.

He rubbed at his eyes, wiping away a silver goo that existed only in his mind now. The scar tissue on his leg where the infected goliath bird had bit him ached in the cold.

That night, a single bonfire had lit up the small ranger camp. In the daylight, he could see that the kjarr nesting grounds followed the forest and disappeared under the mixture of aneda and cypress trees. A sense of guilt kept him from landing among the wingtorn. If his pride had come to their aid, they might still have their wings. He didn't know how they felt about taiga gryphons now. He hoped the new pass through the mountains would help rekindle their friendship.

Off to the south, several spires were in the process of being constructed and dyed bright colors with berry juice. Opinici and gryphons of all sorts worked below, but he only saw one pair of kjarr wings and a head topped with golden feathers. He turned left and headed towards the ground, spooking several feathermanes who circled around Satra like guards.

She tilted her head curiously, not recognizing him.

"Younce of Snowfall," he introduced himself. He almost mantled his wings towards her, but he led a pride now and tried to act like it. "I was wondering if I might steal you away for an hour or two to speak? One pride leader to another."

Satra was more than a pride leader now. She ruled the Ashen Weald. But he hoped this might afford him the privacy to talk to her about Mignet without her guards around.

"I apologize for not recognizing you," Satra said with a smirk. "The reports Thenca sent with the workers described you as being Crestfall pink. She neglected to mention your winter plumage was a shade paler."

She dismissed her guards and motioned for Younce to follow her along a path into the bog. When she saw his trepidation, she added, "Don't worry. We keep watch to make sure there are no starlings near the nesting grounds."

He motioned a wingtip back to the colorful spires. "I've never seen anything like them. What're they for?"

"They're for the fledglings," she explained. "We want to make sure they learn to fly, so we're setting up an obstacle course. As much as our nesting grounds are set up for the wingtorn, I want to see the skies full of kjarr gryphons in the spring."

He could see the wisdom in that. It would also make the weald prides who'd joined the Ashen Weald happy. Hunting competitions were the highlight of the year, and he was sure aerial obstacle courses would be similarly popular.

"So, what brings you west?" she asked.

"Two things." He opened the pocket on his harness and pulled out Mignet's bracelet. "I thought you'd want this back. Mignet doesn't have any close relatives since Vosk's death. I think she'd want you to have it."

Satra was quiet for a moment, but she took the bracelet and traced a paw pad over the heron engraving before returning it to her ankle. "I wasn't sure if I'd see it again. It was all we had that Vosk might want, so it seemed our best shot at making friends of your pride."

"It wasn't just the bracelet I found in Vosk's quarters." He pulled out two of Mignet's feathers and laid them in front of Satra. "These would normally go to her mother, but I don't know if Ellore is still alive."

"Ellore." Satra twitched a long, black ear. "Mignet said her mother had been an opinicus. I didn't know she meant *that* opinicus."

"Ellore was the one who infected the wildlife in the taiga," he said. "She also convinced Vosk to forbid our pride from helping yours when you were captured. We don't hold much love for her in the mountains."

"They still smell like Mignet." Satra wasn't wearing a harness and didn't have a place to put the feathers, so she sat down to hold them in her forepaws. "Ellore's name showed up on a list of blackwing spies. She disappeared before we took New Eyrie. It sounds like she was Ivess's pick for ranger lord after Grenkin surrendered."

Younce frowned. While he didn't wish Ellore harm, he didn't like the idea she might still be out there.

Satra held the feathers close. "I'm surprised we haven't met before now, Pride Leader Younce of Snowfall. Other than the starling's pridelord, you're the only leader south of the Crackling Sea I didn't get to meet."

"That's not true," he said. "We met once after fledging. Do you not remember?"

She shook her head.

"When you and Mignet snuck into Snowfall to use the hot springs?" he prompted.

Her eyes got wide. "I'd forgotten! You and Zeph both."

He laughed.

"Just when we thought we had the springs to ourselves, you two walked in." She joined his laughter.

"Mignet's startled squawk woke half the pride," he said. "You're just lucky it was Deracho who arrived first. How'd you make it back to the kjarr soaking wet?"

Satra's tail twitched back and forth. "He let me hide out in his quarters until I got dry, then he flew me back to Thenca in the morning. *She* gave me hell but didn't tell my dad. Threatened to pluck me if I kept sneaking off. That was the last time I saw Snowfall. After that, I was too afraid to go near the place."

"You should come this year and join us for the holiday," Younce said.

"The Blue-eyed Festival?" Satra looked at his bright blue eyes, and then back at the feathermanes flying over the obstacle course. "I'm not sure my bodyguards will let me."

Younce grinned. "I'll get Deracho to smuggle you back in."

She shook her head.

"It's not just about giving gifts," he said. "It's about remembering the dead. While the festival has gone on as long as taiga gryphons have existed, it changed after the Connixation. Everyone had lost someone. It was a way to remember them without despairing. You, me, Deracho, Thenca, Zeph. We could remember Mignet together."

Satra held the bracelet up to the light so she could see the inscription on it. "Okay, I'll do it. But I'm expecting sugar frogs."

Younce did his best bow and mantle. "Of course. Nothing less for Mignet's favorite."

"You said you had two things to talk to me about?" Satra asked.

"Yes, the other is about Turresh of Crane's Nest." He thought about how to phrase his question. "Her petrel gryphon escorts are still at Snowfall awaiting news. Have you heard anything?"

"Nothing," Satra said, "but tell your fisherfolk guests it's early yet. Thanks to the starlings, the expedition had to walk in. It's a long hike to the Flower. I sent Urious to lead them. He'll make sure she gets home safely."

Younce's fluffy tail curled. If Thenca was right, Satra

had no idea that Urious was the one who had killed Tresh's nieces and nephews.

"Tresh mentioned you'd opened up Hoarfrost to the fisherfolk." Satra asked her statement like a question.

"With the starlings in the south, and the blackwing spies in the north, we're working with everyone we can," he said. Satra would find out that he'd given Ninox the Snowfeather Highlands soon enough. He'd let that news come from someone else. "While you took the fight to the rangers at the Crackling Sea Eyrie, we liberated Sandpiper's Dune and sunk their city of rafts."

"It's strange to have the rangers on our side now," Satra said. "The last few years have been full of surprises, not the least of which was Ranger Lord Grenkin relinquishing the reins of the eyrie."

"How can you trust them?" Younce asked.

Satra tucked Mignet's feathers into her bracelet and motioned for him to follow her back towards the others.

It was a bit of a walk before she finally responded. "I don't, not really. I want to trust them, but it isn't easy. After Impir and Bario, I find it hard to trust the reds, either, but most of them are Orlea's problem now. I just didn't want any more bloodshed. I thought this might give us a chance to heal. To excise the hate."

"From the workers on the path, I hear that the Crackling Sea Eyrie is nearly empty," Younce said. "Do you think if the Blackwing Eyrie's army returns, they'll stand a chance?"

"No," she said. "Not on their own. But I think if the Ashen Weald stands united, we can keep everyone safe. A show of force convinced the blackwings to leave last time. I think that's our only chance."

Younce thought of the independent prides—of the

fisherfolk, Hatzel, Ninox, and Orlea—and wondered if they were better off as part of the Ashen Weald. Only time would tell.

"I should head back," he said. "I'll let the fisherfolk know there hasn't been word yet."

"We'll send our fastest fantail to Snowfall as soon as we hear anything," Satra promised.

He paused before leaving. "I'll be expecting you for the festival. It's on the shortest day of the year."

Satra bowed her head slightly. "It's a promise. If our enemies to the north haven't shown themselves yet, I'll be there."

Younce took to the air and flew east to the taiga. He spared one look back to the kjarr and bog. Tresh, Quess, Urious. He wanted to believe they were okay, but he had a bad feeling.

He wiped at his eyes.

26

THE BOG PRIDE

Tresh clung to the massive shell as they fell past towers and columns and into the depths. Just before they reached the bottom, she leapt back so she wouldn't be next to the turtle when it hit the water.

Small white fish fled in all directions from the impact. The splash echoed across the subterranean ruins where the bog gryphons lived.

Tresh dove deep, but the sunlight only penetrated so far. She'd swum in a lot of strange places but nothing like this. While the current on the surface was strong, pulling south towards the ocean, the deeper she went, the calmer things became. Only the fear of finding more turtles forced her back to the surface.

"Matamata!" came the cries of the ruins' inhabitants. They flocked around the turtle, careful to stay out of range of its beak. Despite the several-story drop into this underground lake, the turtle was still in one piece and biting mad.

Tresh took advantage of the confusion to find a dry place from which to observe the proceedings. There were several collapsed tunnels, once eyrie hallways, around the outer edge of the lake. She found one that gave her cover to scout her surroundings.

On hearing the cry of *matamata*, winged bog gryphons appeared from pillars where they guarded nests. Along the western walls, wingtorn came out of collapsed tunnels or followed paths down from the terraces above.

The bog pride was a hundred gryphons strong, if Tresh had to guess. They were almost all new adults.

And these are just the bog pride gryphons who aren't in the Ashen Weald.

The size of the kjarr pride and its incorporated bog gryphons had been difficult to understand for someone who'd grown up observing the small weald prides.

The herb-gathering gryphon's comments by the dam on being able to fly made a little more sense now that Tresh could see how deep the sinkhole went. Based on how the bottom tunnels looked abandoned, the bog pride was used to the heavy rains that came with being sandwiched between the ocean and the Crackling Sea.

Gryphons working together to build a dam was unusual, but as the entire nesting grounds were built around a massive underground lake of sorts, it made sense that they'd want to keep their homes dry during the wet season.

In contrast to the masonry that had gone into building this forgotten eyrie, the dam had been a crude thing, and Tresh couldn't help but think that a smart gryphon or industrious opinicus would be able to cause it to collapse. She thought back to Biski's harness and the glass vials Piprik had given her.

More shouting at the turtle drew Tresh's attention

back to her current mission. More wingtorn were climbing down the ruins to help.

In fact, every bog gryphon in her range of vision was headed down towards the water except for two. Those two guarded a large, partially submerged passageway.

A stone tower rose out of the wreckage and up to the rim of the sinkhole. The markings were the same ones Henders had seen by the dig site, but there was no way for Tresh to fly up for a closer look without being spotted. The tower seemed to be part of the collapsed bridge.

As she watched the wingtorn climbing the pillars and ruins like a disturbed leafcutter nest, she noticed bog blossom glyphs marking the different paths and passages.

Between the water, the hundred gryphons who would kill her on sight, the angry turtle, and the ruins, she felt overwhelmed. She took a deep breath and closed her eyes. She remembered her brother carrying a salamander. She thought of swimming with Quess. She thought of Rorin's laugh and the way it resonated among the redwoods of Luminaire. She thought of how warm and fluffy Younce was.

Feeling a little better, she opened her eyes again to look for where the prisoners might be kept.

Waves crashed. Wingtorn climbed. Nascent bog witches filled the air. And yet, two wingtorn remained motionless outside the flooded passageway. It was marked with a light blue glyph unlike any of the others. While there was a small dry path into it, the water had filled two thirds of the opening.

That is where I will begin my search.

She lowered herself back into the water. While the guards hadn't strayed from the entrance, their attention was firmly on the turtle. If she were lucky, the flooding would be deep enough for her to get past them unnoticed. Not for the first time, she was grateful for her dark plumage. She'd find the prisoners in no time.

If they did keep prisoners. They could have killed them all.

No, they'd want to interrogate the new ones at least, or so Tresh chose to believe. She was grateful Quess was hidden away far from here.

Tresh swam underneath an overhang full of wingtorn who watched the water, unwilling to get within biting distance of the turtle. Their medicine gryphons dropped pitcher plants of blue paint on its back to make it easier to spot and tried to lure it towards the southern exit and river beyond.

Tresh didn't know how they'd get such a large turtle past the tower to the rest of the river, but that was their problem. She stayed beneath the surface, praying they kept the water next to their home free of sailfins and knife fish.

When a wingtorn fell into the water and distracted the guards, Tresh slipped into the passageway.

TRESH SWAM by some crayfish and an axolotl on her way past the guards. The water had a notable current. The aquatic plants and wildlife suggested that this corridor was always at least partially underwater, even in the dry season.

Does a bog have a dry season?

The passage had high ceilings, and the water didn't fill it. Where the roof had given way, pillars of light impaled the darkness, illuminating a dry path that ran alongside her. As much as she wanted to get out of the cold water, she knew her chances of running into a guard were higher if she took it. Her worry paid off when she heard sounds ahead and was forced to stay still in the unlit sections while several grizzled wingtorn patrolled past. They ignored the underground river.

As she waited for their footsteps to fade away, she inspected the walls. Large sections had collapsed, revealing the limestone behind them.

With the ongoing rebuilding effort at Swan's Rest, there'd been a lot of talk of trying to improve construction before hurricane season arrived at the end of spring. She couldn't remember if limestone had been mentioned—Crane's Nest had other worries—but she knew water ate away at some types of rocks. That could have collapsed the eyrie. It also meant there might be a tributary coming up that led out of the ruins and back into the bog.

Even once the voices had faded into the darkness, Tresh took her time, careful not to splash, praying there were no venomous snakes. Light from another hole in the roof lit up the way ahead, and she could see that the river split off, rising into a crack in the limestone.

The dry path the wingtorn had been patrolling also ended here, becoming some sort of barricade just visible through the murky water. A bog witch and two wingtorn stood guard. This seemed to be where the prisoners were kept.

Well, not everything can be as easy as a leisurely swim.

Tresh latched onto the side of the river to keep from being swept away and listened as best she could without attracting the attention of the guards. It was muffled, but she thought she heard Urious and Erlock talking.

While it was nice to have confirmation they were alive, they weren't what she was listening for. After a few moments, she heard a splash from beyond the barricade. That was a good sign. It meant the river probably curved back around and merged with the passageway.

She took a deep breath and enjoyed the last of the skylights.

It'll just be a few minutes, then it'll meet back, she tried to assure herself. The current here was strong and worked against her, but she fought it, swimming and crawling along as it wound through the limestone darkness.

Things moved in the water. She did her best to ignore them, but when she brushed past something large and slimy, her mind leapt back to the giant salamanders that made Luminaire their home.

She continued on, counting the time in her head until she'd start to run out of air. Despair that she was going in the wrong direction was just settling in when the subterranean river curved back towards the ruins.

Another couple of minutes passed, and her vision went from black to grey. The limestone gave way to stone eyrie walls, and she could just make out an illuminated section ahead.

She swam past the light before surfacing to look around in case there were any guards on this side of the barricade. Inside the oblong chamber were a collection of gryphons and opinici. She ducked back under water and followed the stream a little farther until it disappeared again into a wall, then backtracked and found a spot to poke her head above water.

"Ah! Cave gryphon!" Biski squeaked and fell back.

"For the last time," Erlock sighed, "there're no such thing as cave gryphons. It was just your reflection. Again."

The fantail made her way to the water but stopped when she saw Tresh's face looking up from the stream.

"Oh," Erlock said.

Now Urious had come over, looking even worse than he had after the run-in with the starling at the dig site. He'd been beaten badly. Bruising and dried blood matted his fur and feathers. Black Mask hadn't lied; Urious was the bog gryphon's true target.

Urious borrowed Erlock's voice to say, "See? There's nothing there at all." Then he whispered to a pale ranger with black spots and silver stains under her eyes, "We need some audio cover, if you don't mind, Ellore."

Ellore. Of course she survived.

The ranger lord nodded and brought Xalt, Jer, and the other rangers directly under the largest of the skylights in the prison. They began to complain loudly. The stone room, around twenty feet tall at that section, magnified their cries and projected them through the opening. The sound echoed up into the sunlight, where Tresh caught a glimpse of several light blue feathers.

Urious motioned Biski and Erlock closer. "Tresh, how did you find us? Why are you still here?"

"Blinky has been tracking the bog gryphons for days," Tresh said. "She suspected they were nesting in this area when she saw the break in the trees."

"Blinky's alive, then?" Erlock asked.

Tresh nodded. "Quess, too, barely. How many of you are there?"

At Quess's name, Bruen looked over. When he saw the bandages on Tresh's beak and realized it wasn't Quess, he stayed back and joined in making noise.

"Our original team of six, excluding my kin and you two," Urious counted. "Then we found some of the missing rangers already imprisoned down here. Ellore, Bruen, a redwood ranger, and four blues. So fourteen total. The other rangers all succumbed to the parasite. We saved whomever we could. They forgot to take Biski's harness until later, so we were able to hide away the pumpkin vials."

"A redwood ranger? Mia?" Tresh asked.

Urious pulled the Redwood Valley ranger over.

She balked at seeing Tresh. "You're the one who captured me. You and the dirty taiga gryphon."

Tresh was about to say something snappy until she remembered that Younce had, in fact, been covered in dirt the last time Mia had seen him. "Your sister is looking for you. She asked me to help."

Mia looked skeptical but didn't turn away her only hope for getting out of the prison. "I'm glad Kia's alive. I didn't know about the eyrie fire until the ranger lord arrived."

"You'd be wise to return to calling Grenkin ranger lord," Urious cautioned.

Tresh was surprised that Ellore was unpopular among the Crackling Sea opinici. It was rare for someone to be disliked by both opinici and gryphons. Tresh knew of Ellore from her reputation among the taiga pride and stories of her fight with Younce. Their views on her were not kind, either.

"Can most of you fly?" Tresh asked.

Urious shook his head. "The opinici had their primaries chewed down. Only Erlock is intact."

Erlock nodded. "I think they plan to use me to send a message to the Ashen Weald. What's *your* plan? You didn't come in here just for a preen and a scream, did you?"

Tresh shook her head and explained that Blinky was going to try to lure the starlings here, and it was up to them to escape in the commotion. "The passage I took empties out into flooded eyrie ruins, though, which is full of bog pride and a turtle."

Urious shivered.

Now that she'd seen one, she didn't blame him. "Is there a way up through the holes in the ceiling?"

"No," Erlock said. "They scavenged some opinicus netting and spread it across the openings. Not the war nets, mind you. These are the thick ones used to keep supplies secured to caravans or secure rafts. It takes flight to reach them, which only I can do."

Urious stretched his legs. They were bloody but unbroken. "I might be able to jump that high with some luck."

Erlock looked skeptical. "Either way, we'd need an opinicus blade to saw through them. Beak and claws won't be enough. All the opinicus supplies are on the other side of the nets, and there's no way the guards up there would give us that kind of time."

"You said you found Quess," Mia said. "She was so far gone I don't think they thought to check her flippers for her gutting knife."

"She did not have it on her," Tresh said. She wasn't sure why Quess had given it to Soft Paws, but now wasn't the time for speculation.

"There's one more way out," Erlock said, "but it involves going through the barricade. I haven't been able to find any weaknesses. The skylights might be our only option."

Biski looked at the water. "Well, there's also the way Tresh took in. Could we all swim back?"

Tresh thought about it. It wouldn't be easy to get out of the sinkhole even if they made it that far. It had taken a lot of swimming in a small tunnel. Even with the current working in their favor, it would be close.

She also wasn't sure how long weald gryphons could hold their breath, so she asked. "You would need to hold your breath for at least ten minutes. Can you do that?"

"No," came the answer from everyone.

Mia added, "Can you really hold your breath that long?"

"I can hold mine for about twenty-three minutes, if I am careful." Tresh looked up and tilted her head. "Did the ranger supplies include rope an opinicus could climb up?"

"Yes, it should," Mia said. "All of us kept rope on our harnesses for use on the rafts."

"There's a dozen bog pride up there," Urious said. "Are you planning to subdue them all by yourself and then toss down the rope? There are too many."

"What about when the starlings arrive?" Tresh asked.

The prisoners exchanged a look.

"Honestly, I don't think so," Erlock said. "The ones up top don't leave for anything. The starlings would have to be attacking the eggs to get them to leave. It's a bog witch nest up there. There are three elders who run the show. Based on what we've overheard, one disappeared looking for you. The other two have become shy and stay in the tent."

"Hmm." Tresh decided they may have a problem.

A problem to which Urious had the solution. "What if the starlings *were* right above us?"

She shook her head. "It is too late. I cannot get word to Blinky now that I am here."

Urious twitched his bruised beak into a half-smile. "I think once Blinky arrives we can lure them here."

Watching Urious's beak reminded her of how much

hers hurt now that she was out of the numbing-cold water.

"Lure them here?" Mia asked.

Urious pointed to Erlock. "We have our own starling."

"They will not hesitate to attack Erlock," Tresh protested. "They will not obey her commands."

Urious put up a paw. "We don't need them to obey her, we just need her to get their attention."

Biski looked up from where she'd been sulking. "He's right. The infected starlings recognized her, even if they didn't see her as one of them."

"I can't make that sound, that chittering that calls them to a location," Erlock said. "I just don't know how."

"I can, but they won't react to hearing it from me," Urious said. To prove the point, he made the sound, causing Biski and Mia to jump back. "We have until Blinky lures the starlings here to practice. I believe in you."

Erlock hesitated. "Okay. If you can teach me to make that sound, I'll use it."

"That just leaves our fisherfolk." Mia turned back to Tresh. "How do you plan to get out of here to toss the rope down?"

Tresh thought of the patrols. She might be able to get back out of the caves, but could she escape up the sinkhole unnoticed? There were nests and young bog witches atop all the columns and towers. Even the crumbling bridge was too visible for her tastes.

She looked at the underground river. There would be no light if she followed it farther upstream, but it was worth a try.

She cleared her throat. "Have your opinici keep

making noises so I can find my way back to the tent above. I am going to see if this leads anywhere."

And with that, she slipped back into the underground river and ascended into the watery darkness.

TRESH SWAM through the chilled water, tentatively pawing her way along the bottom, fending off the pinches of crayfish.

After ten minutes underwater, she needed to make a decision. Stop or stay? It shouldn't take her as long to go back with the current if she hit a dead end, so she continued onwards and upwards.

She tried to imagine where this river went underground. Would she end up on the terraces she'd flowed through on her way down into the sinkhole? Or would she find herself away from the eyrie ruins, hidden away safely in the bog?

Gryphons had a tendency to set up outposts or relax around fresh, moving water, so there was a chance she'd surface surrounded by wingtorn. She flexed her claws through the flippers on her feet.

Her lungs were just starting to sound warnings when the black water turned grey and light broke through.

Despite her mental preparedness to surface ready for a fight, she pulled herself out, coughed, and fell over, startling several capybaras drinking from the stream. They squealed at her and disappeared into the underbrush.

Somewhere in the water the bandages around her beak had come loose. The frigid water had kept it numb, but exposed, it began to hurt again.

She looked around, trying to figure out where she was

in case she had to get back. It looked like she was just past the western walls of the eyrie ruins. Through a break in the trees, she could see the killer turtle ponds northeast of her. The moss and underbrush in other directions were thick, suggesting that if the bog wingtorn used this stream for fishing, they did so somewhere farther north.

If this area had been terraced for agriculture like the section along the Jadebeak River, the bog had long ago buried any of the infrastructure. It was all cypress, hanging moss, and exposed kashow roots.

She slipped behind a spiked palm to get a better look at the kashow roots. She was confident that if she needed to avoid the bog pride, she could find her way back here. It was good to know when a stream went underground and ended up somewhere breathable.

Breathable, yes, but dark. She shivered. There were a lot of things moving in the underground expanse of water, things that weren't crayfish or any axolotls she knew of, things she wouldn't want to see in the light.

Though not turtles, thankfully.

Someone had dug down to expose the roots, but it didn't look like anyone had come by recently to collect their sap. Still, it meant she was in an area where bog witches came to collect herbs. It wasn't as safe as it looked. Remembering Blinky's warning, Tresh looked around for any blue flowers, but she was free of prying eyes.

She climbed a few trees until she found one that provided a nice view. She was along the western rim atop the sinkhole. She was nearly forced to abandon her tree perch when several bog gryphons flew out to fetch more blue paint and went right over her.

Erlock had said there was a bog witch hut atop the skylights that illuminated the prison. It should be around here somewhere. The bog witches had flown south, closer to the bridge.

Down below, the local gryphons continued trying to herd the giant turtle out of their home. Tresh almost laughed. While she'd hoped the turtle would cause a distraction, she hadn't expected it to be so effective. With the river mostly blocked by a collapsed tower, they wouldn't get the turtle out that way unless they could convince it to climb over the broken pillars.

With its stubby legs, she didn't think they'd be able to herd it up the small paths that snaked up the eyrie used by the wingtorn, either. They might be stuck with it in their strange, subterranean home.

The fisherfolk in her looked south to orient herself by the ocean. She was just high enough that she could make out the water. Visibility wasn't good enough to let her see the taiga, but she could make out smoke coming from the raftworks.

There'd been several rafts docked there. Perhaps a stray bolt of lightning had caught one of their masts? A storm was in full swing off to the east. Debris kicked up by the wind fluttered above the tree line.

Fluttered.

She looked again at the way the bog moved and realized she wasn't seeing leaves and tree branches, nor even a storm.

The starling swarm was spilling over the canopy chasing Blinky towards the sinkhole.

Tresh glided down from her observation tree and hit the ground running. The way the swarm was moving didn't give her a lot of time to find the hole down to her friends.

She broke through a wall of moss and crashed into an

idle bog gryphon bleeding kashow roots, knocking her into a tangle of thorn vine. The bog gryphon had the usual skull paint on her face, but instead of bones, the pattern on the tops of her wings was floral.

Tresh got ready to pounce.

The bog witch's long, black ears went from back to forward. "Quess? Is that you?"

Tresh paused.

"No, she is my brother's mate." *Was my brother's mate,* Tresh corrected herself. If Quess had really found some solace in the ranger Bruen, Tresh should respect that. "You are the one they call Soft Paws?"

The bog gryphon looked at Tresh's eyes, scarred beak, and flippers before nodding. While she was young, the skull markings made it difficult to say how young. "Tresh. You're Tresh. Quess said you would come. She left you something."

The bog gryphon used her beak to pull a knife out of a medicine pouch and tossed it to Tresh. "She said you'd want this."

Tresh picked it up and secured it to her harness. She sometimes carried a spare for the opinici she worked with, so she had a sheath built in, despite the impracticality of actually using it herself. "Who are you that she gave you this?"

"I looked after her when the infection took," Soft Paws said. "She'd already started chittering. They were going to kill her, but I brought her back with the bog blossoms. She told me about what the wingtorn did to your village, your family. She told me about the Ashen Weald."

Tresh sized Soft Paws up, then turned to leave. Judging by the blood stains where the thorn vine had caught on the bog gryphon's wings, it would take her a few minutes to untangle herself. "I have to save my friends. Please do not alert your kin."

"Wait!" Soft Paws cried out. Tresh ignored her. The starlings would be here any moment. She'd made it a few yards when the tangled gryphon's words reached her. "Is it true the fisherfolk will accept anyone, no matter their past? I've heard that the Ashen Weald is coming."

Tresh stopped.

Like the quiver she'd found at the Flower, Quess's knife had several charms hanging from the end it, secured by strips of leather. Tresh found the small shark charm she'd given Quess and snipped the leather with her claws. She tossed it towards the flower witch. "Yes. If it is true you helped Quess, bring that to Rorin of Swan's Rest or Naya of Sandpiper's Dune and ask for sanctuary. You should leave now. The swarm is coming."

"I don't know where those places are. I've never left the bog." The medicine gryphon was coming free of the vines, and Tresh couldn't risk this being a ruse.

"Follow the coast east to where the bog ends, then fly around the mountains to the dunes." Tresh continued on her way. Whether the bog gryphon was sincere or not, only time—and possibly Quess—would tell. If Soft Paws had really cured Quess using bog blossoms, clearing the kjarr and bog of infected could start as soon as the flowers bloomed.

The chittering of starlings grew louder. Tresh's first instinct was to look up, but the swarm was a ways off.

The sound was coming up through the holes in the ground.

27

WHITE STRIPE

When the gryphon prisoners had said there was a hut over the skylight, Tresh expected the simple huts fisherfolk often constructed in locations like Swan's Rest or Crane's Nest—bamboo with a roof. She'd seen the muddy nests built atop the columns in the eyrie ruins to hold eggs. They'd set a low expectation.

The bog witch hut was something different. It was an old tent framework of scavenged opinicus metal, but instead of cloth or netting, it was using something opinici would never have wasted—scavenged stormcloth.

That explains how the light gets down to the prisoners through the tent. The stormcloth was dirty, and for the first time, she could see glyphs and drawings carved into it. They looked too deep to be from gryphon claws, though given sufficient time, who knew what was possible? The Ashen Weald had managed to break into the Crackling Sea Eyrie's storm curtains with enough determination.

Still, the glyphs reminded her of the ones she'd seen both on the eyrie columns down below and at the dig site. She was left wondering if the bog gryphons had traced the glyphs not knowing what they were or if the storm-cloth had been inscribed by its creators.

Questions for a scholar, and as she'd been reminded by her Ashen Weald traveling companions, now was not a good time to be a scholar.

She counted eight medicine gryphons with wings inside and four wingtorn stationed around the tent. This would be a bad time for *her* if her vine-trapped acquaintance chose this moment to arrive.

Vitra was discussing something with the wingtorn while two of her bog witches yelled down the net-covered hole at Erlock, who was presumably making the chittering sounds after Urious's coaching. He was a good teacher. The starling swarm had shifted away from chasing Blinky and was flooding down into the abyss, splashing through the underground lake as they tried to cross it.

Screams came from the nests. It was a sound Tresh recognized, the primal cry of a gryphon who realizes the eggs are in danger and needs help. *Is this what I've become?* Her brain reasoned that these gryphons would continue to pose a threat to all of the weald and coast, that they had held Quess hostage, but Tresh knew that the loss of life for the bog pride would be terrible. *If there had been a way to approach them, to get Quess back, I would have taken it.*

She wanted the conviction of belief, but she remained uncertain.

A second scream, and Vitra led the medicine gryphons in a panicked run out of the translucent hut. She took the path down with some of the wingtorn while the bog witches flew to help with the starlings, leaving behind only two guards.

Even knowing these weren't the same wingtorn who'd

raided Crane's Nest, Tresh still felt her beak *click* painfully in anticipation. Her heartbeat rose, then dropped into a hunter's steady pace. She had to force her tail to stop twitching.

This is what it means to become a monster.

Younce had warned her about what he'd become while infected, especially when he caught up with the rangers at the nesting grounds. She hadn't needed his warning. She'd seen him at Sandpiper's Dune. He was like a playful gryphlet when he killed. Contrasted with the dead and dying raft rangers, it was not an image she'd forget.

And yet, it had been part of what she found attractive about him. He'd been wild and untamed. Claws, beak, and giant fluffy tail. Pretty rosettes fluttering between rafts. He'd lost himself, yes, but he'd come out of it and helped free Quess. That was why Tresh had come to him that night.

She'd continued flying up to the taiga because it got her away from shore. At Snowfall, no one asked her about rebuilding, about killing, about revenge, about burials. She was free to spend time with Younce without anyone stealing her away to talk about tragedy.

At Sandpiper's Dune, she hadn't understood. Now, getting a taste of the bloodlust he'd experienced, she felt repulsed both at herself and at him.

She would not lose herself. She refused to.

The wingtorn guards seemed disquieted by the sounds welling up from the ruins and subterranean lake. The one closest to the hut entrance went inside to yell down at Erlock.

While that wingtorn was inside, the other wandered around the perimeter, sniffing for starlings. Around the same time it caught her scent, Tresh leapt from her tree and dove at the patrol.

She caught the guard on her side and sent her flying as best Tresh's tiny frame would allow. With one side raked red, the guard rebounded and came at Tresh, trying to trick her into attacking mindlessly like one would do when fighting a starling.

Tresh played along, pretending to stumble forward, until the wingtorn struck, then she did something starlings with their lack of self-preservation instincts never did: she dodged. The wingtorn came off balance and Tresh's claws found purchase on the guard's throat.

The guard's friend inside followed his first instincts and charged Tresh, forgetting he was viewing the fight from inside the hut. He hit the stormcloth at a full sprint and knocked himself unconscious. He was no serpentine whale, shattering the sails of the Crackling Sea rafts. Tresh came inside and finished him off before he recovered.

"You can stop now, Erlock. It is me," she shouted into the hole.

"Tresh?" Urious called up.

"No, Rorin," she quipped. "Yes, Tresh. Who were you expecting?"

She'd been able to scout the hut from outside thanks to the stormcloth, so it only took her a moment to pull out Xalt and Jer's harnesses. The bog gryphons hadn't had a chance to rifle through them yet, and they still had their ropes.

She looked for something to secure the end to. Opinicus fisherfolk could tie knots, but Tresh had never been able to do that with her paws. She ended up pushing the heaviest crates she could manage on one end of it, then tossed the other end down.

Mia was up the rope in no time. Tresh leaned against the netting so Mia could reach through and pull Quess's knife out of Tresh's harness. While Mia sawed away at the heavy netting, Tresh rifled through some Crackling Sea harnesses to locate another blade.

Most of the opinicus blades were meant to handle gutting small sea fish. Several delicate knives had jelly or fish designs on them and looked like they'd snap if anyone tried to actually use them. Tresh found one with a strange, scratched jellyfish badge on it.

This must be Ellore's harness.

The pockets were full of blood-stained pink fish badges. Unlike the ornamental knives of the other harnesses, this one had a long, serrated blade. The sort that would be used for sawing through bone.

Tresh thought of the scar tissue on Vitra's shoulder and Xalt's comments that the rangers assigned to the bog sometimes took matters into their own talons.

She pushed down the bile and unhooked the serrated weapon. Ellore's talons reached through the skylight and Tresh slid the blade to her. It was a cruel reminder of what had happened between the kjarr and Crackling Sea.

Tresh began to bite and claw at the netting, but even with her sharpened claws, she wasn't making any progress. She'd have to make herself useful in other ways.

She took stock of her surroundings. If someone flew by and saw her in here, they'd sound the alarm. On the other paw, she'd splattered the outside of the hut with wingtorn blood. She looked around for some scavenged capybaras pelts to wipe it off with. She hoped it looked like smeared mud and not blood, but she did the best she could before dragging the wingtorn bodies into the woods.

By the time she returned, Mia and Ellore were only about halfway done. Mia had done the eagle's share of the work, and Tresh could see a hint of silver staining the plumage around Ellore's eyes.

Mia swore. "Why did the Crackling Sea have to make such thick nets?"

"They're to keep sharks out of the raftworks," Ellore explained. "You should see the ones they used to try to keep the reeve's pet contained. They were thicker than I am wide."

"You are not very thick," Tresh said, looking at Ellore's ribs and the stains under her eyes. "When did the infection take hold?"

Ellore shook her head. "I'm well enough to get out of this."

Even with the short distance between them, it was hard to hear over the chittering.

"Can you keep it down, Erlock?" Ellore asked. "We don't need the full acoustics anymore. The starlings found us."

"That's not us," Urious shouted back. "The starlings are coming into the passageway. They're fighting with the patrols outside the barricade. We don't have long."

Mia's ranger profanity was impressive in a way that her sister's scholarly frustration could not match. Tresh nearly blushed. *To think they came from the same nest.*

Another section of netting snapped and Ellore pulled herself through and got to work from above while wingless Urious climbed up and ran to stand guard at the front of the tent. A little more sawing and the rest of the opinici would fit through, but they'd need it all gone to get muscular Erlock top side.

More rangers pulled themselves through and began to search through the scavenged goods for weapons. Someone found the metal talons and gave a relieved squawk.

"I don't see any jelly toxin," a ranger said. "Looks like they threw them out. What do we do, Ranger Lord?"

Ellore shook her head, coughing from the effort. "You report to Bruen now. We can't risk having an infected in charge."

Bruen frowned but didn't protest. "They emptied out Ferrick's packs before they knew what the jelly toxin was. With luck, if we can find his field kit, we might have enough to coat a few sets of claws."

Biski's bright blue head pushed through the hole in the ground, and she shook her mane, losing a few feathers in the process. From below, Erlock pushed her orange rump. The feathermane squeezed into the hut and inspected the feather damage. "And my mane was growing in so nicely, too. Oh, Tresh, you lost your bandages!"

Tresh pulled Biski aside. "I met a bog witch who said she treated Quess's infection with bog blossom."

Biski frowned. "They don't bloom this time of year. Was it the plant or the blossom itself?"

Tresh thought back. "The blossom, I think. I believe they store it for winter and use it in the paint and medicines."

Biski went searching through the stolen clay pots stuffed full of herbs and flowers, making a pile of things to put in her harness when she found the vial she was looking for.

"Ha!" Biski said, then stopped herself. "Sorry, they took most of my medicines, but left some they couldn't figure out."

Tresh was nearby and took a sniff. Guano and salt. This was definitely the one Piprik had given Biski.

"Salt—" Tresh began, but Biski hushed her.

"Lots of gryphs and opies are a little touchy about the stuff with the fires and whatnot," the medicine gryphon said, "but Piprik found some on the island where they're holding the starlings. Bario tried to blow up the one of the buildings, but the fuse fizzled. Piprik said it might come in use."

Tresh thought back to Piprik. He'd packed Biski's bag, giving her explosives, but he'd given his broken eyrie badge to Erlock like it was even more dangerous than the saltpeter. Tresh wasn't sure how they'd put either to use, but it was good to have options.

One thought did occur to her. If they could blow the dam, the full might of the floodwaters might catch the starlings and wingtorn off guard. It was too bad the dam was north of them. They'd stand a better chance going to the coast.

"By the depths!" Jer exclaimed. He'd opened a crate larger than the hole and then fallen on his rump. "It's more of those clay jars."

The fact that Ellore, Bruen, and the kjarr nesting ground rangers knew what he meant told Tresh all she needed to know. They'd known about the parasite without having to go to the dig site.

"Are they..." Bruen searched for the word. "Are they alive?"

The ranger was too afraid to look, so Urious walked up and slowly worked the lid off with his paws. He swirled the salts inside with a single claw. "Yes, though dormant."

Ellore came over and collected a small clay orb. She wrapped it in a spare scrap of stormcloth and tied it shut. "They'll want this to test cures with."

Even the rangers gave her a strange look, but as ranger lord, no one tried to stop her. Tresh was about to step in —*ranger lord* didn't mean much to a fisherfolk and the container was an added danger they didn't need—but a hunting party on their way to help the nesting grounds happened to catch sight of the medicine gryphon hut. It was led by a bog witch but contained a familiar face, White Stripe.

WHERE BLINKY'S comments on Black Mask suggested that the bog pride had never fully accepted him back, White Stripe had fared better. He wore the bog wisp flame design across the scars where his wings once connected, and the wingtorn stood behind him in deference. Tresh almost hadn't recognized him at first.

He had on what appeared to be a scavenged opinicus harness, except someone had woven the leaves of the spike palm through it. Their pointed barbs stuck straight up along his back.

"The prisoners are escaping!" he shouted, but the rest of the bog pride were far below at the flooded eyrie ruins protecting the eggs from starlings.

The rangers left the hut to deal with the bog witch and her winged apprentices while Urious and Tresh guarded Ellore and Mia as they finished their work. Only Erlock remained trapped below. The chittering grew louder. Two screams suggested that most, if not all, of the prison wardens were dead.

"The barricade is starting to give," Erlock shouted.

White Stripe and the three unarmored wingtorn circled Tresh and Urious.

Urious's tail twitched. "I don't like these odds."

The nearby hooting of an owl caught Tresh's attention. "Go one way around the hut, I will go the other. Divide them up. I hope you have salted fish bars."

Urious's eyes widened in understanding. Luck was on their side, and the wingtorn split to chase Tresh and Urious rather than going inside to slow down the opinici sawing through the last of the shark netting. White Stripe made a beeline for Urious while two of the other bog gryphons chased Tresh.

She took to the air, finally getting to stretch her wings. A wingtorn leapt after her but was caught midair by Blinky, looking disheveled after guiding the starlings out of the eastern kjarr.

When the other wingtorn turned to look at the owl gryphon, Tresh pivoted and caught him in the center of his back, thankful they didn't all have spikes.

Through the stormcloth, Tresh saw Biski and Ellore pulling Erlock into the tent while Mia sawed away at the last of the netting.

"We need to save Urious, then get inside and help," Tresh said to Blinky. "The crate should block the hole once Erlock is through."

Blinky blinked, and they took to the air, Urious's no-flying commandment forgotten. Now that the entire starling swarm was here, there was no reason to remain earthbound.

Tresh and Blinky came from behind White Stripe,

giving Urious the opportunity to see them. He leapt into the air with a roar, and the two bog wingtorn leapt after him.

Tresh's dive caught a wingtorn in the face and drove him into the ground. Catching things on a dive was what she did best.

Blinky had less luck, with White Stripe twisting midair to avoid being vivisected. Blinky got a side full of quills for her trouble, but the twist put him off balance.

He landed hard, breaking both of his back legs.

"Yield, friend," Urious said. "We'll help your leg and you can flee west and avoid the starlings."

White Stripe tried to stand but cried out. "This isn't the sort of injury you walk away from."

"Then I'll carry you," Urious repeated.

This time, White Stripe laughed, though the sound was tinged with pain. "You always had too much hope for the future. Just like the new batch, you and Thenca were eggs through the worst of it. You didn't see what the Kjarr did to us."

"The new batch?" Tresh asked.

White Stripe realized his mistake. He began to shout for help, projecting his voice the way the mockingbird gryphons were best known for.

Blinky silenced him with a single slash. "We need to close the hole before the starlings come through it."

Urious stared at the body of White Stripe. Tresh wanted to ask him if they'd been close but knew now wasn't the time. He panted to cool himself off after the battle and padded towards the hut.

Tʀᴇsʜ, Blinky, and Urious arrived in time for the fantail pride leader to burst through the hole in the ground.

"I hope you have a way of closing that, the starlings are in the cavern." Erlock had a few bite marks on her flank.

"We do. Push!" Tresh commanded.

It took all of their strength, gryphon and opinicus alike, but they managed to get the crate of jars over the opening.

"Time to collect our ranger friends and fly out of here," Mia said. Her foretalons were blistered from the effort of sawing thick rope.

"Well, not fly," Urious scolded.

Mia's nares turned red. "I didn't mean, I'm sorry."

He pointed to her wingtorn-chewed primaries. "Only Tresh, Erlock, and Blinky can do any sort of flying."

"Speaking of which, those opinicus friends of ours need help," Erlock said. Without pristine primaries, the rangers were able to get some lift, but not stay aloft or direct their flight. Three were dead and the others were having trouble dealing with the bog witch crone and her pristine-winged apprentices.

Blinky made her way to the door. "I will fix this."

"Does our rescuer have a plan for what's next?" the ranger lord asked, gesturing to Tresh.

"I saw smoke at the raftworks. It could be fisherfolk," Tresh explained. "We managed to get a few of the rafts that drifted to Sandpiper's Dune working. The last time I was at the raftworks, several rafts were nearly complete. We might be able to sail one east."

Ellore frowned. "East? To Sandpiper's Dune? If any town has reason to hate the rangers, it's that one."

"Hoarfrost is next door if you would rather try your luck with the taiga pride," Tresh hissed. Ellore was insane if she thought Sandpiper's Dune held a grudge for their internment that compared to the hatred felt by the survivors of Crane's Nest.

Ellore's eyes narrowed. "I heard them talking when you visited the cave earlier. You are *playing opinicus* with Vosk's successor, yes?"

Tresh didn't dignify her with an answer. Her personal life was her own business and no one else's. "If you surrender to Sandpiper's Dune, I can promise you will be sent north of Glacial Run without incident so the Ashen Weald can pick you up."

The words *Ashen Weald* didn't seem to reassure Ellore. "Your word will have to be good enough. Let's go."

The addition of Blinky, Urious, and Erlock helped bring down the last of the bog hunting party. Tresh looked at the body of the elder bog witch. There'd been three that broke the healthy starling's wing back at the dig site, based on Blinky's story. There was still one more out there to deal with. And Vitra.

Blinky dragged the body of White Stripe over to Urious, horrifying gryphons and opinici alike. "Put the harness on. Use your voice to imitate your friend if we get into trouble. The spikes will protect you from above and hide your identity."

Urious hesitated. He reached out, but his paw was shaking. Mia and Bruen came over and unfastened the spiked harness and put it on him.

The freed prisoners continued east to the ruined bridge and looked down upon the lake and nesting grounds.

Starlings and bog gryphons were locked in combat. The bog pride was tenacious, but the starlings numbered beyond counting. So long as the nests on the cliffs were in danger, the bog pride refused to abandon its home. So long as there was food ahead of them, the starlings wouldn't stop, either.

Tresh frowned. "The starlings flow west like a red tide, poisoning all they touch."

There must be some way of stopping this. They are like grains of sand on the shore.

Erlock looked towards the Emerald Jungle. She'd recovered the broken eyrie badge Piprik had given her at the start of their journey and was holding it in her paw.

"It's time to go, fantail," Ranger Captain Bruen said. Everyone deferred to Urious, but the opinici were all bunched around the captain, except Mia and Henders, who guarded Biski.

"I'm not going back," Erlock said. She held up a paw to allay argument. "Everything that's happened in the bog has been terrible, but if the infected starlings start flowing back into the Emerald Jungle with the parasite, there may not be a safe place on the continent. Someone has to warn them, and I'm the only one here they'll talk to."

Biski shook her head. "I don't think they'll listen to you. Even if you're part starling, you're more weald."

Erlock held up the cracked badge. "Piprik said he knew of one who might. I need to try."

"If you are going north first, there is something you could do to help," Tresh said. She pointed to Biski, who reached into her bag for the two orange vials. "They have set up a dam and created an artificial lake. If the dam blows, the water would wash away most of the infected starlings below."

She didn't mention that this would allow the remaining bog witch apprentices to save what eggs they could find and escape. With their home full of turtles and starlings, they'd need to relocate, but at least they'd survive. If the battle raging on below continued for too much longer, she worried they'd all be lost. As much grief as they'd caused her, she didn't want to see them wiped out. She would not be Urious or Younce. She would not be like the survivors of Crane's Nest. She saw a better way.

Biski tossed over the saltpeter. The rangers and other gryphons all stepped back when they realized what it was. "Can you work flint and tinder fungus?"

Erlock shook her head. "I don't have the coordination of an Askel or Triddle. Or our door-opening petrel friend."

Ranger Lord Ellore pulled a set out from her packs, starting another coughing fit. "I don't have much strength left in me. I won't make it to the coast, but I'll do what I can to help my rangers. If you can help me scale the terraces up to the dam, I'll light the saltpeter."

Bruen gave her a look of understanding. Tresh was left wondering what had passed between those two. Whatever the look meant, Ellore had prepared him for this. She gave him a pouch of Crackling Sea Eyrie badges, keeping only one for herself.

Her serrated blade was back in its harness sheath, but Tresh wasn't the only one staring at it. Urious's eyes narrowed when he saw what she carried.

"Ranger lord," Bruen said.

"Ranger lord," the other opinici echoed.

"No, just Ellore. Your ranger lord is Grenkin. Don't forget that." Ellore looked at Bruen. "If your petrel friend is still alive, consider giving it a chance."

Urious whistled to get everyone's attention. "Okay, it's a long way to the coast and longer to the raftworks. Let's get going!"

28

RANGER LORD OF THE CRACKLING SEA

Ellore and Erlock, ranger lord and pride leader, made their way north to the dam. When they reached the waterfall, the fantail gryphon grabbed the infected opinicus's harness and helped pull her up the stone terraces.

The indignity of an opinicus being carried anywhere by a gryphon was unbearable, let alone the indignity of a ranger lord being carried by a weald gryphon, but Ellore had learned to deal with the unbearable over the last few months.

For the first month of her internment at the Flower, Ellore had been certain the rangers would show up at any moment to save her. Rangers never leave their own behind. It was unthinkable.

Thus, when they entered the second month of living off dry crate rations, she came to the conclusion that the Crackling Sea Eyrie must no longer exist. Satra the Kjarr must have purged the eyries, reducing New Eyrie to ash as she had the Redwood Valley Eyrie and scourging the cliffs of the Crackling Sea of all opinicus life. It was the only reason she could think of that she hadn't been saved yet.

While she'd lost faith that they'd be rescued, she hadn't lost faith in the eyries. If the Crackling Sea had fallen, she'd lead these rangers north. There, she'd give them an option: join the Blackwing Eyrie or go their separate ways. Mia would probably return to search for her siblings, Kia and Olan. That was fine. But some of the others would want to rejoin civilization despite past grudges. She was certain of it.

She'd worked hard to encourage all of them, to keep their spirits up. She'd promised they'd make an attempt for the raftworks if supplies began to run low. She'd come to see Mia as a friend, Bruen as a worthy successor, Quess as a potential ally, and the others as solid rangers.

Late at night, while Bruen and Quess whispered sweet nothings to each other, Ellore and Mia had made escape plans. They'd planned for almost everything, poring over old kjarr maps, considering their best options.

Northeast would take them into the paws of the old kjarr nesting grounds, now likely controlled by Satra. Directly east put them in the taiga or weald. Neither were ideal, but the taiga was particularly problematic if her manipulation of Vosk was now common knowledge. Southeast led to the fisherfolk. Quess had no power to bargain, but she'd promised to plead on their behalf.

West was where the starlings lived, and north led to hope. Ultimately, their escape plan hinged on the goodwill of their ex-prisoner. The next time flooding came, Quess offered to lead the starlings into the ocean. They seemed to have trouble with water, which should let her get a head start. Then she'd risk the shark-infested coastline to get the starlings away from the Flower so the opinici could fly north.

It was a good plan. Had Vitra not tricked them into

heading west to try to rescue trapped rangers, Ellore would like to think it would've worked.

If they'd felt like prisoners trapped in the Flower, they would have traded anything to go back to those days once the bog pride had them. Their numbers had dwindled. Eating the meat the bog pride gave them led to the parasite infecting them all. The blue paste the bog witches offered wasn't a cure, only a stop gap measure.

Ellore had attempted to hide several vials of pumpkin in the cave before the bog gryphons learned to take their harnesses—one of the rangers had hidden a knife and tried to fly up and saw through the netting. The next day, they were stripped and had their flight feathers chewed down. The hidden vials were found in the search.

When Ferrick worsened, Ellore didn't have her hidden pumpkin vials to help him. His infection had been resistant even before their capture. Ultimately, the bog witches had taken Ferrick and released him.

That had given her a new idea. She'd started taking less of the blue goo, allowing her eyes to take on the silvery sheen of the infected. If she could trick them into believing she was too far gone, she might be able to hide some blue goo in her craw and cure herself with it once she was released.

The only problem had come when the new prisoners arrived. Seeing the wingtorn, weald gryphons, and opinici working together wasn't the worst of it. She was happy anyone had come to look for them. But seeing the rangers there, rangers who'd waited months before searching for them, that broke her heart.

Despite their differences, she'd always believed Grenkin to be a fair opinicus. Finding out he'd spent months helping the wingtorn instead of searching for his own kind fundamentally changed her. It was the moment she knew she was never going back to the Crackling Sea.

Impir had been right about everything.

So when the fantail offered this opportunity to separate and head north, Ellore had taken it. She didn't have any pumpkin with her, but she had something more powerful: a clay jar of the parasites. With that, she'd barter with Impir for the antidote.

If she could get north in time.

She wiped silver goo from her eyes.

"Watch my harness," Ellore scolded. "I don't need your claws cutting through the straps.

She'd lost her footing near the top of the waterfalls, and Erlock had been forced to fly over and catch her before she went over the edge.

"I'm doing the best I can," the fantail said. "If you can't tell, I'm missing most of my rudder."

Ellore wiped her eyes. She hadn't taken a close look, honestly. It had been dark down in the pit. "What happened to your tail?"

"Your lot did," the fantail said. "You dropped saltpeter on my nest. I was lucky to escape at all. I was on fire when Satra and Thenca found me. You're equally lucky I don't drop *you* on someone's nest."

"Different department," Ellore said, though that wasn't entirely true. Her captain status meant she'd sat through the meetings where Bario and Jonas had suggested using the saltpeter to burn down the weald for farmland and hadn't spoken up. Only Grenkin had protested, but as the Crackling Sea reeve's consort, Jonas outranked him, and the ultimate decision had landed on Reeve Brevin's shoulders.

Erlock caught Ellore mid-stumble again. "We're just about there. I know it's hard, but the sooner we do this, the sooner our friends will be safe."

Ellore ignored her and concentrated on keeping one foot in front of the other. Erlock went airborne to check the distance again, leaving Ellore on the ground.

It was interesting that Erlock used the term 'friends.' Ellore felt a camaraderie with Bruen and Mia but mostly felt a duty to the rangers under her command. That Erlock had traveled here with a Reeve's Guard, wingtorn, fisherfolk, weald gryphon, and two rangers—and considered them friends—was a strange thing. Ellore would not have guessed that the Ashen Weald's bonds would hold, but if Erlock were any indication, they had.

It wouldn't be enough to stop the Blackwing Eyrie, though. Impir had shown her the wider world. Surrendering to the blackwings was their best bet. Other eyries had done so and survived, even thrived, as their ally.

A rustling came from the thick underbrush and three young bog witches came bounding towards her. They nearly crashed into her when one let out a hiss. They seemed unsure what to do. The signs of her infection kept them at bay.

"There's no reason to walk," she told them. "The starlings are here. Fly, fly to your home. Save what you can."

They looked at each other. Despite the skull makeup, she could see desperation in their faces. Two took flight and left her alone.

The third stared into her eyes. His long, black ears went straight back. He hissed a challenge at her, another young upstart seeking glory. She played weak and wounded but tightened her grip on the metal talons around her right foreleg.

She slumped down, and he reached out with a tentative strike. He wasn't prepared for how quickly she could still move. The metal talons nearly removed his head.

Just like old times.

It was a pity it had come to this, that the young were used in war. All that time as the bog pride's prisoner, all that time being interrogated by wingtorn with blue flames painted on their sides. It had taken her a while to realize what was going on, where this hidden army had come from. She wondered what Satra would think when she figured it out—especially if the starlings and water killed them all.

Ellore sifted through his primitive medicine bag until she finally found the blue paste. She imbibed half of it and slipped the other half into her harness pocket. She wiped her beak and metal talons off and pushed the body down the terrace and into the river. Erlock came back a few minutes later.

"I cleared out the guards at the dam. We're almost there." The gryphon sniffed the air. "Fresh blood. Did something happen?"

Ellore did her best to give a reassuring smile. "Just a starling kill. I'm fine. Better than fine, even."

She closed the pouch on her harness.

WITH SOME HELP from the fantail leader, Ellore arrived at the makeshift dam. It looked like something an animal would've constructed, but despite her design critiques, she had to admit it'd been effective. The bog pride had succeeded in turning the floodwaters into a massive lake.

"It's old and rotting in some places," Erlock told her. "They must have been using it like this for a few years now."

Ellore looked her over. "After the weald fire, did you expect to be taking saltpeter to blow up another pride's nesting grounds?"

Erlock's ears went back. "This is a little different. The bog pride has declared their own private war on the Ashen Weald. Unlike you, I waited until the fighting began to take drastic actions."

Ellore coughed. She'd intended to laugh, but it hadn't come out that way. "Wait until you're starving and see what you consider an act of war. We couldn't manage to feed our children when the kjarr pride came in and stole our food."

"Enough," Erlock cut her off. "Do you wish to spend the end of your life bickering? Light the fuse. Finish this."

Ellore wiped silver goo from her eyes. "Help me on top of the dam."

Erlock pulled Ellore up, and she located the best place to put the saltpeter. Vials weren't an ideal way to store it, but there should be enough here to take care of the makeshift dam.

"You should fly away now, gryphon," Ellore said.

Erlock looked at her. "Don't you want me to fly you to safety?"

"This is as good a place to die as any," Ellore said. "I'd rather not risk wandering through the wilderness and spreading the infection."

"I hope it's a quick death," Erlock said. "Thank you for doing this."

"Do you really think you can talk to the starlings?" Ellore asked.

Erlock checked to see that she still had Piprik's badge. "I think someone needs to try."

"The explosion could be huge," Ellore said. "Start flying west to get some distance, then I'll light it. Don't turn back for anything. You don't want to look directly at the explosion."

"You die a good death today," Erlock said. Then she took to the air and began to fly west, towards the Emerald Jungle.

"Not today," Ellore whispered for her own sake. She checked to make sure she still had the medicine she'd taken off the bog witch. With any luck, it would last her until she made it to Crestfall.

She searched for some vines to use as a makeshift fuse and instead found sun-scorched moss. She was hopeful that if she got it going, it'd take a few moments to burn down to the saltpeter.

Out of habit, she nearly said *for the crackling sea!* Instead, having been abandoned in a swamp for months, she considered a new battle cry. She scraped the fish paint off the badge Impir had given her, revealing the Black-wing Eyrie symbol beneath it. She stuck it to her harness.

"For Rakesh, Bruen, and Ferrick," she yelled. "May the Crackling Sea Eyrie sink to the depths!"

She lit the moss and flew north as fast as her weakened wings would allow.

29

THE RUINED BRIDGE

Tresh and the escapees picked their way south along the edge of the sinkhole, slipping through tangles of thorn vine and past bog blossoms. Down below, the bog gryphons were fighting starlings and trying to relocate their eggs, using the river to escape the madness.

Tresh hoped if they crossed along the walls of the eyrie, across the broken bridge, no one would take notice of them. They might be able to slip down to the river and cross between the bog gryphons. They'd just started their descent and begun to question if the saltpeter was still working when an explosion wracked the swamp.

More of the bridge collapsed, sending a giant pillar and the southern section of the sinkhole careening into the water below. The sound echoed up from the abyss, alarming the starlings and bog pride. When nothing else gave way, they went back to fighting.

Tresh looked north to the rapids and terrace that had brought her to the sinkhole originally. She traced the line of the river and waterfalls she'd braved. She could just make out the initial waterfall that fed into the turtle-infested ruins.

It took half a minute, but the effect of the dam explosion showed itself in a surge of water crashing over the ledge. She thought she saw several chunks of shore disappear into the water, possibly more giant turtles. The river and the turtle ponds disappeared under the deluge as it cascaded down the terrace, erasing it from view, and into the eyrie below.

The impact created a wave ten gryphons tall that crashed into the sides like a serpentine whale. It washed away the majority of wingtorn and also the starlings who failed to get into the air in time. Even several bog witches who managed to catch flight were caught unawares when the wave crashed against the walled ruins and splashed back, pulling them down with it.

Below Tresh's vantage point, the surge flung gryphons against the stone pillars where the nests had been kept. Thankfully, most of the eggs had been moved to keep them out of reach of the starlings, but the results of the dam explosion had caught many on both sides by surprise.

The lucky ones were washed further south, under the bridge and out the river at the southern edge of the sinkhole. As the wave passed by the expedition's vantage point, it splashed above the rim, soaking Urious and nearly washing away Xalt and Jer. Whether or not the tidal wave would dissipate before it reached the ocean, Tresh didn't know.

It could've been her imagination, but she thought she caught sight of a one-winged gryphon with bog-blossom blue plumage. To her disappointment, Vitra didn't crash against the stone tower but was washed away.

"Well, even if we were willing to climb down, there's no way to wade across the river now," Xalt said. "It's too wide, and the current is too swift. Looks like this is our only option."

Urious was at the edge of the broken bridge, looking down at the ruined eyrie pillars quickly disappearing under the unleashed floodwaters. The drop was a dozen stories straight down into the turtle and gryphon soup.

"With some help from the winged among us," he said, "we could cross it."

Tresh looked at Blinky. The owl gryphon was panting and covered in scratch marks. Maybe with Erlock's help, Urious's plan would be possible, but it'd been a long day already, and Tresh's energy had started flagging when she had to swim through an underground river. Blinky didn't look any better for flying and fighting all afternoon.

"No one else can fly?" Henders asked. "Was anyone mid-molt when they were captured? Anyone getting primaries back in?"

There were a few murmurs of no. At Bruen's suggestion, Urious had taken White Stripe's spiked harness to protect him from any bog witches they came across, so Blinky and Tresh both grabbed hold of different halves of the harness and tried to beat their wings to get airborne.

Blinky was already giving the spines on the harness a dirty look. All along her side were red splotches from her dive against White Stripe. The venom in the spike palm wasn't fatal but caused a burning sensation no gryphon soon forgot.

Henders and Mia used some of rope to create loops through the harness straps for Tresh and Blinky to hold onto. The flighted gryphons grabbed the loops. They were secured to the underside of the armor so the spikes would be facing away from them, leaving Urious upside-down. They just managed to get him off the ground but couldn't hold him up for more than a few moments.

Blinky shook her head. "I cannot do this. We would need another flighted gryphon."

Tresh looked back the way they'd come, hoping Erlock had changed her mind and returned. No such luck. The top of the cliffs was a tangle of moss with some of the bog blossoms they'd passed by earlier.

Bog blossoms that, as Blinky had taught her, were not in bloom. The flowers were in a pattern she'd seen before.

She chirped at the flowers and the wing they were painted on pulled itself away to reveal a blue skull.

The bog witch apprentice she'd left tangled in the vines tentatively approached the group. Tresh put a paw on Blinky to hold her back.

"I can help you fly your friends across, if you will grant me sanctuary," Soft Paws said.

Tresh turned to face the group. "This bog witch said she helped save Quess's life when I met her earlier. Is that true?"

One of the rangers who had been captured with Ellore whispered something to Bruen. Bruen nodded and inspected the bog gryphon. She spread her wings, showing the skeletal pattern underneath and blossoms on top. Her skull face paint was smudged a little where she'd hit the ground after Tresh pushed her earlier. The tops of her front paws were painted blue.

He placed his talons on her back leg and pulled it straight, revealing bite marks.

The apprentice winced.

"Probably," Bruen said. "The rangers who were here with Quess said she bit the one who was treating her."

While Tresh had mentally given up the mantle of leader of Crane's Nest, she had yet to formally resign or tell anyone else of her intentions. She cleared her throat and tried to sound official, not an easy task with the pain in her beak. "I, Turresh of Crane's Nest, grant you sanctuary among the fisherfolk."

"Is that her full name?" Mia whispered to Biski, who nodded. "It's a beakful."

The Crackling Sea opinici looked appalled that Tresh had let a bog gryphon into her village, but there was no other way to get them all across and this one seemed to have Quess's trust.

The rangers secured another loop of rope to Urious's harness and stood back.

Tresh, the bog witch, and Blinky each picked up a different section of Urious and lifted him across the chasm to the ledge on the other side. The landing wasn't gentle, nor was it upside-right, but he was in one piece. An opinicus would help remove the ropes and get him back on his paws once they were across.

Tresh paused to catch her breath. Thankfully, she didn't remember anymore chasms between here and the raftworks. Most of what she'd thought of as rock in this section of the bog seemed to be submerged eyrie ruins.

Once their wingtorn guide was safe, getting the others with chewed primaries across was just a matter of having them flap their wings while someone with intact flight feathers caught their harness and kept them going straight. They were all tired by the time it was done, but no one wanted to sit idle. The water was draining out of the canyon, and Tresh didn't want to stick around to see if any of the starlings or surviving bog pride had caught sight of them.

HAVING Soft Paws with them proved to be more useful than Tresh would have thought. Their new bog witch traveling companion was used to guiding the flightless through the hidden paths along the bog and kjarr and was able to get them most of the way to the raftworks before nightfall. Were it not for the occasional starling stragglers, they'd have continued through the night instead of settling into a hideaway to wait for daybreak. Like most of the bog outposts, it was an abandoned turtle hole hidden by a spike palm.

Tresh and Blinky took first watch, accepting some food from Jer before he crawled into the hole to sleep. Tresh felt like she was going to fall over at any moment. She could sleep through a thousand starlings chittering at this point. She'd only volunteered for first watch because she knew Blinky's owl senses would make up for her own exhaustion.

Biski snored loudly from inside the hunting hideaway. Henders mumbled something about Foultner in his sleep.

Tresh yawned and turned to Blinky. "We need to get Quess. Can you find your way back to your old hiding place?"

Blinky nodded. "When the night is darkest, I will go back and retrieve her. We will meet you at the raftworks."

The bandages made it hard for Tresh to talk. Biski had insisted on a new batch of them along with some paste Soft Paws had suggested.

"I would like to go with you," Tresh said.

Blinky blinked. "You are too loud. It will be difficult to get Quess south quietly. I do not want to worry about two of you. You may wait at the raftworks. Yes?"

"Okay." Tresh knew Blinky was right. She just hoped Quess hadn't wandered off. Tresh had given her two full vials of pumpkin, enough to cure all but the most resistant infections.

A sound caught Blinky's attention, and she peered into the darkness for several moments in silence before continuing their conversation. "There are still starlings and a few bog gryphons moving through the night. Do not wait for us at the raftworks. We will fly out to meet you over the water. It will be safer."

Tresh nodded but not in response to Blinky. Instead, her head slipped down into her paws, and she dozed off. Her conscious mind was fading when she felt Blinky lick her forehead and begin to groom her.

There's nothing that annoys owl gryphons more than poorly-groomed feathers, Tresh thought, *and I'm about as poorly-groomed as they come right now.*

It was strangely soothing.

30

THE RAFTWORKS

The next morning, Tresh was still outside. The other shifts of the night watch had come and gone around her while she slept. None had been willing to move her inside the hideaway.

Not that it would have been easy to move me through the spike palm guarding the hideaway entrance.

Their bog witch had given Tresh a tuber to alleviate the worst of her beak pain, leaving Tresh feeling the best she'd felt since her swim through the frigid underground stream. It tingled a little and speech was difficult, but she was grateful for any relief.

She stood up, stretched her wings, and started her morning grooming only to find the sticks and gunk from the hike yesterday gone.

She thought back and could just remember Blinky starting to preen her last night. Now Tresh found herself groomed, both in plumage and fur, but fluffy. Petrel gryphon feathers were designed to be waterproof, but owl gryphons lacked the necessary oil glands.

Thank the stars Rorin cannot see me now.

She took a few steps.

I'm...bouncy.

She took a few more. Her feathers had puffed up to twice their usual fluff level. She pushed aside the spines of the palm in front of the hideaway and poked her head inside. There was no sign of Blinky. If all had gone well, she was retrieving Quess. Tresh took advantage of her absence to attempt to regroom her feathers so they'd stay dry if she had to swim.

She'd just finished when Soft Paws returned with breakfast, a dead monitor.

"Newly dead," the young bog witch assured them. She hadn't removed her skull face paint even to sleep, leaving Tresh wondering if she ever took it off. "Still tasty."

Tresh prayed she wouldn't end up on a raft full of gryphons with upset stomachs. Biski cut the pieces small and loosened the bandages to let Tresh eat a little. She tried a few beakfuls of the sailfin monitor. It was a testament to what they'd been through that none of their Redwood Valley members complained. Neither Mia nor Henders flinched at the thought of consuming raw lizard. Biski made a face but still ate.

They finished in the morning light. Biski and the bog witch chirped back and forth about herbs and treatments. Soft Paws was curious about bees and honey, while Biski wanted to know about the bog blossoms. The blue extract put the parasites into a type of hibernation. While this wasn't as useful as the pumpkins, which killed them outright, when spring came, the kjarr and bog would be alight in blue flowers. This bought them time to grow more pumpkins. *The Ashen Weald may find they need food scholars like Kia or Cherine more than Piprik.*

Tresh walked over to Bruen, Mia, and the rest of the

rangers. Xalt and Jer had fallen in line under the rescued captain. However many rangers Vitra had captured at the Flower and raftworks, only a pawful remained. They looked like they'd been through their own ordeal.

"Are your rangers okay, Captain?" she asked Bruen.

"No." He secured a harness on one of the weaker rangers. "We'll see what the trip home brings, but I'm not certain they'll all make it."

She looked at their eyes. There was a little crusted silver but not much. They wouldn't have to worry about anyone turning before they reached Sandpiper's Dune.

He gestured to the bog gryphon. "Your witch friend's blue goo keeps it in check, but they've been without proper nutrition for months. We could lose most of them at any moment."

Tresh stood on her back paws to get a better look at the rangers. It wasn't her most majestic pose, but she'd gotten used to dealing with tall heron and crane opinici back home.

One of the rangers backed away when he saw the scarring on the side of her beak peeking through the bandages, but Xalt put a talon on his shoulder. "It's okay. She's a friend now."

Tresh finished her inspection. "We have some pumpkins at Sandpiper's Dune. We will see them cured before we escort them north to the Ashen Weald's lands."

"You have *our* pumpkins," Mia said. When she got a glare from Bruen, she corrected herself. "I mean, you have the pumpkins I left there."

"Spoils of war, Ranger," Bruen said.

"They did not spoil," Tresh said, turning to Mia. "Under your sister, they thrived."

The red-plumed ranger chewed on a talon while she

thought. "What of my parents and Olan? Did they make it to New Eyrie?"

Tresh shook her head. "At the bottom of the world, we just hear snippets. Kia does not know, either."

"Why didn't she go check?" Mia asked.

"I do not believe she is welcome among the Ashen Weald." Tresh was speculating, but she'd wondered the same things Mia gave voice to now.

Urious had come up behind them with Henders in tow. "Kia was instrumental in saving the wingtorn gryphlets. I can't imagine there are hard feelings there."

"According to the wanted posters in the New Eyrie Reeve's Guard barracks, Kia was instrumental in blowing up the Redwood Valley Eyrie," Henders said. "I don't know if that's true or not, but whatever the wingtorn think of her, she's not popular among the Redwood Valley opinici who now live in tents, Mia. There are bad feelings even now. An inquiry."

Tresh's ear cocked to the side. Neither Naya nor Orlea had spoken of an inquiry, but this wasn't the first time Henders had hinted at one. What did that mean?

No one said anything for a few moments, giving Urious time to take control. "If you mockingbirds are done making gossip, maybe we could get out of here before the starlings double back?"

The bog gryphon had finished reapplying her feather and fur paint. Tresh realized she'd never seen her newest recruit without her paint on. Tresh wasn't sure she'd be able to recognize the bog gryphon clean. She hadn't even remembered to ask if Soft Paws was her real name.

The bog witch pushed aside a tangle of vines, revealing a path through the spike palm and thorn vines heading south to the coast.

TRESH and the rest of her expedition followed their new bog friend towards the raftworks. The mangrove roots made it hard to traverse, and several dislodged crabs pinched at paws and tails. The path wasn't designed for the tall nor the winged, leaving many of their Crackling Sea companions with thorns or spines to pull out when they stopped to rest and drink.

There was no talking on the path, but the mood had changed. Tresh remembered walking into the bog with many of these same gryphons and opinici. Somewhere on their journey, she'd come to like them. She hadn't realized it until she found Quess and decided to go back in for the rest.

Even Mia, whom Tresh had helped capture once, didn't raise her hackles anymore. Tresh had spent hours listening to Kia talk about how she and Mia would play at Crater Lake as kids. It had helped Tresh relate. Mia still seemed skeptical of the fisherfolk, but her stance was softening as she saw Henders and the rangers interact with Tresh.

They were forced to pause several times while small pockets of five to eight starlings passed by. Soft Paws had insisted they rub the thorn vine on themselves, and when the starlings appeared, she used her wings to shield the others from view. The chittering of the main swarm at the bog nesting grounds continued pulling pockets of infected west.

While Erlock's warning about the starlings re-infecting the Emerald Jungle echoed in Tresh's head, the fact that the swarm had moved west meant Tresh's expedition should be able to get around the mountains to Sandpiper's Dune without trouble. Deracho would still be watching from Williwaw, and if no new storms developed, he'd see them as they got closer.

The expedition would be home before they knew it. The bog witch chirped the all clear, and they continued. *And then I need to explain why I brought a bog gryphon with me. And what a bog gryphon is.* That was a problem for tomorrow.

They hit the boardwalk midmorning and followed it over the floodwaters south to the raftworks. It was eerie approaching from the north.

The last time Tresh had been here was with Zeph Reevesbane and Quess. Much of the raftworks looked the same now. The raft construction hangar on the shore was still abandoned. There were goliath bird carts overturned near the entrance. The carts had been chewed on by capybaras, though the large rodents had made themselves scarce.

Three things, however, had changed. The remains of a fire smoldered in the courtyard, proving that the smoke she'd seen the day before hadn't been a trick of the light. One of the rafts that had been floating in the lake had now been tied to shore and prepared with a makeshift, but workable, sail.

Lastly, the storm shutters in the main building had been closed and secured. Not just secured, locked shut. She was certain they'd all been open when she'd investigated with the Reeve's Bane.

I should like a title. Turresh of the Depths. Turresh Fishbane. Turresh Bogbane. Tresh Wingtornbane. Too long. Not specific enough.

Urious's words came back to her. *We called you 'The*

Shark.' Tresh smiled and her numb beak didn't pulse in pain. It was a good name.

Everyone was moving towards the raft, but Tresh hissed, catching even Biski off guard. Tresh pointed to the main building and its closed shutters.

Opinici secured their metal talons. Tresh put on her flippers. Urious stretched his bruised legs. They took a few steps towards the main building when, from the construction hangar and mangrove scrub, a dozen bog witches appeared.

Tresh looked up at the tower again. Why had they closed it? How had they closed it? *I could not work the mechanism with gryphon paws last time I was here.*

Vitra stepped out from behind the main building. She looked at the expedition's last remaining wingtorn and the bog traitor. "Hello, Urious. Hello, little one."

Urious growled low in his throat. His ears were straight back. He looked like hell.

Vitra the Kjarr's fur and feathers stood on end, making her look twice her normal size. Her tail was more like a pinecone in design. She wore no paint, letting her natural brown and blue plumage stand on its own.

She turned to Bruen. "You and your *opinici* may take your raft and sail home. This is family business. Leave the traitors."

If Vitra looked twice her normal size, Soft Paws had sulked down to half her normal height. Her short tail was tucked between her legs. Tresh stepped in front of her.

"You, too, fisherfolk," Vitra said. "Swim home, little minnow."

"No," Tresh said. "I am Turresh the Shark, and Soft Paws is a member of Crane's Nest now. You may not have her."

Bruen and his rangers stood their ground. He pulled out a netted bag full of eyrie badges and tossed them on the ground. "The Crackling Sea remembers its dead. The raftworks, the Flower, the lumber mill, the capybara ranch. We found enough harnesses in your bog witch hut to account for most of them. You'll answer for your crimes here and now."

"My crimes?" Vitra's voice was floodwaters and rage. "My *crimes*. Yes, I hunted down every ranger who desecrated this sacred bog. Is it a crime to defend one's homeland? You cut off our wings and left us to die. My mother bled out before my eyes. Now you, a *ranger*, are going to judge me? The bog has no love for you and your Kjarr, you and your reeves."

The bog pride's circle constricted a gryphon length. Some of them hissed.

"I cannot fathom why no one put you down before now, Urious," Vitra spat. "You and Thenca were always lifting your tails when Jun passed. *Oh Jun, thank you for saving us. Oh Jun, you're so much better than your father.* Jun could've released the bog pride at any moment, but he kept us like pets. They deserved what they got."

"What they got? Have you forgotten you're speaking of your father, your pride?" Urious pointed his beak at her. "You're more kjarr blood than I am."

"I'm kjarr in blood only," she retorted. "You're kjarr in soul. You think the bog gryphons don't know that the kjarr pride wanted to breed us out into a single mongrel pride? A society of half-kjarr, half-bog? You think it a coincidence Jun took a bog mate?"

The wind picked up, pushing the smell of smoke into Tresh's eyes. The fire still smoldered. Whoever lit it hadn't had time to go far. If it had been a fisherfolk expedition, why hadn't they made themselves known?

"There's still hope." The newest member of Crane's Nest found her courage. Soft Paws mantled her painted blue wings to look larger. "We could join the Ashen Weald. There are more bog gryphons there. We could be whole again, could ask to be made independent."

Vitra's voice softened. "Your parents died in the eyrie depths, Soft Paws. Don't let the words of traitors poison you to the truth. We don't need anyone's permission to be free."

Urious turned and really looked at the traitor, Soft Paws, for the first time. Tresh tried to see what he was seeing. Soft Paws's ears were kjarr black. Her plumage was just past fledgling status.

A growl returned to his throat.

"What is it?" Tresh looked from the bog witch to Urious, but all she saw was the skull, bone, and flower markings. Soft Paws had black ears, a short tail, and long legs, but the rest was hard to make out.

"Grenkin took our gryphlets as hostages," Urious said between gritted tomia, "but not all of the eggs had hatched, just the early season ones. We never heard what happened to the remaining eggs."

Bruen spoke up. "We held them at the nesting grounds in the kjarr because we were afraid they might be damaged if we tried to move them."

One of the other rangers who'd been stationed there confirmed it. "We went chasing bog wisps right before a heavy storm hit. By the time we rushed back to move the eggs to higher ground, they'd already disappeared. I'm sorry."

Bog wisps? Tresh thought back to the flame symbols

some of the medicine gryphons and bog pride painted on their sides.

Urious licked his paw and wiped some of the paint off Soft Paws's face and wing. Without the bog blossom blue, what Urious had seen became obvious to Tresh.

Soft Paws didn't have the shrike or mockingbird mask that Urious, Thenca, or the other bog gryphons all shared. Her front half was the spitting image of Satra and Jun. Her back half was speckled like Ari.

Tresh looked around at the other young winged gryphons surrounding them. Only two showed signs of bog markings or colors.

This was where the missing kjarr eggs had gone, not lost in the storm but hatched and raised by the medicine gryphons who'd abandoned Jun for two years while their parents were locked up in the Crackling Sea Eyrie or sent to the Redwood Valley to attack the fisherfolk.

"You are all kjarr," Tresh said to the gryphons surrounding them.

"Kjarr in blood," Vitra said. "Bog in soul. One pride, just like Jun and his father always wanted."

Urious turned to the circle of gryphons around them. "You are not bog pride. You are stolen kjarr eggs. You will be welcome in the Ashen Weald. Step back—"

Vitra pounced before Urious's words could hold sway, sending him into the side of the raftworks. He managed to catch the building with his paws and push off, knocking Vitra onto her back.

She rolled, using her wing to give her leverage. They bit and slashed, Vitra getting the better of Urious's stolen armor by virtue of being in better health. By the time Urious managed to disengage himself, he was the bloodier of the two, and his previous wounds had reopened.

Both the bog pride and the expedition held back. Neither willing to strike until they saw what happened with their leaders.

Urious pounced, but his jump gave Vitra time to slip aside. Still, he caught her back paw with his claws, and she screeched and slashed at him.

Tresh couldn't tell who had the upper paw. Vitra had likely been leading raids since the bog medicine gryphons liberated her. Her single wing gave her a counterbalance that allowed her to move in strange ways. Urious, however, had proven his fighting prowess in campaigns across the bog, kjarr, and weald. He'd been at the battles for Crane's Nest, Crackling Sea, and New Eyrie.

Two days of being beaten in confinement, not to mention the starling's bite, had taken their toll on him. When the fur and feathers settled, they were at the foot of the main tower, and Vitra had him by the throat with her claws.

"You have flooded our nests, killed our children, and betrayed your own kind," she said. "You will die. Then my kin in the wingtorn camp will lead me to Satra, and she will die. I will make sure your Ashen Weald and fisherfolk friends here pay for helping you."

Vitra was so caught up in her anger that she didn't hear the storm shutter open above her.

Tresh saw a face very similar to her own with silver tear stains. The eyes were clear, though, and the infection had finally broken.

Quess had locked herself in the tower—Tresh had left the key in Blinky's hideout when she emptied her pockets.

Quess must have been the one who had lit the fire, too, and gotten the raft ready. The pumpkin had finally worked. Had she awoken and found Blinky and Tresh gone and come looking for them? Had Blinky arrived to find an empty turtle hole? Quess was holding Beaky's javelins.

Quess of Crane's Nest dove the way a petrel dives into the sea to get fish. Instead of using her beak, she held a javelin made of bamboo. It pierced through Vitra's spine and into Urious's shoulder.

Vitra went limp. The light left her eyes.

Tresh rushed over.

Quess's beak shook. Her whole body shook. There were silver tears coming out of her eyes as she looked at Urious.

"Y-y-you killed my children," she managed.

Urious's eyes were wide, in pain or shock, Tresh didn't know.

"You k-k-killed my mate."

Urious nodded. Blood pooled behind him, a mixture of his own and Vitra's.

Tresh gently gripped the spear in her paws and pulled it out of Vitra. The dead gryphon's body fell atop Urious.

Tresh tried to take the spear from Quess, but her brother's mate pulled it away and placed it against Urious's throat. The point of the spear was as unsteady as Quess.

"I still hear the screams of the gryphlets and chicks when I sleep," he said. "I knew one of their parents would find me. It's okay. Please, end this. I'm so sorry."

Despite everything Tresh had been thinking since the attack, she found herself putting a paw over Quess's talons.

"The dead cannot forgive," Tresh said. The dreams of

her nephews and nieces played in her head. "We must forgive for them."

Quess quivered. "They are restless in the ocean of s-s-stars."

This time it was Bruen who put his talons on Quess's shoulder. "This is how you quiet them. You do what they cannot."

Tresh's heart beat in her chest, over and over, a hundred times before Quess's grip slackened. Bruen carefully took the javelin from her and held her while she cried.

Biski and Soft Paws rushed forward to stop Urious's bleeding. Soft Paws looked relieved that Quess had recovered.

Tresh turned to the winged bog pride. They seemed unsure what to do without their leader. She looked down to Urious, and he nodded at her.

"Your pride is gone," she said. "From the starlings or the flood waters, take your pick. Most of you were eggs when you were stolen from your parents. Now is the time to go and meet your kin in the Ashen Weald."

Two of the youngest, newly fledged, looked nervously at each other. By their markings, they were true bog gryphons.

Tresh walked over to them. "I am sure you are welcome with the bog gryphons in the Ashen Weald. Urious and Thenca are heroes there, after all. If you are worried, you may come with me and Soft Paws to Crane's Nest. All are welcome among the fisherfolk."

The remaining bog pride relaxed. One of them stepped forward. "I will be Ashen Weald."

Another spoke up. "I will follow Soft Paws of Crane's Nest."

A third gryphon, complete with skull paint, began to ask Biski about *weald witch bee magic.*

After talking among themselves, three would go with the expedition east and investigate the Ashen Weald, fisherfolk, and other prides. The others would head back west and continue to search for survivors. Many of the eggs had been evacuated before the tidal wave hit, and they hoped that without Vitra and the elders, they'd be able to convince their kin to rejoin gryphon society.

Urious looked about to pass out, but he still had enough strength for a few more words. "We should leave before starlings find us here. Will you handle Vitra's body? She should be one with the bog."

Tresh nodded. She'd done the same for the dead wingtorn and fisherfolk alike by Swan's Rest. These waters were different, but Soft Paws would know the funeral rites for a bog gryphon.

"The Ashen Weald is one pride but also many?" one of the bog gryphons asked Biski.

"Yes, that's right," Biski said. "I'm a member of the feathermane pride, the medicine gryphons, and the Ashen Weald."

The bog gryphon thought it over. "I will not be kjarr, but I will join the Ashen Weald as a member of the bog pride, to be certain we have representation."

Once Vitra's funeral was over, the remaining survivors of the bog piled onto the raft. Blinky arrived just in time to join them, having spent all night and morning searching for Quess. One of the Crackling Sea rangers had spent time at the raftworks and helped get it into the ocean. The bog gryphons who planned to search for survivors waited until the sail was deployed, then disappeared into the hidden path through the mangroves like bog wisps.

Tresh looked over the side of the raft into the ocean depths. She felt better over water than land. She was bringing Quess home, and that's what she'd set out to do. The wind was with them, and they would reach Sandpiper's Dune around midnight if it held.

She put her wing around Quess to help keep her warm.

They were just within sight of Williwaw when the last of the sun's light faded. Tresh looked up into the sky, but there were no stars present, just the black depths of the sky-ocean.

The dead held their own counsel tonight.

EPILOGUE

Cherine had just finished taking notes for the day when the stone door to the workshop slid open.

A brown owl gryphon hooted the code word and rushed to Cherine. "It's happening! Ninox is laying her eggs."

Cherine dropped the pen. "Eggs? More than one?"

"Yes!" the messenger said. "At least two, according to the medicine gryphon. You should be with her."

He stuffed his notebook into his harness, not waiting for the ink to dry. He'd just closed up his inkwell when the door opened again. This time, there was no greeting or code word.

He shouted a warning to the owls, but they'd already taken to the rafters or found cover.

He was expecting an army of blackwing opinici to walk through the door. Instead, a bomb was thrown through the opening. He ducked for cover, but no explosion came, only smoke. Smoke with a strange smell. It wasn't saltpeter, more like incense. It was a familiar scent, but he didn't place it at first. It wasn't a flower or herb he'd worked with. It wasn't like the meat of the capy-baras, a smell he'd never forget. No, it was something with bees.

It was the incense used to keep the bees unconscious when they had to transport them from one food experi-ment site to another.

"We have to get out!" he shouted to the owl gryphons. "Without any ventilation, this will knock us unconscious."

The owl gryphons didn't respond verbally, but one of them grabbed the smoke bomb in her beak and dove out the door with it, tossing it as she flew. Cherine and the other three owls were right behind her. She flew straight into a net and fell unconscious when a ranger scratched her with a poisoned metal talon.

Cherine dove south, towards the grove, while the other three owls split up, one taking flight while the other two pounced rangers with nets.

He couldn't get a good feel for how many rangers there were, but more than a few. The outside guards were unconscious and wrapped up. That couldn't have been an easy task for the rangers, trying to catch owl gryphons unawares. His first thought was that the invaders had arrived at last—who else knew about the secret work-shop?—but interposing himself between Cherine and the grove of trees was a gryphon he'd hoped to never see again. He would recognize Merin's size and hooked beak anywhere.

The pride leader had a few new scars from the Crack-ling Sea campaign but looked much the same as he had during their last encounter. The only additions were five metal bracelets—four on his paws, one on his tail. He held himself more upright, with a confidence he hadn't had before. Where once he'd controlled one of the lesser weald prides, now he was a major leader in the Ashen Weald.

While the smarter action would have been to fetch help from the rest of the Strix pride, by the sounds of the opinicus screams, at least two of the owl gryphons had decided to fight. Cherine hoped the third had gone for help because he knew the odds of him besting Merin were not in his favor. They'd chosen to subdue the Strix gryphons instead of killing them, probably to avoid a larger incident, but he couldn't be sure that same courtesy would extend to him. If the owl gryphons killed any of the rangers, he wasn't sure how it would go for them, either.

"I know you," Merin's voice was unsure. "Where do I know you from?"

"Probably Orlea's pride," Cherine lied. Merin's wings were spread wide, and he was sideways, as if challenging Cherine to attack. Cherine didn't think of himself as a small opinicus, but he didn't have the muscle mass of a gryphon. His time with Hatzel's pride had shown him that gryphons who seemed small were incredibly strong and agile. He didn't know if Merin was agile, but he felt certain the gryphon could kill him without breaking a sweat.

While it had been two of Merin's children who had beaten Cherine and broken his beak, Merin had been the one to initially capture him by the ranger outpost in the weald. Cherine had a problem on his talons.

"No." Merin was starting to work it out. His voice dropped. "From before the eyrie fell."

Cherine felt that, as an opinicus facing a gryphon, if he could put enough distance between himself and Merin, he could probably outfly him. Cherine just wasn't sure how to do that. The more he waited, the sooner the owl gryphons would be rendered unconscious by the jelly toxin. He didn't think he could outmaneuver the Crackling Sea rangers. *Ashen Weald rangers now, I suppose.*

One of the rangers managed a lucky strike on another owl gryphon, leaving it unconscious. They were heading inside the workshop now to fetch the prisoners.

Merin looked at the tip of Cherine's beak, and his eyes widened. "You! You placed the explosives near my nesting grounds. You fell into the river in the cave and disappeared. I was sure you were dead."

Cherine hadn't been sure he was going to survive Triddle's plan of being pulled up the river, either, but he didn't stick around while Merin worked out the details of his resurrection.

Cherine leapt into the air and tried to gain as much altitude as his wings allowed, hoping Merin wouldn't be able to replicate the trick. Cherine didn't look back, and for a moment, he thought he would make it. Then he felt Merin's paws wrap around his back legs and pull him straight down.

Merin slowed their descent a little with his wings, but flung Cherine to the ground and put a paw on his chest, claws extended into his skin. Cherine tried to catch his breath through the pressure. One of the rangers came over with a collar and chain.

"It's a good thing we found spares," a ranger was saying as he fastened the collar around Cherine's neck. "Is it wise to take one of the owl's allies prisoner? Who is he?"

Merin growled. "Ninox needs to learn that her pride remains independent at Satra's whim. He was part of the Redwood Valley that blew up most of the weald. He was the one who tried to blow up my home. He got away from me once, but this time, he'll face justice."

Cherine expected them to knock him out, but it

seemed they thought it would be easier if he could fly of his own accord. He counted the unconscious bodies of the owl gryphons outside the workshop and could only see five. One had escaped.

The ranger looked at Cherine's ink-stained harness and shook his head. "Not a good time to be a scholar. You should've fled north with the rest of your kind."

Once the collar was secure, and the leash held by a surly-looking ranger, Cherine was shoved next to the blackwing and cockatiel prisoners. It was a small concession that both of them were similarly restrained. However the Ashen Weald had managed to locate the workshop, they didn't consider the invaders to be friends.

When the cockatiel saw that Cherine was also in chains, his crest perked up. "How exciting! Now we'll get to be prisoners together." Then, in a whisper, "You'll probably want to save yourself before *our* rescue arrives."

Cherine stared at the grinning cockatiel and wondered what came next. He expected they would be led west, either to the Crackling Sea or the kjarr nesting grounds. Instead, their captors led them south, into the weald.

K. VALE NAGLE
REEVESBANE
GRYPHON INSURRECTION: BOOK FOUR

AUTHOR'S NOTE

PERUVIAN DIVING PETRELS REVISITED

So if you read this far and you're hoping to find out how long a Peruvian diving petrel can hold its breath, I'm going to warn you up front, I don't know yet. I'm still looking into it. So far, my bird scientist resources have been of limited help, except that many believe petrel diving numbers were inflated by early studies. The difficulty in finding solid answers seems to revolve around the fact that they're small birds and the old transmitters are too heavy for them. I'll keep you posted as author's notes continue. Hopefully we have a few more books together before the series ends!

What I wanted to talk about today is my team. No, I don't have a ghost writer. I'm not secretly fifteen people writing under the same name. There's a lot that goes into the books that aren't writing, and I'd like to take a moment here in book three to thank everyone.

First, I'd like to thank my spouse. He's my first reader. He's the one who complained that fantasy books have too many human protagonists and not enough gryphons, something I'm attempting to remedy here. If you look back at pictures of us as teenagers (we were friends even then), as often as not we're wearing silver gryphon shirts. No one gives as in-depth feedback as he does because his love for gryphons knows no bounds. He's never afraid to give honest feedback, and he never pulls a punch.

While each beta reader will get their own shout out, I'd like to thank Tara Richardson Connolly first because she went above and beyond several times. When I was on a deadline and needed feedback, she made it happen. *Ashen Weald* in particular was imbued with her help. It had many heavy revisions before going into beta, and she was there every step of the way helping me. And it's not just books. She's the kind of person who looks out for her friends in all aspects of her life. Ever since I was a scared little 14-year-old kid volunteering at a local museum, she's watched out for me.

Let me rewind a moment to when *Eyrie*'s first draft was done. I have a good friend who handles gryphon covers for other authors and has won all the awards. She'd agreed to paint the cover, but a medical problem came up, and I was happy to bow out of her schedule while she recovered enough to handle her usual work load.

I hadn't thought about other cover artists before then, so I began to reach out. (I have no say over my literary fiction, but for my fantasy, I have full say on my covers.) I'd seen Jeff Brown's beautiful castles and spaceships, but someone pointed me in the direction of his dragon lich painting. I sent him an e-mail asking him about gryphons, unsure if I'd hear back or not.

Nineteen minutes later, I had an email. It wasn't just a response that he was interested, he'd sent a concept sketch cover for *Eyrie* without even knowing its name. He even included a little ground parrot. He was so excited to work on gryphons, I said yes and stopped my search right then. I don't think he had any idea what he was getting himself into—we're very particular about gryphons in this household—but his patience and skill deserve all the praise they get. As I'm typing this author's note, almost as though summoned, he just sent the penultimate cover of *Reevesbane* and it looks amazing.

Have you been enjoying the chapter headings and ornamented scene breaks? If so, Crystal Gafford from Crafty as a Coyote is to thank. If you've seen the little adorable gryphons holding hearts that show up on social media and my website around the holidays, those are also hers. She's great to talk to, does solid work for myself and other STET Publishing authors, and I think all the gryphon books are classier for her skill.

A relatively late addition to the team was Brenda Lyons, but that doesn't make her any less important. For over a year, we'd been planning on working together on a different project. Just as *Eyrie*'s proofs were coming in, Brenda was sending me sketches of Rorin and Tresh for the future project before she began painting.

The sketches were amazing. Her paintings already fill the walls of my office, but I didn't know about her amazing graphite skills. We're both fans of the Larry Dixon interior art pieces in the '90s gryphon books, so we started talking about the possibility of her doing interior pieces for the future project when I realized there was just enough time to have her do two for *Eyrie* before it came out.

Thus were Hatzel and Brevin brought to life. They're two of my favorite characters, but saber-beaked gryphons and peafowl opinici aren't easy to draw. She did an amazing job. It made me teary-eyed. I hope it did the same for you. I'm grateful every day that she said yes to doing the interior art pieces for this series.

Beta readers are tricky to find. I think everyone starts by looking to their friends, then quickly realizes that not all of their friends read fantasy or like gryphons. I had the benefit of starting out with my literary fiction beta readers, a few of whom were willing to try out fantasy. In particular, Judy Pomerantz and Vickie Bills took the dive into fantasy with me and offered their feedback. Judy has gone on to read all 20+ of the Valdemar books on our shelf, and Vickie has been providing helpful proofreading services for me.

Of the other beta readers who went above and beyond, Andrew Vilc has a tendency to beta test games and dig deep into them. He used that same skill set to dig into my novel, challenging me on nature and technology. John Bailey joined as an opinicus fan and provided hours of gryphon talk. He's my opinicus special advisor. He has his own gryphon books that'll be out shortly, complete with opinici. Joel Procell spent our time at the gym helping me troubleshoot business and writing matters and is an avid fantasy reader. I probably owe him more for keeping me healthy than writing, but to do so would underplay how many hours' worth of fantasy conversations we've had over the last two years. Finally, there's Hawkie: I recorded the audio proofread for her, and she was nice enough to provide feedback that shaped several characters drastically.

My line edits were done by Tim Marquitz, author of over twenty fantasy books. By the time you read this, he's probably already written another dozen science fiction books with Craig Martelle and Michael Anderle. Coming from having written literary short stories for the traditional market, let's just say that I had a lot to learn about writing novels. Tim helped me through that. He also knew about fantasy conventions because he's a fantasy author. That saved a lot of time and headaches. I'm grateful to him.

Dustin Porta served as developmental editor and occasional life coach during this project. When he first received *Eyrie*, I wasn't sure if we'd be a good match. Words are sacred, and it can be hard to get developmental feedback. Thankfully, the suggestions he offered showed he knew what he was doing. I hope a novel about gryphons surprised him the same way I was surprised about how useful his feedback was.

Last, but not least, I'd like to thank my family. They've supported my literary fiction and my fantasy. When I'm having a bad day, they're the ones who encourage me to write. While I'd love to say that no one needs permission to write, my spouse's support has been life changing in this regard. My mom has offered her support time and time again. Even my in-laws have sent me emails with suggestions on how to make my gryphons better. And let's not forget my two cats, who keep my feet warm in winter and encourage me to take breaks.

Did I just say "last"? Well, I lied. There's actually one more part of the team not listed above.

It's you.

You've now read three books. If you purchased them, you're helping me make a living. If you got them from the library, you still have my gratitude, and please encourage your librarians to buy the series. And if you just happened to borrow the books from a friend, consider recommending them, writing a review, or letting me know what you think. Start the email with "my favorite gryphon is..." and you can't go wrong.

Would I write gryphon books without you, dear reader? Yes, I would. I love gryphon books as much or even more than you do. But would I write so many so often? No, I wouldn't. You make more gryphon books happen, like a magician pulling gryphons out of a hat. I'd like to think that means you're making the world a better place.

-Vale

ABOUT THE AUTHOR

K. Vale Nagle is alarmingly hard to kill. While he's written his entire life, after surviving a pulmonary embolism and multiple organ failure, he began to take his writing more seriously and worked to get a degree in creative writing while recovering.

During that time another embolism struck and failed to kill him, at which point the doctors discovered an undiagnosed autoimmune disorder and patched him back up. Having used up two of his nine lives, he began publishing short stories and novels. When the doctors said that lung surgery was a 95% certainty, he dyed his hair dark blue, which is when he discovered that he was so unwell that his hair wasn't growing. A year later, and a switch from dark blue to teal, and his hair has finally started growing again (albeit silver instead of its pre-embolism black) and he's writing like a fiend.

Now, Vale writes feral fantasy—books with mythological creatures and nature-based settings, often involving gryphons and conflict.

He can be found online at kvalenagle.com, via his newsletter, or on Patreon.com/KValeNagle.

facebook.com/kvalenagle

twitter.com/kvalenagle

bookbub.com/authors/k-vale-nagle

amazon.com/K-Vale-Nagle/e/B07ND33BHW

patreon.com/kvalenagle

instagram.com/kvalenagle

ALSO BY K. VALE NAGLE

The Gryphon Insurrection

Eyrie

Ashen Weald

Starling

Reevesbane

The Ruins of Crestfall

The Crackling Sea

Opinicus

Pridelord

Short Story Collections and Anthologies

Blue Eyes and Other Tales

Tales of Feathers and Flames

CHARACTER LIST

I've had a few requests for an updated character list being included with each new book. It's a great idea, so here you go! Ideally, the entries here don't spoil anything that happens in *Starling*, but *Eyrie* and *Ashen Weald* spoilers are fair game.

The gryphons listed here have four cat paws, a cat tail, and cat ears unless otherwise noted. For example, Zeph has a feathered tail, as do all fantail gryphons. The opinici lack external ears and have bird forelegs and tails. Fisherfolk can go either way. While it's mostly a societal construct, having avian forelegs which allow one to use tools or a pen is often used as the definition of what makes an opinicus.

The characters are sorted by pride or eyrie in the following order:
Hatzel's Pride
Merin's Pride

Taiga Pride (Snowfall)
Redwood Valley Eyrie
Fisherfolk
Kjarr Pride
Bog Pride
Strix's Pride (The Strix Pride)
Parrotface Pride
Fantail Pride
Feathermane Pride
Crackling Sea Eyrie

HATZEL'S PRIDE

Hatzel's pride controls a small stretch of land in the northwest corner of the weald, nestled between the taiga and grasslands. They're usually magpies or Cooper's hawks, except for Hatzel, of course.

Hatzel the Saberbeak

Hatzel is a Haast's eagle and a saber-toothed tiger gryphon. She's the last saberbeak gryphon in the weald. She was born in Poisonmaw in a valley up north, but the monitor plague forced her pride to the weald. Most of her pride were killed fighting monitors. What remained combined with the magpie and copper hawk prides to become what is now Hatzel's pride.

She survived the plague, one of three so-called plague-born, and grew close to Vosk, with whom she attempted to have plague-resistant children with for years. They still sent messages and gifts of shiny rocks after giving up. She is the largest gryphon in the weald.

In *Eyrie*, she rescued Cherine and led the rescue effort to get Satra and the kjarr gryphlets out of the eyrie. After the fire, her pride took in refugees—both gryphons and opinici—as word of the "Pride of the Reeve's Bane" continued to spread.

In *Ashen Weald*, she traveled to the taiga and discovered that her old friend, Vosk, had been aiding the opinici. She killed him and helped Younce retake the kjarr nesting grounds before retreating into the taiga. She's now back to managing her pride and helping find a balance between the gryphon traditions and the influx of opinicus refugees who have joined.

Zeph Reevesbane

Zeph is a Cooper's hawk (copper hawk) plus North American cougar gryphon. He was born in the taiga and is a hatchmate of Younce and Mignet. Because his plumage and fur weren't suited for the taiga, he was moved to the weald at a young age and traded parrots with the eyrie. He has tail feathers despite being a gryphon.

In *Eyrie*, he killed Reeve Brevin on the night of the conflagration. He likes being left alone to hunt parrots, but after seeing how deep the schism between gryphon and opinicus really is, he's been working hard to try to mend relations. He's referred to as "The Reeve's Bane," "Zeph Reevesbane," or, formerly, "Zeph Parrotsbane."

In *Ashen Weald*, he brought supplies to the shore to help the pumpkin growing efforts and ended up going with Tresh to investigate the raftworks. He later went north to warn Satra of the starlings, but he was waylaid in Hoarfrost by the infected. He arrived at New Eyrie in time to warn the Ashen Weald, but during the battle, he escaped back to Luminaire with Reeve Brevin's youngest daughter, where he's remained ever since.

Xavi

Xavi is a magpie gryphon and the den father of Hatzel's pride, not to mention Hatzel's second in command. All of his children have Pink Paw as their mother. He's Zeph's friend and once claimed to kill a three-Hatzels-length snake, though we all know nothing is as big as three Hatzels.

In *Eyrie*, he traveled south with word of the wingtorn army but was captured by Rakesh before he could deliver it to the fisherfolk. In *Ashen Weald*, he was rescued by Carru and recovered on Luminaire Island before Kia came down to fetch him. He's now back to taking care of the gryphlets and opinicus chicks for Hatzel's pride.

Pink Paw

Pink Paw is a Cooper's hawk (copper hawk) plus North American cougar gryphon. Her back left paw has pink pads instead of black. All of her children have Xavi as their father. She's a skilled hunter and resents acting as den mother when Xavi is indisposed.

In *Eyrie*, she went with Triddle to blow up the flameworks the night of the fire. In *Ashen Weald*, hinting at a deleted scene, she served as Hatzel's messenger to the Ashen Weald declining their invitation. No one seems to remember what her real name is. Now that she's been reunited with Xavi, she's gone back to hunting. She has a name despite being a cameo character because she's usually in several scenes that get cut during editing. Sorry, Pink Paw.

MERIN'S PRIDE

Merin's pride controls a medium-sized stretch of land in the northern weald located south of Hatzel and north of Glacial Run. His pride are often eagles of some sort, usually harpy eagles.

Merin

Merin is a dark brown harpy eagle plus lion gryphon. He's the second largest gryphon in the weald. His most notable feature is his hooked beak, which turns down at the tip. His father was killed when a grasslands experiment went awry and a goliath bird stampede went through the old nesting grounds.

In *Eyrie*, he caught Cherine by a saltpeter crate and had him thrown into a cave near the Snowfeather River where two of his children nearly killed the opinicus. On the night of the fire, he ordered two of his offspring and Askel to sneak away during the rescue operation and light the place on fire. He freed Satra from the eyrie but didn't tell anyone about finding her over Jonas with a bloody saw.

During *Ashen Weald*, he befriended Foultner, which slowly changed how he felt about opinici in general. He fought the commander of New Eyrie with Zrim Feathermane's help until the starlings interrupted the fighting.

He's been absent from council meetings, though his children have been around. No one is sure where he went or what he's been up to.

Askel

Askel is a chestnut-colored golden eagle gryphon with a feathery tail. He's inseparable from Triddle, and together, they often go out on adventures that end with something or someone soaking wet or with scorched feathers.

In *Eyrie*, under Merin's orders, he used the waterworks

to spread oil across the underbough of the eyrie. He then lit it on fire, causing the Redwood Valley Eyrie to burn down. He was captured by Reeve's Guard, then brought along with Bario and Impir to the Crackling Sea.

In *Ashen Weald*, he was held at New Eyrie by Impir. He escaped from his prison, saved Levin, and was ultimately saved himself by Foultner.

After the events of *Ashen Weald*, he's been reunited with Triddle and is working on the new pass through the mountains. He spends his evenings attempting to train guard parrots with limited success.

Triddle

Triddle is a blue harpy eagle plus lion gryphon with a crest of feathers. He likes water, especially redirecting it to cause small floods.

In *Eyrie*, he blew up the flameworks to cause a distraction with the help of Pink Paw. Before the saltpeter went off, he dragged Bario to safety. With Ninox's help, he blew up the bridge over Glacial Run and organized the firefighting measures.

In *Ashen Weald*, he spent most of the time unable to function without Askel. During the battle at New Eyrie, he helped tear a hole in the gates. Now that he's been reunited with Askel, he's working on the new pass through the mountains. He hasn't yet told Askel that you can't train a ground parrot to guard anything.

Merin's Eldest Son

Merin's eldest disappeared on an expedition to find the starling prides. Carru went looking for him, but there was no trace of where he went after he reached the bog.

Carru

See: FISHERFOLK.

TAIGA PRIDE

The taiga pride controls the mountain range from the northern goliath bird pass, which starts at Crater Lake, down to the ocean. They are often snowy owl or gyrfalcon birds crossed with snow leopard cats, though there are a few lynxes hidden in there. They used to be made up of several prides. Williwaw, Hoarfrost, and Snowfeather used to be their own prides before the Connixation wiped them out. (If you haven't heard the word connixation before reading *Eyrie*, think of a con-flagr-ation with the Latin word for fire replaced with the word for snow.) Now, only the Snowfall Pride remains.

Vosk

Vosk is a gyrfalcon plus snow leopard gryphon. He's one of the three gryphons who survived the plague, along with Hatzel. They grew close after their two years spent in the medicine gryphon caves as children, trading pretty rocks once they grew up and returned home. They tried to have plague-resistant children for several years before giving up. He went on to have Mignet with a Crackling Sea opinicus, Ellore. When Mignet died and Jun refused to turn Satra over to the taiga, Vosk decreed that no taiga gryphon would help a kjarr gryphon ever again.

In *Ashen Weald*, he was caught conspiring with Ellore and was killed by Hatzel.

Younce

Younce is a gyrfalcon plus snow leopard gryphon and

one of Zeph and Mignet's hatchmates. He currently rules the taiga pride and is in the process of expanding several smaller outposts to help watch for starlings attempting to cross the ice and snow. He's often referred to as grumpy.

In *Eyrie*, he helped guide the gryphon insurrection through the mountains to sneak up on the flameworks from the north.

In *Ashen Weald*, he helped free Sandpiper's Dune from the rangers with Biski's help. He uncovered Vosk's betrayal, leading to the pride leader's death. He led an attack on the kjarr nesting grounds to free it from Ellore's rangers.

Since then, he's begun to build a pass through the mountains for goliath birds and wingtorn just north of Glacial Run. Tresh comes to visit him every other week. He's opted not to join the Ashen Weald. He opened up Hoarfrost and Williwaw as joint fisherfolk-taiga outposts to watch for starlings.

Zeph's Mom

Zeph's mom was a gyrfalcon plus snow leopard gryphon. She was killed in an avalanche soon after Zeph was moved to Hatzel's pride to be with his father.

Deracho

Deracho is a snowy owl plus snow leopard gryphon and Younce's best friend. Many years ago, he fell in love with Thenca, but she forbid him from helping the kjarr pride against the Crackling Sea. He talks a lot to make up for Younce's quiet. He was assigned to help expand Hoarfrost into a joint taiga-fisherfolk outpost to watch for starlings attempting to cross the taiga into the weald.

Biski's New Apprentice

Biski's medicine apprentice is a snowy owl plus lynx gryphon. He has a bobbed tail but lacks the snow leopard rosettes of most of his pride. He can't read common. There are rumors of a taiga pride like him that once existed in the northern mountains who disappeared during the Connixation.

Mignet

Mignet was a gyrfalcon plus snow leopard gryphon who had long, beautiful tailfeathers because her mother, Ellore, is an opinicus. Her first hunting grounds bordered Satra's, and the two quickly fell in love. When the ice gave way beneath them, Mignet drowned in the freezing water. She had a small bracelet with a blue heron on it to remind her of her Crackling Sea heritage. She was born at the eyrie, but when her forepaws were cat-like, she was dropped off with Vosk at Snowfall.

REDWOOD VALLEY EYRIE

The Redwood Valley Eyrie was the last eyrie built on the continent. Rumors say that it was gifted to a peafowl opinicus who saved the lord of all reeves from a giant cobra, though there's no evidence of that in the historical texts. When it was created, a dam was built along the Snowfeather River to form Crater Lake, and an aqueduct system was added in. All of its leaders, male and female, have had green male peacock plumage up until Ivess. It is currently an ashen ruin located at the northern tip of the Redwood Valley.

Kia

Kia is a red-winged parrot plus orange tabby cat opinicus who often paints green designs into her tabby fur so it matches her front half. She was an apprentice flora and fauna scholar at the university before it burned down. She used to date Cherine. She has a sister named Mia and a brother named Olan.

During *Eyrie*, she was sent by Headmaster Neider to look for Cherine, who had gone missing. She enlisted the help of Zeph, discovered Satra and the wingtorn, and traveled to the weald to warn the gryphons of the explosives. She helped evacuate the kjarr gryphlets, blow up the Snowfeather Dam, and saved Zeph from drowning.

In *Ashen Weald*, she hadn't reacted well to seeing Zeph kill Reeve Brevin, nor Headmaster Neider admitting to working with the northern eyries. Worried about her sister, Mia, and her brother, Olan, she traveled to Luminaire and then Sandpiper's Dune. In exchange for the fisherfolk attempting to bring Mia back from the kjarr safely, too, Kia used her scholarly skills to help their growing and fishing efforts. She hasn't returned to the weald or eyrie.

Mia

Mia is a red-winged parrot plus orange tabby cat opinicus, though with much more red plumage than her sister has. She's one of the few Redwood Valley opinici who became a ranger. She often fought with her parents. She was assigned to help Rakesh along the fisherfolk coast.

In *Ashen Weald*, she was captured by Tresh and Younce but escaped in the confusion and fled to the raftworks.

Cherine

Cherine is a golden eagle plus cougar opinicus scholar specializing in food. He lost his little brother to the monitor plague and worked as a butcher before he was given a scholarship by Neider to attend the university. He dated Kia for a few years. Kia described him as "kind when it is not easy to be so."

In *Eyrie*, he was beaten within an inch of his life by Merin's children, losing the tip of his beak in the process. Triddle and Hatzel rescued Cherine and brought him to the medicine gryphons, who fixed him up and added a metal tip to his beak. His journal and information were instrumental in warning the gryphons about the explosives.

In *Ashen Weald*, he spent time helping the opinici scavenge food and supplies while searching for his family. When Ninox brought him a copy of a notebook written by Mally the Nighthaunt, he set off exploring the northern mountains with her, finding only mass graves. When they finally returned back to Ninox's makeshift nesting grounds, her scouts had caught three Blackwing Eyrie spies. Since that time, Ninox and he have grown close.

Foultner

Foultner is a house sparrow (nest sparrow) plus tabby cat opinicus poacher. She grew up in a constant state of hunger and in trouble with the law. She holds the reeves accountable for the poor conditions in the underbough.

In *Eyrie*, she has a brief cameo helping with the fire fighting efforts near the end. In *Ashen Weald*, she joins Satra's forces as a spy to help free the wingtorn. Her infiltration of New Eyrie helped save Askel from the blackwing spies, earning her a pair of shiny metal talons and some black leather armor. She grew close to Blinky during that time and became Satra's intelligence officer. She was promised that wherever the Ashen Weald holds land, she's allowed to hunt and fish there. May secretly return Henders's affections.

Orlea

Orlea is a female cardinal plus house cat opinicus. She used to be a hunter with her mate until the Reeve's Hunting Grounds were declared off limits, then they became poachers to survive. Her mate was killed by the Reeve's Guard, and she was nearly killed by some Redwood Valley rangers until Zeph saved her. On the night of the fire, she rallied the opinicus refugees to keep the fire from spreading into the grasslands and forest. She reformed them as an opinicus pride. She was once a rival of Foultner's.

Since *Eyrie*, she's been working on chronicling everything that happened the night of the fire. She corresponds and trades with Naya of Sandpiper's Dune, who is also trying to figure out who started the fire.

Reeve Brevin

Reeve Brevin was an emerald peafowl opinicus who ruled the Redwood Valley Eyrie. Despite feeling no attraction for anyone and never taking a consort, she had several children to help continue the family line. When the Crackling Sea Eyrie came under siege, she sent the full might of the Redwood Valley there to help. When it looked like the Crackling Sea might starve, she refocused the university to figure out a way to keep everyone fed.

Where once the eyrie and gryphons were relatively friendly with each other, when a fire destroyed a large swath of the weald, she cut down the burnt trees to develop farm and grasslands.

In *Eyrie*, she attempted to burn down the rest of the weald to create more farmlands. She also planned to scourge the gryphons and fisherfolk from the valley to avoid a situation like the one between the Crackling Sea Eyrie and the kjarr pride.

On the night of the conflagration, Strix attempted to assassinate her but failed. She later ran into Zeph Parrotsbane by the Snowfeather Dam and was killed in the ensuing conflict. She had seven children, at least one of whom, Levin, has survived.

Headmaster Neider

Neider is the eagle owl opinicus who used to lead the university. He would pretend to be forgetful, a valuable ruse for a spy. He was recruited into helping the Blackwing Eyrie by Felicio the Phoenix sometime before the Crackling Sea came under attack. He seems to genuinely care for the scholars under his care despite the espionage. He met Cherine during the monitor plagues when Cherine's brother passed away. When Neider later saw Cherine working at a butchery to help salt meat to make it safe from disease, he offered Cherine a scholarship for the university. The headmaster once led an expedition into the bog to search for swamp iron.

In *Eyrie*, he sent Kia to search for Cherine. Later, when Kia found out about the wingtorn and Reeve Brevin's plans, Neider brought her to a meeting so she can learn the rest. When the eyrie was lit on fire, he ran off with the cockatiel forger to the north.

In *Ashen Weald*, it was revealed that the headmaster had maintained contact with Bario, Impir, Rakesh, and

Ellore through his spy network. Whether the clay jars were his idea or that of his blackwing masters is unclear.

Cockatiel Forger

The name of this black cockatiel opinicus is unknown. He followed the headmaster around taking notes. He's able to forge most documents down to the handwriting. He's a red fern addict.

In *Eyrie*, Kia used his addiction to allow her to steal back Cherine's notes on where the explosives were being stored. Later, he escaped with Headmaster Neider on the night of the fire to meet with their blackwing allies. At the end of *Ashen Weald*, he was caught leading a small team of blackwing opinici back to the Redwood Valley by Ninox's pride. He's currently being held in a secret workshop and being questioned by Cherine. Ninox refuses to hand him over to the Ashen Weald, fearing that he was attempting to meet someone there.

Ivess, Grand Reeve of the Twin Eyries

Ivess was a blue peafowl opinicus, Brevin's middle child, and her favorite snake was the leaf-nosed snake.

In *Eyrie*, she was nearly killed by Strix. She tried to lay claim to the title of Reeve after her mother died, freeing Impir from prison. In *Ashen Weald*, she was ultimately killed by Impir, working under orders from the Blackwing Eyrie, just before the Ashen Weald took New Eyrie.

Levin

Levin is an emerald peafowl opinicus and Brevin's youngest child. She was nicknamed "Lei" or "little lightning bolt." Her father was Larren, a Reeve's Guard captain killed by Satra when she came to free the wingtorn. Levin has only just finished fledging. Her favorite snake is the krait.

In *Ashen Weald*, she was malnourished and living at New Eyrie with Ivess. During the fighting, Askel freed her and brought her to Zeph, who flew her down to Luminaire so she could be safe among the fisherfolk. While Ivess is definitely dead, it's unclear if any of her other sisters survived. They were stationed on the island where Bario met with his blackwing allies, and there are rumors that there were only four dead peafowl opinici there.

Since *Ashen Weald*, Levin has been receiving tutoring lessons from Piprik. He's warned her that there are two types of leaders in the world: those who serve and those who rule. Her mother was a ruler, but Levin will need to decide for herself what path to take.

Reeve's Guard Captain Henders

Henders is a peregrine falcon plus house cat opinicus who used to guard the botanical gardens at the Redwood Valley. There's a brief unnamed cameo of him in *Eyrie* when Kia is attempting to steal red fern. He's friendly, though perhaps not the smartest opinicus in the flock. He was befriended, tricked, and then later saved by Foultner, who was pretending to be a Reeve's Guard. He's currently one of a few New Eyrie refugees who are working at the ranch with the Ashen Weald.

Mally the Nighthaunt

None of the characters seem to remember what bird and cat Mally resembles. His beak and talons are blood-red, which is caused by a genetic blood-iron disorder. He was found to be experimenting on mothers, eggs, and chicks and exiled. His research prevented a lot of children from dying. The *Nachlass Mal* was a book of his unpublished research that doctors still use today.

While he hasn't been seen in the Redwood Valley since, the underbough chicks tell stories of something that haunts the night. While the events of Eyrie suggest that this could have been Strix, the rumors started long before the owl pride leader began his serial killer spree in the eyrie's depths. Impir, Neider, and Felicio all worked with Mally in the early days, though none speak of him now. Where did he go after his exile?

Cherine and Ninox found one of his old laboratories hidden north of the eyrie, along with several mass graves of mothers and chicks. They also found someone's attempt to make a copy of a new book of research by him. Did he join the Blackwing Eyrie? Or has he gone somewhere else? Piprik mentions having worked with him after his exile, though it's unclear if that took place at the Blackwing Eyrie or Piprik's home eyrie. The New Eyrie refugees still tell stories of a nighthaunt slipping in and out of their camps when the moon is in its darkest phase.

Impir the Mad

Impir is a blue peafowl opinicus who was locked up for attempting to continue the experiments of his master, Mally the Nighthaunt. He claims that he was spared by Reeve Brevin because he developed a formula that allowed her to pass her emerald peafowl appearance on to six of her seven children. He also claims to be the father of Ivess, though that's never been confirmed.

He continued publishing monographs from prison until he was freed by Ivess the night of the fire. He watches out for Bario because he "owes a debt to Felicio." His madness may be a pretense to make others feel better about not executing him. He gave Ellore a hidden Black-wing Eyrie badge so she can flee north when the time is right. Before the Ashen Weald breached the walls of New Eyrie, Impir poisoned the Reeve's Guard and killed Ivess. Then he fled north with clay jars of the parasite. The jars were shattered, but Impir escaped.

Felicio the Phoenix

Felicio is the cardinal opinicus scholar who first went north in search of knowledge. He developed mining techniques which improved the Redwood Valley's metal-working abilities, leading to the discovery of the first saltpeter mine. Both the mine and Felicio were destroyed in an explosion. His blast shadow still hangs in the new flameworks building. He recruited Neider, Impir, and Bario into the spy network.

Bario the Phoenix

Bario is Felicio's son, a cardinal opinicus. He developed a leaching process to create saltpeter without needing to mine it, but while the mine was still producing, he couldn't get funds from Reeve Brevin to continue his research—until his father died under mysterious circumstances. He was saved by Triddle, who said his name was Askel, during the night of the fire. In return, he let the real Askel out of jail in his escape and taught Askel a little about what it means to be a scholar. The scentless braziers that once lit the Redwood Valley Eyrie were Bario's invention. While he was captured at the Crackling Sea Eyrie, he used a hidden explosive to kill his guards and escape from the library, where he met his blackwing opinicus allies on an island. Now, he's presumed to be hiding out at the Blackwing Eyrie up north with Headmaster Neider, Impir, and any other scholar spies.

FISHERFOLK

The strange fisherfolk are made up of gryphons and opinici who have rejected the eyries and prides and come together to live in harmony. All are welcome among the fisherfolk. They had three large settlements along the southern shore of the Redwood Valley: Sandpiper's Dune, Crane's Nest, and Swan's Rest. Nest and Rest were destroyed by wingtorn, though Swan's Rest is in the process of being rebuilt. There are also many small groups of fisherfolk who live in tiny settlements built on islands south of Luminaire, including one made up of ex-taiga gryphons.

Rorin the Hunter

Rorin is a japanese crane plus van cat opinicus, despite sometimes being compared to a sandhill crane. He has a splash of red on his chest that came from his grosbeak mother. According to Jonas's intelligence reports, "When the great beasts of the sea arrive on the southern shore, it is Rorin who sends them back to the depths." He leads Swan's Rest and likes spears. He has a soft spot for Tresh.

In *Eyrie*, he killed Jun the Kjarr and helped rescue several eggs from Swan's Rest. In *Ashen Weald*, he helped liberate Sandpiper's Dune, killing the elder and helping destroy the city of rafts.

Since then, he's worked on improving the fisherfolk's abilities to fish, hunt, and grow food with Kia's help. He reached a peace with Satra, with the condition that no wingtorn cross south of Glacial Run. He often worries about Tresh and is secretly glad that she has no cold tolerance and probably won't run away to the taiga to be with Younce.

Turresh the Shark

Tresh is a peruvian diving petrel plus melanistic fishing cat gryphon. She has angular breaks on her beak that give it a shark-tooth appearance, caused by a run-in with a rock crab when she was a gryphlet. She didn't speak until after she'd fledged, and while she speaks with confidence now, she has trouble with some words. Her inability to roll the double R's in Turresh is why she started to go by Tresh.

She's an excellent swimmer and the only gryphon born into a family of opinici. She dislikes it when would-be suitors try to treat her as an opinicus because of that. All of her family died during the wingtorn's assault on Crane's Nest. Despite having spent the last few years living in Swan's Rest, she is the acting leader of the Crane's Nest refugees. She's the only fisherfolk leader who refused to reach a peace agreement with the Ashen Weald. She lured in a serpentine whale to destroy the rangers' city of rafts.

Since *Ashen Weald*, she's made several attempts to get into the kjarr to search for her sister-in-law but has been rebuked by starlings. She's been sneaking up to Snowfall every other week to be with Younce.

Naya

Naya is a sandy and cream-colored gryphon. She's the current leader of Sandpiper's Dune after the death of her older brother.

In *Ashen Weald*, she led the gryphon refugees into the taiga, where they were infected by parasites set loose by

Rakesh. She found Younce and Biski up there, who helped cure her gryphons and retake Sandpiper's Dune. Then she went north in search of answers, where she opened a trade route to Orlea. They're both trying to work out what happened the night of the fire.

Gressle

Gressle is a blue heron opinicus who emigrated from the Crackling Sea to Swan's Rest. She used to trade with the eyrie and weald. In *Eyrie*, she met Kia and Zeph outside of the eyrie and gave them salted fish bars. In *Ashen Weald*, she was part of the expedition that freed Xavi and killed Rakesh. Currently, she's been helping Sandpiper's Dune stay on the straight and narrow path while managing the bambooworks.

Carru the Goliath Bird

Carru is a huge blue harpy eagle plus lion gryphon and Merin's son. He once fell in love with an opinicus. They planned to run off to the fisherfolk together, but she didn't show at the last moment, so he went alone. He used to share a hunting territory border with Xavi and Pink Paw, whom he became friends with. In *Ashen Weald*, he helped free Sandpiper's Dune from the rangers and got the bambooworks up and running again. Now, he's working with Rorin to try to recreate the Crackling Sea nets, rafts, sails, and other technology. He may have a crush on Kia.

Quess

Quess is a peruvian diving petrel plus panther opinicus. She was married to Tresh's brother and had several kids with him. She was the only petrel opinicus to learn how to swim like Tresh could. During the wingtorn attack on Crane's Nest, she was out fishing with Tresh. Now she's driven to find the wingtorn and rangers responsible. She followed the rangers fleeing from Sandpiper's Dune across the dunes, through the mangrove swamp, and into the bog months ago and hasn't reported back.

Piprik

Piprik is a white-tailed kite opinicus. He says he came from the north, where he was a scholar of some sort, though now he serves as a medicine opinicus. He owns a lot of expensive glass instruments and seems to have known Mally the Nighthaunt. His white plumage and the black circles around his eyes are completely unknown in the bog, kjarr, taiga, Crackling Sea, weald, and Redwood Valley. If his stories are to be believed, he once dissected a taiga gryphon and was part of an opinicus expedition into the Emerald Jungle. He's now on loan to the Ashen Weald as a sign of good faith from Rorin, helping figure out a cure for the parasite afflicting the starlings.

KJARR PRIDE

Kjarr is an archaic spelling of carr, which refers to a flooded forest in the process of becoming a bog, swamp, or marsh. The kjarr pride once existed in conflict with the bog pride, fighting over the stretch of land between the taiga and the Emerald Jungle. Eventually, the kjarr pride took over the bog pride, assimilating them. When Jun's son was caught stealing food, it launched the conflict that ended with the kjarr pride becoming the wingtorn. They often have black-backed ears and long legs like a caracal, though a few have cheetah markings.

Jun the Kjarr

Jun was a hawk plus caracal wingtorn gryphon often called the "Scourge of the Crackling Sea." The opinici caught his son stealing from the farms and strung him up as an example, so Jun salted their farms and began his own private war against the blue opinici. He ultimately surrendered to the Crackling Sea Eyrie after they took his children. In exchange for his surrender, Satra was allowed to keep her wings. He was killed by Rorin the Hunter at Swan's Rest. Despite being kinder to the bog gryphons than his father was, he still did not free them and was ultimately responsible for them ending up as wingtorn.

Vitra

Vitra was a shrike plus caracal gryphon. She was Satra's older sister, though she has a bog mother, whom she disappeared into the bog with when Jun surrendered. She used to love blue feather and fur paint. She was presumed dead, based on the records of the rangers, who claim they used her body to capture her mother. She didn't get along with Satra.

Satra the Kjarr

Satra is a golden-crowned kinglet plus caracal gryphon with golden feathers on her face and head. She's Jun's youngest daughter. She was held hostage at the bottom of the Redwood Valley Eyrie. Gryphons often referred to her as a murderer due to an incident with a taiga gryphon, Mignet. She became the new Kjarr on Jun's death and now leads the Ashen Weald. Because her father was often busy, Thenca and Urious often took care of Satra.

In *Eyrie,* she schemed to free the kjarr gryphlets

hidden in the Redwood Valley Eyrie. She had an opinicus saw modified to be used with gryphon paws and poisoned Jonas, but she couldn't bring herself to go through with sawing off his wings. Instead, she left him unconscious as the eyrie burst into flames.

In *Ashen Weald*, she led an army to take the Crackling Sea Eyrie and New Eyrie. She liberated the bog and kjarr wingtorn from both locations. While she now controls her old nesting grounds, she hasn't been able to push into the kjarr and bog because of the starling problem. She allowed the Crackling Sea opinici to join the Ashen Weald with Ranger Lord Grenkin as their leader. She hasn't allowed the Redwood Valley opinici at New Eyrie to join until they elect someone to represent them.

Ari

Ari is a cheetah wingtorn gryphon and the kjarr pride den mother. She's remained at the Strix Plateau watching the fledglings until it's safe to bring them back to their ancestral nesting grounds. There are rumors that she and Urious have become close.

BOG PRIDE

The bog gryphons were once their own pride before the kjarr pride took them over. Both Jun and Satra promised to set them free, though neither has done so. After becoming wingtorn, the fighting between kjarr and bog was so severe that their opinicus jailors had to separate them. They often have shrike or mockingbird markings with masks and tails that resemble a raccoon, despite being feline in nature.

Thenca

Thenca is a mockingbird wingtorn gryphon and Urious's twin sister. She can imitate almost any sound or voice. She was one of the last eggs to hatch before the bog pride was integrated into the kjarr pride. She was fiercely loyal to Jun and helped raise Satra. She had a snowy owl gryphon lover, Deracho, in the taiga she would visit. Her loyalty to the Kjarr helped keep the bog pride in line. She was the one who found Satra and Mignet and protected Satra from the taiga pride.

In *Eyrie*, she attacked Swan's Rest with Jun. In *Ashen Weald*, she climbed Snowfall Mountain to appeal to the taiga pride. With Vosk's death, she's remained up there ever since to be with Deracho. Once the mountain pass is finished, she hopes to be reunited with her brother.

Urious

Urious is a mockingbird wingtorn gryphon and Thenca's twin brother. He can imitate almost any sound or voice and was one of the last eggs to hatch before the bog pride was integrated into the kjarr pride. Unlike Thenca, he has scarring on his tail. With his mask pattern and bushy tail, he resembles a raccoon. He's always had a crush on Ari. He helped raise Satra and keeps the bog pride from rebelling against the Kjarr.

In *Eyrie*, he led the attack on Crane's Nest that killed Tresh's brother, nieces, and nephews. In *Ashen Weald*, he fought Ranger Lord Grenkin and convinced the opinicus to surrender. He's slowly losing control of the bog pride.

White Stripe

White Stripe is the nickname of a shrike plus African wildcat wingtorn gryphon with white feathers and cream-colored fur. His eponymous 'mask' is two white stripes instead of one black one. He holds no loyalty to Satra.

In *Ashen Weald*, he was leading the bog gryphons imprisoned in the depths of the Crackling Sea Eyrie. He fought at New Eyrie.

Black Mask

Black Mask is a shrike plus panther wingtorn gryphon. His mask markings take up most of his face. He hates the kjarr pride, but generally holds Urious and Thenca in high regard. He was rescued from the Crackling Sea Eyrie and fought at New Eyrie, but still holds antagonistic views towards Satra and the kjarr pride.

STRIX'S PRIDE

Strix's pride is made up of nocturnal owls. Unlike most gryphons, they rarely have cat ears. They've only recently adopted the common language, and Strix was one of the few fluent speakers in it. After his death, half of his pride split off to become the Strix Pride under Ninox, while the others remained in the Ashen Weald. Those who remained have not elected a new pride leader. Instead, Ninox's brothers formed a council to make decisions together.

Strix

Strix was a black and red owl gryphon. Unlike most gryphons, he didn't have any cat ears. He was an excellent night hunter. He was friends with Jun and the first owl pride leader to start having his pridemates learn the common language in addition to owlish. He disappeared the night of the fire while fighting Commander Wolden, but Ninox found his burnt body in the ruins of the Redwood Valley Eyrie.

While he's remembered well for helping rescue Satra and the gryphlets, in his point of view chapters in *Eyrie*, it's revealed that he was the one who killed the capybaras and started Zeph and Kia on their mission. It's also revealed that he's sought out harder and harder prey, eventually ending up hunting opinici in the Redwood Valley Eyrie.

Ninox

Ninox is a black and red owl gryphon. Like most gryphons, but unlike most owl gryphons, she has cat ears, though she doesn't remember to move them like a gryphon does. Her mother was a fantail. She runs into a lot of branches. She appreciates a smart gryphon or opinicus. She still has trouble speaking common. She left her old pride to create the Strix Pride, which controls the northern mountains. Many of the other prides don't appreciate her leaving the Ashen Weald. She's grown very close to Cherine, who has been teaching her how to read and understand mathematics. She believes that the future lays in smarter gryphons.

In *Eyrie*, she captured and held the Reeve's Guard headquarters the night of the fire. Then she helped Triddle destroy the bridge to prevent the fire from jumping Glacial Run.

In *Ashen Weald*, she searched the northern mountains for signs of the blackwing invaders and the eyrie ruins for signs of her dead father. She found a hidden workshop and a mysterious book, which she brought to Cherine. She formed her own pride when her brothers wanted to join the Ashen Weald, then searched the northern mountains for signs of Mally the Nighthaunt, finding mass graves and, in the epilogue, three blackwing scouts.

Blinky

Blinky is a black and red owl gryphon who is not one of Strix's children. She was one of six owl gryphons assigned to help assault the Crackling Sea Eyrie and New Eyrie and took a metal claw to the face while saving Askel. She's good friends with Foultner, though they don't always see eye-to-eye, and loves fish.

PARROTFACE PRIDE

The parrotface pride controls most of the weald north of Glacial Run. They're often kakapo plus cougar gryphons. They enjoy using berry juice to stain their feathers a violet color. They also enjoy beads. They prefer walking to flying, and their prey is often rimu olives, berries, nuts, eggfruit, or edible roots. Zeph commented in *Ashen Weald* that he believes one of the three plagueborn came from the Parrotface Pride, though that hasn't been confirmed.

Parrotface Elder

The parrotface elder from *Eyrie* is a kakapo plus cougar gryphon. Since kakapo always look old, no one is sure about her age. Like all parrotfaces, she prefers walking to flying and tends to scavenge rimu olives and eggfruit rather than hunt. Despite being a relatively peaceful pride leader, she controls most of the northern weald. She paints her fur with violet berry juice and wears small rocks and beads. Unlike the other Ashen Weald pride leaders, she's opted to remain in the weald and continue food-gathering efforts. Despite joining the alliance of prides, she continues trading with everyone and counts the head medicine gryphon as an old friend.

FANTAIL PRIDE

The fantail pride is the only gryphon pride where all members have long, feathery tails. They're not made up of specific cats or birds. Their long wings and feathery tails give them an advantage in flight. They're the only gryphon pride that can fly as well as the opinici can. Their home territory was burned down and their nesting grounds destroyed by saltpeter bombs. They've taken roost in the kjarr until spring.

Erlock Chartail

Erlock Fantail, now Erlock Chartail, is an unnamed bird and cat mix, but she has 42 tail feathers exactly, and there's a hint of starling in her dark plumage. She's the leader of the fantail pride. Her tailfeathers were burnt off by an explosion at her nesting grounds, so she's had shorter red feathers imped over top of them until her next molt. The fantail pride's hunting grounds were completely destroyed in the weald fire. She's currently stationed at the kjarr nesting grounds as a member of the Ashen Weald council.

In *Ashen Weald*, she fought off the rangers in the weald until an explosion knocked her out of the sky and lit her tail on fire. Satra and Thenca saved her, and she went on to be a founding member of the Ashen Weald. She stayed behind to guard the gryphlets at the plateau until she molts again and gets her feathers back.

Since then, she relocated her pride to the kjarr and has been seen going back and forth from the island prison where the few surviving starlings from New Eyrie are kept.

FEATHERMANE PRIDE

The feathermanes all have large, feathery manes. They're often half lion, though the front half varies wildly. Even the ones who don't have lion back halves still have floofy manes. They're noted for their ferocity and loud roars. The feathermanes founded the medicine gryphons, though after the monitor plague, other prides have joined in. The weald fire in *Eyrie* destroyed all of their hunting grounds. After Zrim's death, no one has become the new leader, though they've been seen hanging out with Merin's pride.

Zrim Feathermane

Zrim was a golden eagle plus lion gryphon with a huge, bushy mane that used to drag on the ground when he walked. He disapproved of the 'younger' prides like Merin's and Hatzel's. He split the southern weald with the fantails, controlling the southwest, which borders the dunes, taiga, and fisherfolk shore.

In *Ashen Weald*, he became a founding member of the Ashen Weald, leading the winged gryphons against the Crackling Sea Eyrie and New Eyrie. Ultimately, Zrim was killed by starlings while attempting to defeat New Eyrie's commander. He has not been replaced.

Medicine Gryphon Leader

The old medicine gryphon is a golden eagle plus lion gryphon who has lost most of her eyesight. She treated the original monitor plague victims, setting up the medicine gryphon caves where the three "plagueborn" survivors grew up. She prefers to teach now but has taken a more active role after the night of the fire. While the medicine gryphons are technically neutral, she should control the Feathermane Pride after Zrim's death. Instead, she maintains her neutrality and refuses to acknowledge the Ashen Weald.

Biski

Biski is a bossy blue jay plus jaguar gryphon who was called the "mismatched medicine apprentice" in *Eyrie*. She's a new adult who is just now getting her eponymous mane of feathers. She's been training a new taiga apprentice off and on, though it's never stated if she's been promoted from apprentice to full medicine gryphon. Either way, she acts like she was.

After saving the gryphons of Sandpiper's Dune from ending up like the starlings, they've constructed sand gryphons in her honor and are naming their children after her, much to the chagrin of Younce. She's currently working with a contingent of medicine gryphons on an island who are attempting to find better treatments for starlings.

CRACKLING SEA EYRIE

The Crackling Sea Eyrie is made up of blue heron opinici. Before their reeve was assassinated, they used to be a major trading hub, and many of the blue opinici show hints of other eyrie and even gryphon pride heritage. Their storm curtains, translucent and over a foot thick, were considered a modern marvel.

Blackwing assassins killed their reeve and his family but failed to take control of the Crackling Sea. It's unclear what forced the blackwing forces to retreat, though the

Crackling Sea and Redwood Valley Eyries claim it was their combined show of force. During the rebuilding efforts, conflict rekindled between the opinici and the kjarr pride. After the kjarr salted the farms, the Crackling Sea took their nesting grounds and held their children hostage. The kjarr gryphons surrendered and became the wingtorn.

The Crackling Sea Eyrie was controlled by the reeve's consort, Jonas, until he disappeared the night of the Redwood Valley Eyrie fire. Ranger Lord Grenkin took over in his absence.

Crackling Sea Reeve

The unnamed Crackling Sea reeve was killed by a blackwing assassin. While he had a male consort, he still had many children to continue his line. They were all killed in the same attack. Since his assassination, his eyrie stands without a reeve. Little is known about the blue reeve, except that Ellore, Rakesh, and Grenkin found his body.

Jonas

Jonas was once a merchant who owned the largest goliath bird ranch on the Crackling Sea, but he gave it all up to become the reeve's consort. After the reeve's death, he took over the eyrie. It was his decision to kill Jun's son and subjugate the kjarr and bog prides. He opened a fishing village on the far side of the shore that became New Eyrie and worked with the Redwood Valley opinici to try to fix the food shortages. Many at the Redwood Valley were unaware of his importance, believing him to still be a merchant. He went missing the night of the fire, presumed dead. Satra drugged him and left him in his home, which later collapsed into the fire.

In the days since the reeve's assassination, the Crackling Sea slowly fractured into two factions. One held regret for what they'd done and flocked to Ranger Lord Grenkin. Others, those who believed drastic times called for drastic measures, became Jonas loyalists. While Jonas is dead, there are many opinici who believe they have nothing to apologize for. They continue on and see Jonas as the savior who fought off the Blackwing Eyrie and kjarr pride, a ranch owner who became a reeve in his own right.

Ranger Lord Grenkin

Grenkin is a blue heron opinicus who is missing an eye and several digits from his left foreleg, bitten off by Ari when he captured the kjarr pride's gryphlets. He leads the Crackling Sea's military efforts, the rangers in particular. He disagreed with Jonas's policies and decisions and has been working on rooting out the Jonas loyalists ever since the consort's disappearance. In Jonas's absence, he has become the leader of the Crackling Sea. He surrendered the Crackling Sea to Satra, who was forced to give it back to him when she didn't have the forces to hold it. He helped fight the starlings at New Eyrie. Ultimately, he led the push which led to the Crackling Sea opinici joining the Ashen Weald, leading to a divide between him and the Redwood Valley refugees at New Eyrie, who remain lost and leaderless.

Ranger Captain Ellore

Ellore is a blue heron plus snow leopard opinicus and Mignet's mother. She was the ranger captain assigned to hold the old kjarr nesting grounds because she was believed to be a Jonas loyalist and Grenkin didn't want her assigned to the eyrie. It was later revealed that her loyalties lie with the Blackwing Eyrie. She attempted to force Vosk to join the Crackling Sea Eyrie, but when the other gryphons found out, they killed Vosk. She hates Satra for causing Mignet's death. She was assigned to find out what happened to the missing opinicus outposts in the bog by Grand Reeve Ivess, who temporarily promoted her to ranger lord on the incorrect assumption that Ranger Lord Grenkin had been killed by the Ashen Weald.

Ranger Captain Rakesh

Rakesh's bird and cat species remain unnamed, but he's described as an emaciated combination of grey and green. He was sent deep into the bog as a cadet and came back changed. He was once Ellore's best friend. Jonas assigned him to the combined forces sent to the dunes. Ellore gave him metal talons with a small moth engraved on them when he was made captain. He captured Xavi before the gryphon could warn Sandpiper's Dune but was ultimately killed by Carru several days later. Carru gave Rakesh's metal talons to Quess.

Bruen

Bruen is a blue heron plus caracal opinicus. He's been Ellore's second-in-command for as long as she's been a captain. His kjarr ancestry keeps him from being promoted.

Oh my goodness! Did you read through the entire character list? You're a hero.

Here's a bonus fact. Most big cats can either roar or purr but can't do both. It was believed that a partially ossified hyoid bone is what allowed a big cat to roar, but it's actually due to other factors. The one cat that can't roar OR purr is the snow leopard. (It can make a funny purr-like sound when it exhales, but that's about it.) None of the taiga pride who have the pretty snow leopard rosettes can roar.

www.ingramcontent.com/pod-product-compliance
Lightning Source LLC
Chambersburg PA
CBHW051554100726
47898CB00001B/96